SIRENS

SIRENS

✳ LOST WORLD
BOOK 2

T.L. ZALECKI

First edition of *Sirens: Lost World* published 2015.

Editing by Kindle Press.

Early editing by Maxann Dobson,

The Polished Pen, www.polished-pen.com

Cover design by: Andrew Bouve

Interior Design by E.M. Tippetts Book Design

www.emtippettsbookdesigns.com

For Will and Ava,
may your imaginations always be wild.

ONE
LOREL

September 19, 2098
Kotte, Sri Lanka

BUTTERFLIES WINGED THROUGH LOREL'S chest as she walked in step with her colleagues down the bowed planks of Kotte's marina dock. Nauseous wafts of diesel served as a reminder of how behind Sri Lanka was in fueling technology. And how far she was from home. Her neck dripped with sweat beneath a thick curtain of hair.

Just put one foot in front of the other, Lorelei. And breathe.

Obediently, she sucked in hot air then threaded her fingers through the damp curls, lifting the strands to feel a small breeze. The urge to pull her hair into a ponytail was curbed by the need to maintain what privacy the long auburn waves offered.

It had only been a day and a half since she and her colleagues from the Department of Oceanic

Administration touched down in Kotte, but the time had passed too quickly. Lorel swallowed thinking of her irrevocable choice. It had set things in action, things that she hoped were falling into place. And in a few days, she would be *there*. Rodinia. The thought sent excitement through her, penetrating the layer of anxiety like a ray of sunlight through clouds. Still, she did not feel ready.

Had she made the right decision?

Tears threatened as she pictured her father on a sterile hospital bed back in Washington, DC. She had left him at his darkest moment, and the fact that he thought it was for a work trip almost made it worse. She would drop any commitment in a heartbeat if it meant being with her father in his last days. What must he think of her? But there was consolation in the reason beneath it all — she was here to save his life. She could only hope for the chance to explain everything to him one day soon. Rodinia may have a come-and-never-leave policy, but there were some rules in the world that did not apply to her.

She didn't need to be told by PanDivinity, the global entity in power of most people's minds, bodies, and souls, not to steal from one of their Hubs — her honesty would never allow it.

She didn't need municipals breathing down her neck about muzzling her transgenic cat on city streets — the safety of other people was paramount to her already. And she didn't need the queen of Rodinia telling her she could never return to her home for fear she would betray the sirens' location to the human world — Lorel cared too much.

She cared so deeply for the rare species, in fact, that she was risking her own life to come to their island and defend them against Francis Galton, the CEO of DiviniGen, and whatever posse accompanied him in pursuit of the Poseidon Project. Deep down she had her selfish reasons. She would save her father in the process, but the bottom line remained the same. They had asked her to their island out of need, and she had obliged. If her loyalty and dedication weren't proof enough to the queen that she was worthy of exception, then Lorel would find her own way home. She had come too far to let her father die alone.

But Jake would be there for him, she reminded herself, remembering her one plea to her Navy SEAL boyfriend before she left DC. At the thought of him, the tears surfaced. Things had become complicated. *Love felt like an anchor stuck in murky weeds, too entangled to lift, paralyzing her.* For now, it was easiest not to think about him. It would only weigh her down. She wiped the tears away before her Department colleagues noticed.

Beyond the harbor, the Laccadive Sea glittered under the bright morning sun. It was no different than any other sea she had seen in her twenty-five years. Beautiful and blinding. A rippling scape of emerald water suggested a plentitude of sea life flourishing in its depths. But looks were deceiving.

At the end of the dock, her colleagues huddled in a cluster of white coats. A hush fell over the group. Lorel's blackglass eyeband darkened, shading her eyes, as she peered up at the research vessel awaiting them in the boat slip between two official Sri Lankan ships. It was humble in size, appearing no longer than Jake's forty-foot catamaran, but nothing else about it was modest.

Slick white sides gleamed from bow to stern as though just waxed. Beneath a painted American flag were the words *US Department of Oceanic Administration*. Lorel was not surprised that her boss, Benjamin Reshing, had the resources to summon a federal ship halfway across the world for their small-scale, undisclosed research expedition. Some might even consider it insignificant.

Those who did not know the worth of a rare purple plant existing only in a place beyond the world's reach, Lorel thought, biting her lip.

An A-frame crane stood fixed to the stern and a diving bell hung from the side along with a couple lifeboats. Multiple antennae and solar reflective panels covered the two-story hull. Among them, she spotted a holographic GPS, meteorological-satellite and echo-sounding equipment. At the stern was the dive platform stacked with scuba gear, submarine holocams, and a weatherproof blackglass wall displaying oceanic charts in real time.

Under normal circumstances, Lorel would be brimming with pride. This was the trip she had always dreamed of as a marine biologist. But how things had changed. This moment now marked the beginning of a very different journey. She shrugged her bag farther up her shoulder and squeezed the strap until her nails dug into her palm. At least they had gotten the compass watch to her, albeit last minute. Her only tool to guide her to the meeting spot, the watch was programmed with the exact coordinates and synced with their own GPS device so that they — the ones she felt so far away from at the moment — would have a constant read on her status. After Reshing unknowingly thwarted her first attempt to retrieve it, she had lost hope. It wasn't until moments before leaving her hotel room earlier that morning when an unmarked Dragonfly delivered the watch to her window's receiving drawer.

"That baby's for us?" A colleague stumbled up behind her holding a microscope under one arm and a small duffel bag in his hand.

"Look at that diving bell," cooed the powder-pink-haired woman next to him in awe.

A few others murmured similar sentiments. Lorel remained silent. She had been trying to keep a distance from the rest of the team. It was possible any one of them could inadvertently throw a wrench in her plan. That is, if Reshing didn't first. She clenched her jaw as Reshing turned to address the team, fixing his unblinking eyes directly on her.

"Welcome to the *Riptide 113*, the Department's finest oceanic research vessel," he said, stepping onto the drop stairs that led up to the first deck.

She wasn't used to seeing her boss outside the lab. Instead of his usual white lab coat over a suit, he wore a light blue button-down shirt and khakis. His mouse-brown hair tufted in a casual windblown look. But the permanent crease between his brows was still there and his lips maintained the pursed look of condescension she had become so familiar with.

Two Sri Lankans followed him toting a suitcase and a large box of lab supplies. Reshing leaned over the shiny chrome railing to face the team of eager scientists below. "I hope you all enjoyed your first few hours in Kotte. I know you're jetlagged and tired, but that's what coffee is for. Work begins now. Get your kits set up, check your cultures, be prepared for receiving your live samples. Oh, and everyone find a partner for the duration of the trip. This person will accompany you on the dives each day, make sure you are accounted for. We wouldn't want any of you to get lost at sea."

A few people snickered. One woman raised her hand and said in a nervous voice, "Doctor, there's fifteen of us."

"Hmm, yes. Ms. Phoenix, you will be my partner," he said, looking once again at Lorel. "Breakfast will be waiting for everyone below deck."

Two long and uneventful days had passed, mainly spent pouring over algae samples dredged up by the submersible, and everyone aboard was itching to begin their first dive. The midday tropical sun beat down outside, streaming in the circular windows. Lorel and the rest of the team sat cramped in the second-story hull among the lab equipment. Holos displaying ocean temperature and depth, algal bloom conditions, and live organism alerts slid across the interactive holographic blackglass wall behind Reshing. Microscope lights cast a purplish glow around the room.

Lorel smoothed her hand down her thigh to stop her leg from bouncing. They were about to drop anchor at their destination, the remains of an old shipwreck. The ship had run aground in the nineteenth century against a reef, now thirty feet deep, but back then probably only inches below the surface. It was just another reminder of the swelling ocean. People tried to ignore it, go about their lives, but the water was always there in the distance, lapping at the edges of their cities. Hungry.

Lorel could sense the undercurrent of animosity people felt toward the ocean. All the talk over the past couple of decades about how humans would one day live in it, farm its floors, build settlements, industrialize. It was all spoken of with such an air of entitlement it made her sad. After all, look what people had done to the land — depleted it of almost all its natural resources. What little beauty and life left in the sea would be exploited and ruined like the rest of the earth. It was as though the purity and vastness of the water taunted people, challenged them to claim it with some sort of misguided vengeance.

Despite the dazzling technological advances snowballing into the twenty-second century, submarine colonization still seemed far-fetched. Most people had believed it impossible — until DiviniGen's announcement of the Poseidon Project. Deep down, she feared Galton may have finally found a way.

No, she thought, *they would not succeed.* Galton had no idea what would be awaiting them on the phantom island he chased, if he ever reached it. The sirens were still holding out hope that DiviniGen would lose its way. Rodinia had a long history of evading human eyes. Their existence was only alive in the human world through legend, and their home was nothing more than an inconsequential island among many scattered in the loneliest part of the sea. Though, before now, no one knew to look.

Reshing tapped an earpiece and ordered the captain to cut the engine. The boat slowed, bobbing in the choppy waves. "You will have two hours, then we meet back here," he announced as a crewmember handed out oxygen tanks. "Remember who your partner is, and when you return, make sure you account for their presence."

Lorel avoided his piercing gaze that followed, staring out the window at the vast expanse of water. Her stomach felt oily and a lump rose in her throat. She swallowed hard but it persisted. Two biologists who worked on the green algae project were peppering Reshing with questions about the respiratory equipment. Not everyone had a lifetime of scuba experience. At least she did not have to fret those details.

She bit her nails, ready to get through the instructional lecture and dive in. Her sleek new wetsuit, the one Reshing had given her as a gift, was tight and made her feel constricted. Trapped.

"Ms. Phoenix, your attention please." His demand

snapped her gaze back. "As I was saying, you have two hours before your oxygen runs out. Your gauges are connected to your watches, so keep an eye on them. When your watch begins flashing you'll have twenty minutes to surface. Do not waste any time getting back to the boat. The tides here become tumultuous at dusk, and the ship will depart promptly once everyone has returned aboard."

Only half listening, Lorel slipped her wrist behind her back, hoping no one would notice that she wore two watches.

"Doctor Reshing, should we expect any predatory sea life here?" the intern, Brian, asked, raking fingers through his spikey burgundy hair. "Just remembering that orca beaching last month. I heard they found a body in one of them." Snickers filled the room and he added, "Not that I really believed it."

Lorel froze at the comment, awaiting Reshing's reaction, but his face was as unreadable as always.

"No, I'm sure you did not. How absurd." His voice took on a serious tone. "However, this is the middle of the ocean. It may be severely depleted, but it is not empty. You should be prepared to see anything. Any other questions?"

Silence, except for the waves lapping against the side of the boat below.

"Good. Now explore as much as you can in the time that you have down there. You will find quite a variety of algal species throughout the site, inside the ship, on the coral, even free floating. You will see cyanobacteria, of course, but we've all seen plenty of that. What we're looking for are the more rare variants. Examine the blooms that have less chlorophyll—the lichens, brown and red algae. Keep your eyes out for anything *unusual*. And make a mental note of where the particular sample is growing. We will spend the evening in the lab and prepare for onsite analysis."

Lorel fiddled with her dive belt, watching his face from beneath her lashes. He was practically foaming at the mouth. His eyes seemed to burn with anticipation as though he could almost taste the purple algae. No one else saw it. But she did.

Don't hold your breath, Ben.

She cursed him in her mind for the hundredth time since they had met at the airport. He had been so strangely attentive: carrying her bag, opening doors, and then forcing her into his limousine for her *safety*. The overly protective, almost chivalrous display repelled her but also induced wonder. There had always been a strange tension emanating from him at work, a nervous energy, and she had not ruled out the possibility that he was attracted to her. Maybe he felt the freedom to be casual with her outside the lab, or maybe his motives were more Machiavellian.

Did he know she was on to him? That he'd been using her as a pawn in his game to find the algae?

His comment in the limo the day before had been cryptic, and she could still feel the chill his hand sent through her as he placed it on her knee under the guise of concern. *I know what happened in your apartment,* he had whispered, then muttered something about how he would protect her. His reference to the man in black who had attacked her and Link in her home, who Jake had killed in her defense, was unnerving. The man she was *sure* had been working for Francis Galton. Maybe Reshing was suspicious that she had pieced together his call with Galton that she had overheard in the office. Maybe his connections with the shady CEO had led him to the information about her attack. But he couldn't possibly know the true extent of her involvement, she assured herself.

How he underestimated her.

After fielding a few stray questions from the team about the best strategy for scraping algae samples, Reshing led them to the lower deck and everyone began climbing into their gear. Stats scrolled across the blackglass wall.

> *Ocean temperature — 21 degrees Celsius*
> *Depth — 9 meters*
> *Green algal bloom — High*

The sun reflecting on the water made it impossible to see below the surface, and Lorel could barely keep her eyes open. She pulled flippers on over her booties and lined up behind the others as they plopped into the water one by one.

A hand slipped across her shoulder sending a chill through her despite the heat. "You know what to look for," he whispered in her ear, too close, and she resisted the urge to shove him away.

"Of course," she said, staring straight ahead.

"Good girl." He patted her back and, just as he was about to jump in, paused.

"Lorel," he said taking her hand in both of his, "what is this?"

She jerked her wrist back as he examined the compass watch. "It's just a dive watch my Dad gave me. I still have the navy one too, see?" She held out her other wrist.

"What a wonderful gadget. See you back here in a couple hours," he said with lingering eyes. "Good luck."

"Yes, you too," she said.

He pulled his facemask on and jumped in leaving her alone on the edge of the deck.

She glanced at her watch. *13.28.16 UTC. Right on time. And right in place. Coordinates, 5.409, 75.546.* Luckily, the research vessel had not veered off course or timeline despite the heavy winds they had faced on the way out.

Lorel looked down at the gently cresting water beneath her and felt a well of emotion in her chest. She jiggled her limbs around, loosening her body, and double-checked her equipment. The oxygen tank and weight belt were heavy, especially with the additional satchel full of collection tubes and tools. Soon she would feel weightless.

Ready to take the plunge, she secured her mouthpiece, checked the pressure gauge, and jumped. Cool water washed over her, cooling the impermeable skin of her wetsuit, and she hovered for a few minutes to assess her surroundings.

She loved how the world turned silent once she was underwater. The only sound was the metallic *whoosh* of her breathing. Visibility was better than she had expected. Rays of sun sliced through the algae-laden water like strobe lights, quivering in the current and casting a greenish glow over the landscape. Bleached coral projected from the sea floor in various shades of white and gray, some columnar like Greek ruins and others like scattered bones. It had the eerie feel of a visit to the catacombs.

At the bottom lay the ship, twisted and half buried. The propeller shaft and stern rose out of the sand, and a slivered mast pierced through the water reaching eternally for the surface. She swam down toward the others who were already dispersing throughout the sunken ruins. Reshing signaled her to follow as he disappeared into a large hatch on the bow, Brian trailing after.

Brian seemed enamored by Reshing and eager to impress. *Maybe the intern will keep him sufficiently distracted,* she hoped.

The ship looked like it had been buried in its watery grave for centuries. Barnacles, shellfish, and algae covered every surface. As Lorel swam over the bow oysters snapped closed in a wave of bubbles beneath her passing shadow. Instead of following Reshing through the hatch, she swam in the opposite direction. At the other end of the ship, she plunged headfirst through a window into the wheelhouse and felt a rush of dizziness.

The floor was ahead of her where the wall should have

been, and the ship's wheel jutted in her face, its knobby wooden spokes green and covered with slime. An eel slithered out from beneath the helmsman's chair and swirled around Lorel's head like a ribbon. It opened its mouth in a slow yawn, annoyed that she had just woken it from deep sleep. She lurched backward, surprised at seeing the rare serpentine creature. It was beautiful. Still, goosebumps prickled against her wetsuit. She hovered for a moment to collect herself, then checked her watch again.

13.44.56 UTC. Almost one forty five on the dot. Time.

She thought back to their planning session back in DC. In the most discreet, back alley coffee shop they could find, their voices barely audible over the drone of house music, Sam Bishop, his wife Isla, and George Oberbach had walked Lorel through the fine details of her escape plan, first to their submarine meeting place and then beyond. She had felt numb then, filled with anger toward Galton and DiviniGen. All they had done to make her life a living hell and threaten so much that was good in the world had fueled her decision to leave. That moment suddenly seemed surreal, belonging to another world, as though she had dreamed it all up and was now about to jump off a cliff with no safety net. All she could do was have faith it would all fall into place as Sam had promised. As they had parted in the alley, Link whimpering on a leash in Sam's hands with sad yellow eyes, Lorel almost called it all off.

But she hadn't. With an echoing deep breath through her equipment, Lorel shimmied back out the window of the wheelhouse. No one else was in sight. Their noses were probably buried in thick clumps of algae, scraping samples in the bowels of the ship somewhere. Sucking a deep breath from her oxygen tank, Lorel checked her compass, then shoved off the deck in a southbound direction.

Don't look back.

With a surge of adrenaline she propelled forward, pumping her flippers, and swam for her life. *Or from her life,* she thought. No time for doubt. Her fate was about to be sealed. The bed of coral below her tapered off to a submarine desert of white sand. At first, the seafloor was visible. Despite them being in the middle of the ocean, the shipwreck site rested on a raised plateau which at one time had probably been a sandbar at low tide before the ocean levels rose. Now, the sandbar quickly diminished to a steep degradation until the sea floor was no longer visible and all she could see was darkening blue below her. Her watch lit up with a sharp temperature decline. The current strengthened and she felt like she was running against the wind.

Or was nature telling her to turn back?

She swam lower into the darkness, switching on her headlamp. Her equipment purred with a pressure adjustment but her body remained warm inside the wetsuit. A dark murky seafloor appeared below her in the broad beam of light. The sand sloped to a deeper plane, though sparse vegetation indicated she was still at a level far above maximum depth. The swaying plants thickened to a vast tangle of giant kelp at least fifteen feet high. It looked like an enchanted forest. Or a haunted one. She swallowed. Two rockfish darted out from the edge and made a beeline in the direction of the reef as though escaping. Lorel shuddered at the thought of entering.

She paused for a moment to glance back at the shipwreck and felt a rush of relief. There was still no one in sight, and she had managed to put a good distance between her and her colleagues. They would not know she was gone for at least another half hour. With a fresh burst of adrenaline and all the courage she could muster, she swam toward the kelp forest.

It was only a few yards ahead, but to her dismay she realized she was swimming in place. The current was too strong. Every muscle in her body ached and her legs were turning to rubber. It was like a bad dream. Gasping for breath through the oxygen tank was insufficient and for a moment she thought she would hyperventilate. Despite her desperate kicking, she could feel herself inching backward as though the forest was repelling her, warning her to stay away.

Suddenly a surge of current parted the wall of kelp stalks to reveal a pair of large round eyes staring at her from the dark recesses. It was a man. He stood with his feet firmly planted to the sandy ground. His bare chest looked like a steel barrel of muscle, and a thick mane of silvery hair swirled around his head. In his hand the blade of a knife glinted in a flicker of light.

For a moment Lorel felt hypnotized. His owl eyes held her in a trance as the current sucked her backward. He stretched his arms in her direction, beckoning her.

She tried to swim forward, but it was impossible to make anything but negative progress. *Was he just going to stand there while she struggled in the current?*

He raised both of his arms above his head then lowered them until he was pointing at her. He nodded, emitting a sonorous clicking sound that caused Lorel's entire body to flinch. Two sets of beady eyes appeared near his head and she could barely make out the shape of their large bodies.

Dolphins!

Her heart jumped, unable to believe what was before her. But despite trying to swim toward them, she moved backward swiftly now, back toward the ship. She pulled at the water with flailing arms but the resistance was too much, and she felt a burst of anger.

Wasn't he supposed to help her? She was an exceptionally strong swimmer in most conditions, but this tumultuous, unwelcome part of the ocean was too much. This was his territory, not hers.

The man lifted his arms again, this time in front of his chest, and began moving them in a circular motion, one over the other, faster and faster as if he was pulling the water toward him. She was close to giving up, her body turning to jelly as it helplessly drifted backward, but then the current shifted. She felt it churn and swirl around her, tugging at her body. With sudden imposing force it yanked her back toward the kelp forest, toward him. She resisted the urge to fight it and let herself be hurled along, all the way into his arms.

He caught her thrashing body and clasped her tightly,

standing firm as the powerful flow of water eased. For a long moment their eyes locked, hers unblinking from beneath her mask, his wide and deep blue, and incredibly alive. She felt a burst of emotion, fear mixed with marvel and bewildering awe. A siren was cradling her in his arms. And he was the most magnificent man she had ever laid eyes on.

So you must be Mello, she thought.

Breaking the stare, he acted quickly, yanking down the zipper of her wetsuit and ripping it off. She shivered as the water fully enveloped her half-naked body, but his slippery hands felt warm against her bare skin. The oxygen tank was the last to go and with a nod to make sure she understood, he began to unfasten it. Lorel nodded in response and drew in a long breath just before her final lifeline detached and floated away like a balloon in the sky.

Panic loomed. She struggled to stay calm, clinging to Mello's shoulders. *Just like freediving,* she assured herself, remembering Jake's confidence in her breath-holding skills. With one hand Mello held her tightly against him, and with the other he took a knife and began slashing her wetsuit to shreds, then released it into the current. The tattered material floated up toward the oxygen tank, which was now bobbing at the surface. All she had left now were the flippers, goggles and the two wristwatches, one of which she flung off. It began flashing as it floated away.

She was now untraceable.

Mello nodded, signaling they were ready, and pulled

her hands around his neck from behind, leading her into the forest. The dolphins followed at her heels. She held on tight, floating along behind him like a cape in the wind as he walked.

He was walking, not swimming, she noticed with confusion.

But his strides were wide and fast and they moved at a steady clip. His body stayed weighted to the ground as though gravity were no different on the ocean floor than on the sidewalk. Patches of sunlight streamed through the seaweed creating shadowy hues of aquamarine and the sandy floor declined to a steep slope. As they descended, the floor became smoother and she realized they were no longer inside the forest, but *underneath* the forest. A canopy of kelp hovered above them like a dense green cloud, and in the murky distance she could see a blinking red light.

The submarine! They were almost there.

Her lungs felt like a balloon about to burst and every blood vessel in her body throbbed. A dizzy, lightheaded feeling began to overtake her. *What was she doing here again?* She had a burning desire to close her eyes and just float.

Mello looked at her with widening eyes, then picked up the pace, dragging her swiftly along like a ragdoll. The dolphins nudged at her feet, her legs. *Thump, thump, thump.* Her entire body throbbed now, pulsating with her strained heart.

Suddenly, a few feet ahead she could see herself and Mello. Their images moved in slow motion. It was like she was looking in the mirror. But the mirror shimmered and bowed as though breathing, and her image distorted as they approached. Then the reflective watercraft was upon them, a behemoth of camouflaged metal hovering inches above the seafloor.

Mello darted up to the hatch on top and began twisting a gear, then pulled it open with a creak. He motioned for her to crawl inside.

At the sight of the dark cavity, her mind jerked out of the dreamy haze and she stared in horror. Its opening was the size of a manhole, black and hollow. Mello gestured again in frantic motion for her to get inside. She shook her head. It went against every instinct in her body.

"Can't we just go by boat?" she had asked Sam.

"No, our chances of being discovered would be too high. The only road to Rodinia is along the seafloor."

"And this guy, this siren, he'll keep me safe? He won't let me drown?"

"Yes. You have to trust him underwater. He's all you will have," Sam had told her.

If she did not trust him, she would drown here anyway. She scrambled inside and curled into fetal position. Her mass of hair swirled above trying to escape the chamber, and she yanked it inside with her just before Mello slammed the hatch shut with a resonating thud. In the following silence, a feeling of doom crept in.

Don't panic, don't panic, don't panic.

Her lungs burned like wildfire, on the verge of exploding. Panic. She kicked, tried to scream but water flooded her mouth, intensifying the feeling of terror. In desperation, she pounded her fists against the ceiling of the hatch. *This was it, this was how she was going to die.*

Just before she lost consciousness, an image of Jake smiling, a single curl hanging over his forehead, appeared in her mind, then the gurgling sound of a drain erupted in her ears.

TWO

JAKE

Washington, DC
September 22, 2098

JAKE EXITED DIVINCARE HOSPITAL and yanked down his germ mask to take a deep breath. The heavy air offered no relief, but at least it didn't smell of death. Pedestrians streamed around him on the Centercity sidewalk, but he felt miles away from them. Everything still felt numb, surreal, as though this day was a nightmare he would soon awake from. Exhaling, he lifted his face upward. The white skyscrapers seemed to lean in, undulating in a dizzy display of lights. Jake used to find the colorful sight exhilarating, but now it felt oppressive, a concrete maze meant to trap and confuse him. His tablet buzzed against his thigh and he pulled it out to check the voicemail.

"Dude, call me. Crazy shit is happening out here at the factory. I think they've got some sort of aliens or something." Jake clicked delete and the holo image of his twin brother Leo disappeared into the blackglass. Another one followed. "Bro, call me."

For the past twenty-four hours Jake had ignored a dozen calls, from his brother, his Commanding Officer, several friends offering condolences. The news about Lorel still reeled in his mind and spending the last few hours with Henry had only made it worse. Two men, helpless and grieving. As much as he cared for Lorel's father, Jake was glad to be alone. He did not want to talk to anyone else unless it was the Kotte authorities. Or Lorel.

But her message had breathed life into him. And hope. He could not stop analyzing her note, hand written and tucked carefully inside the seashell. It had been addressed to her father, but when Jake closed his eyes he could feel her whisper the words directly to him.

. . . I may be far away, but I will be back.

They haunted him now. Did she mean she would be back in a week as planned and for her Dad to keep his spirits high while she was gone? Was she not dead? Was it some cryptic message meant to let them know that although the world may think she had drowned at sea, she was alive somewhere? Or maybe it was just some prank, by the same people who had been following her.

Regardless, Jake felt like he had just been injected with a syringe of adrenaline. He was on a mission. And the first step was talking to Leo. In the back of his mind, he wondered if the strange activity Leo had mentioned regarding the DiviniGen factory—Reshing's appearance,

23

people covered in black cloth—had to do with whatever Lorel was involved in before she left. On the surface it seemed unrelated. But there was one link.

Reshing.

Jake mounted his bike, revved the engine, and sped away from the hospital, headed for the freeway. The Skirts. At the familiar Fort Miller exit, he squealed off and began to taper his speed. The full moon looked brighter outside of the city and cast a bluish hue on the crumbling sidewalks. With a burst of eagerness he hopped off his bike and crossed the lawn to the front door. It would be good to see Leo. He was the only family Jake had left.

And right now he needed family.

As the chiming of the old-fashioned doorbell faded inside, Jake frowned. The front porch light was off and the house was dark. Maybe he should have announced his visit ahead of time, but Leo was always home in the evenings. His whole life was in this neighborhood. And he was the heart of it. The neighbors loved his brother, who shared his fresh garden yields and taught lessons in agricultural survival, a valuable skill in the Skirts, where the only food was PeterPan or DivinCakes.

PanDivinity still had their claws in tightly out here, Jake thought. Maybe even more so than in the city. The people were poorer, less educated, and easier to take advantage of.

Jake banged on the door one more time then walked around to the back of the house. No sign of Leo. He crossed the patio and peered into the bay window of the kitchen. At first Jake thought his eyes were playing tricks on him. He rubbed them.

The figure of a body lay splayed across the floor near the dishwasher. Barely discernable was a puddle of dark liquid surrounding it. Jake stomach plummeted. *It's not what you think,* he said to himself, though his heartbeat intensified.

Spotting a nearby decorative stone, he picked it up and tossed it through the window of the back door, then reached inside and turned the old manual lock. With the flip of the light switch, Jake's worst fear was realized.

His brother lay dead on the floor. The clear demarcation of a las-gun through his forehead sent a shudder of grief through Jake so powerful he fell forward, grabbing the kitchen counter to steady himself.

He began shaking uncontrollably and let out a bellowing cry. *Who had done this?*

No sooner had he asked himself the question then he knew the answer.

THREE
LOREL

Indian Ocean
September 22, 2098

A FACE MATERIALIZED IN FRONT of her as she slowly came to. Mello. He stood at her bedside. The sight of the siren sent a rush of heat through her body and suddenly she was fully alert. He started as though caught in a moment, and she realized he had been watching her.

"Hi." She sat up and held out her hand, hoping the expression on her face did not betray the spellbound delight she felt inside. "I'm Lorel."

Instead of the handshake she expected, Mello took her hand gently in his and kissed it. When he looked up his cheeks were flushed. Sparks lit beneath her skin where his lips touched, and she stopped breathing for a moment.

"I'm Mello. Nice to meet you." His eyes flickered all over her at once. "Welcome to the Barracuda."

There was something about him, something familiar. She opened her mouth to ask if they had met, then realized how ridiculous it would sound.

"Nice to meet you, Mello," she managed with a weak smile.

He returned the smile, revealing fine square teeth, humanlike but for the canines, which were wide at the top and tapered to a sharp point. His hair was a silvery shimmering blond like none she had ever seen. It fell in damp waves across his forehead, curling around his ears and just grazing his neck. A single black streak shot from his widow's peak winding around his temple and tucking behind his ear before reappearing in a swirl at the nape of his neck. His skin was deeply tanned, hairless and smooth as polished stone, but raw pink scars slashed across his chest, face, and arms interrupting the flawless texture. The lines were precise and symmetrical, like medical incisions.

Lorel remembered what Sam had told her. Mello had experienced something real, something torturous during his captivity in DiviniGen. The evidence ran deeper than the scars. It glinted at the corners of his mouth and in the depths of his eyes. A profound pain. She felt a burst of sympathy for this strange man before her. And then anger.

Damn you, Galton.

An agonizing desire to touch him seized her. If she could just run her fingers across his chest, along the facets of his fresh scars maybe she could ease his pain. But an invisible force seemed to stop her, the barrier of two worlds refusing to mix. His face had three, one running horizontally across his forehead and the other two slashing downward across his cheeks toward his nose like tribal markings. The structure of his facial bones was strong and angular, but there was something soft, almost vulnerable, beneath his exquisite masculinity.

"I can't thank you enough," she said softly.

"You can pay me back in pirate's gold," he replied, with a hint of a smile.

"What?" She had never heard anyone but her father say the quirky phrase.

Mello blushed. "It's just a saying. You owe me nothing."

"Thank you, Mello."

Silence stretched before them.

"So how did you do it?" she asked, straightening up in the bed. "How did you change the current?"

"There's no magic to reveal, I'm afraid. Sirens just know the water the same way birds know the wind." He took a seat at the foot of her bed, his head bent low to avoid bumping the top bunk. With a smile he said, "You seem disappointed."

"It almost seemed like you could control the tide."

"Well, if you blow hard, you can direct the current of the air. I guess what we do is similar. Not control so much as manipulation," he said shrugging. "It's just an instinctual part of how we interact with the water."

"It's beautiful," Lorel said. There was so much to discover about this new species. Hopefully she could learn more from Mello. He seemed kind, and open to sharing the capabilities of a siren. He exuded a delicate balance of pride and humility that disarmed her.

In another stretch of silence, his gaze remained fixed on Lorel, and blood rushed to her cheeks. He was so close she could feel the heat emanating from his body. She knew she should pull away, but he drew her in. Second by second the barrier melted away. Unable to return his piercing gaze any longer without losing focus, she glanced around, soaking in her new surroundings.

"I hope you're comfortable here," he said.

"I am. Thank you."

The room was tiny, to be expected in a submarine, but cozy. Soft LED lights burned from dots in the ceiling and bounced off the pocked metal walls, brightening the space. A metal dresser was built into the far wall. Next to it was a heavy-looking door with a round window mirroring the one a few inches from her on the wall. Still in nothing but underwear, she sat wrapped in an oversized plush robe on the lower mattress of the bunk bed. Someone had seen to it that she was warm and dry on board.

Her eyes magnetically returned to his. "Mello?"

With a flit of self-awareness, he broke his gaze and stood up from the foot of her bed. "Sorry to stare, it's just that . . ." he started, a note of apology in his voice, "I've only seen brown eyes a couple times in my life. Yours are enchanting." His candor startled her and heat coursed through her body.

"Thanks. They're a gift from my dad. From the Italian side, not the Irish," she said, then wondered if sirens understood Mendelian inheritance.

"I heard your father is sick. I'm sorry," Mello said.

Lorel closed her eyes, trying not to think of what pain she was causing her father. He would be hearing the news of her death anytime now, maybe already had.

"Thank you. Today is his birthday." Out the round window she could see only blackness and a stream of bubbles. It appeared they were moving fast. "So, how far are we? And . . . how deep?"

"Very deep. We have another few hours. You passed out in the hatch, then awoke in bed only to fall right back into a ten-hour slumber." He smiled. "I think you needed it."

As he turned and walked toward the door, she noticed a tattoo at the nape of his neck. Several concentric circles darkened to a center of solid black like a whirlpool.

"No wonder I feel so awake now," she said pulling the covers off and sliding her legs over the side of the bed.

"Unfortunately, you'll need to stay in here for the rest of the trip. Quarantine," he said with an apologetic tilt of his head.

"Oh." She looked down, suddenly feeling like a leper.

"Don't worry, it is just a precaution. You know, different germs and all that."

"Of course." She nodded. "Just one more question though. Rodinia is not . . . *entirely* underwater, is it?"

He chuckled. "Only half."

She laughed nervously in return, relieved. It was silly, but for a terrifying moment, she thought maybe she had overlooked a major detail. *How little she knew of this place.*

"Don't worry, you can keep your land legs for now. I'll be back to check on you. In the meantime, there is someone eager to say hello."

As Mello slipped out the door, Link, her transgenic big cat, slid in with a deep guttural purr. His golden eyes danced with joy, so unlike the sadness she'd seen in them when he'd departed with Sam back in DC. Relieved he had made the journey, she jumped up, clasping her hands over her chest.

"Hey buddy! Did Sam take good care of you?"

In response, he pounced at Lorel. All one hundred and twenty pounds of feline weight shoved her back on the bed where he began smothering her face in rough wet kisses.

F O U R

JAKE

September 23, 2098
Washington, DC

IN A WINDOWLESS BOOTH of the PanDivinity Hub just off DuPont Circle, Jake pressed his finger to the blackglass table to pay for another timeslot of holo streaming. A green light confirmed print recognition and the timer began, accumulating his bill. He tapped a red bottle icon to order his third BullCoke, despite the fact that his hands and feet were already shaking and a current of energy ripped through his body every few seconds.

Only yesterday he had discovered his brother dead on the floor of their childhood home. The entirety of the previous night was spent in the Skirts with a slew of cops and investigators. Upon realizing that Jake was the same person who had killed a man in self-defense only days earlier in the city, they had dragged him to the Fort Miller station. It was salt in the wound. He had murdered someone to save Lorel's life, only for her to lose it days later. In his state of grief, they interrogated him beneath scathing heat lamps. Jake could hardly believe the nightmarish events. If it were not for his commanding officer swooping in to defend his name, he would probably be behind bars, or worse.

Part of him wondered if PanDivinity was behind Leo's death. After all, everything that his brother stood for conflicted with the values the omnipotent company propagated. Where they touted greed, indulgence and blind faith in a corporate god, Leo stood for humility, self-restraint, and freedom from anything material. He had a spiritual respect for the earth, understanding that humans benefitted most from enjoying a symbiotic relationship with it. He was loved by the people in his community and spread his values to them. He taught them that they did not have to depend on a corporation for every human need.

There were rumors that PanDivinity kept lists of people who were subversive, people who threatened the way of life they had so successfully ingrained in humans. A way so beneficial to them and only them. But would they go so far as to kill people? It seemed so medieval. Plus, Jake felt the cause behind Leo's death may be closer to home, perhaps related to certain events he'd been trying to make sense of.

He needed to remain laser-focused. The tragedy had only made his mission more clear. Someone had killed Leo. Someone had possibly killed Lorel—or left her for dead—and Jake knew who was behind it. He had to be.

For the tenth time since sitting down, he restarted the news vid from earlier in the day.

I'm going to kill you, you piece of shit.

I'm going to find you, and I'm going to kill you.

Jake clutched the edge of the table as the holo lit up in three dimensions beneath the glass. The image sent a fresh rush of blood to his face. Benjamin Reshing stepping off the Naval plane and onto the tarmac, tanned and smiling as if he had just returned from the tropical vacation, the other scientists trailing behind him looking jetlagged and weary. Jake's chest tightened.

Reporters swarmed around the celebrity scientist, shoving microphones in his face and peppering him with questions. *Has Ms. Phoenix's family been notified? How long did you wait before turning the boat around? Do you feel like the Kotte authorities conducted a proper search? Were pirates responsible? Was she married?*

The last question clenched at his heart. A ring, hidden beneath the mattress of his sailboat home, flashed to mind in cruel memory. *Almost.*

Reshing answered each question in turn with poise and a touch of feigned sympathy then looked directly into the camera. "Lorelei Phoenix was a great scientist, dedicated to oceanic preservation and the pursuit of scientific advancement. The Department is deeply saddened by her death and our heart goes out to her father, Henry Phoenix, who is her only surviving family member."

Her death. The elegiac lament disgusted Jake. They

had not even found her body, and this man was already dismissing her as dead. It seemed like everyone had. Reshing may fool the rest of the world, but he was not fooling Jake. There was more to the story.

"Dr. Reshing, can you tell us what type of assignment Ms. Phoenix was on?"

"I cannot discuss the details of Ms. Phoenix's research."

The reporter pursed her lips but continued. "Just one more question, Doctor. There have been reports that her dive equipment surfaced during the search and that her wetsuit was torn to shreds. Has there been any confirmation that sharks devoured her body?"

Jake paused the video as Reshing responded to the reporter's crass question. For a split second the camera caught a look that confirmed all of Jake's suspicions. Reshing smiled at the woman, but Jake saw it in the twitch of his lip and hardening of his jaw.

Something darker than guilt. Satisfaction. "I won't be commenting on any more details until we speak personally with her father. Thank you," he replied coldly, then bowed his head and pushed his way out of the cluster of reporters. A black limousine just off the tarmac pulled up to him and he ducked inside.

The camera panned to the onsite anchor, an attractive man sporting a coif of black hair with stylish blue streaks and a theatrical look of sympathy. "Well, folks, a big loss for the US Department of Oceanic Administration. Budding scientist Lorelei Phoenix lost at sea, presumed dead."

A picture of Lorel flashed on screen. It must have been supplied by the Department. She wore a suit and stood at a podium smiling next to Reshing, whose arm wound proudly — *possessively* — around her shoulder. Behind them was a royal-blue drop curtain with the logo of the *Sea Ethics Foundation*. "We'll keep viewers posted if there are any new developments in this story. Mike, back to you at the station."

Jake slammed his fist against the blackglass, splashing his BullCoke on the smooth surface. A couple at a nearby station who had been accumulating a pile of shopping bags next to their glowing screen turned to glare at him. He sunk lower in his seat. Disgust, anguish, and rage were the only emotions he was capable of lately and he did not want to scare anyone. He had to stop obsessing and do something.

Leo was gone. He had been onto something at the factory, and now he was dead. There was nothing Jake could do but mourn the death of his only living family member. But in Lorel there was a glimmer of hope. The intentions behind her note were unclear, and her words floated through his mind in a cloud of mystery. But the more he thought about it, the more certain he felt that her message was a call for help. She had disappeared, and she *knew* for some reason that that would be her fate. Wherever she was, she was alive. She needed him.

And he was going to find her.

Later that night Jake scanned Lorel's apartment from the center of her living room. It was possible she had never taken her personal tablet to Sri Lanka since she had her work-issued one. Where would she have kept it? If he could get into her tablet, he was sure Ben Reshing's address would be in there. It was unlisted on every website Jake had searched on the Internet, but he was determined to pay the doctor a visit.

He sighed in frustration at Lorel's stubborn resistance to certain technologies. If she had a synced hologram screen he could easily retrieve her contacts. Now he was forced to search for a small slab of blackglass that she could have stashed anywhere. After rummaging through every drawer and cabinet, beneath every cushion of the couch, he sat on her bed with his face in his hands. Something hard slid under his heel as he moved his foot. He reached under the dust ruffle and pulled out a tablet half tucked inside a manila envelope.

He stared at it in wonder. It was too big to be her palm tablet and there was no personalization to be seen on its casing. Even more perplexing, the screen was shattered with a large piece missing, and Jake could find no way of turning it on. The manila wrapping was just as mysterious. A string of random numbers was scribbled across it in Lorel's handwriting.

Jake reached inside to see if there was anything else

in the envelope. He pulled out a small plastic card and, recognizing it as a business card, swiped his finger across it. Letters lit up in green.

> *George Oberbach*
> *IT Systems, Private Contractor, DiviniGen, Inc.*
> *Home Office:*
> *54 Ironside Drive, Washington, DC 20007*

Jake stared at the man's name with furrowed brows. Lorel had never mentioned anyone named George before. And why would she be associating with someone from DiviniGen? She passionately avoided people who worked for the greedy megacorps, the "corp zombies" as she called them. Lorel and Jake used to spend endless hours bemoaning the state of the nation, how PanDivinity corporations had hijacked the government and left the people helpless as they elected puppets for politicians.

But this was something, Jake thought. This was a clue to what Lorel was doing in the weeks before she left. He had to pursue it.

Jake scanned the address into his tablet, yanked on his navy hoodie, and headed down to the street to catch a cab.

FIVE
LOREL

September 23, 2098
Indian Ocean

SITTING ON HER BUNK, Lorel tugged on her lip in thrilling anticipation as she glided her fingers over the corner of the colorful papyrus map. Isla, the first and only siren Lorel had ever met, had given it to her to study the lay of the land, and Lorel felt like she had been handed a Dead Sea Scroll. At the top of the map was a series of numbers. She traced them with her finger. Only a few weeks ago she had stared at the mysterious sequence of numbers in bewilderment. Now, here she was.

INDIAN OCEAN
ARCHIPELAGO # -6.111, 72.085
(RODINIA)

The map also included maritime trade routes, but the

island was not within the crosshairs of a single one. At the bottom, a man's name was printed in tiny letters.

SIR CHRISTOPHER SAXTON
CARTOGRAPHER & DESIGNATED GUARDIAN
BEACON, 1908

The detailed sketch of the island looked like a tropical paradise frozen in time, a warped time where things were different. It was a circular chain of five mountainous islands, each with their own names, but marked as "Land Realm." Swampy marine forests called "The Mangroves" loosely linked the five islands. Rocky islets were scattered around the outside perimeter labeled "Open Sea Realm." Inside the ring was the heart of the island, a round expanse of water named "The Eye." Penned in larger letters across it was "Blue Hole Realm." She shivered at the thought of the geological wonder that lay beneath the Eye: the blue oceanic sinkhole plunging a thousand feet to a sea floor flourishing with life.

A portal to another world.

Lorel noticed a tiny star symbol in the center of the blue hole and referenced the map's key in the bottom right corner. Next to the star read: "Abyssal Plane — See Separate Map, Council Approval Only." The reference only made her more curious. Where was the map? And what dictated Council approval? The base of the blue hole was a tightly guarded area of Rodinia. *And where the algae grew,* she thought.

A ring of coral that receded into the inner shores of

the islands served as a perimeter: "The Eye Atoll". Each island's beach corresponded with the name of the island itself.

The varying topography was fascinating. Some islands appeared to have a smooth landscape of greenery, while others were rocky. All boasted tall spires of mountains.

"Volcanically formed," she whispered to herself.

One island, labeled "Paraíso," seemed to be taken up almost entirely by a single volcano — the Vulcan. Its sides cascaded down in jagged, jungly terrain, which turned to a mix of forests, then sandy dunes, and finally smoothing into beach. Paraíso Beach. Paradise. The name struck her as odd for some reason.

Lorel stared down at the Blue Hole Realm. She knew from her studies that the gaping watery cavity in the center had a cave system of rock that formed the surrounding walls, tunneling far beyond the perimeter of the island ring itself. Did they actually inhabit the caves?

The population of sirens was about fifteen thousand. Which meant that was about the number of sirens in the entire world. *That certainly classified them as an endangered species,* Lorel thought, raking a finger through her tangle of salty hair.

Her allegiance to these people was growing stronger. Even just the two sirens she had met possessed something special, an authentic ease with their own existence, like they had figured out the secret to life. Old souls. They had a comfort in their own skin that Lorel had never known but always searched for.

She peered closer at the sketch of the Land Realm. Sam said they would be staying on Baltra. It was hard to tell from the map, but the key feature of the land there seemed to be cliffs. And from the contour lines, they looked magnificently high. Imagining them in reality, her stomach fluttered.

A light rapping at her door made her jump. Sam Bishop peeked through the round window of her door. She waved him in. His grey-flecked hair was tousled, and he looked at her with concerned blue eyes through his wire-rimmed glasses. Though most people used PAPs, DiviniGen's patented phenotype altering pills, to correct vision, Sam stuck with old-fashioned glasses. Lorel saw them as his trademark, adding to his academic look. He smiled and the warmth on his face made her think of home. Although she had only known him for a few weeks after he'd mysteriously introduced himself in DC as a fellow marine biologist, he had changed her life. He had imparted knowledge to her of the sirens. He had led her here.

"Hi Sam." She placed the map gently on the bed and walked over to him. He wrapped her in a bear hug and emotion welled in her chest. "I made it."

"You made it." He sighed, pulling away to look at her and shaking his head in relief. "I got a little worried when you didn't meet our courier at the Sri Lankan airport to get the watch."

"I got a little worried when Mello shoved me into that tank full of water and I thought I was going to die!"

They laughed, breaking the heaviness of the moment.

Sam glanced at the map she had spread out on the bed. "Have you memorized all your realms yet?"

"I have to admit, I'm looking forward to seeing this place. It's a volcanic island chain, isn't it?" She asked. Sam always brought out the curious scientist in her.

He took a seat on the bed and peered over her shoulder. "Yes. And see these jagged lines?" He slid his finger along faint lines that divided the whole map like a jigsaw puzzle. "These delineate the tectonic plates."

Lorel pressed a finger to her lips, digging to retrieve her geological knowledge. "The plates collide right underneath the island, and it's volcanic so there's a mantle plume beneath it churning lava, which means—Rodinia is on a hotspot?"

Sam smiled. "Precisely."

Lorel exhaled with excitement. "Just like the Galapagos are."

"Or were," Sam corrected her.

They looked at each other in silence.

"So are you feeling ready for all this?" he asked gently.

She nodded. There was no use in dwelling on the darker reasons they were here. "I'm ready."

"Not much longer to go. I'll see you soon." Sam put a hand on her shoulder and squeezed, then walked out the door, leaving her alone once again.

As she started to roll up the map she noticed a smudge mark on the island marked "Paraíso". She peered closer but still could not decipher the letters. *Why had someone tried to cover up a landmark?*

43

She finished rolling it up and set it on the bed. A stack of her clothes lay folded on the dresser. She untied the terry cloth robe and let it drop to the floor, shivering as the cool air hit her naked body. She pulled on the jeans and white T-shirt that smelled of her laundry detergent and looked around for something long sleeved. Inside the top drawer of the dresser was a tunic unlike any fashion she had seen at home. Its design was simple, and the undyed fabric seemed suited for hot weather. She ran her fingers along the soft threading then pulled it over her head. It was too big but warm and smelled of the sea.

She began to hum, pacing the room and staring out the window, which was still black with a constant stream of bubbles. They must be close. So what now? There was no way she was sleeping another wink. The trip seemed to be taking forever and the thought of arriving in Rodinia loomed in her mind in an intoxication of wonder and dread.

It would not be a paradise during her visit. *Visit* was the word she had been using in her mind. *To go and stay for a temporary period of time.* She would get back home. She would either convince the queen, or she would find her own way out.

Just hold on, Dad. Please hold on.

Jake was probably there with him right now, protecting him, comforting him. Hopefully one of them had understood her message, read in between the lines — or found some hope she could still be alive. Although it was crucial that the rest of the world believe it, she could not bear the idea of Jake and her father thinking she was dead. It had been so hard not to tell Jake. When they made love the night before she left, her heart was filled with sorrow and she had tried her best to hide her tears. She had almost broken.

Maybe if things had been different, if he had been more receptive when she asked him to move from New Charleston to DC with her, she would feel more open around him. But he forced her to put another brick in the wall, continue blocking him out. It was her best tool for self-preservation, one she had developed as a child.

Traveling around the world to remote and often primitive countries had prevented her from making many friends throughout her childhood. There were times when she did make strong connections only to realize that she was forced to sever them when it was time to move on. It made for a lonely life, but it gave her control. No one could abandon her again the way her mother had. There was a comfort in that.

But as the thought of her mother surfaced with a dull pang in her chest, Lorel knew it was a wound that had never heeled. The primal love for a mother was too powerful to overcome, even after twenty-five years. Maybe it didn't work both ways though. Her mother had been able to walk away. Her father had searched for her for years, holding out hope they could one day reunite, until he learned she had died. The finality of her death was salt in his would, and it only made Lorel more furious with the woman who had left her motherless and broken her father's heart. The resentment that Lorel had never been able to shake weighed on her like a heavy cloak, blocking her true self from others.

With Jake it was not only her emotional blockage that prevented her from telling him everything. It was also fear of getting him involved in such a dangerous situation, not that he couldn't handle it. He was professionally trained to defend, after all. But that was part of the problem. When it came to protecting her, sometimes he was too brazen for his own good. She would never forget how he saved her from the attacker in her apartment—the blood was still fresh on his hands—but where was that loyalty when it came to commitment?

What dominated Jake was his temper, his passion. Add his combative skills, and sometimes his drinking, and it could be explosive. If he knew she was in danger, he would head straight for the man behind the curtain, like a bull charging a matador. This was not some pervert on the street whistling at her, this was Francis Galton—the CEO of a PanDivinity company. He was too powerful an adversary, even for Jake. She would never forgive herself if something happened to him because of her.

She sighed, smoothing the tunic against her skin. It was better this way.

Walking over to the mirror hanging above the dresser, she looked at her reflection. Her soft waves had turned to tight curls from the saltwater and dark bags hung under her eyes. She pulled her fingers through her hair and wiped a smudge of eyeliner that had crept below her lash line. She looked like a girl in need of rescue.

But she was not. She had chosen this path that trailed off the grid leaving no breadcrumbs. The fear that she might never see Jake again pressed against her chest like a weight, and she took a deep breath.

"We'll see him again, won't we, Link?" She kneeled to pet the giant spotted cat curled comfortably in a ball next to her bed. He purred, the sound of gently rolling thunder, oblivious to the gravity of their journey. *Of course we will.*

She would be back.

SIX

LOREL

September 23, 2098
Indian Ocean

"WE'RE A HUNDRED YARDS out! Change the ballast tank to neutral buoyancy and cut the propeller," Mello shouted from out in the control room.

Lorel clutched the metal bedpost as a series of loud beeps echoed into the sleeping chambers. They were ascending. Her stomach somersaulted at the sudden change in pressure. The Barracuda rose adeptly, like the fish it was named for.

She scrambled to her bunk and peered through the tiny window. Bright lights popped on illuminating the undersea environment that had before been a black abyss. She looked out and released a slow breath, steaming the window. A knot formed in her stomach.

Not one, not two, but three sunken ships emerged

within her span of view. The wreckage looked ancient, ships half-buried in the sand like the one at the research dive. Along the sea floor at about ten yard intervals, spiked metal spheres the size of bowling balls floated ominously in the water, suspended to the bottom with chains.

Mines.

These ships had not wrecked from natural causes. This was the sirens' homemade Bermuda Triangle.

Who are these people? she wondered with a shiver. The watercraft continued to rise, shedding light on the expansive ship graveyard. She shuddered at the thought of how many human bones must lay buried within. But it all made sense. The whole perimeter of Rodinia was probably surrounded with remnants of ships that had the misfortune of getting too close to the forbidden island.

Lorel remembered the myth of the mermaids attracting sailors to jagged rocks, luring them to their death with hypnotic voices. But surely the sirens had not intentionally attracted humans to Rodinia. They had reacted only in defense. It was self-preservation, the instinct of all species. This was how the sirens had kept their home a secret, at least in the past, before using sleight of hand with satellite images. Before Beacon. Still, it left an unsettling feeling in her stomach.

The ghost ships disappeared into the depths as the Barracuda rose toward the surface, pausing about ten feet below with a gurgling *whoosh*. Lorel realized she had been squeezing her eyes shut. She opened them with a burst of excitement. It would not be long before she set foot on Rodinian soil.

A knock sounded at her door.

"Lorel, come look."

It was Mello.

"You mean I can come out of quarantine?"

"I think you've served your time." He grabbed her hand and led her out of the room, down a narrow hall full of blinking red lights and into an open space full of what appeared to be navigation equipment.

"Just below maximum buoyancy," called Isla as she pulled a lever. She stood at a dizzying display of controls just below a large protruding window.

Noticing Lorel enter, Isla cast her a warm smile. A surreal feeling passed through Lorel, just as it had when Sam Bishop introduced her to his wife back in DC. Already, the siren seemed more in her element. She wore a simple white tunic that gathered just above her belly, which looked about to pop, and shiny cornsilk hair fell around her shoulders.

The ship jerked and Lorel's hands shot out to steady herself.

"Sorry, Lorel. I'll hold it here until we're ready to surface." Isla's hands danced across the knobs, twisting and pulling. Bubbles rushed over the window's surface making visibility near impossible.

Off to the side of the control board, Sam clutched a long pipe that extended from the ceiling. He pressed his face against a glass device at its base, deep in concentration.

"Is that a periscope?" Lorel asked, approaching.

Sam pulled away, red circles imprinted around his eyes. "I think you deserve a turn here, Dr. Phoenix," he said spinning the eyepiece in her direction.

"Thanks," she whispered, pulling it against her face. At first the brightness was blinding, but after a moment her eyes adjusted.

It was dawn and the sun had just begun to peak over the horizon. The water was calm, mirroring the gray sky, and was only interrupted by statuesque rocks that emerged from the surface like chess pieces standing guard over the land beyond. They were clustered together so densely it was a wonder how any ship could navigate between them. In the distance, Lorel could make out green mountainous peaks piercing through a dense ring of fog and up into the low-lying clouds.

There it was. Rodinia.

A hand touched her shoulder. "Are you ready?"

She pulled away and turned to Sam. He looked years younger, wearing linen pants and a buttoned tunic like the one she had found in her room. His eyes glistened with excitement. "The boat is here for us."

"Boat?" she blinked, looking down at her comfy clothes in relief. "Nice."

"You didn't think we were going to make you swim, did you?" Isla winked from her chair by the control board.

Lorel shrugged. "Let's just say nothing would surprise me at this point. I'll go gather my things."

On the way to her room, the Barracuda began rocking more violently. She used the walls to steady herself and practically fell to her knees inside the room. The small rolling suitcase Sam had toted from DC for her stood next to the bed. She grabbed it then secured a leash to Link's pink leather collar and returned to join the group.

Out in the bridge of the inner hull, multiple holocam monitors flashed with sceneries of their surroundings. The Barracuda groaned loudly.

"Take a seat, Lorel. It's a bumpy ride to the surface." Mello gestured to a stool bolted to the ground and she collapsed into it as the room swayed.

Mello and Isla seemed to maintain balance, clambering around by the control board pressing buttons and pulling levers, but Sam clutched his stool with white knuckles.

"So where do they park this thing? I assume not out in the open ocean." She raised a brow at Sam.

"No. It has a slip in the grottoes, inside the blue hole about a mile down."

"So you can get inside Rodinia from underwater?"

"Not exactly. The ocean and the blue hole don't connect. They are separated by a seawall of rock, but there is one tunnel. Its entrance is widened for the Barracuda to fit in just enough to be hidden. Then it narrows to a swimming passage. The sirens keep it barricaded at all times though, so that no predators or anything else could enter Rodinia from below. Mello and Isla will secure the sub there, then swim up through the blue hole to the beach."

"Up through the Eye," Lorel murmured.

"I see you've been studying. But hold onto that map.

This place has more geological nooks and crannies than you could imagine. Some you don't want to stumble on by surprise."

Lorel felt confident despite Sam's cautionary tone. Navigating new territory was a forte she had developed from accompanying her father around the world on his archeological digs. She was ready for the challenge.

After a few more minutes of nauseating movement, the Barracuda slowed and then broke through the surface. Mello cut the engine and the vessel gently bobbed. Lorel placed a hand to her stomach to counteract a wave of nausea.

"Sam, you and Lorel can debark now." Mello called over his shoulder, still focused on the controls.

"Let's do it." Sam stood and the color returned to his face. "Follow me."

With Link in tow, she followed Sam down the hallway. He opened a door at the end to reveal a ladder. Lorel peeked her head in to see that it led up to a hatch.

"Oh." A fresh memory of being trapped inside the watery cavity made her halt.

"Don't worry, this time you'll open that hatch to the freshest air you have ever breathed."

"I like the sound of that," she said with relief. "After you." Heaving their luggage, they climbed up the ladder and Sam pushed open the hatch above. Sunlight streamed in, and she felt a rush of hot air and smelled salt.

"Lorel, meet Silas."

No sooner had Lorel pulled herself out onto the curved surface of the half-exposed submarine when a hand reached up toward her, long webbed fingers outstretched in greeting.

"Welcome." Silas nodded and his long black hair, dreaded and woven with creeper vines, blew in a light breeze. The siren looked no older than sixteen. He smiled up at her bashfully with one foot in a small wooden canoe boat and the other balancing on a rung of the ladder. "Please, let me help you down."

She grabbed his hand, and as he clasped hers tightly she felt the webbing. It was smooth and collagenous. Clumsily she stepped into the boat followed by a surefooted Link, then Sam and their luggage. Woven straw cushions padded the seats and a bouquet of bright orange and white flowers hung from the curved wooden bow.

They rode in the serene silence of the morning as Silas paddled adeptly around the towering rock structures that guarded the shore. Geological structures here seemed purposeful as though they had evolved to protect their island just as living things did. *Little pawns defending their king,* she thought. The shape of the island and all of its jutting peaks reminded her of a royal crown.

She closed her eyes, then opened them to make sure it was all real. Home seemed so far away, another world. Another life. The dip and pull of Silas's oar was the only sound other than the distant shriek of birds. Clusters of white gulls swarmed around the rocky shore. Something sacred emanated from the presence of the island, and Lorel felt a warmth flow through her.

"Sam," she whispered.

"Yes?" he replied, then added in a whisper, "Don't worry, there's no one to hear us for miles."

She laughed.

"Don't get me wrong, I know why we're here, but I feel so . . . peaceful." She lifted her face to the brightening sky and the sun warmed her cheeks. "Like I'm coming home."

Sam was silent then cleared his throat.

"Lorel, there's something I need to talk to you about. As soon as you get settled in your hut, we can meet on the beach."

"Sure." She smiled. "Dare I ask, do they have coffee in Rodinia?"

"The best."

The sand of Baltra's inner beach felt warm and welcoming underneath her feet compared to the rocky outer beach that they had landed on, and the sun had burned off the fog to expose a clear panoramic view of the archipelago. Lorel, Link, and Sam followed Silas across the beach as he led them to Lorel's hut, but she had to stop and soak in the full vista.

"Link, isn't it beautiful?" she whispered, kneeling down to release his leash.

True to the map, Rodinia was a tight ring of islands surrounding a sapphire-blue body of water. Lorel squinted toward the north to see the view of the other islands from Baltra. The diameter of the ring appeared to be a couple miles at most and the farthest islands shimmered in a distant haze. They were all mountainous, revealing their volcanic origin. The dense mangroves between each island gave the impression the land was all connected, a closed circuit.

The island to the northeast, Paraíso, was a single volcanic mountain that stretched toward the sky, its mouth gaping open at the zenith as if ready to slurp rain straight from the clouds. Lorel's gaze fixed on the grand geological structure.

"That is the Vulcan, the only active volcano in Rodinia. See its flat top? You can peer down into the crater if you hike up there. Though I wouldn't recommend it," Silas said as he carried her suitcase up the beach toward a line of palm trees.

"Does it ever erupt?" Lorel asked, noticing a faint trail of white swirling from the top as the clouds parted.

"No way, she's all smoke and no fire. She hasn't erupted in five thousand years, and won't again. Unless we ask her to," Silas replied with a cryptic smile.

"Don't worry, Lorel. You're safe here," Sam said.

"At least from natural disasters," she added under her breath.

They were now treading on a soft bed of pine needles and Lorel noticed the temperature drop with the thickening trees. The forest felt ancient, as though souls of the sirens' ancestors hovered in the shadows. A multilayer canopy of leaves blocked the light except for scattered gaps where fallen trees had invited in the sun. Trunks of varying diameters competed in height, all reaching for the sky. Woody debris covered the ground, sprouting assortments of springy ferns and sprawling vines.

Lorel inhaled the oxygen rich air, taking in the loamy scent of earth and decay. She noticed a leafless tree, its hardwood trunk pocked with holes and buzzing with insects. Thick vines tumbled from the highest branches all the way to the ground. The tree's skeleton still stood strong, towering above its neighbors. It had been allowed to reach the end of its lifespan. *This was a virgin forest,* she realized. *Maybe the only one left in the world.*

Ahead a large meadow spread out, creating a clearing with a single tree in its center. Lorel's lips fell apart as she soaked in the sight. It was like no tree she had ever seen. It was weeping, but not like a cherry or a willow. Grander, taller, wider. And most breathtaking were the leaves. The bluish green foliage glimmered in the sun, catching wind and light in a rippling mass. Around the tree, herbaceous plants sprawled every which way in a mishmash of texture and height. Lorel inhaled the sweet scent of basil mixed with the pungent odor of wild green onions, her eyes still fixed on the centerpiece.

"This is the Waterfall Tree," Silas said, pausing to take a sip of water from his canteen.

"I can see how it got its name. It's beautiful. Is the species extinct? I mean, in our world."

"It's indigenous to Rodinia. Never existed anywhere else," said Silas with a hint of pride, then handed Lorel the canteen. "It's a good marker if you ever get lost."

"Or if you get sick," Sam added, removing his glasses, which had fogged from the humidity, and rubbing them against his sweaty shirt. "The untamed botanicals you see here yield the widest herb selection in Rodinia. Sirens know the medicinal uses for every single one."

"But don't eat anything unless you know what it is. Especially the mushrooms," Silas warned, kicking his boot into a small patch of pale yellow mushrooms.

"Got it." Lorel glanced at a bluish, gilled mushroom protruding by her foot. "So is there a central town on each island or are sirens scattered about in their houses . . . cabins?" Blood rushed to her cheeks. "Sorry, I don't even know what you all live in."

Silas and Sam glanced at each other.

"We've had such little time to prepare Lorel for this visit," Sam said, clearing his throat.

"Don't worry," said Silas. "It's actually a point of contention among the sirens. Over the last several years, the younger generation began sleeping on land instead of in the grottoes. At first it was just a night on the beach here and there, but then they started to build huts and really move in. The Elders see it as a risk." Silas shrugged with the nonchalance of an adolescent. "But what can I say, we like the breeze."

"So some still sleep in the grottoes, underwater?" Lorel tilted her head. "How does that work? I mean, with the time limit on oxygen."

"The grottoes are chambers embedded in the wall of rock that surrounds the blue hole's shaft. But they all have air pockets. The air is thin, but there are microorganisms that regenerate the used oxygen. So sirens go back and forth among the rooms allowing for oxygen regeneration. There are clusters of rooms that connect too, so often a clan will inhabit those."

"Like little apartments! I didn't realize how intricate the cave system down there is," Lorel said.

"And no bulldozer required to build them," Sam grimaced, wiping a layer of sweat from his forehead.

"The Blue Hole Realm is our true home," Silas continued, "but sirens have always spent plenty of time in the Land Realm. We have lodges and above-ground caves hidden throughout all the islands. It's just never been common practice for us to establish settlement on land. Until now." Silas's eyes glinted with pride.

Lorel looked at Sam. He had fallen quiet, taking a backseat to educating her on sirens now that one was present in the flesh. "So you and Isla must live in a hut then. Will it be near mine?"

"Yes and yes," Sam replied. "Although I'd give anything for the experience of sleeping in an underwater cave."

Lorel could see how much Sam yearned to be deeper within Isla's world. "I guess humans can never fully experience Rodinia," she said with a hint of sadness.

"Got that right. But don't worry, we're good storytellers, right, Sam?" Silas patted Sam's shoulder affectionately. "Next bonfire, just ask someone to tell you what it's like down there."

"Thanks, Silas. I'll be sure to do that," she said, knowing it would never compare to the true experience.

"Shall we carry on?" Silas slung his canteen back on his shoulder and walked at a brisk pace around the Waterfall Tree.

He was leading them deeper into the forest. Ferns still wet with dew sprung up from the ground everywhere, and an earthy smell mixed with the salt-laden air. Moss thicker than a shag rug covered the ground beneath the brush and crept up tree roots that towered over her head. Here and there she spotted flowers, but none of them were recognizable.

"Sam, is the vegetation on land as preserved as the marine life is?" she asked, her breath shortening as the incline increased.

The air was thick with moisture and her T-shirt stuck to her body with sweat. She had rolled her jeans up as far as they could go and fern fronds tickled her ankles as she passed by.

"It's not my area, but I know they have flora that the most trained botanist couldn't identify. To us it's extinct," Sam said, grabbing a leaf as he passed. "Just look at this one. It's a perfect circle."

"That's a moonleaf," Silas called from up ahead.

Lorel marveled at the biological rarities surrounding her. A tiny red flower on the border of the path peeked out among the ferns, and she couldn't resist plucking it and tucking the feathery plant behind her ear. Somewhere above birds erupted in a loud chorus, then what sounded like a monkey's cry.

"What about the fauna?" Lorel asked with heightening awareness.

"Just stay close by in the woods, Lorel," Sam replied. "And if you are ever alone, keep Link at your side."

"Here, boy." She pulled the slack of Link's leash as

goose bumps rose on her arms.

Soon they were hiking steeply up an acclivity on the rough trail, and the trees began to thin out to tall grasses. After twenty minutes, they plateaued. A grassy meadow extended in every direction.

"This is the only place on Baltra where you can see the Eye and the ocean at the same time. But it gets pretty windy," Silas's voice rose above a strong breeze gusting from the ocean.

Lorel pulled her hair into a ponytail and shoved on her eyeband, thankful she had remembered it. The sight took her breath away.

"We're just over here," Silas called.

Lorel and Sam fell into pace with one another behind Silas.

"So can Isla walk all the way up here in her condition? That trail was pretty rough."

Sam's face clouded. "She'll be sleeping in the grottoes until the baby is born, with her sister. She's terrified of birthing the baby on land."

"But if the baby is half human, wouldn't that be dangerous?" Lorel asked.

"There are grottoes dedicated to birthing with warm water pools. Isla can labor and birth beneath the water and surface as soon as the baby is out. Sirens have lungs to, you know. Not gills."

"Right," said Lorel. "Humans sometimes do water births in tubs. It makes sense."

"But there is no way for me to enter the grottoes. I just wish I could be there for her." He shook his head.

"Don't worry, Sam, I'm sure everything will go fine. I know it must feel strange to be left out of your child's birth, but Isla will have all the help she needs down there."

"What I worry more about is DiviniGen. Those people know she's pregnant. They were spying on us in our own home," he said, then added under his breath, "thanks to Mello."

"But they don't know you came back here, right? They don't know any of us did. Right, Sam?"

"No. They couldn't possibly know."

Lorel didn't like the way his voice wavered. But he was a man with a lot at stake.

"We're almost there. See?" Sam pointed toward the Eye where a thick line of trees and shrubbery edged the meadow.

The huts were so well camouflaged that it took her a few seconds to realize they were there. Several wooden structures with thatched roofs huddled under the shelter of the trees. Each one could not be more than one room large.

"Let's go, Link!" Lorel bounded toward the huts after Silas.

"Lorel, be careful!" Sam cried over the wind. "There's a cliff on the other side of the huts."

"Thanks," she called back to him, grabbing Link and refastening his leash. She slowed her pace and walked up to Silas who was standing by one particular hut smothered in a flowering vine and partially hidden by some low-hanging tree branches.

"This one is yours. The front door is over here." Silas wound around to the far side of the hut motioning for her to follow.

Lorel gasped as she exited the thick cluster of trees. Sam was not kidding. The back, or rather, the front yard led to a sheer drop off. Her stomach spun like a pinwheel as she looked down on a flock of seagulls swooping by. Immediately below was the white half-moon of Baltra's inner beach. She backed up slowly until her back pressed against a tree, but her eyes followed the edge of the cliff all the way out to the end. There it jutted out to a rocky point that hovered directly over the water.

"That's where they cliff dive," Sam said, appearing at her side. "I would not recommend it."

Inside her hut, Lorel was alone for the first time in the strange new place. The clicking and chirping of wildlife mixed with the sound of sea winds bellowing through the trees. Homesickness racked her heart and fear clawed at her conscience. Fear of the unknown, of rocky cliffs, and of shipwrecked ghosts of sailors past. Suddenly the threat of DiviniGen seemed small and far away.

But it wasn't.

She shook herself out of the trance and looked around her new home. The simplicity was comforting. A mattress with a white downy cover and a fluffy pillow occupied one corner, and a bamboo dresser stood against the opposite wall. On top, a straw basket held strange, colorful fruits and a wooden cup with a pitcher of water next to it. Above were three shelves filled with plates and eating utensils. No fridge. No plastics. No hologram screens.

Behind one of the two closed doors Lorel found a small bathroom with a sink and toilet and breathed a sigh of relief that Rodinia had modern plumbing. Behind the other door was a shallow closet, empty but for something on the top shelf. Lorel reached up and pulled down a burlap sack and emptied its contents onto the floor.

Inside was a wooden bow with little arrowheads intricately carved from stone, a small hand knife, and a hatchet. Lorel kneeled down and ran her fingers over the weapons. Not the average closet contents she would see back home. But here they had purpose. *Sirens were hunters, apparently on land as well as sea.*

Lorel realized how little she really knew about survival. And why should she? All her life she had been surrounded by armed municipals and grocery stores and restaurants. The ubiquitous DivinWay. PeterPan's hollow but addictive burgers. Meals of any kind packaged and delivered by Dragonfly to your window with one click of the tablet. Never once did she have to look an animal that she was about to devour in the eye.

Suddenly she felt helpless. Maybe PanDivinity had wanted it that way. She'd always grown up believing that she held some freedom from their lifestyle by the mere fact that she didn't subscribe to their narcissistic philosophies. But maybe they'd had more control over her life than she realized. She took a deep breath. Not anymore. If she was going to be as self-sufficient as the rest of the Rodinians, she had better start learning. And a big part of it was physical fitness. Sirens did not pop Muscle Ripper and Pulmonary Efficiency PAPs or Fatty Cell Eliminators here to stay fit. She pinched the soft muscle of her triceps with a frown. Lorel had always prided herself on going the natural route — exercise — but it had fallen off since her move to DC. Desk time had won out.

She dropped down on the floor and began a set of push-ups, then sit-ups, until sweat beaded along her upper lip. Something about this place made her want to use her body for its original purpose, but when she thought about it, she was not totally sure what that purpose was, only that she was closer to finding out. With every breath here she felt more . . . in touch.

Panting, Lorel stood up feeling satisfied with the burn in her muscles. She picked up the hatchet and ran her finger along the smooth side, catching the reflection of her large brown eyes in the shiny steel.

Across the room white muslin curtains covering the north-facing window billowed letting in a warm breeze and cooling the fresh layer of sweat on her skin. She pushed open the shutters and light filled the hut. The glassless frame looked out over the Eye and the archipelago beyond reminding her of her height above sea level.

A whiny huff came from the corner, and she turned to see Link restlessly circling the room. "I hope you have a healthy fear of heights, buddy. Let's find you a place to rest."

With an extra blanket from the closet, she rolled up a little bed in the corner. Within minutes Link was purring loudly, sound asleep.

"Well, you seem settled in."

She was tempted to join him for a nap. The last couple days had left her weak and exhausted. And she had so much ahead. Then she remembered her promise to meet Sam. He had made it seem urgent. Leaving Link to snooze, she headed out across the meadow and down the footpath that led to the beach.

Sam was sitting next to a rock by the line of palms and curling seagrape trees that bordered the beach. The sandy shore curved around on either side, hugging the Eye, and Lorel looked back at the sheer face of rock. Her hut above was barely visible.

Upon approach she noticed two steaming wooden mugs on the flat part of the rock that Sam was using as a table.

"Coffee?" he asked, holding one out to her. "With coconut cream."

"Thanks." Lorel took a sip and rich nutty liquid flooded her taste buds. "This is fantastic."

"Everything here tastes better somehow." Sam sipped his own mug, looking out at the water.

Was she imagining things or was he avoiding eye contact?

"I bet the sunsets aren't too shabby either. We should watch it tonight." Lorel wanted to relish in the little time she had to discover Rodinia in peace.

Sam's face darkened. "After we meet with Lalique. There is much to discuss, much to prepare for in the next three days." His gaze stayed fixed outward.

"*If* George's intelligence is correct," Lorel said. She had felt a shadow of doubt when George reported Galton's estimated arrival. If they sent a hit man after her and bugged Mello, how were they not onto the mole yet? George was good, but was he that good?

"You're right. *If* it's correct, we have three more sunsets to enjoy in peace," he said.

Lorel stared at Sam's profile, listening to the buzz of insects in the woods. His shaded eyeband had replaced his glasses. It reflected the sparkling water and towering mountains in front of him, shielding his full expression.

"Sam, what did you need to talk to me about?"

He tugged at his lips, rubbed his jawline. Beads of sweat glistened in the fresh stubble of his salt-and-pepper beard. Lorel shifted uncomfortably. Was it her dad? Jake?

Sam took his eyeband off and wiped sweat from the bridge of his nose then looked at her with troubled eyes.

"Lorel, it's just that, well," he shifted positions on the sand, and she noticed his briefcase leaning against the rock. "It's time you know the truth."

"The truth?" Lorel's back stiffened. What had he been hiding?

"I'm sorry, I wanted to tell you before but . . ." His voice trailed off weakly, and with shaking fingers, he unlatched the briefcase. Inside was a tablet.

"Here it is." He downed the last of his coffee and placed the tablet between them on the smooth stone. A holo emerged, barely visible in the shade of the palm fronds, but Lorel could clearly see the word *confidential* glowing in red letters. Underneath it was her full name and birth date.

Lorelei Lyn Phoenix. May 22, 2073.

"You have a file on me?" Her muscles tensed. All the trust she had built up began to melt into a puddle of doubt. "What the hell, Sam?"

"Lorel," he started, clearing his throat, "as a young child, you were diagnosed with mosaicism. Yes?"

He put a hand on her knee and she drew away.

"How do you know that?" Her rare congenital disease was the last thing in the world she had expected him to broach.

In response, he swiped the hologram, scrolling to reveal a photograph of herself as a young girl. A hot flush raced up her neck.

Sam continued to tap and slide his index finger across the glossy surface until he retrieved a sub-file labeled "Census H." He tapped in a passcode.

"Lorel, Isla and I have been on a long-term intelligence assignment since living in DC. We manage a list called Census H."

She jerked her head back. "Okay. And what's Census H.?"

"The Census of the Hybrids, people that are half

human and half siren. Lalique mandated that we keep a vigilant watch on the mainland, in case any siren visits from the past had resulted in hybrid offspring. It's a measure of protection for the sirens, you understand. If humans ever discovered the existence of a hybrid, the entire siren species could be in danger of discovery."

"A siren-human hybrid." She mulled the words on her tongue, and remembered the image of the Poseidon Prototype. "It sounds like DiviniGen's dream species."

He laughed nervously. "Oh yes. A hybrid to them would be worth more than its weight in gold. The genetic work they are attempting would be done. They could just clone, or use the gene for a PAP. Whatever their plan, it would save them billions in research and development."

"Are they aware of any hybrids?" Lorel asked.

"To be honest, I wasn't even sure any existed. I thought Lalique was being paranoid. Census H has been a list of blank spaces until a few years ago. Lorel," Sam said softly, "I have a file on you because of *this*."

He swiped open an album file with photographs labeled "Hybrid Features." She leaned in. The glowing pictures hovered a few inches above the tablet in a virtual stack and then spread like a deck of cards. The images raised the hair on her arms.

A close up of unusually large, round eyes — pale blue. Then a set of analogous brown eyes. Another of skin, perhaps of the forearm, on someone whose face was not shown. The skin in one picture was flaky and peeling. In the next it was submerged in water and shone iridescent. Her stomach fluttered as she flashed back to her first time in the ocean — the shock, then fear of seeing her skin turn pearly. The embarrassment of its constant, hideous flaking and bleeding since childhood. She stared down at her arm now in awe.

"See this one?" Sam pointed to an emerging image.

Lorel gasped and turned her head, recognizing the defect immediately. It was the nape of a neck with a pitted indentation similar to a belly button. She lifted her hand to the back of her own neck, sliding it gingerly across the indented scar, the scar she had always believed came from a childhood accident. Her fingers began to shake.

"Sam, what the . . ." Her voice caught in her throat.

All of the features displayed in front of her were strikingly similar to the ones she had lived with for twenty-five years, the ones that her doctors had attributed to her mosaicism.

"Lorel," Sam's voice was now rising in a frenzied excitement. "Mosaicism is not, as you have been told, a disease at all. On the contrary, it is a collection of characteristics that, while not useful to our species, have very purposefully developed in another."

She stared blankly out at the blinding water, frozen. The panoramic scenery began closing in on her.

Sam stood up, shoved his eyeband back on. "You see, the markings of your condition, oversized unlobed lungs, excess iron content in your blood, hyperreactive pupil dilation, skin that peels and bleeds. All of these perceived anatomical defects serve a purpose if placed in the correct context." He kneeled in front of her, placing a hand on her shoulder.

"Lorel, do you understand what I'm saying?"

Her head spun and the heat of the island felt like a boa constrictor wrapping around her body. Her breath caught in her throat as she whispered the words.

"I'm a siren."

SEVEN
JAKE

September 23, 2098
Washington, DC

R IDING ALONG CONNECTICUT AVENUE in the autocab, Jake fingered the las-gun in his pocket, feeling only a little guilty that he was abusing his special ops privileges. Regular citizens were not allowed to carry guns, and tonight he was nothing more than a civilian. But he could take no chances.

Whatever Lorel was involved in before she left was beginning to smell foul. Whether it was this George character or Reshing or a person unknown, someone had played a role in her current whereabouts, the details of which remained a mystery. Now, in light of Leo's murder, Jake felt even more certain. Lorel was not shark meat at the bottom of the Laccadive Sea. She was alive.

And she was in danger.

He exited the cab and stepped out onto the busy

Centercity sidewalk. The white stucco high-rise loomed above him, its façade illuminated in a rainbow of colliding colors. Jake found DC's floodlights to be much more patterned and complex than New Charleston's, reflecting the intensity of the capitol city. But they turned the buildings into glowing works of art.

To his relief he passed through the lobby easily by mentioning he was a visitor of George Oberbach's. The pink-haired teenage girl working the front desk waved him up without hesitation.

"Forty-third floor. Right off the elevator," she said flatly, then returned to reading her tablet.

He stepped inside and pressed the button. The elevator burst upward swiftly, increasing Jake's anxiety. *Who was this guy?*

Potential scenarios ran through his mind. If George was just a friend of Lorel's, maybe he could enlighten Jake about what had been bothering her for the past few weeks. Maybe he even had insight into Ben Reshing's intentions with her. But what if George was one of the *sources* of her duress? He thought of the envelope, the shattered tablet. *No.* It seemed as if George had been giving Lorel some sort of information, trying to help her.

Another more irrational thought nipped at the back of his mind. Maybe Lorel had *been with him.* Jake wrapped his index finger into the trigger of the las-gun as he approached unit 4308. He knocked three times on the door, hard.

No answer. Jake pressed his ear to the door and could hear sound booming from a holospeaker. It was

73

some sort of fast beat house music.

"George?" he called, leaning his forehead against the door, "my name's Jake Ryder. I'm a friend of Lorel Phoenix."

He knocked again louder but still no response. Then Jake noticed the retina scan pad by the door was cracked. Jake's SEAL instincts kicked in. With a strong jolt he tried forcing the knob, but it didn't budge. He pulled out the las-gun and trained it on the deadbolt. With one silent ray it blasted the lock. Jake stepped inside the apartment.

For a moment he froze, disoriented. The place was more like a spaceship than the bachelor pad he had expected. Blinking and buzzing consoles full of sleek computer screens and 3-D holo boards filled the entire space. The only sign that anything with a heartbeat occupied the dwelling was a black leather couch squished in between two glowing wall panels that displayed maps and a conglomerate of complex graphs. A styrofoam box of half-eaten DivinCakes food sat on the coffee table next to an oversize bottle of blue soda.

At the far end of the room a bank of computers beeped loudly above the throbbing music. Jake rushed toward it to read the red letters flashing from each of the screens.

SECURITY BREACH!

Was this DiviniGen equipment or personal? He tapped the glass surface of the desk to see what information he could retrieve. It lit up with a scrolling banner. *Ghost Control Center.*

Ghost? It seemed like a code name for something.

Jake's brow furrowed in confusion. Then he remembered George. Where was he?

A groan sounded from the back room. Jake eyed the closed door to what he guessed was the bedroom. Someone was inside. He swung open the door and aimed his las-gun into darkness.

"Help," came a voice from the far side of the bed.

Jake flicked on the light and scrambled around the bed. A pudgy young man wearing flannel pajama pants and a worn white T-shirt lay on the ground. He slumped awkwardly against the nightstand. Blood trickled down his forehead, across his plump cheekbone, and into his short stubbly beard.

"Where is the wound?" Jake dropped to the floor and began checking George's vitals. His heart rate had slowed. His blood pressure was dangerously low from loss of blood.

George lifted a weak hand toward his left ear, pointing. Jake gulped. A gaping hole the size of a dime oozed a mix of blood and brain matter. Jake ripped off his hoody and pressed the fabric against the man's head to halt the blood flow. With his free hand he reached into his pocket to retrieve his tablet. If medics did not get here quickly, George would die. Jake clicked their GPS location and ordered an EMT. A confirmation beep sounded within a few seconds.

"Medics are on the way." Jake looked reassuringly into George's drooping eyes, but he did not feel confident. The man was going to lose consciousness any second.

"Who are you?" George whispered in a hoarse voice,

staring at Jake in bewilderment.

"I'm Jake Ryder. Lorel's boyfriend."

"Lorel," George whispered her name with familiarity, almost sadness.

"You know her. George, listen, can you tell me anything about where she may be? I know she's alive."

"How do you know that?" A look of suspicion passed over George's face.

"Doesn't matter. Look," Jake reached into his back pocket and pulled out the envelope with the numbers scribbled on it. "I found this in her apartment, from you. What does it mean?"

George's eyes grew wide with a sudden burst of life. He gasped.

"George, do you know where she is?" Jake's eyes pleaded.

George stared at him as though trying to determine whether to reveal something.

"George, if you care at all about Lorel please tell me. I know she's in trouble. I want to find her and help her. I love her." Jake's voice cracked and he squeezed George's shoulder. "Please, where is she, man?"

George's eyes softened and something inside him seemed to relinquish any resistance to Jake, to life. He was letting go.

"George!" Jake felt a twinge of panic. This man could not die now.

George pointed to the envelope in Jake's hand. "She's there," he mumbled.

Jake stared down at the numbers. "What do you

mean, *here*? This is just a string of random numbers!"

"It's the island."

"Island! What island?" Jake desperately needed more clarification. He watched in dismay as George's heavy lids closed. "George, wait. Tell me who did this to you!"

"Galton," he whispered.

The CEO of DiviniGen. What the hell was going on here? Jake's mind raced. He now had more pieces to a very fuzzy puzzle.

Suddenly George grabbed Jake's hand. "Help them!" he croaked desperately. Then his head lolled to the side. Jake felt his pulse.

George Oberbach was dead.

Having slipped out of the building before the medics arrived, Jake decided to walk back to Lorel's apartment and blend in with the city's late night clubbing crowd. He had so much to think about, so much to decipher.

Lorel on an island?

He looked again at the numbers. If you divided them in the middle, then inserted a decimal after the first digit of the separate number strings, it was the right length to be coordinates. As soon as he was back, he'd map it.

An island! But why . . . and how?

The idea seemed surreal, but the more he thought about it, the more it explained certain things. Like how Lorel could have disappeared in the middle of the ocean.

If someone had taken her to an island, perhaps in a submarine, then that explained why they never found her body.

But they found her wetsuit, torn to shreds, Jake's conscience cruelly reminded him. Maybe it was all a hoax and Lorel really was gone. But, if someone *had* smuggled her away underwater, there were only two entities that could pull it off. A PanDivinity company or a federal agency. Pirates didn't have the resources. Certainly no US civilians did. Two possible individuals came immediately to mind.

Galton and Reshing.

Both had endless funds and connections. And both Jake could link in one way or another to Lorel . . . and to Leo in the weeks before he died. But the links were random, unclear. Jake clenched his jaw and marched forward with glazed eyes, unaware of the stream of dazzlingly dressed people parting in his path.

Halfway home, his mind virtually arranging and rearranging puzzle pieces, Jake reached the DuPont Circle fountain. It gushed into the air changing colors every few seconds. Black iron benches set against manicured shrubs surrounded the circular marble footpath. Jake took a seat and stared into the mesmerizing fountain. Red faded to pink, then orange, then yellow.

Groups of teenagers walked by, decked out in flashy and revealing night attire. Their hip hairstyles matched the colors of the water. DiviniGen's PAPs had certainly made the world a more colorful place, if not a little too reliant on pills.

Suddenly a flash blinded Jake from the side. He swiveled around on the bench to see a man in a dark coat standing behind an oak tree. He held a camera in his hand. It flashed again as he snapped another one. Jake stood up and chased him into the sparse woods of the Circle. The man was short and stocky and his pace was no match for Jake's. Jake clobbered him onto the grass next to another oak tree.

"What the hell are you doing?" Jake grabbed the camera from him and began scrolling through the holo pictures while the man tried desperately to release himself from Jake's iron grasp.

"Let me explain," the man sputtered, gasping for air as Jake pinned his neck down against a protruding tree root with one hand.

First, Jake saw a holo of himself on the bench, then another of him walking down the street. The next one was of him and Lorel standing in front of the DivinCare hospital. Then the pictures of Lorel began. They went all the way back to New Charleston. Jake lifted the man's face up to his, and growled, "Who are you?"

"I'm Frank Ludlow. I work for Dr. Ben Reshing," he said between gasping coughs.

Jake's adrenaline soared.

"Take me to him." Jake released his grasp on the man with a shove then discreetly pulled out his las-gun. "Now."

"All right, all right. Get your hands off me." The flustered man stood up and brushed the dirt and grass off his clothes in exasperation. "He wants to see you anyway."

Hiding his surprise, Jake jabbed the gun into Frank's side and walked to the edge of the round park where the autocabs were circling. One came to a halt and they slid inside.

"Eighteen-hundred Kalorama," Frank commanded into the cab's console.

A sense of unease crept under Jake's skin. *He* was the one suspicious of Reshing. *He* was the one secretly investigating the dubious events surrounding Lorel's disappearance. So why did Reshing want to see him?

EIGHT

MELLO

September 23, 2098
Baltra, Rodinia

I T WAS DUSK AND the buzz of dragonflies filled the otherwise quiet woods. Mello pulled open the burlap curtain in the doorway and walked out onto the stoop of his hut. It was a lone dwelling nestled into the giant buttressing roots of a kapok tree. The kapok was ancient, like most of the trees in Rodinia, and its leafy umbrella spread out a hundred feet above. Mello used the waxy, palmlike leaves to thatch his roof and stretch hammocks from the thick lower branches. Its thorny gray trunk alone was nine feet wide. Mello found solace and protection in the arboreal giant. Still, it dwarfed in comparison to the Waterfall Tree, about fifty yards inland.

He sat down on the wood planks, dipping his feet into the cool freshwater lagoon that served as the front yard. Under the glassy water was a small sinkhole that tunneled below the island all the way to the Eye. Mello had never used the narrow connecting tunnel, but it was a good escape route should he ever need one. Mostly he used the lagoon for refreshing swims, but the main reason he'd chosen the spot was because of its privacy.

The air felt oppressively hot, and he sucked in a deep, meditative breath. It was hard to shake the feeling that a dark presence would soon be upon them. He had been attempting to quell his burning anger at Galton. This was more personal to him than the rest of the sirens, on many levels, and he hated himself for picturing Galton choking, sputtering, dying at his hands.

All day he had shut himself inside, brainstorming ways to deal peacefully with Galton and DiviniGen even though it went against every instinct he had. But if they were to save their island, and themselves, all signs pointed to violent measures for defense. And nothing shamed the sirens more.

Mello could only hope Lalique had some more diplomatic ideas, at least for Plan A. He headed out toward the beach to begin the trek to her caverns. The strategy meeting with the Council was in an hour.

The soft dirt trail meandering through the pits and mounds of the forest floor gradually turned to white sand and Mello strode out onto the beach. The sun hung low on the western horizon, saturating the islands in an array of oranges, reds, and pinks. Light glittered on the calm surface of the Eye, transforming its blue iris to gold.

A girl sat on the sand, and her long hair fell in ripples down her back, which appeared to be shaking. He squinted into the sun and walked toward her. Excitement rushed through him when he saw her face.

"Lorel!" he called, and she lifted her head from her knees.

Tears streamed down her face and her beautiful brown eyes were bloodshot and puffy. She sucked in a sob and sat straight up as he approached, wiping her eyes with the back of her hand. *She knows,* he realized.

"Hi," she mumbled, cheeks flushing pinker than the sky. "So, do you know . . . about me?"

"I just learned from my mother this morning." He sat down next to her. "I had so many questions about why we would invite a human here, no offense."

She looked down at the sand. "None taken."

"Anyway, I'm glad you're here now. You'll be safe with us. With me," he said trying to catch her eyes.

She looked up at him and a fresh well of tears spilled over. She swiped them away with reddening cheeks. "Thanks, Mello."

He wasn't sure what more to say. *"Congratulations, you now have aquatic abilities"?* It was obvious she wasn't sure what to think of it all. Her world had been turned upside down, and she was thousands of miles from everyone she loved. But to Mello she had somehow become more beautiful than before. Lorel had transcended the divide between two species and become extraordinary.

"You are a very special person. One in a million, I'd say."

She looked at him strangely then laughed. "I've been sitting here for hours, thinking about things. All the

83

implications. Like, my parents. My mother must have been a siren. I lived my whole life thinking she was a deadbeat who abandoned me. I've spent so much energy hating her, but there must be more to her story. How did she get to the US? Was she forced to leave, discovered and then punished? Maybe she never really died! I'll never know, and that kills me. And my father! Did he know this the whole time? Has he been lying to me? I'm just so . . ." She punched the sand with a loud groan.

"Hurt, confused, angry," Mello finished for her then placed his hand on her knee. "It's okay to feel that way."

"Good, because I feel all of those," she said.

Mello paused in thought and said, "You know, I have an idea of how she may have met your father."

Mello told Lorel about Post 505 and the Lamplighter. How it used to be a coming-of-age enlightenment for young sirens, a chance to go on mainland and experience a slice of the human world. How it used to be the Choice every siren was given.

"It's no longer an option now, but your mother would certainly have taken the journey. That has to be how she met your father. Maybe he was in the United Kingdom at the time she was in Penzance," Mello suggested.

"So my mother must have decided to stay in the human world then. I bet it was because she had fallen in love with my father!"

Her voice stirred with hope, and Mello shifted uncomfortably on the sand. He tugged at his bottom lip, searching her face.

"What?"

"The only thing is, Lorel, if a siren *did* decide to stay on mainland, an extremely rare choice to make, there were two rules. First, they were forbidden from revealing their true identity to any human. Second, they were never, under any circumstances, allowed to mate with a human. Breaking these rules incurred severe consequences."

"So my mother must have been a rebel."

"I guess so," he said.

"Mello . . ." Lorel stood up on the sand and began pacing back and forth, biting her nails. "Do you think she could be here in Rodinia? I mean, if she broke a rule, they must have forced her to come back home, right?"

Mello averted his eyes from her expectant gaze. "I don't think so. My mother is a superior within the Sieve Council."

"The Sieve Council?"

"It's a portion of the Rodinia's governing body. They sift through the world's available technology and decide what to import from what Beacon offers to us. But it's not just material objects. Information is sifted through the Council too. They oversee all mainland intelligence issues, including any human and siren interactions that may occur. If your mother had been caught, I would have heard about it. That's a situation I would remember because it's never happened before, at least that the sirens know of." He cleared his throat and looked down at the darkening sand.

Lorel was silent as though trying to come up with a reason to prove him wrong.

"Sirens and humans mating is very rare, Lorel. Sam

and Isla have really broken new ground, against the odds and against a siren's ethical code, but it's possible. Here you are." He smiled.

"Hm. Maybe she had to leave my dad to *hide* then. Maybe she's hiding out in the States somewhere."

Mello could understand Lorel's persistence in wanting to find a narrative in which her mother was alive, but he didn't want to give her false hope. He stood up and placed his hands on her shoulders, forcing her to stop frantically pacing the sand.

"Lorel, listen to me. The most likely scenario is that your mother is dead as your father told you. I know how sirens work. The Council and the Guardian of Beacon, whoever they were at that time, would never *ever* have let her escape. Sirens that chose to stay on mainland were watched closely. If she were alive, they would have found her. And yes, they would have dragged her back here faster than she could blink."

"Wouldn't there still be a record of a missing siren though?" Lorel asked.

"Well, I guess there would. Look, I'll ask my mother to check the records. I just don't want you to be disappointed when nothing turns up," he said.

Lorel dropped to the sand and pulled her knees back to her chest again.

"I'm sorry," he said softly.

"No. You're just being honest with me. I can't say that for most people I come across these days." She kicked her legs out and leaned back on the sand, staring out at the setting sun.

There was something about Lorel that made him want to confide in her, unburden the secret he had been keeping for so long. He sunk to his knees next to her. "Can I tell you something?"

"Of course," she replied. Her surprised look reminded him they were hardly more than strangers.

"But you have to promise to never say a word to anyone."

A disarming smile swept across her face. "Promise."

"You know how everyone is so furious that I went into the city on mainland?"

"Into DC? Yeah, I saw it all over Sam's face when he first told me. And in Isla too. I think maybe people just don't understand why you would have risked it." Her voice rose at the end as though she were one of those people.

He nodded. "It was incredibly selfish, and foolish. I'd put so much faith in Galton. I never imagined he would turn on us, that it would come to this. He had a target on my back, and I walked right into his trap. But I didn't just go because I was curious to see a human city. I went because I wanted to find the body of my daughter."

His heart dipped at the sound of the words . . . *my daughter*. He had never said them aloud before.

"Your . . . daughter?"

"When I was sixteen, I went on *my* journey to the Lamplighter. I had decided to return to Rodinia, but Penzance had not satiated my desire to learn more about humans. So I snuck away to London. I met a girl there, a human girl named Lea, and I fell in love with her. We spent only a few weeks together, but it was enough. I believe we conceived a child. Lorel, I think I have . . . er . . . *had* a daughter."

He mustered all his effort to suppress the salty tear that hovered at the corner of his eye.

"Wait, *you think*?" Lorel arched one auburn brow. "So you're not sure."

"Well, not totally. But that day I was in DC I heard something in the news about a girl who washed up in the body of an orca whale. She had silver hair with a black streak, and she was young, a teenager. The whales were in their migration path from the British Isles across the Atlantic toward the States. Maybe she was following them. I'm not sure why, and I know this sounds crazy, but I swear she was mine." He fingered the black streak of hair at the side of his face, then noticed Lorel focus her gaze on it.

She cleared her throat, returning her focus back to his eyes. "And Lea never told you she was pregnant?"

"She said she thought she was, but I never heard if it was true. She never could have reached me. You see, I was caught in London and punished severely when I got home. Luckily, my mother saved me from being exiled, or worse. But I never saw Lea again. Then when Lalique came into power later that year, she banished the Choice forever. And I know it was all because of me. I have never told a soul that I'm the one who ruined it for everyone."

"Mello, wait." Lorel scooted forward and stared at him with widening eyes. "I was there. I saw her!"

Mello listened as she spilled the details of what she

had seen on the beach in New Charleston a month prior. It all added up to the same incident he'd heard on the radio that day. The beaching of the whales, the body of someone inhuman, then the attempted cover up. Lorel had been an eyewitness, and they — DiviniGen — had tried to force her into silence.

"But I did tell," she said. "I reported it anonymously, though it was dismissed as a false report by the press. I've always wondered about the girl's body because it was so mysterious. How did she end up in the belly of a whale unless she'd been swimming in the middle of the ocean? Plus, she didn't *look* human. But then she was so bloody and . . ." She stopped short and her hand flew over her mouth. "I'm so sorry, I should never have said that."

Mello swallowed hard as the image entered his mind. "It could only be a siren. It was her, I'm sure of it. And DiviniGen has been covering it up. They took possession of the whale bodies for genetic research, and I know they're doing the same with her. That's how they discovered we exist in the first place. I need to find her, give her a proper burial." Mello felt a resurgence of hope. "If only I could find Lea again, but it's impossible. I wonder if she even knows what happened."

"Mello, you have a chance to find your daughter. Galton will be here soon enough. Maybe you can talk to him," Lorel offered.

"I'll find her. He won't leave this island alive until I do."

"You will then, if you want it that bad." Lorel reached

out and drew the black strand of his hair into her fingers. Staring at it, she said, "And I think you're right, that she has to be your daughter. She had this too." She glided her fingers down the lock of hair until they rested at his collarbone. A shiver passed through him at her touch.

"Thank you," he said. "For telling me all of this."

She nodded, breaking their locked gaze to look out at the water. "Thinking about her swimming out in the ocean makes me wonder about myself, what I'm capable of. She was a hybrid just like me."

"I imagine you are capable of a lot," Mello said.

A long stretch of silence followed. He watched her trail her fingers along the length of her calves deep in thought.

"Why does my skin bleed?" she asked. "All my life I've dealt with these random episodes of pinprick bleeding, like little beads of sweat that break out on patches of my skin. It's painless, but it's traumatized me many times, appearing when I'm in public, and I don't notice until I look in the mirror. Some of the high school episodes were downright mortifying."

Mello got up and walked to the water. He leaned over and swirled his arms in the water then returned to Lorel's side. She had so much to learn.

"See that?" He held up his arm. The skin on his forearm shimmered like a fish in the sun.

"What is it?"

"We have scales." He smiled at her. "You wouldn't know it from looking at us when we're dry, but these are special scales called placoids. They're microscopic and don't grow larger, they just slough off and regenerate. If you aren't swimming in saltwater on a regular basis, which I'm guessing you weren't, the skin won't properly exfoliate and the scales will poke through. I would imagine that's your pinpricks."

"Scales," she whispered, staring at her own arm.

"Watch." He took her forearm and firmly rubbed some sand grains against it.

"Ouch, you're rubbing me raw!"

"Sorry, almost done. We have to get past the top layer of your epidermis."

She squeezed her eyes shut and her arm went limp, submitting to his rough massage. After a few minutes, he moistened her skin with his damp palms.

Lorel lifted her arm up and the sun glinted on the fresh skin to reveal a subtle sheen of iridescence. A look of wonder lit her face. "It's beautiful."

She turned to him and reached for his hand. Her fingers were soft and warm and they sent a tingle through his body.

"May I?" she asked.

Mello relinquished his hand to hers and watched as she examined it with astute curiosity. Gingerly, as though she were handling a fragile object, she ran her index finger along his wrist, his fingers, the delicate webbing in between.

He laughed nervously then flushed.

"I don't have this," she said.

"No. But you have this." He pulled her hair around her neck and tucked it against her shoulder, touching the indentation on the back of her neck. "It's only covered by a thin layer of skin."

He dared to let his fingers linger for a few seconds on the soft down along her hairline.

"But doesn't that make it useless?"

"Well, there is one thing we could do to restore it." A smile crept across his face. "If you're willing."

"Really?" Her eyes lit up and Mello felt a burst of relief. She was going to embrace her siren side.

"It would only involve a minor surgery. Slitting the skin and stitching it off to the side to reveal the opening that always should have been there. And with a long salt water swim and some algae, it would be healed in a day."

"So, assuming my siren anatomy is all intact, I'd have a fully functioning blowhole?" She grimaced. "I can't believe I'm even saying this."

He laughed. "Yes. Pretty much just an extra nostril. With a few fancy capabilities."

She stared at him with lips slightly parted. It looked as though she had stopped breathing for a moment, then she frowned. "Are there doctors here?"

He laughed. "I promise, one of these days I will convince you we are not living in the dark ages."

"Sorry," she said, cheeks flushing red.

"If you really want to do this, I know a surgeon. He's not on Baltra. He lives in the grottoes and usually works out of the hotel."

Her brows rose to points. "You mean hospital?"

Mello pointed to one of islands in the distance. "I mean hotel, on that island over there. Paraíso. It's a long story," he added watching her face twist into a frown.

"So we'd go there for the procedure?"

Mello opened his mouth to affirm, but something stopped him. "You know, I'm sure Dr. Seaton would come to you. I'll talk to him today, see if he can come to your hut first thing in the morning. That is, if you're sure."

"You move fast, Mr. Seaford."

"I think you've waited long enough."

"Only twenty-five years." Her head fell to the side with a smile. "It's worth a try, just to see what I'm capable of. I'll do it. But I want you next to me when I do."

His heart danced. "Your wish is my command."

A rustling sound in the woods caused them both to turn around at the same time, bumping heads. They laughed.

"Hey, you two, the meeting starts in a few minutes. Come walk with us," Isla shouted as she and Sam emerged from the dark line of palms and ambled down the beach. The buzz of crickets pulsed loudly from the dune grasses, reminding Mello it was dusk.

"So how did it go today?" he asked, standing and wiping the sand from his pants.

Isla stopped to catch her breath, then leaned over and grabbed her belly with both hands. "Ouch."

"You okay?" Mello and Sam both rushed to her side.

She straightened up. "I'm fine. It's just my body practicing. Really," she added. They backed away, but the worry lines remained on Sam's face.

Isla had stopped by Mello's hut in the morning for a

pep talk before she and Sam met with the High Council to confess the news of her pregnancy.

"Today was okay. I've never seen Lalique look so upset, but it was almost like she was sad more than angry. It was strange, to be honest. But they were so distracted by DiviniGen that they didn't even talk about how to handle it. You were right, Mello." Isla sighed with relief and rubbed her belly. "I'm just glad it's over."

She turned to Lorel and her face brightened. "I'm so glad you know the truth now. You are one of us." She pulled Lorel into a tight embrace. "Always."

Mello noticed Lorel stiffen at first, but then she returned the hug and said, "Thanks, Isla. I'm still in shock."

"We wanted to tell you, but we couldn't until now," said Isla, shaking her head.

"I know. Sam explained."

Sam placed a hand on Lorel's shoulder. "Once you get used to it, you may even like it. You have new powers to discover."

"You make it sound like I'm a superhero."

"He's just jealous," Isla nudged Sam in the side.

"Well," Lorel hid a smile, "Mello has already convinced me to unlock one of my *superpowers*."

"Do tell," Sam said as they all fell in step together headed toward Lalique's caverns.

Mello walked ahead, listening as Lorel informed Sam and Isla of her surgical plans. The sun had almost set and the Eye had lost its shimmer under a violet sky. He looked across the water at Paraíso, already fading into the dark.

Recessed in the trees he could see the behemoth shadow of the crumbling hotel where the doctor's equipment resided.

Tomorrow he would bring Dr.Seaton back to Lorel, and by afternoon she would be breathing underwater. He had known Lorel for such little time, but she brought something out in him. A light had sparked inside his gloomy soul. Maybe it was that her nascency as a siren gave him the opportunity to impart his own knowledge. The past month he had felt useless. No, worse than useless, a *liability*. It felt good to help someone.

"You think the doc could operate on me?" Sam joked. "I may have a blowhole under there somewhere."

"My poor Sam." Isla smiled playfully at Lorel as she slung her arm around her husband's neck. Her belly was so big Mello worried she may go into labor any moment.

Despite the light banter, the group grew tense as they neared Lalique's caverns. Isla seemed to feel a renewed sense of anxiety over another public appearance with her ripe belly. The stakes were high for everyone, and they had only a few days to prepare all of Rodinia for the enemy's arrival. Lalique had met privately with the consuls of all five islands to devise a plan based on information provided by George. In the end, nothing had been decided and everyone remained on edge.

This was new territory.

When they reached the westernmost point of Baltra's beach, the roar of the waterfall overpowered all other sounds. They halted in front of a swirling pool of water that received the falls.

"With two humans and a very pregnant siren, swimming beneath is not an option. We'll have to go behind the falls to get in," Mello shouted.

One by one he led them across the rocky footbridge smothered in thick green moss. It traversed the frothy and tumultuous pool. Tiny rainbows lingered in the mist until the dark shade of the cliff wall erased them.

"Be careful. It's slippery," Mello called as they crept along the narrow stone ledge behind the roaring sheet of water. His heart lurched as he noticed Lorel's foot slip, but she caught herself quickly on a protruding tuft of vines. Finally they reached the arched entryway.

Inside, the cavern glowed from dozens of lanterns on the walls and ceiling. Mello turned back to watch Lorel soak in the enchanted space. Her eyes lifted upward, brightening in awe as she noticed the glittering constellation of gems embedded in the gold-leafed ceiling. But as soon as she faced forward her smile faded.

On the far side of the chasmal space, up the marble stairs on a platform of polished gold was a long shale table filled with sirens. The Sieve Council. Mello cast Lorel a reassuring glance and led them toward the stairway.

At least twelve council members chatted busily among themselves at the grand table. The Triumvirate clustered in a row at the head, Lalique's great whalebone chair towering above Siri and Assyria, who sat as still as statues. Mello thought of how strange they looked above water. It was only for the direst of meetings that they departed from the Realms they oversaw, the Blue Hole and the Open Sea at the outer perimeter beach.

Their presence only heightened the tension he felt in the atmosphere.

Mello briefly caught his mother's eye. She and Warren Brimland seemed to be in a heated debate at the other end. Four chairs near them remained empty. The table fell to a hush as the group approached.

Mello squinted at the glowing sphere of blue and green hovering in orbit a few feet above the center of the table. It displayed a nautical map of the maritime routes. The portable holoprojector below fanned out in the shape of a small starfish. He noticed his mother fiddling nervously with the control panel embedded in the glass before her.

Lorel, who had slowed to a snail's pace, was hiding behind Sam. Mello reached back and put his hand on her shoulder.

"It's okay," he whispered in her ear. "They're all glad you're here. They know who you are."

Lorel cast him an appreciative glance.

Lalique stood, acknowledging the arrival of the foursome. She wore a powder blue gown of satin and organza. Her red hair was swept up into a pile of tight, silky braids and woven with thin blue ribbons. Tiny gems ornately beaded the edges of her large sapphire eyes as if a part of her skin. They matched the diamond that hung in the center of her forehead just below her widow's peak.

"Your Highness, consuls, the Council . . ." Mello addressed the silent crowd of Rodinian leaders. He bowed then reached back and took Lorel's hand, guiding her into the light of the grand chandelier that hung over the table. "I would like to introduce Lorelei Phoenix."

Mello escorted her toward Lalique. He could feel all eyes glued on them. *They were watching Lorel, not him,* he reminded himself. Regardless of people's opinions on hybrids, her mere presence seemed to inspire awe.

Despite the jaw-dropping stares, Lorel held her chin high. At the foot of Lalique's chair, she took another bow then looked squarely into the queen's face. "Thank you, Your Highness, and all of you, for inviting me here," she said, nodding to the queen, then the rest of the table.

"Ms. Phoenix, would you like to say a few words, introduce yourself to the Council?" Mello offered.

"We won't bite," a male siren called out from the far side of the room.

Lorel laughed nervously then drew in a breath. "I only hope that I can be helpful. I feel a responsibility, as many of my fellow humans would, to help preserve this beautiful place . . . and the people that call it home. I'm sorry it has come to this. Please know that we are not all full of greed and self-interest. Humans are compassionate and kind people, not so different from all of you. I share hope, as I know some of you do," she glanced back at Mello, "that we can find a way to coexist. I think the best future for everyone is one in which we are together."

Mello noticed his mother smile and a few heads nod.

"And after all of this is finished, I want to be a part of making that happen." Lorel paused, cleared her throat. "But my own future cannot be here. As soon as Rodinia is safe from DiviniGen and your anonymity is restored," she continued, with a slight raise of her chin, "I will return home to be with my father who is ill. Thank you."

Lorel's declaration was punctuated by silence. Although her fists squeezed into tight little balls and her chest fluttered, Mello caught a twinkle in her eye that said she meant it. Judging from the expressions around the room, he was not the only one shocked that she would broach the topic of returning home within the first moments of meeting the siren queen. She knew the consequences of coming to their island. She had been warned. Though he couldn't help but admire her determination. It was possible Lorel was as headstrong as he was.

Lalique's mouth hung open in an uncharacteristic moment of bewilderment. The queen had always been an enigma to her people, who were never sure of where she stood, but only of her strong and resolute character. Would she be cold to Lorel, this hybrid who stood for everything the sirens forbid? Or would she respond softly, revealing an empathy with the siren youth?

Everyone sat on the edge of their whalebone chairs, awaiting Lalique's reaction. Lorel's presence in Rodinia had already been accepted under formality, but Mello knew people were confused by it. They were on the lookout for clues as to the real reason she was there.

"Well," Lalique cleared her throat loudly and stretched her hands toward Lorel. "Welcome, Lorelei Phoenix."

Mello silently exhaled.

"Please, call me Lorel."

"Very well, Lorel."

Lalique clasped Lorel's hands in hers in a gesture of welcome. Mello found it strange that the queen's hands trembled.

"We embrace you today as a siren, as one of us. Rodinia will always be home to you," said the queen. "Always."

Mello wondered if a darker imperative lingered underneath her words, denying Lorel's plea to leave, or if it was a genuine welcome. Regardless, murmurs of agreement echoed down the table from the other sirens.

"Thank you, Your Highness," Lorel said. "Thank you all." Her eyes flitted around the room until they met Sam's, who pulled out the last open chair next to him. She sat, joining them.

"Now let us get down to business," said Lalique then looked at Mello's mother. "Cora, please display DiviniGen's route."

Cora tapped her fingertips against the control panel in front of her to zoom in on the holo. A route illuminated in red. From Washington, DC, it traversed the Atlantic Ocean then snaked through the ever-widening waterway that divided North Africa and Western Europe, down through the Arabian Sea and finally to a point flashing about ten miles west of Rodinia in the Indian Ocean.

"Based on their GPS program," said Cora, "we believe the trail of breadcrumbs they are following ends here. It is roughly where Mello ejected their tracker from the submarine. They have performed analyses to determine the remainder of the route, and unfortunately, their technology is good. It puts them only a couple miles west of Rodinia," she finished, tapping the glass to zoom back out.

"From there they can find us with binoculars," Warren said tossing his hands up and leaning back in his seat. He glared at Mello.

Mello averted his eyes.

"Thank you, Cora. Please retrieve the fleet now," said Lalique.

With another swirl against the glass, Cora pulled up an image displaying various ships. "And this is why we need a strategy," she said.

People squinted, examining the glowing ship figures to piece together exactly what they were looking at. No one had expected a fleet. Mello swallowed. *If only DiviniGen's resources could be put to better use in this world . . . but that would never happen with Galton at the helm.* "Do we know what kinds of ships these are?"

"George sent us the details," said Warren frowning into his tablet. "One aircraft carrier, an amphibious warfare ship, two cruisers, mobile logistics and a variety of support ships."

"Are they coming to conduct a science experiment or to wage a full-blown war?" One of the consuls blurted out as the hologram rotated through images of the various warfare ships.

"Well, they are obviously expecting resistance," said a woman. "Let's give it to them."

"Are they expecting resistance or do they just come prepared to a strange and unknown territory?" Lalique challenged. "Certainly they are confident with this private army. But they enter the fray not knowing our strengths, only assuming our weaknesses."

"They think we're some primitive tribe," said Temple, the consul of Baltra, rolling her eyes.

"Or Neanderthals!" added the siren next to her.

"And this is the point. We are none of these. We are sirens," Lalique said. "They do not know what that means, but we do. Now it's time to decide how we respond. Because how we respond defines who we are."

Murmurs of agreement rippled through the room. But as the group began hashing out details, reality set in. Mello listened in silence as several ideas were generated, discussed at length, then discarded. There was no easy way to deal with DiviniGen peacefully. Fear began to dominate the discussion. His mind raced, trying to come up with a solution.

A debate broke out over whether to attempt diplomacy or take a hostile position immediately with a preemptive attack. In the end it was decided to prepare for both.

"So, in summary, Plan A," said Warren, clearing his throat and propping the tablet up in his hands. "Lalique and the High Council will preemptively greet Galton's fleet at their pinpointed destination, a couple miles offshore. Lalique will make Galton an offer—an unlimited supply of algae on the conditions that they abort the Poseidon Project initiative and return home with lips sealed."

"This tells them, in no uncertain terms," added

Lalique, "that they are unwelcome. That Rodinia is the point of no return. Should they choose to enter our waters, Plan B will be implemented."

"And none of us want that," said Warren, sitting back down.

Cora tapped the glass and the projected image was sucked back into the starfish base. The room dimmed to a golden glow. "I, for one, feel confident with Plan A."

"Yes, this whole mess can be turned around," said a siren across the table. "They just need to hear from our queen, listen to *reason*." He flashed Mello a steely glance. "Since the last diplomat wasn't effective."

"I was never meant to be a diplomat," Mello shot back. "I was forced to be anonymous, remember?"

"We *all*," interrupted Cora, "have faith in our queen. I believe the plan will work. But if it doesn't, we will be prepared."

Mello sunk back in his chair. Hope lit the faces around him, but inside he shuddered envisioning Plan A. The siren queen and the CEO. A frightening clash of worlds. Deep down he knew it would inevitably lead to Plan B. Galton would not bow to their queen. He would only look past her, his eye on the prize, the land beyond. The war no one wanted would ensue, and the sirens would find themselves on the defensive. Plan A would only serve to compromise them, tangle them in the hope and then failure of a naïve course of action. Mello breathed a sigh of relief when Sam broke in to voice his doubts.

"If I may, from a human's perspective . . ." Sam stood, adjusting his glasses across his nose, "this plan is flawed.

It assumes Galton and his people will listen to reason. They won't. This company is a steamroller. They will proceed with their plans no matter what the resistance. Lalique is capable of powerful persuasion, but her words will fall on deaf ears. Galton has already promised the world his Poseidon Prototype."

Lorel cleared her throat next to Sam, soliciting the attention of the room. "He has promised them more than that. He has promised them the world, a solution to all their problems, a brand new frontier under the sea. He will not back down on his promise. And sadly, people believe his plans are in their best interest." She paused, shaking her head. "That couldn't be further from the truth."

"Humans can be gullible," Sam continued in agreement, "especially when they are vulnerable. But humans are also good. Often you can find a way to their sympathies, appeal to their emotions. But Galton and these guys, they're different. They are programmed to carry out what they consider to be divine plans."

"*Pan*Divine plans," Lorel muttered under her breath, catching Mello's eye.

Mello scanned the faces around him awaiting the reaction. Faces wrought with frustration as they struggled to understand their sister species. Sighs rippled around the table. Lalique chewed on her lower lip in contemplation.

"Sam and Lorel are right," Isla said. "We should listen to them. If Lalique can't persuade Galton to turn around, then we've already put our cards on the table and lost the advantage in defending ourselves."

"I think you lost your voice at this table once you allowed *that* to happen," said a siren with a tight blonde bun shoving a finger in the direction of Isla's belly.

"Hey!" Sam shot the woman a look.

More debate followed. Heated opinions on coexistence, the dangers of mixing with humans, and what to do with DiviniGen bounced around the table like ping-pong balls. So many people were talking across each other, at each other, Mello leaned quietly back in his chair.

"Enough!" Lalique shouted. "We will stick to the plan, unless someone has something better in mind."

Silence. Only the gushing echo of the waterfall could be heard. "Just as I thought. Warren, let's detail this. We need an action plan for every island."

As Warren laid out plans for how each consul would congregate weapons and prepare their people, an idea took form in Mello's head. It was late and everyone had dark circles of exhaustion beneath their eyes, but it was now or never.

"Wait, I have an idea." Everyone turned to look at him, and he could read their faces.

You, the one who got us into this?

You have no say.

You have failed us.

"Please, Mello. Do tell us," said Lalique, not hiding her exasperation.

"What if we go along with it . . . I mean, for a while. Let them get comfortable, set themselves up here. We can even offer them the hotel on Paraíso to set up their labs."

"Sure, while you watch safely from your island's cliffs," said Jett, the consul of Paraíso, his voice edged with resentment. "As if the Vulcan weren't enough burden to our island."

"If it were a burden, make no mistake, it would be so to the entire archipelago," Mello said, then sighed lifting his hands in the air. "Look, hear me out. The infrastructure they need is there already. A real building, a place to conduct their work. We can show them our hospitality, make them feel at home. Then we can see what they really plan to do to us, in detail. And we can make smarter decisions to defend ourselves. Let them at least think we are unable, or unwilling, to resist their plans. These people are businessmen on a mission, not warring soldiers."

"Too risky!" shouted Warren, his face red.

"Agreed," said Jett.

"And they have a private army, right?" Temple asked with raised brows, "that we just welcome in too?"

"Yes, PanElite," Mello replied. "But they're only there for risk management. Think of them as security backup for their operation, not army troops. If they think they're getting what they want, they'll have no reason to throw the first stone. They don't *want* any trouble, they just anticipate it as a potential part of their mission." He looked over at Sam. "Am I right?"

"I would have to agree," said Sam. "They expect resistance, but if they don't get it, the PanElites will just be silent, albeit intimidating, bystanders."

Mello nodded to Sam, but heads shook around the table.

An elder siren next to Isla stood up, fists clenched at his side. "This idea is absurd. They will treat us like animals!"

"And how many sirens might we lose to their *labs*, Mello? How many operated on? Sliced apart for genetic experimentation? You of all people to suggest this . . ."

Mello's heart fell to see his mother publicly rebuke his idea. But as her head fell in her hands, he realized why. "I haven't forgotten, Mother," he said.

"And not just that," said Warren. "These people are sick. They want our genes. They'll surely be after our pregnant women," he cast a steely glance at Isla, "and you can only hope they don't know what *you* carry."

"They will not know of her existence here at all," Sam replied through gritted teeth.

"Fine, let's hope. But can we protect all of our women if we just let these people in freely?" Warren said, gripping the table with white knuckles. "I'm sure you've all considered our women could be raped."

His words were met with gasps, but Mello had suffered the thought himself. No one knew how far Galton would be willing to go. No one but him.

"Our women are quite capable of protecting themselves," said Lalique. "And those who are compromised," she glanced at Isla, "can take shelter in the water or a bunker. There is no shortage of places to hide on our island."

"Or beneath it," added Siri from Lalique's side.

Assyria nodded in agreement, and added, "The perimeter will serve as protection from the outside. The weapons in the deep may be ancient, but they work. Only a year ago, I watched a stray thresher shark bump into one during a kill. It was not pretty."

Mello felt a chill at her reference to the sea mines floating just yards off the microcontinent's shelf. They had been erected by Beacon in the seventeenth century. People liked to pretend they had forgotten. The sirens rarely saw Assyria since her job was to guard the outside perimeter and swimming in the Open Sea Realm was forbidden. It made it easy to forget about the mines and the violent threat they posed to anyone, or anything, that dared enter Rodinian waters. But suddenly the built in defense of the minefield was a comfort.

"Sirens have found many ways throughout the centuries to protect our island. Whatever course of action we take now," said the queen, "I want each individual to be prepared. Every man and woman should keep their spearguns on them at all times."

"Of course." Mello stood, thrusting his arms out in appeal. "We can't—we *won't*—let those things happen to our men or our women. The sirens who have chosen to live on land will surely be in more danger than the ones in the grottoes. But we will all be on guard. This is *our* terrain. Our jungles and mangroves and grottoes are their labyrinths."

"Or their graves, if they make the wrong move," added Warren.

"Or *our* graves!" Jett replied. "What if these

mercenaries are triggered to action?"

"The PanElites are just killers for hire," said Mello. "They have no passion, no spearguns made from the very rock we stand on. They have nothing worth fighting from the heart for. We do. We can do this."

Some faces around the table softened and a few people leaned back in their chairs. His mother caught his eye and nodded. This was right. This was the way.

Mello leaned over the table, lowering his voice. "Look, our island has eyes. Beacon's old surveillance cameras still work. Now they have a real purpose. We will use them to watch Galton and his people every second they're here. We don't have to be brash. Instead of reacting, we can watch their every move until we figure out how to stop their game for good. And then we act."

"But we are first on the battlefield," argued Jett. "We have the home advantage. We should strike while they are on light ground."

"Yes, they enter our island blindly, but it isn't a battlefield yet. Our terrain can still serve as an advantage to us without an initial direct attack," reasoned Mello, trying to refrain from raising his voice.

Couldn't they see the wisdom in laying low?

Jett and Warren opened their mouths in unison to disagree, but Lalique held up her hand. "True, it is not a battlefield yet. No war has been waged. Yet. But we must be smart. Anything is possible and we must think that way, preparing for the worst but acting with finesse. We cannot be naive to the nuances of war. It is an art, and one our people used to know well. There is hope in Mello's idea. Hope that violence will not be initiated by them if unprovoked. Hope that we can maintain the integrity of our people by avoiding bloodshed. The High Council will continue the conversation. Thank you, Mello."

"Of course, Your Grace," he said with a reverent nod.

"Now," said the queen, "everyone go home and begin getting the word out. We will be defending ourselves one way or another very soon." She stood in adjournment.

As everyone descended the steps and headed toward the curtain of falls at the far end of the cavern, he felt a hand on his shoulder. "Mello, may I speak with you?"

He turned to see Lalique. Her face was softer, almost welcoming, despite the anger he had felt from her since his return. "Of course."

"Your idea is good. It's smart."

"Thank you," he said, trying not to stammer.

"You may have made some mistakes, but I believe we would have come to this moment at some point regardless of your actions. What brought us here was a risk, a risk you led the charge on, but one for which I have stood behind. And so have others. Some may be angry and confused about the role you played in this, but deep down they look up to you. I believe, Mello, that you could be king of Rodinia one day."

Mello felt his breath catch in his chest. No words surfaced in his mind to express how he felt, how much Lalique's words meant to him. "I—"

"Mello, I understand why you did what you did. I understand because I have wanted that human connection as well. I have done things I regret too, in the name of that desire."

"And now we have a human connection before our eyes." He looked back at Lorel walking toward the falls with Sam and Isla. "She's proof that there's still hope."

Lalique followed his gaze to Lorel. Her eyes glistened with anguish. It was a feeling he recognized only because he had seen it in himself. "She is a very special girl, very special indeed," she said.

"Thank you, Your Grace, for telling me this. Thank you for understanding," Mello whispered knowing his words could not fully express his gratitude.

She nodded, the stoicism in her face returning. "Go. There is much to prepare for," she said, turning from him with a swish of her gown.

Mello walked down the steps and let out a quiet breath of relief. Not only had Lalique revealed the degree to which she sympathized with him, he had succeeded in convincing her that war was not the solution, at least not yet. Sirens were not barbarians wielding weapons and attacking living beings at whim. They had risen above that long ago. That's why they were going to put DiviniGen in a silent checkmate—or a deadly one, if Galton made the wrong move.

"Hey, Mello!" Lorel called through the darkness as they parted ways at the Waterfall Tree.

"Yeah?" He stopped in his tracks and turned to face

her.

"I think you did great in there. I mean, I think it's a good idea," she said approaching him.

He thought she blushed, but it was hard to tell in the moonlight.

"Thanks." Warmth surged through him followed by an uncomfortable silence. He was suddenly aware of how close she stood to him. Her human scent was different, intoxicating as it mixed with the herbs and lavender sprouting from the ground. He looked up at the sky.

"You can see more stars here than anywhere I've ever been," she said, following his gaze skyward. "And I've been a lot of places."

He laughed over a sting of inferiority. "I wish I could say the same."

"I may have seen more of the world above, but think of all you've seen below." She swung her arm playfully around a branch, leaning in closer to him.

"True," he said. "I guess together we've seen it all."

She laughed, brushing a strand of hair from her eyes. He thought how much harder they were to read, the brown iris blending into the black pupil shrouded the emotion he searched for. But her lips gave away more, hovering between a friendly smile and something more. "I guess so," she said.

The warmth running through his body had risen to a simmer, now a boil, and he felt an overpowering urge to pull her into his arms the way he had in the kelp forest.

"They look like the crystals, don't they?"

Mello jolted from his trance. Lorel still stared at the

sky. Stars glittered against the velvety blackness.

"You know," she said, "like the ones hanging from Lalique's cavern. They were everywhere. What are they?"

"Oh, yeah, the diamonds," he said.

"Diamonds. Do you have any idea how rare those are? And the gold! Gold is as extinct as the polar bear, at least in the rest of the world. Do you know what it would cost to buy just a tiny chip from Lalique's floor? More than I could make in my entire life. I had no idea Rodinia had such precious metals and stones. Where do they come from?"

"The deep-sea mineral mines beneath the Abyssal Plane. Tunneling through the seabed beneath any thermal vent would lead you to caverns full of geological gems. Most of the metals, like the gold, came from under the Vulcan. But now they're all closed up." Mello averted his eyes, hoping she would not ask more.

"This place is like the Garden of Eden. The whole planet used to be that way until we pruned it down to nothing." Her face darkened. "Mello, let's hope Galton doesn't find out. He'd never resist getting his hands on those mines."

"That would be bad. Catastrophic, actually. But trust me, it's the least of our worries. DiviniGen will never find out about the mines, much less penetrate them."

"How can you be so sure?"

Because it's impossible, Mello thought.

He looked at her disturbed expression, wondering if he could get back to a few moments ago. He swore he had seen a flicker of desire in her. Maybe she was resisting too, or maybe it was just wishful thinking.

"First of all, humans would never be able to get down there alive. But even if they could get dredges down there, let's just say the mines have minds of their own. And they've decided to close for business." He smiled, attempting to quell her worry. "Even we can't mine them anymore."

"I hope you are right. Can I ask you one more question?"

"But of course." He was eager to move on.

"Why are sirens so ashamed of violence? I mean, I respect it, but they are completely in their right to defend their home against an invading group of hostile corporate zombies. I'd say it's justified."

Mello took a deep breath and looked up at the moon that was almost full. It lit up the clearing in a pale bluish light.

"Did Sam ever tell you about the Dark Submersion?" he asked.

"No. He started to. It was when we were at his house in DC, when he told me everything. I had just met Isla. I remember she was upset already, and she stopped him saying she couldn't take any more sadness. I've been wanting to learn more ever since, like it's a part of siren history I should know." Lorel pulled herself up onto a low branch and straddled it. She leaned forward on her elbows, looking down at him with alluring brown eyes. "Tell me."

Mello hopped up on a lower branch so their faces

were level. He could see her lust was for more knowledge of Rodinia, not for him, but still he relished the intimacy of the moment. "I'll tell you anything you want to know. There should be no secrets from you, not after all you've been through. I'll warn you though, it's not pleasant."

"I guessed as much," she said.

"About three hundred years ago, humans were living on Rodinia. Only a handful of Beacon members from London. They had built trust with the sirens, and the relationship was working. The network of paramilitary intel hubs and bunkers they'd constructed were discreet, mostly underground, and served the sirens as much as Beacon."

"So this was around the time that the sirens' were still sinking Portuguese ships that threatened the East India Company, right?" Lorel asked, then added, "I read some letters about it."

"Yes. The East India Company formed Beacon as a secret subsidiary to protect their seafaring operations with no restrictions. Rodinia was the perfect place to set up their defense base."

"What did the sirens get out of it? Why would they allow humans into their home?"

"Beacon offered the sirens plentiful resources and protection from the world. The human population was growing exponentially, exploring more ground. The sirens knew they wouldn't be able to hide forever without help. So they offered their land, and they began doing Beacon's dirty work."

"Sinking the ships."

"Dutch ships, Portuguese ships, even pirate ships. Anything that threatened the EIC's revenue stream."

"Ships with people on them," Lorel said.

"Yes." Mello sighed. "You saw the graveyard, the mines."

"I did." Lorel said.

"But that wasn't the worst of it."

"So what happened?"

"The Portuguese empire was powerful, and their goal was to be the next Rome. They were aggressively conquering land overseas. Any island along the trade route between India and Portugal was game. They would stake their claim, build fortresses, military bases, whatever suited their fancy. There was fierce competition in the seas for their colonizing body, the Portuguese State of India. The Dutch East India Company and the East India Company were also colonizing every new land they found along the trade route. When the Portuguese realized one of their competitors, the EIC, was somehow behind all their lost ships, they began spying. That's how they found Rodinia."

"How did they even know to look for Rodinia, much less locate it?" Lorel asked.

"The Portuguese planted a mole in the EIC, and he discovered Beacon. Once they discovered that Beacon operated from a secret island equipped strategically for defense, the Portuguese State of India planned a siege. To locate the island, they abducted and tortured Beacon's Guardian until he revealed the coordinates. Luckily, information didn't spread so fast in that time. The only ones that knew were confined on one galleon ship. They came armed in the night, and murdered every human on the island over the course of twenty-four hours."

Lorel gasped. "How horrible! What about the sirens?"

"They were underwater, in their grottoes, when the Portuguese came. And as soon as they peaked above the surface of the water and saw what had happened, they submerged again. For a year."

"A year?"

"Yes, they hid. Every siren in Rodinia stayed underwater in the grottoes, breathing in the air pockets, and only surfacing late at night to see what the Portuguese were up to. The humans never saw a trace of them. Some had heard rumors of sea-people and would search and search the waters. But eventually, they chalked it up as a myth created by drunk sailors."

"So what *were* the Portuguese up to, when not siren hunting?" Lorel asked.

"They began settling the land, using the bunkers and hubs that Beacon had built as their defense headquarters. They got word back to Portugal and three more ships arrived filled with people and building supplies. They began to erect a large building on one of the inner beaches of Paraíso. It was a fortress."

"You mean the hotel? That building you pointed out earlier?"

"Yes, the hotel."

"Only in name I assume. Since this is an island with no visitors."

He laughed. "For the most part. But before it became

our hotel—and library and banquet hall and makeshift hospital—it was Fortress Paraíso. It looked like a castle, strong and built of a stone the sirens had never seen before. It was a massive structure, with wings branching from the center. There were windows that glowed with candlelight at night from the rooms where they slept. They staked their flag in front of it, began building smaller cottages in the surrounding area. It soon became obvious that they intended to bring back more people, colonize Rodinia. The sirens decided they had had enough. They had to defend their home." Mello glanced down, biting hard on his lower lip.

"What did they do?" Lorel pressed.

"You have to understand, they felt cornered. Trapped. And they were angry."

"Mello, I'm not judging."

Her assuring nod softened his guard and he continued. "One night when the moon was new and the sky was at its darkest, they all rose to the surface at the same time. Sirens poured from the Eye onto the land like ants. They marched inland and slaughtered every single human in Rodinia. They were scared to leave anyone alive, for fear word would get back to the mainland about their existence. Hundreds died that night, Lorel, even children, which the sirens had not anticipated."

"Children?" Lorel placed a hand to her mouth.

"Who knows, maybe in the chaos, the darkness, no one realized. But children died at the sirens' hands. So much life was lost. Young, old, human, siren . . . they were all people." Mello swallowed a bitter tang in his mouth. "It used to be second nature for sirens to sink ships full of humans. The ships would just turn into watery tombs. They never had to see the bodies, stare into faces so similar to their own. But this time they did. The sight of the bloody massacre was enough to send the sirens into such abysmal shame that they vowed never to lower themselves to such brutal measures again. Killing a human being is not only against the rules in Rodinia, it is a disgrace to our people and a black mark on the soul."

Lorel's jaw hung open, and for a moment Mello felt like she was looking at him in disgust, like he had shed that blood himself.

"What a horrible tragedy. I . . . I don't even know what to say." She glanced around, seeming to soak in their surroundings in a new light.

Had he repelled her?

He slid around the tree trunk, closer to her. She didn't move away, but the look in her eyes remained distant. He became aware of how small she seemed next to him, how her head barely reached his chest.

She looked off in the direction of Paraíso even though the horizon was just a dark smudge. "How is it so beautiful now? It looks more like a hotel than a military fortress."

"Decades later, Beacon returned. They helped reconstruct the fortress so that it could be used for good purpose, so that it no longer symbolized tragedy. They added the library, the dining hall, turned the sleeping quarters into rooms resembling a hotel where their people could stay. Brightly painted stucco covered the gray stone. They built gardens, a veranda, an aquarium where we put our most beautiful fish on display. It became known from then on as Hotel Paraíso."

"Paradise Hotel," Lorel said. "Sort of ironic."

"I'm sorry. I wish that wasn't a part of our history, of *your* history." He lifted her chin up so that she stared up at him. Behind the look of surprise he saw desire. But she dismissed it with a friendly smile. He dropped his hand, feeling a sting of rejection.

"Don't apologize for something your people did so long ago. Trust me, humans have done way worse."

"Sometimes I feel like the sirens were just being used by Beacon, puppets in a game of possession on the sea. It's almost like they perverted our desires to be safe into something that made us into ugly creatures."

"Hmm. Sounds exactly like what PanDivinity does to humans."

"Beacon protects the sirens though, they've been good to us," he said, unconvinced.

"That's what people think PanDivinity does for them. Protect them, offer them the safety of an Afterworld. Give them stuff. Those material possessions are carrots dangling in front of them, making good people act ugly."

Mello frowned. "The parallels between Beacon and PanDivinity are disturbing. The sirens would never want to think of their protector that way, or of themselves that way."

"It's not bad to question things, Mello. It's healthy. Sirens seem like such wise and gentle souls. I'm sure they are. The Dark Submersion was one point in history."

"I guess anyone is capable of ugliness."

"Anyone is capable of anything. Which is why kindness is such a beautiful thing. It's a choice."

She looked so deeply into his eyes he feared she was staring at his soul.

So close.

Her breath was warm on his face, and a buzz of electricity sparked in the distance between their lips. His parted slightly.

She sucked in a breath, and Mello stopped breathing completely. Then her eyes darted away. The spell was broken.

"Goodnight, Mello

NINE
LOREL

September 25, 2098
Baltra, Rodinia

A LOW RUMBLING SOUND STARTLED Lorel from a restless sleep. She bolted upright in bed to survey the inside of her hut. It was day three on the island, the day of DiviniGen's predicted arrival into Rodinian waters, and a queasy feeling churned in the pit of her stomach. Only this morning she had been lavishing in the ephemeral paradise, learning to spearfish with Isla and her friends. If only she could slow time down. Except, the sooner they dealt with Galton, the sooner she could get back to her father.

She had been formulating a plan of escape from Rodinia in case Lalique refused her permission to leave. Lorel found the queen intimidating. Though she had not grown up predisposed to revere Lalique as a ruler, it was something in her eyes, the striking cold beauty of her face, and the power she wielded so confidently that had made Lorel feel shaky in the knees. Yet, she had also felt an undercurrent of warmth. It gave her hope that Lalique had a soft side and would allow her to return home . . . *with* a plentiful supply of algae.

In the corner of the room she eyed her pile of belongings, the only remnants of her temporarily abandoned life. The day she packed her modest bag for Sam to take on the submarine she had been faced with the cliché question: *If you were going to be stranded on a desert island, what would you bring?*

Rodinia was not exactly deserted, but sirens had less need for certain conveniences she had grown accustomed to. Her essentials included a pair of jeans, three cotton tees, one pair of socks and sneakers, leather sandals, a light purple windbreaker, her red bikini, underwear, a hair brush, lip gloss, and black eyeliner—the only items of makeup she could never live without. Against reason, her light blue maxi dress, an elegant strapless piece with an empire waist and a gathering of eyelet fabric ruffled across the top. And finally, the one piece of jewelry she had ever cared about—a necklace her father had given her for high school graduation. It was an ancient shipwreck coin set in a ring of gold with the figure of Neptune riding a dolphin. A tiny crystal twinkled in the dolphin's eye. The necklace had been excavated on one of his archaeological digs.

I gave it to your mother when we first met. She left it behind, for you, her father had said as he fastened the gold chain around her neck. *Just like she left us behind,* Lorel remembered thinking with bitterness. Still, she cherished the necklace, the only piece of her mother she had. She would often rub it when she was stressed, keeping the metal untarnished.

Link paced back and forth inside the hut impatiently. The thundering sound persisted.

"Link, what do you think that noise is?" She cupped her ear. "I don't hear rain."

He stared at the door, his yellow eyes begging her to let him out.

"Well, you should never have let me sleep so long. Here." She jumped out of bed and opened the door. The rumble was louder outside. Link slid through the door, spoiled by his new roaming liberties in Rodinia. The thick wood at the backside of the hut offered more critters for him to hunt than he could catch in a lifetime.

Lorel rubbed her eyes. Late afternoon light filtered through the muslin curtains casting a rosy glow around the room. Her midday nap, or rather collapse from exhaustion, had left her groggy and disoriented, and she was still lagging on Washington, DC, time. Earlier that morning she had felt an eerie calm on the island. In the still of the trees and the placid surface of the Eye. Mello predicted rain.

Had the storm arrived?

The pressure of the air felt different. It was still and smelled salty and sweet, like the sea mixed with the aromatic scent of the sapphire clematis that bloomed on the roof and crept into her hut through tiny gaps. She padded over to the window to assess the weather. The panorama of endless sky and water served as a crystal ball portending the mood of the atmosphere. She looked down at the Eye and it returned her gaze, sapphire and unblinking.

A whole world lay at the bottom.

Would she have a chance to visit the Abyssal Plane or would the ensuing chaos prevent her from ever seeing where the algae grew? And how?

As she leaned out the window, a heavy gust of wind blew the curtains outward like billowing sails to reveal dark cumulus clouds rolling in from the distance. Lorel squinted. They were too far away for such loud thunder, and bright sunbeams sliced through breaks in the waffled cloud layer overhead, touching down across Rodinia in a prismatic scattering of light. She leaned farther out the window and looked directly below at Baltra's inner beach.

Yesterday George had revised DiviniGen's ETA to be well past midnight instead of early afternoon. Everyone had breathed a little easier at the news. But this morning when they tried to get another update, George never responded. Regardless, the sirens were ready. The Machiavellian plan Mello seeded was in place—*keeping the enemy close*—and they were set to *amiably* receive Galton and his crew.

The sirens would appear cooperative on the surface, but they would be carefully watching. All of the underground bunkers were set up with communication and monitoring systems so at a moment's notice they could switch into defensive mode. The sirens' long game would be anything but cooperative if DiviniGen became hostile.

Lorel knew what a mammoth DiviniGen was, and the lengths they were willing to go to ensure they got the genetic formulation for their perfect aquatic human, but Lorel had faith in the sirens.

Now all of the islands had been put on guard and every siren in Rodinia was aware of the pending visit, which was why Lorel was surprised to see signs of what appeared to be a colossal celebration. The beach and all the avenues leading to it were flooded with sirens, dancing, marching, undulating to the beat like a swelling wave.

Maybe this was their welcome party.

The rhythmic sound grew louder in a crescendo of percussive melody. It was impossible to categorize, a tribal beat of steel pans and skin drums fused with tinkling mallet instruments. Heady voices carried on the wind and echoed against the cliffs, saturating the air. The beat invaded her body in a wave of ticklish vibrations, tugging at her on a primal level.

This was something she had to be a part of. With a burst of excitement she pulled on her Maxi dress, then shoved her feet into the leather sandals and ran out the door.

"Come on, Link, we're missing the party!"

Link darted out of the shrubbery licking his lips with a satisfied expression and bounded after her down the winding, thicketed path toward the beach. The dense woods muffled the music, but she could still feel the thumping vibrations in her bones. There were so many sirens she could hardly believe it.

Would they look at her strangely? Would they know she was a human? *Or part human,* Lorel thought with newfound pride. Her feelings about the recent self-discovery vacillated from thrill to terror, but ultimately it was propelling her into an enlightened state of self-acceptance.

She thought of one of her father's maxims. *Know thyself.* That was how to reach life's plateau, he had always assured her.

She pulled her hair, matted from the morning swim, up into a ponytail in order to flaunt her newest feature. Yesterday the skin on the back of her neck had been tender and swollen where the doctor had made the incision, but today it was fully healed from the algae. With a thrill she traced her finger around the slit.

Her blowhole.

Mello had been a godsend, teaching her to swim with it in the shallows and in the lagoon outside his hut. How to cast a spout. Her body tingled thinking about the thrill of her training, and the sound of Mello's voice, firm and commanding.

"Don't freak out under water, that's lesson one," he had said.

Lorel stood on the porch of his hut. The rustic planks jutted out over the placid lagoon. Looking down, she could see her reflection. Her hair dangled in long matted curls, and her slender body poised for the dive. Next to her a large masculine figure appeared and slipped his hand into hers.

"Ready?"

She nodded. "As I'll ever be."

"This is cake, I promise. And we can test out how much siren you really have in you."

"What if it's not enough?"

"It will be. Remember what the doc said? Your blowhole is fully functional, your rib cage is sized for siren lungs, your red blood cell count is right on par with ours. You got this."

"It looks so dark down there. Will my eyes see like a siren? Mine are so..."

"Brown? Have I told you how much I love your eyes? So what if you're blind underwater?"

She laughed. "Yes, beauty over function."

"Just take a deep breath."

Lorel looked above her at the tree vines swaying in the light breeze, then down to their reflections, the shimmering images of clouds floating across the sky, the glassy water. Mello. At the precipice of discovering what she was truly capable of, there was no one she would rather be standing beside. They jumped in with a huge splash.

Instead of swimming up to the surface as her instinct would lead her to do, she remained below, floating. Blood rushed from her extremities to her core, and her heart rate slowed until it felt as though she were moving through time in slow motion. Staying as still as she could, she opened her eyes. At first it was dark, and a curtain of bubbles from their entrance surrounded her in a murky cloud. She didn't breath in. She didn't breath out. The intolerable moment she had dreaded, where her lungs turned to lead and unconsciousness lapped at the edges of her mind loomed.

But it never came.

The bubbles dissipated and her eyes began to adjust. There was a golden glow to the water. A few yards below, translucent green weeds undulated from the current created by her gentle movements. A face appeared in front of her. As soon as her eyes met his, he smiled. She could see the joy on his face. He was proud of her.

Instead of panicking from the oncoming feeling of suffocation, she willed herself to stay calm and focused on his face. He squeezed her hands and gave her a nod. After a few moments, the feeling passed, and she no longer felt the threat of drowning. Her body felt one with the water around her. A bright blue angel fish passed between their faces and she laughed, emitting a few bubbles. Suddenly the distance between her and that fish, between her and the world around her, seemed smaller. She felt connected.

After several hours of training, testing her spout, her breathing and vision abilities, they climbed out of the water and back onto Mello's porch, naked and dripping wet.

She squeezed the water from her hair and wrapped herself in a cloth Mello had draped over the porch rail. "So how'd I do? Did I make the cut?"

Mello plopped down beside her with two wooden mugs of coconut juice and handed her one. "I'll give you an A."

"A? That's below my standards. What about A+?"

He laughed. "You've got most of it down. In fact, I'm amazed that you adapted so instinctually to the water. It's like your body just knew what to do. But some things take time. Like submarine communication. The doc said your skull is shaped the right way. You have a hollowness in your frontal *bone that should allow for biosonar, but it's a language thing. It has to be learned."*

"Are you saying I could talk to fish one day?"

"You could, but they won't talk back. Dolphins on the other hand, they're chatterboxes."

Thirst still ravaged her from the physical demands of the swim, and she downed the rest of her coconut juice then stood up. "This is the most amazing thing I have ever experienced in my life. Thank you for today, for teaching me how to — " she paused in thought. "How to be myself."

Mello stood, their bodies close. Before she could think of a reason not to, she threw her arms around him and squeezed. The smoothness of his bare skin and the feel of his sinewy muscles sent a shiver of delight through her. He returned the hug, full and wholeheartedly. The sunlight felt warm on her back, and his presence felt warm surrounding her. It was a moment she would never forget. The moment she discovered what she was truly capable of.

"Anytime, darlin'. Anytime," he replied with a squeeze before releasing her.

Remembering the embrace gave her the sensation of warmth all over again.

Now, she felt like she truly belonged in this strange world. The hut she stood in felt more like home. The siren in her was alive. It gave her power. And a chance to take things into her own hands if a more watery escape home was necessary.

The most amazing thing was that the strange dimpled scar in her neck that had once symbolized all her insecurities now made her extraordinary. Her altered anatomy had transformed into working condition, and the perplexing mysteries of her skin, blood, scars had all been solved. She was no longer human. She was *superhuman.*

The notion seemed silly, but a shiver of elation ran through her. The extent of what a siren could do in — and with — water was still a mystery to her, but whatever Mello had done with the tide that day was staggering enough. One day she would uncover it all.

The steep trail evened to level ground, and the trees thinned to a forest of pines leading out to the beach. Sirens milled around everywhere. As she stepped into a pool of light, her heart quickened.

A group of sirens played instruments a few feet away. Some sat on logs or the bed of pine needles, others danced. One swayed to the slower layer of the rhythm while another jammed to the faster beat. Her proximity to the group was exhilarating, but she moved along and attempted to blend in with the crowd.

A hobbyist musician herself, Lorel was not a stranger to jam sessions, but this one was on a grand scale. It had the intimacy of a campfire but the vastness of a festival. Despite the size it still maintained a cohesive harmony, each individual's music coalescing into a single anthem. *How were they so in sync?* The sirens had turned the entire island, maybe even the whole archipelago, into a single song of gale force.

"Here, want this?" said a childlike voice beside her.

A small girl wearing a cream tunic with curling blonde ponytails stood before her. Her siren eyes looked even larger on her little heart-shaped face. She held up an instrument Lorel didn't recognize. It looked like a bamboo drum with strings. Six strings, she noticed. It couldn't be so different than her mandolin.

"Thank you." She kneeled down, eye level with the little girl.

"You're pretty. How come your eyes are brown?" she asked, wrinkling her nose.

Lorel laughed. "It's a secret. Maybe I'll tell you one day."

The girl smiled wide then ran away. Lorel wondered with a heavy heart what DiviniGen's presence would mean for the children on the island. *There was so much to protect.*

A few feet away, Link had bolted over to befriend a woman leaning against a nearby tree. She gasped and jumped in the air, frightened and partly amused.

"Sorry!" Lorel called to her. "Link, stay by my side!"

He bounded back to her heels obediently. They shuffled through the crowd with the bamboo instrument clutched in Lorel's hand.

Out on the beach the celebration continued. The smell of cooking fish filled the air and smoke swirled into the sky from bonfires scattered along the beach. *If they were trying to stall Galton's arrival, smoke signals were not going to help,* she thought.

"Coconut juice?" A man shoved a sliced coconut shell in her hand with a smile.

"Thanks." Lorel sipped the sweet pulpy juice. How did they do it? Nothing cost money here. They didn't even have a currency.

Most of the sirens were dry and clothed, but there were a few scattered in the shallow waters. Spouts jetted into the air like fountains as they darted in and out of the breakers near the coral atoll. Lorel walked toward the water.

Calm waves lapped gently at the shore in a delicate white froth. She did a double take and gasped in delight as someone rose out of the water on the back of a dolphin. It seemed the animals served the same purpose that dogs and cats did to humans — companionship.

Jake would be in bliss here. It saddened her to think she couldn't share it with him.

She slipped off her sandals and meandered along the beach, letting the music pulse in her veins and lift her spirit. The sand, still warm from baking in the sun all day, was soft under her feet. She sighed at the tactile pleasure.

Link pranced beside her on all fours, stopping every few feet to paw at the pearly white granules. There was a sense of euphoria that was contagious here. She inhaled the salt-laden air then glanced at the sky. Beyond the island ring, the burgeoning thunderheads still approached, but nobody seemed to care. After all, what was rain to a siren?

Still, Lorel couldn't help thinking the storm was a harbinger of things to come. A cool gust of wind sent goose bumps along her skin. The air pressure was changing as the warm and cold fronts neared collision. She began to pick at the strings of her exotic new instrument. It twanged in a dissonance of hollow notes. Thankfully, her off-key strumming was drowned out by the more pleasant soundscape.

In the distance, where the beach curved inward and hugged the iris of the Eye, a large outcropping of craggy rocks jutted into the water. It beckoned her, the perfect place to people-watch from afar. As she approached she noticed someone else had had the same idea.

On the high contour of rock sat a man with his elbows on his knees and his chin in his hand, gazing inland. An image of The Thinker flashed through Lorel's mind. Before she could say anything, Link scampered over to the outcropping and up the rocks. Lorel watched in horror as he began licking the man's face. The man laughed and turned in her direction.

"Mello!" She gasped in surprise.

"Lorel, hi," he said with an ear-to-ear grin, ruffling Link's mane.

She put her sandals back on and climbed up to him, taking a seat on the smoothest surface she could find. The water churned and eddied around the base of the rocks, periodically spraying them with a cool mist.

"What is all of this?" She gestured to the crowded beach. "They know what's happening soon, right?"

"They do. That's why they're celebrating," he said in a melancholy tone, flicking a small rock into the water.

"I don't get it."

"They know it could mean war. So why not go into battle with your spirits soaring? It's harder to bring you down that way." He laughed, but it was tainted by a dark undercurrent. "Don't get me wrong. The consuls on every islet have been preparing their people for the worst-case scenario. They've been up earlier than the sun stashing bunkers and grottoes, stationing weapons at strategic landmarks on land and water. They know very well what could be in store. There was a time when . . ."

"When this was second nature," Lorel finished. "They sure don't seem scared though." She watched a nearby circle of sirens dance, their feet splashing in the shallow waves.

"Sirens are courageous people, always have been. They have faith in themselves. They used to have faith in me, at least the young ones. The elders always doubted me." Mello looked down at his feet, and Lorel realized what was bothering him.

"Mello, you going into DC to look for your daughter . . . I think it was brave. You never meant to put your people in danger. In fact, everything you've done is to make Rodinia a better place. I know the DiviniGen deal started off with the best of intentions."

"And sky-high hopes." He sighed. "Thanks, Lorel. It means a lot."

"And now we can only hope you find out more about your daughter. See, we all have a silver lining in this."

"What's yours?" he asked.

"To return home and save my father's life with your algae." She smiled matter-of-factly.

"So Sam tells me. I wish you luck. If only he could have gotten it as soon as he was diagnosed, through your health system. That's how it was supposed to work. They were supposed to make it available to the people who needed it."

"Well, it ended up in the hands of the richest people, most of whom weren't even sick. They just wanted it for the other benefits."

Lorel watched as Mello clenched his jaw.

"But that's just the way the PanDivinity companies do business. You couldn't have known, unless you'd grown up in our world. Even then, most people still don't see them for what they really are."

Mello nodded. "I suppose we see what we want to see."

They both stared out at the shore full of sirens engaged in the melodious festivities. Then his face lit up. "Hey, wanna go for a swim?"

He stood and extended his hand down to her.

"Now?" The idea seemed foolish considering all that was going on, but then, everyone else seemed to have forgotten the storm ahead, at least for the night.

"Yes, now. Trust me, there may not be another chance. Plus, we still have a few days until they come."

"So they say," she shrugged. "I don't know, Mello. I'm new at this siren thing, and I still felt like a fish out of water swimming with Isla this morning."

"But you've already acclimated. Your lungs are ready. Now you just need to tap into your buried instincts and ready your mind." He tapped his temple, raising an eyebrow at her.

She took his hand hesitantly and pulled herself up, unsteady on the rocky surface. Her mouth twisted in contemplation. "Look at all the people around. I don't have my bathing suit," she said, aware her excuse was weak. A gust of wind blew her dress up to reveal her bare legs.

Mello smiled. "I'm sure you've noticed that sirens don't even own bathing suits. Your body is not something to be ashamed of, it's who you are. It's natural."

She laughed, shaking her head in defeat. "You know that would be quite the line back home."

"Yeah, well, you're not in Kansas anymore, are you?"

"It amazes me how full of human cultural references you are."

"We are studious creatures," he said with a wink. "So, what do you say?"

She noticed they were still holding hands. "You aren't going to let this go, are you?"

"Definitely not."

"All right. Let's go."

"Great, because I want to show you something." His eyes shone with mischief.

"Wait, what do you mean?" she demanded, suddenly suspicious. "This is just a swim, right?" She had spent the last couple days acclimating underwater, getting used to her nascent breathing apparatus. Still, she did not feel confident in the depths.

"Come on, trust me," he said as he scurried down the rocks.

Before she could answer, her breath stopped short. Mello had dropped his pants and tunic to the sand and stood naked before her. Maybe this was the norm for sirens, but Lorel was still half human. She felt a pulsating heat rush through her at the sight of his bare body, smooth and sculpted. It wasn't the first time she had seen him exposed. They had trained naked. But somehow, the more she knew him, the more emotions he elicited from her. Emotions she was not yet willing to explore. She allowed her eyes to soak in his body. The sea spray coated his skin, leaving it shining in beads of iridescence. A dimple formed in his cheek as he smiled up at her.

She did trust him.

"All right, Link. Be good. I'll be back in a bit." She kissed his furry head then climbed down the rocks next to Mello and dropped her maxi dress to the sand.

They waded in the warm water out to their chests. "Just hold my hand when we get past the Eye Atoll, okay? Then follow my lead with the strokes," Mello instructed. "And don't be scared!"

Lorel nodded, then looked out at the horizon. The sun had sunk below the line of storm clouds and brilliant beams of light danced on the water and illuminated the festival on shore.

Pushing her toes into the cool sandy floor she shoved off, falling into pace with Mello in a smooth breaststroke.

TEN
JAKE

September 23, 2098
A couple days earlier
Washington, DC

JAKE STARED UP AT the dizzyingly tall building as he slid out of the cab. Ben Reshing lived in the penthouse of one of the highest residential skyscrapers in the city. After leading them past several burly doormen and security guards, Frank stepped into the separate penthouse elevator and scanned his eyes in front of the retina-recognition security panel.

"You said he wanted to see me. Why?" Jake said as the elevator barreled skyward.

"I cannot say. My employer prefers to speak for himself."

Jake yanked the man's collar and shoved him against the mirrored wall. "Don't screw with me. Did he get the wrong guy when he killed my brother, is that what this

139

is?"

"Yes, I'm very sorry about that." Frank said in a choked voice.

Jake squeezed his neck harder. "What does he know about it?"

Frank's plump face was turning dangerously red and the elevator beeped as they bypassed the eightieth floor.

"You can ask him yourself."

Jake pulled the las-gun out, pressing it into Frank's side. "Give me one reason not to walk right in there and use this on your employer the second that door opens."

"That, my friend, would be foolish. Dr. Reshing needs your help. Someone is in trouble." Frank's mouth twisted into a sly curl. He peered from the corner of his eye to gauge Jake's reaction. "Someone you may know."

Jake let go of his neck and Frank stumbled back to standing position. They both stared out the elevator at the colorfully glowing city below.

So Ben Reshing needed him? Maybe it was true. Maybe he was not responsible for Leo's death. Jake realized he had to be strategic. A hot head might lose him the opportunity to uncover the truth. And the truth led to Lorel. A terrifying thought entered his head. *Jake needed Reshing as much as Reshing needed him.*

The elevator doors parted to a palatial foyer of marble. The sound of Beethoven's Ninth Symphony floated from unseen speakers. Shards of sparkling zircon crystal hung in geometric patterns from a domed ceiling. Ahead, a half-moon couch hugged a sleek glass coffee table, still glowing with remnants of a recent hologram display.

Beyond the couch stood the figure of a man, short in stature and dressed in casual attire that seemed out of place amid the opulence. The man held a tumbler filled with dark liquor and stared out the wall of glass. Glancing at the view beyond, Jake could see where the city ended and the barrier canals began. Filled with boat traffic, they looked like moving rivers of lights. Past it, the ocean stretched out to meet the night horizon at a point impossible to discern.

"Dr. Reshing, he insisted I bring him here." Frank announced waving a hand in the air.

"Mr. Ryder. Welcome to my home. Can I offer you a drink of brandy?" Reshing walked toward Jake with an extended hand. "By the way, when I saw you approaching the building, I asked my guards to spare you the indecency of being frisked. I trust you will be keeping that gun in your pocket?"

In person, this man did not look as Jake had imagined. Lorel would never have been sexually involved with him, at least not willingly. He was subtly repulsive, and his pale blue eyes protruded from his avian face with startling intensity. Jake couldn't pinpoint it to any one feature, but despite his diminutive stature, the man's presence was commanding, almost foreboding.

But was he capable of murder?

"Unless you give me a reason to bring it out." Jake said, both hands still in his pockets.

Reshing lowered his hand back to his side and sipped his drink, all the while eyeing Jake in an open stare. "I see . . . you think I killed him, don't you? You think I killed your brother."

Jake's jaw muscles twitched. "You were there. At the factory. He saw something going on there, and you knew it."

"You are correct. And I know exactly what he saw. But I did not kill him. I'm not the one with anything to hide. I want to show you something. It will explain a lot."

"Like who the hell *did* kill my brother? Because that's what I want to know first. And second," he edged closer to Reshing until he could smell the whiskey on his breath, "I want to know where Lorel is."

"I see you speak of her in the present," Reshing said with a slight tilt of his head.

"I know she's alive. And I intend to find her," Jake said. "Now tell me what you know."

Reshing put his hand up. "All right, Mr. Ryder. Please, take a seat. Let me start at the beginning."

"Start with why you have this man snapping pictures of me and Lorel." He gestured to Frank, who was slipping out the door. "She's my girlfriend, though I assume you already know that."

"I do. And the pictures are a way of keeping track of things. Lorel mainly, before. But now you too."

"Yeah, see you're going to have to explain that." Jake inserted his hand in his pocket to emphasize his point.

Reshing's face remained expressionless, but for a subtle pursing of his thin lips. "No one has ever called you patient, have they?" He took a seat on the couch and rand his fingers over the snow globe of an ocean scene sitting on the side table. "This is quite a confidential matter, but under the circumstances, I must tell you. I've been in charge of protecting Lorel, keeping her close under my wing."

Jake snorted and a sarcastic laugh escaped his lips. "Of course you have. From who?"

"From a very powerful man who wants her for . . . business purposes," Reshing said. He gestured for Jake to sit down next to him and began pouring something from a decanter on the holo table. "But I've failed. Brandy?"

Jake narrowed his eyes, searching Reshing's face for the truth.

He handed Jake a snifter. "I'll take your silence as a yes."

Jake took the glass then sat down on the pristine white couch. Three leather cushions separated him from Reshing. He gulped down the potent spirit. "So who is this *powerful man*?"

"The same man who is responsible for the death of your brother. Francis Galton," Reshing said plainly.

Jake's heart kicked into a gallop, but he kept a poker face. "Why should I believe you? Leo knew something, didn't he?"

Reshing raised his chin with narrowing eyes. "You don't think the CEO of DiviniGen would let a lowly employee get in the way of big business plans, do you?"

Jake squeezed his snifter, inhaling the sweet woody smell of the brandy, and tried to stay focused. "And what does this bastard have to do with my girlfriend?" The ice cubes clanked together as his hand shook.

"There is no way to answer that question easily. Let

me show you something, Mr. Ryder." Reshing slid closer to Jake on the couch then leaned forward to swipe his finger across the glass surface of the table. It lit up with a display of photos.

"What is this?" Jake set down his glass and leaned in closer to examine them.

"These are photos courtesy of Frank, my trusted private investigator. I've had him on Galton and a particular team of DiviniGen scientists for a few months now. See for yourself what they are doing in the name of modern science."

Jake blinked rapidly, making sense of the images. There were bodies of people, strange people that seemed almost inhuman, though he couldn't put his finger on exactly why. They were in a medical setting of some sort, lying on brushed steel gurneys. Most had gaping incisions where organs had been extracted and hung in liquid containers above the bodies. Other pictures showed people in white coats examining the organs. Raw hearts, livers, kidneys, and some organs Jake couldn't recognize floated in suspensions with indecipherable labels. The background contained microscopes, test tubes, monitors, and other lab equipment.

"These are the people Leo saw. This is at the Fort Miller factory?" Jake looked at Reshing for confirmation.

"Yes, the Skirts was a place where they could get away with it. Apparently their subterranean lab had some sort of security breach."

"It's DiviniGen. They can get away with pretty much anything."

"Yes, but not this. This is on a whole new level of scientific experimentation. Not even PanDivinity would allow it."

"So they have been operating outside of big daddy's authority?"

"Yes. Galton is the wolf among black sheep. He has gone rogue. And this is something for which the man would—and did—kill to keep secret. You may recall in the news DiviniGen's new transgenic project to create an aquatic human . . . the *Poseidon Prototype*?"

"Yes," Jake remembered his conversation with Leo. "Their plan to colonize the sea."

"That is the long game. And these," Reshing's face tightened and he tapped the glass surface, "are the people they are using to make that business goal a reality."

"Are they alive?" Jake asked, staring at the bodies.

"Yes, but only because these are the only five that the scientists have in their possession. Galton needs many more. These people are rare. And special, very special."

"Galton doesn't give a shit about special. I'm not surprised DiviniGen would do this, with all their *divine mandates*," Jake said bitterly.

Reshing's voice softened and he stared down at his hands. "I can't tell you how much this has affected me, changed my entire view on things. See, Francis Galton and I used to be acquaintances, on a professional level that is. But this has changed everything for me."

"Are they still at the factory? We have to get them out of there."

"Impossible. There are PanElites guarding it day and

night. I considered telling someone at PanDivinity, but that would get complicated."

"PanDivinity? Good luck finding that someone." Jake shook his head then narrowed his eyes.

"I have my ways. Connections. But it wouldn't be a good idea, for this particular situation."

"Why wouldn't you just call in the authorities, the feds?"

"No, it would expose them." Reshing leaned toward Jake, lowering his voice. "Mr. Ryder, these people are not human. They are very similar to us in appearance, but they have amphibious capabilities. They can survive underwater. Though not forever, as you can see from this one's body."

He clicked on a photo of a blanched and bloated body. "Drowned in an endurance test."

"Not human. I don't understand." Jake frowned. "What are they?"

"The scientific name would be *Homo sapiens sirenia*. But they are called sirens."

"This is bullshit." Jake stood, blood rushing to his face, and stabbed a finger at Reshing. "You're bullshitting me."

"Mr. Ryder, please. You must hear me out. Don't you want to know how this leads back to your amore?"

Jake sunk to the couch. The music in the room seemed louder, throbbing in an erratic beat, and the twinkling city lights below seemed to laugh at him. Spikes of heat rushed his body. The drink, the thin atmosphere. He couldn't think straight. As he watched his fists clench and release in his lap, he saw Lorel's face in his mind and looked up.

"Go on," Jake said, steeling his gaze on Reshing.

With a pleased nod, Reshing scrolled through the holos and then enlarged one with a wide swipe. It began playing in silent video mode. "This young woman was their first experiment, their prize discovery. She was already dead when they found her. But what they did with her body . . ."

Jake stared at the holo. It followed a tall, white-haired man in a suit from behind as he walked through a door. The man approached a cadaver on a medical table and began examining it. The body was neatly sliced into pieces like a loaf of bread. Glass discs separated the carnal sections to allow for scientific observation. The man leaned in, carefully examining each one.

Then the camera panned in on the head, fully intact, and the face. Jake swallowed hard. This had been a young girl. He could see she was beautiful, because her face had been perfectly preserved. Astonishingly large blue eyes, now glassy with death, faceted within an oval face. Her hair spilled down over the white table like a shimmering silver waterfall. A single black streak of hair framed one side of her face. Jake jerked his head back.

"That's the girl Lorel saw on the beach!"

"Yes," said Reshing in a calm voice. "She told me about it. She reported it to the news despite my insistence that she shouldn't. They didn't believe her anyway. But I did. I knew."

"Then this is why. Why he took her!" Jake stood,

breathless. Suddenly, his heightened senses zeroed in on Reshing. "You. You were with her though. Out there in the middle of the ocean. You were in on it. Where is this goddamn island?"

"Lower your voice, Mr. Ryder. I was not. I'm puzzled as to how she did it myself."

"Did what?" Jake said through clenched teeth.

"Went to the island."

"Are you saying she *went*, as in went there of her own accord?" Hurt stung him at the thought. *Did he really know her?*

Reshing stood abruptly and began pacing by the window.

"There is no time to fully explain. What I will tell you is that this torture is going to happen on a massive scale on these people's native land."

"Native land. Where?"

"The ones you saw in the pictures were the rare few that lived here among us, but the rest of them are all together, isolated from the human world. They inhabit an island in the Indian Ocean called Rodinia. And this is where Lorel has gone, I believe, to help save them."

Jake walked over to the window and leaned, pressing his palms against the cold glass. The distant ocean was a black void taunting him with answers beyond his reach.

"Galton and a crew of scientists and PanElites are on their way to the island now," Reshing continued. "They are on a private fleet of armed ships. And once they get there, they will stop at nothing to achieve their master plan."

"The creation of their aquatic human." Jake murmured, his breath fogging the glass.

"Yes, this *Poseidon Prototype*. They want to wrap these siren genes in a pill and sell them to humans as a promise of long life and the ability to colonize the ocean floor and reclaim the drowned cities."

"So if these people, the sirens, resist, it could get ugly."

"They *will* resist. It's their home. And from what I understand, they are not a weak species. They are highly evolved. But DiviniGen is prepared to get their hands dirty. And their actions will be shielded from the world. This will be a silent war, but a deadly one."

Jake's palms sweat on the glass, causing his hands to slide. He ran them through his hair, trying to breathe. The notes of Beethoven's symphony transitioned abruptly from the calm andante movement to a surging crescendo until the urgency of the melody filled his chest. He looked at Reshing.

"Lorel will be in the middle of a war zone."

"We must help her," Reshing said. "This is why I need you."

"Wait, you said your job was to protect her. What do you mean by that? She was your employee."

He paused as though expecting the question. "Tell me, are you familiar with the East India Company?"

"The old English trade company?"

"Yes." Reshing glanced around the empty room then cleared his throat. "I used to be part of an organization, a secret subsidiary to the EIC, called Beacon. It is a very powerful entity. Its members are behind the scenes of every major maritime outfit in the world, from the United State's NOAA to the China Maritime Safety Administration to the . . ." he raised an eyebrow at Jake, ". . . Navy SEALs."

"I'm listening," Jake said, a chill replacing his anger.

"Beacon has known about the presence of this rare species for centuries. They help the sirens stay hidden from the world. A long time ago, I was tasked with watching over Ms. Phoenix because of, or rather *in spite of*, my position with this organization. I was under special orders, for a special person." His eyes clouded over and he blinked a few times.

"Lorel saw a siren the day of the orca beaching, but what does she have to do with Beacon?" Jake asked.

"Nothing. But you ask the wrong question. What does she have to do with the island? That answer, Mr. Ryder, will lead you to why Galton has been after her."

Jake's head spun. He remembered how Reshing had handpicked Lorel in college to work for him, how he had seemed so possessive . . . or was it just protective? Either way, one goal was clear now. "How do I get there?"

"Good question. And one we both need answered. You must go to help Lorel. And I must be there to stop Galton at his game. But this is where I need you, Mr. Ryder. I need you to tell me what those coordinates are." Reshing stepped closer, his breath quickening.

So they were *coordinates.* Jake stepped back from Reshing, fingering the folded envelope in his pocket. "Don't you know where this island is, through your ties to Beacon?"

"No. The location is under lock and key. Only the Guardian knows it."

"Then ask him," Jake challenged.

"I can't do that. Beacon cannot know about this. They would be furious. Plus, my privileges have been revoked." Reshing put his fist to his lips in frustration, then mumbled, "Maybe if I . . . no, it's too risky."

Jake's eyes narrowed. "If the people meant to protect this place won't help you, why would I?"

"It's not what you think," Reshing snapped.

"Then what is it?"

"There's no time to explain, I told you. We need to get there now. Now, do you not understand?"

No, said a voice inside Jake's head. Something still wasn't right. This man had motives of his own.

"Dr. Reshing, thank you for the information. I'll take it from here."

"Mr. Ryder, you cannot do this alone," he said, adding with an edge of desperation, "please."

With a salute of his hand, Jake headed for the private elevator and hit the L button. As the doors closed, the two men stared at each other. Ben Reshing stood unmoving, but his eyes shot arrows of fury at Jake.

Two hours later, after a quick visit to the hospital to check on Henry and then a mad rush around Lorel's apartment to toss his belongings into an overnight bag, Jake headed across town to the marina. In the autocab he took one more look at the map and shook his head. The coordinates of this supposed island showed only water on the public GPS.

Zooming out, the general area, which was smack in the middle of the Indian Ocean, was marked as British territory. But his navy map displayed a more detailed picture. A discrepancy in the readings indicated there could be land there. And if there was, he intended to find it.

Now his path was charted. He boarded the sailboat and untied the riggings, then began the conversion to hydrofoil. Sailing would not suffice. This journey required him to take full advantage of the boat's high tech speed capabilities. After coasting several yards out from the docks, he ignited the diesel engine, activated the hydrofoils and erected the aerodynamic windshield at the helm. He entered the coordinates into the blackglass embedded in the control panel before him.

Within minutes the boat was elevated several feet above the surface, picking up speed. He watched as the speedometer needle approached one hundred and eighty miles per hour, then two hundred. Soon he was zooming at maximum speed across the open Atlantic, the wind at his back and a full moon above him.

ELEVEN
LOREL

September 25, 2098
Baltra, Rodinia

WITH A BURST OF courage and a big gulp of air, Lorel sunk beneath the water's surface. Mello hovered in place. His skin had already taken on a pearlescent appearance, shimmering like his silvery hair. With a sharp nod, he emitted a strange clicking sound and three dolphins appeared. Lorel nodded, half expecting them to nod back.

Mello motioned for her to follow, then turned and swam ahead. Two of the dolphins joined him. The third hovered in place a few inches away as though waiting. Lorel made eye contact with its black saucer eyes, and for a moment she was sure it smiled at her. With a flip of its tail, the animal glided after Mello, and she followed with a galloping heart. For several yards they all swam near the surface, slicing in and out of the water to suck oxygen

153

through their blowholes.

Lorel noticed Mello and the dolphins engage in what appeared to be conversation. She was far from understanding her biosonar capabilities, if they even functioned, so the only way to communicate was by gesture. But she planned to stay at Mello's side anyway. She knew where he was taking her.

The water of the Eye was clear as a diamond, unlike the rest of earth's cloudy green oceans, and she could see ahead for what seemed like miles. She blinked rapidly in the salty water, still amazed that it didn't sting her eyes. Her newly discovered vision opened up a whole new universe.

Still, nerves threatened to suppress her siren instincts, and the familiar panicky feeling of drowning set in as it had in the lagoon. Her lungs began to burn and every cell in her body was screaming for her to take a breath. Then she felt herself submit. Her heartbeat slowed, and she could feel her arteries constrict like muscles. And this was how it worked . . . the efficiency of one breath. One that would last her up to three hours.

That beats the sperm whale, Lorel marveled. The most amazing thing was that the oxygen reserve had always been there, she had just never known how to tap into it.

With fluid motions her body cut through the silent water, following Mello's lead. He stayed low, pointing out little sea crabs and lobsters that burrowed in and out of the sandy floor. Tufts of sea grass thickened to an oscillating green carpet as they approached the Eye Atoll. Just beyond it was the drop-off where the oceanic sinkhole opened to a dark, gaping chasm.

Lorel swallowed hard.

Fish were everywhere, and most of them she hardly recognized—they'd been extinct for so long. Every color was represented in a rainbow of flashing scales and fins. The coral itself was abundant in a variety of species. Soft corals bunched like bouquets of gelatinous flowers quivered in an array of pink and peach. Branches and twigs of polyped stony corals reached toward the light, their honeycombed surfaces hosting delicate red fan corals. Sea anemones bloomed and recoiled in an alternating display of pastels.

A dense school of striped damselfish swam in front of them like tiny zebras, blocking Lorel's vision. Her head spun in momentary confusion, and the dolphin nudged her shoulder, pointing her in Mello's direction. He grabbed her hand then yanked her body against his, tucking her underneath him as they swam forward in tandem.

As the school of fish parted, a long thin animal swam by making Lorel's skin crawl. It was like no fish she had ever seen, longer than an eel and three times as thick, with the skin and teeth of a shark. The prehistoric looking beast snaked gracefully by them within a few feet and glared at Lorel with dead eyes. Mello kept their course, swimming over the coral, then released her with a reassuring nod.

No sooner had her relief come when a fresh fear emerged. They had reached the precipice of the blue hole. The drop-off into the deep, dark pupil of the Eye.

They paused. Lorel had never jumped out of an airplane, but she imagined this felt similar. She knew she was not going to turn back, despite her pounding heart. Mello pointed upward, and they swam to the surface, breaking through with big splashes.

"Ready to see the real Rodinia?" he asked with a smile.

"I knew you were up to something." She frowned, sputtering water. "I hope I am."

"I know you are. Let's start with full tanks though." He inhaled slowly through his nostrils and Lorel watched as his chest muscles swelled above the water line. Then he sunk in a cloud of bubbles.

Something encircled her ankle and she looked below to see him run his fingers along her calf, the back of her knee. She paddled in place, stalling. He gently tugged at her big toe and she smiled.

Now or never, Lorel.

She sucked in an enormous breath and relaxed her muscles, allowing her body to sink below. Mello and the dolphins hovered before her. He nodded with raised brows.

Lorel closed her eyes for a long moment. She was ready. She nodded in response. Hand in hand they dove headfirst into the darkness, the dolphins at their heels. Mello's hips began undulating in a powerful stroke propelling them downward faster and faster. Lorel tried to mimic his body movements, but her speed was still no match for his, and he dragged her faster and faster into the endless pit of blackness. The resistance was too much and her legs were turning to rubber, but she persisted.

As they descended, the expansive limestone shaft narrowed swiftly. The decreasing diameter put a downward pressure on the water, and soon Lorel felt like she was swimming downstream. A stream filled with unseen obstacles.

The temperature of the water plummeted, sending shivers through her body despite her burning muscles. But a more chilling feeling overwhelmed her. It felt as though someone was piling bricks on top of her chest. With every downward stroke, she felt the pressure increase brick by brick. And then her body did something strange. Her ribcage collapsed in a painless, silent cracking.

Lorel tore her hand from Mello's and grabbed her chest in shock. What was happening to her? She knew. She had been told, but they never practiced deep diving in the lagoon. Terror flooded her senses.

Mello grasped her, pleading with his eyes for her to calm down. Realizing she was on the verge of panic, he grabbed her arm and dragged her sideways until they were up against cold stone. He slid her into a narrow passage that sliced into the wall and then shoved her upward.

With a sputter, she realized she was in air and began gasping frantically as her head bobbed at the surface. *A grotto.* The cave-like space glowed a soft green. Mello slid up next to her from beneath, surfacing with his face inches from her own. The length of their bodies pressed against each other in the cramped space, sending a jolt through her. As soon as she caught her breath, she released the tension in a tirade.

"How could you not warn me?" she spat. "I felt like my body was going to collapse!"

"Shh, calm down. Breathe," he commanded, clasping her shoulders. "I know we explained the mechanics, but I should have told you how intense it felt."

"Intense? I felt like someone was squeezing me in a vice."

"I know, but it's natural. And it's great. This is how you are supposed to work underwater. You just can't panic, okay?"

Don't panic. It was one of the first lessons she learned in scuba diving. "Okay."

"I don't think I can believe you unless I get a laugh out of you," said Mello, his dimple appearing with a sly smile.

"Very funny. I'm trying not to be terrified. I can't laugh."

"Maybe I can make you."

She squinted at him with suspicion. "Mello—"

Before she could stop him he was tickling her, and it was more than she could resist. She yelped, begging him to stop between an uncontrollable mix of laughter and shrieks. They echoed through the cave. "Please, I'm begging you!"

He finally pulled his hands from her side and shoved them in the air in surrender. "Done, promise. But it was nice to hear you laugh."

"You've got a lot of nerve. That was cruel. I should

get you back." She reached her hand up but he grabbed her forearm in midair and pulled it down to his side. She was now holding his waist. He pulled her closer to him, and she suddenly felt as though she was melting. Her heart quickened and she drew in a breath, her lips brushing up against his chest muscles. For a moment, she let them rest there.

Silence replaced the echoing laughter in the cave.

Mello lifted her chin until they were looking straight into each other's eyes. Her breath caught. She closed her eyes breaking the stare and releasing all resistance. He pulled her face close and pressed his lips to hers. It felt like a million tiny stars exploded inside her body, shattering any thoughts of inhibition. Nothing but raw emotion, desire. She responded, pressing hard against him, feeling his entire body envelop hers.

But deep down she knew it was wrong. Her life was straddled between two worlds, neither of which she fully belonged to now. That had to be figured out. "Mello—"

He pulled away, keeping his arms around her lower body, and scanned her face with questioning eyes.

"I'm sorry, but I can't."

She watched his sensuous grin fade as he read it, and his dimple disappeared. "It's okay. Please, don't be sorry."

They stared at each other until Lorel spoke in attempt to break the awkward silence. "So, here we are. In a cave under the ocean. I almost forgot for a second."

He laughed. "Glad I could help with that. You ready to keep going? We're not far from the Event Horizon."

She looked at him with narrowing eyes. "Dare I ask, what's that?"

"You'll know it when you see it. And feel it."

She sighed in reluctant agreement. "All right, I'm ready. At least I get to reset my oxygen," she said, sucking in a big breath. "Wait, how did you find this air pocket so quickly? It's pitch black out there."

"Biosonar." Mello winked. "Baby steps."

He shimmied down and out of the cave nook, his body rippling against hers again as he passed. Lorel drew in a deep breath, still recovering from the heat of his touch, and followed him back out to the shaft. After several more excruciating minutes, the water began to grow warmer and brighter as if someone had turned on a lamp down below. The shaft began to widen and the downward current weakened.

Lorel jerked her head around. Suddenly she was no longer propelled forward. Another pressure change racked her bones, and her body tumbled as she desperately paddled to rebalance. Time and space seemed to stand still. She and Mello floated, suspended in the vastness. Their surroundings had disappeared. Lorel shivered with a new sense of vulnerability.

The Event Horizon.

She squinted in the still water. In front of her, Mello's hair floated around his face, bright against the dimness of the strange atmosphere. The dolphins that had been at their side moved slowly about in the periphery of her vision. Her eyes continued to focus, pupils pushing their limits beyond human capability.

And then there was light.

Crystalloluminescence!

Sam had explained that the hydrothermal vents ubiquitous on the Abyssal Plane produced a faint glow from the salt crystals in the water responding to the intense heat. That light, combined with the lava streams that flowed in the form of rivers, creeks, and tributaries, created radiance at the bottom of the sea.

"It's more like moonshine than sunshine." Isla had clarified. *"But it's lovely, like an eternal twilight."*

The burnishing glow grew brighter as they descended. In the distance she could make out a fuzzy image of the landscape. Mello released her hand and signaled a slower froglike stroke. Lorel followed with newfound ease. Together they swam headfirst toward the brightening Abyss.

The aerial view came slowly into focus, and she had to blink several times to believe her eyes. It was like she was skydiving in slow motion to the ground. Mello turned to face her, and a wide smile swept his face.

She responded with a hand to her heart. He was welcoming her into his treasured underworld. This was the heart of Rodinia.

The topography was a complex contour of volcanic thermal vents that rose in clusters like small mountain ranges, geysers of white plumes billowing at the lazy pace of smokestacks in an industrial park. The orange lava streams, which originated from pools within the mountain range, cascaded in gushing falls and then slowed and snaked through the valleys, winding and pulsing. In some places they swelled into bubbling lakes, and in others they thinned to streams.

Lorel was glad she couldn't speak underwater. There were no words to describe what she felt. No planet in the universe could offer more alien beauty than what lay before her.

Mello gripped her hand again, guiding her down to a small plateau of elevated land that edged out to a narrow cliff. They turned upright and Lorel stared down at her feet in delight. She could stand. It wasn't quite the same as gravity on land, but something in the balance between her inner fluid and the ocean salinity allowed her to plant her feet firmly to the ground.

She moonwalked to the edge of the cliff and looked down at the Martian landscape. Glowing organisms floated through the water like slow moving glitter filling the aquatic atmosphere, and strange animals roamed the land below. The rolling grassland, dotted with tree-size kelps and a patchwork of sea grasses, reminded Lorel of her visit to the African bush land. But this aquatic biome was home to animals no human had laid eyes on in the past century, if ever.

Sea cows the size of bison grazed lazily among the grassy prairies, and giant stingrays soared through the water like little spaceships. A school of dolphins swam by in synchronized motion. Mello lowered his chin to his chest as they passed, emitting a few clicks, and they responded with their own echoing sounds.

Lorel stood in awe, trying to keep her jaw from dropping. A swarm of phosphorescent fish darted past them like a flock of birds shimmering in the twilight. She squeezed Mello's hand in excitement.

But where was the purple algae?

She was dying to finally uncover the mystery. Without waiting to be led, she dove off the edge of the cliff, soaring swiftly to the valley below. Mello followed close behind in strong, fluid strokes. They landed near an enormous kelp tree where a group of glowing fish were nibbling at a hole in the trunk like a swarm of hungry bees. Around the base of the tree were tufts of pink sea anemones that squeezed shut as Lorel leaned toward them.

Off in the distance hydrothermal vents rose from the ground, spewing clouds of particle dust. Beyond them loomed a wall of earth, extending upward as far as Lorel could see. She guessed it was part of the base of the island. Its roots. Wide horizontal gradations cut across the lower portion as though a giant had carved steps into earth. A grand stairway. It reached so high that she couldn't make out where it ended.

Did it lead somewhere?

She gestured toward it but Mello shook his head with a frown. He began swimming toward some white smokers and Lorel followed. As they approached the current grew stronger and the temperature of the water turned warmer, increasing to the brink of intolerable. It felt like she was swimming through a giant hot tub.

But as they reached the valley and looked up at the ascending volcanic hills, she noticed it. The ground everywhere was smothered in a mossy carpet of macro and microalgae in purplish hues.

Porphuraphyceae was an extremophile!

The scientist inside her was bursting at the seam. It all made sense. The algae converted sulfuric acid and other chemicals from the thermal vents into useable energy. The scientific community was well aware that these tiny deep-sea pores in the earth's crust could sustain a diversity of organisms, ones specially adapted to withstand the high temperatures and pressures around the mouths of the vents.

Shrimps, limpets, clams, giant tubeworms, and very rarely some forms of algae. Usually sulfuric traces were found in their chemical composition, a critical clue Lorel never uncovered during her research. But here it was, the buried treasure, thriving beneath the spewing gas.

Mello reached down and grabbed a tuft of the macro plant matter and stuck it in his mouth, gesturing for Lorel to try it. She leaned down and tugged at the slimy blades. They were much stronger in their habitat, not the delicate thread sample she had at the lab. With a yank she pulled out a strand and hesitantly inserted some in her mouth.

All she could taste was salt water, but the slippery rubber texture was not pleasant. She closed her eyes and gulped. It slid down her throat like a raw oyster, and she imagined its contents dispersing into her system; the essential fatty acids, antioxidants, and deep-sea phytonutrients, mending and healing her cells.

Despite the food's wonders, she wrinkled her nose. This was the ultimate proof that a food's taste was inversely proportionate to its nutritional value. The stuff was repulsive.

Mello watched Lorel's face in amusement. They both began laughing silent, underwater belly laughs.

They spent the next hour meandering through the kelp forest, Lorel darting off course after exotic fish and strange marine mammals until finally Mello gestured that it was time to surface. He made a loud clicking sound. Within seconds the two dolphins were hovering at his side. They rubbed up against his thighs with high-pitched squeaks and clicks.

He pointed to Lorel and one obediently darted to her side. She stroked it by the dorsal fin, and it nuzzled her thigh in response gesturing for her to grab on. Soon they were soaring upward into the darkness of the Eye.

The dolphins released them before they had reached the light of the surface. Lorel could barely make out Mello's figure a few feet away. She could tell they were on the ledge of the blue hole, but which way was up? She had expected to still see light streaming through. Almost three hours had passed. The sky must have darkened with the pending storm.

Finally, after flailing in the dark currents around the Eye Atoll, they broke through the choppy surface and inhaled electrified air. Torrents of rain pelted them, and the waves slammed against their faces. The gale had arrived. A bolt of electric blue light sliced through the sky, followed by a bellowing crack of thunder. This time it was the real thing.

They tore through the water, fighting against the current to reach the shore. Physically wasted and scared, Lorel gripped Mello's hand tightly as they trudged through the breakers and onto the empty beach.

No sign of the festive celebration remained, only the violently swaying tree line of palms and the deafening roar of the storm.

Link! She'd left him alone. Surely he would have found his way to shelter. Lorel began yelling his name, running down the beach toward the outcropping of rocks now barely visible through the sheets of rain.

And then she saw it, looming like a giant black insect on the beach, the noise of its engine drowned out by the howling winds. Before her loomed a helicopter, its propellers still spinning, spewing rain sideways through the air. A bright light blinked from its roof, alternating blue then green, as the spinning blades cut the beams in a dizzying display.

"Mello!" Lorel screamed at the top of her lungs. Water streamed in rivulets down the curves of her naked body and she began to shake, struggling to stay calm. "They're here!"

T W E L V E
MELLO

September 25, 2098
Baltra, Rodinia

MELLO STARED AT THE helicopter several yards down the beach. Time stood still. His ears silenced the rain and all he could hear was his heart pounding inside his chest. The last estimate had put Galton's fleet of ships arriving several hours from now. And there had been no intelligence warning of an aircraft landing inside the island. He must have sent a reconnaissance party in ahead.

Or George had been misinformed.

The lights inside the helicopter popped on and a door opened. Lorel stood frozen on the beach halfway between the helicopter and the jetty.

"Lorel, come back," he yelled over the sound of the rain.

She broke from her daze and ran toward him. They

167

both crouched behind the jetty as the waves crashed against their naked bodies.

"I've got to see who's in there. Stay down!" Mello scrambled up the rocks and peered over.

A woman hopped down from the passenger side. Clad in black, she was barely visible but for her long blonde hair and pale skin that glowed in the stormy dusk. Even from a distance Mello recognized her. Madelyn Maddox, the DiviniGen business associate who'd first recognized him as a siren on the mainland. She was with Lucas Keating, the other associate who had also been at the marina on the fateful day Mello exposed himself.

Lucas and two men with clipper las-guns strapped to their backs rushed around from the other side to meet Madelyn. Together the foursome jogged toward the line of palms seeking shelter from the downpour. Tiny flashes of light from their tablets lit up like fireflies in the forest.

They were reporting back to Galton, as they always did. Anger swirled inside Mello as he remembered the last time he saw them on the dock, how they pretended everything was normal. He had lost his cloaking disguise after saving the human baby that had fallen into the marina. And they turned him over like a stray animal, betrayed him.

You betrayed yourself, his conscience chastised.

Mello scrambled back down the rocks and crouched next to Lorel.

She grabbed his arm and huddled closer. "Who is it?"

"Galton's two right hands, and a couple PanElites. Probably here to take the lay of the land and do the initial talking. That's what they're good at."

"I just can't believe they're here already. Do you think the sirens know?" Lorel asked, her wet hair whipping around her face.

"I don't know. It's a good sign that the beach is clear. They may have detected the helicopter's presence," Mello shoved his hands through his hair and squeezed, sending streams of water down his chest.

"So what now?" Lorel asked as Mello peeled his clothes from the top of the rock and put them on.

Her dress sat crumpled on the sand. She grabbed it and pulled it over her head. It stuck to her body like glue and Mello tried not to let his eyes linger on her curves. She had just been naked, but her clothed form still held such mystery.

He cleared his throat. "We have to warn Lalique and the Council. Let's go."

They darted up the beach, making sure to keep a distance from the new arrivals, and into the forest. Branches and vines slapped against their bodies as they ran through the thickening woods toward his hut.

"Over here!" he called to Lorel as they burst into the clearing of the Waterfall Tree.

The torrents of rain slowed to a drizzle and clouds parted above to reveal a full moon rising. They crossed the clearing and blazed down the narrow trail snaking inland toward the hut.

Soon the kapok tree appeared, towering over the shadowy lagoon. Its bristly humped roots shone like dinosaur skin in the moonlight. They wound around the water to his front door.

"First things first. Dry clothes." He pushed open the door and guided Lorel inside, then lit a lantern hanging on the ceiling.

She stood shivering, her dress dripping a pool of water onto his straw mat in the center of the room. He dashed to the bamboo bureau and rifled through the top drawer before pulling out a few garments.

"This one's for you, madame." He tossed a long muslin tunic with a silky cream sash.

"Thanks." Lorel peeled off her wet dress allowing her skin to air dry for a few moments before yanking the tunic over her head.

Looking at her standing in his hut made him want to forget everything, forget what they saw on the beach, and just be there, in the moment. But his mind raced and his heart thumped against his ribcage in a fury. He pulled on a dry tunic and pants. "Time to go down."

She planted her feet. "Under the water again? You must be joking."

"Underground."

He led them both around to the other side of the tree. A thick curtain of foliage draped across two six-foot high roots like a tent. Mello pulled it aside to reveal double doors of copper that had oxidized to green. They lay at a forty-five degree angle. A numbered dial in the shape of a sunburst surrounded the handles, serving as a lock of solid gold.

"Where do these lead?" Lorel paused, staring at the hidden doors with a frown.

"This is one of the entries to the Baltra bunker, one of the old paramilitary stations built by Beacon."

"So these house the intel stations, the cameras, the weapon supplies?"

"Yes, all the islands have at least one. The consuls have been ensuring they are stocked and all the systems are working." He leaned down and began turning the dial. "If you ever need to open this, just remember the numbers 1602."

"Any significance?" Lorel leaned in next to him.

"It's the year Beacon was founded," he said.

"You said this is one of the entries. How many are there?"

"Only this one and then another hatch near the Waterfall Tree. It's on the map."

Lorel stared at him, twisting her mouth in question.

"Our map, nothing they would see. Trust me, these are like fortresses. Beacon knew what they were doing when they built these bunkers."

"I was just thinking of Isla. She'll need a safe place."

Mello steeled his gaze on her and took her shoulders in his hands, gripping with more force than he meant to. "I will keep Isla safe. And I will keep you safe. Believe that."

Lorel looked at him with bright eyes and pressed a palm to his cheek. "I do."

Heat radiated through his chest. It was all the affirmation he needed. He pulled open a door to reveal a small stone landing with a ladder dropping from the edge. He walked in to the loamy scent of metal and earth and lowered himself down. The ladder was secured to the underground network of kapok roots, but the space extended away from the tree to a small room.

At the bottom of the steps Mello's pupils dilated to adjust to the pitch-black room. Lorel was on her way down, but he was unsure if her half-human eyes could see in such darkness.

"Pull it shut behind you, and be careful not to trip." he called up to her, his voice echoing through the chamber.

The door slammed shut with a bang. She lowered herself down and landed with a hop on the smooth concrete ground. "I'm completely blind. I feel like a mole."

"Let's hope you're not," he smiled through the darkness.

"Sorry, wrong choice of words."

"Here, take my hand." He wound his fingers through hers. "The control room will be brighter, this is an entrance tunnel. Here's the door, just over this way."

Mello fumbled at the heavy manual lock until he pushed open the door. Clean circulated air replaced the mustiness. He hadn't been in the bunker for years before the past few days. Only the sirens assigned to intelligence and monitoring frequented them. After the Dark Submersion, they had been left abandoned for decades, filled with the dead bodies. They were reminders of the ugliness. But Beacon finally forced the sirens to face reality, clean them up and begin using the structures that they had built so long ago.

Now, a smooth concrete floor gave way to clean metal

walls that curved around the control room. Tunnels fanned off every several feet leading to other areas of the bunker and tiny canned lights in the ceiling cast a bright glow in the underground space.

"Wow." Lorel gasped. "This is more than I expected. Where does the island get its electricity?"

"The waterfalls. We just use it sparingly," Mello replied.

The furnishings were state of the art. A few small blackglass conference tables with white leather chairs edged the wall. Each had tablets stacked on them. In the center stood an island console of blackglass supporting an array of hi-tech equipment: a hologram screen, several blinking computer monitors, 3-D printers, and a wall full of dials and controls. A few sirens sat around with headsets on, staring into the screens.

Mello dashed to one of the monitors and swiped it, then commanded, "Baltra, Area One-Two-Four, inner beach."

A siren next to him slid off her headset. "Everything okay?"

"No," Mello shook his head as the image of the beach appeared on screen. "Have you been monitoring the inner beach?"

"We are monitoring everything, but there are cameras everywhere, on every island so . . ." The siren rolled back from her screen, which displayed several split images of scenes around Baltra, then cocked her head. "Why?"

"Because of this." Mello leaned over her to magnify one of the screens.

"Oh." Her jaw dropped.

The others gathered around Mello at the screen. Lorel edged closer as they all stared at live feed of the black helicopter. Its propellers had stilled and its lights were now off.

"Alert all the consuls. I'll contact Lalique and the Council myself." Mello pushed back from the screen and crossed his arms. "And find out exactly where these people went. We saw them run into the woods."

Sirens bustled around the monitors, pulling up other live video feeds around Baltra and the other islands. Mello dragged Lorel over to one of the conference tables at the perimeter.

"Are the cameras really everywhere?" Lorel looked at him with widening eyes. "We need to check the outer beach too. The rest of them could be out there now."

Mello placed his fingers to his forehead, then ran them along his brows with a deep breath. "We have them everywhere. On every island, every lodge, every hut cluster. Inside the hotel, of course. Even underwater in the grottoes."

"Good," she said leaning into the tablet Mello had powered on.

"Lalique," he said into the screen.

After a few moments, he set it down with a thud. "Dammit. Not answering." He crossed his arms. "I'll try in another minute."

Lorel fidgeted with her hands, then said, "I have to admit, I had no idea you were so—"

"Advanced?" Mello broke focus to glance at her.

"Sorry, I don't mean to offend, it's just that—"

"We aren't using Morse code? Telescopes? Messenger pigeons?" He laughed as Lorel's cheeks flushed. "It's okay. But there is no way we could have hidden from humanity this long without certain amenities."

"But you don't see sirens walking around with their heads buried in a tablet. I like that."

"We embrace technology in a different way than you do. More for protection than entertainment. The Sieve Council is constantly getting information, gadgets, all sorts of technology from Beacon that they have to sift through. A lot of it we don't need. They analyze and decide what to import from what Beacon offers to us."

"So is this all supplied by Beacon?" Lorel raised a brow, glancing around. "That's a heavy reliance on Beacon, isn't it? I mean, to trust that they are really showing the sirens everything, giving them a clear picture of these technologies and how they could be utilized."

"I've always thought the same thing," he said, surprised at how unguarded he felt around Lorel. "It feels like too much control, but no one want to question it, bite the hand that feeds them so to speak. And Lalique and the Council seem to trust them, so the rest of the sirens follow suit."

"Except for you. That's part of why you've pushed so hard. It's more than coming out of isolation, isn't it? It's becoming independent."

"Yes," he whispered as though someone were listening. "How is it you see the world so much the way I do?"

"Our worlds aren't really so different." She frowned. "Do you ever wonder why the Council never got a satellite through Beacon? Why did you have to get it from DiviniGen?"

"It was something they never wanted us to have. Too risky, they say. Signals could be traced," Mello said.

"Need I mention the word controlling again?"

"*Big brother* controlling."

"*PanDivinity* controlling," she said, topping him.

He smirked. "Exactly."

"The way the sirens revere Beacon, it reminds me of, well I hate to make this comparison, but of the corporate zombies."

"The who?"

"Never mind." She shook her head. "It just seems like some people forget that it's okay to question."

"Something maybe I came late to myself. I looked up to Galton. It disgusts me to think about it now, but I did. Now, I question what had me so enamored with human culture at all." He swept his arm out toward the computer station, lowering his voice. "These things . . . these glowing screens and magic microchips . . . do they really make life better? Or do they keep you from living with your eyes open?"

Lorel stared at him, her eyes ensnaring his for several seconds before blinking. "Should you try Lalique again?"

Refocusing, Mello swirled his finger on the tablet and a glowing orb the size of a beach ball materialized. "I just need to check one thing first."

"What is it?" Lorel's face, glistening from rain and

sweat, glowed in the holo.

"Earth. With the maritime overlay map."

Its virtual blue sea rippled and thin lines crisscrossed the surface, mostly PanDivinity trade routes. The continents glowed in a variety of colors. Small black font denoted the countries and bodies of water. He zoomed in on the Indian Ocean, then Rodinia. With his index finger, he explored the area around it.

"Dammit, George!" He pounded his fist on the table.

"When was the last time anyone talked to him?" Lorel gripped the edge of the table, her voice quivering.

"Over a day. And the satellite feed is not showing their ships anymore." Mello cursed under his breath again and stood up to rake fingers through his hair. "Unless our connection is reinstated, we don't have a read on their location. Though with Madelyn and Lucas here already, it's obvious they're close. Time to make the call."

Mello returned to the island banked with monitors and dialed Lalique's cavern on the hologram. Lorel leaned in toward the screen.

The queen materialized on the screen in full figure. The stalactites and dangling lanterns of her cavern glowed dimly and behind her. He noticed a few people seated around her table in the background. Two PanElites stood stiffly against the far wall, shouldering giant las-guns. All he had to do was take one look at Lalique's face and he knew.

"They're with you," he said quietly, then pressed Lorel gently away from of the screen's view. *How could they possibly have known?*

"Yes, Mello, our special guests arrived right at my doorstep." She turned from the screen so Mello could see Madelyn and Lucas in view at the table with a few other sirens. "I believe you two are acquainted with Mello Seaford."

Mello froze. He was far from ready to face them without exploding. They had taken advantage of a vulnerable moment back in DC, a moment that was now changing the course of his people's history. The marina flashed through his mind—saving the baby from the murky water, losing all elements of his human cloak, emitting a spout. They had pretended they didn't notice. They had deceived him.

He squeezed his fists into balls, too aware of the absence of his nails, which had been plucked from his fingers one by one during his subsequent torture. Lucas and Madelyn had turned him in like he was nothing more than an escaped lab rat. Upon seeing Mello's face on screen, his old associates turned white as ghosts.

Was it guilt? Fear? After all, they were on his turf now.

"Mello, so nice to see you again," Madelyn said in a choked voice. "We are honored to be here."

Lucas nodded. "Hello, Seaford."

"Madelyn, Lucas," he said with a stoic nod.

From the uncomfortable looks on their faces they were taken off guard by the queen's welcome. They had expected a more hostile greeting from the natives. He saw relief in their eyes, but the PanElites looked hungry for some action.

"Well, you can all reconnect when we take our friends here to the hotel," Lalique continued in a cheerful voice. She turned to Mello. "The rest of their party is ported at an islet in the Open Sea Realm and will enter Rodinia tomorrow morning. They've come quite a long way and we want to make them feel at home."

"Of course," Mello said, clenching his jaw.

A smile spread across Lalique's face, but didn't reach her eyes. "Please spread the word."

"Right away. Thank you, Your Highness," Mello said, pressing a shaky finger to end the call. "We'll meet you on Paraíso at dawn."

Lalique's image faded to black.

Mello stared at Lorel, her lips parted and face ashen. A realization overtook them both.

"Isla," Lorel whispered.

Mello's heart sunk. Some were in more danger than others, his dearest friend among them. He swiped the screen again and Sam's face appeared with eyes wide in anticipation.

"It's starting," Mello said in a calm voice. "Bring Isla to the bunker. Don't waste a second."

Under a clear blue morning sky, Mello, Lorel, and Sam sat inside a canoe as Silas paddled them across the smooth Eye toward Paraíso. The mood of the group did not reflect the peaceful surroundings. Sam kept shaking his feet incessantly, rocking the boat. They all decided he should be at the welcome brunch for DiviniGen that was to take place inside the hotel. Isla had been ushered to the bunker under the care of her younger sister, Harper.

"Sam, she'll be safe there, don't worry. Any word from George?" Mello asked.

"None. And all communication from the *Ghost* is down," Sam replied in a somber tone.

Mello frowned. "I noticed."

"I hope he's okay." Lorel shook her head with concern.

"I never should have asked so much of George. If anything has happened to him . . ." Sam placed his palms to his face and took a deep breath, then released them. When he looked up his face was weary and eyes bloodshot. "I've been trying all night long to reach him. His tablet, our private network. I even sent a Dragonfly to his home and his office. Nothing."

"If they've caught onto George, it's bad news for all of us," Mello said.

They all fell silent. Only the sound of the paddles in the water could be heard.

"We have to focus." Mello's voice jerked their attention back. "DiviniGen's fleet is *here*. Their ships are resting in port at an outer islet. We all hope George is safe, but we'll just have to get our intel first hand now."

The canoe scraped against the shallow shore. Silas jumped out and pulled the boat onto the beach.

The hotel towered above them. Its coral stucco façade had faded to light pink, and paint peeled from the decorative trim. An overgrowth of vines reached to the structure's highest peaks as though the thick forest was attempting to swallow it whole. Across the front a wide veranda with elegant concrete spindles jutted out toward the beach. It looked lonely, in need of al fresco diners and cocktail sipping tourists. Shiny limestone tiles paved the front stairs and a walkway cut through the dunes all the way to the beach.

"It's beautiful. The Portuguese never had a chance to use this place, right?" Lorel trotted up the beach next to Mello.

"No, not even as a fortress. The sirens never let it get that far."

Lorel shaded her eyes, lifting her face to the sun to take in the full spectrum of the building before her. "You mentioned there was a library in the building, right?"

"The grandest of libraries."

"I'd love to see it, well . . ." she shook her head, "not now, of course."

"I left some books for you in your hut. I hear they're hard to come by where you're from."

"That was you! Thank you. If only there were time to read," she said with longing then squinted. "What does that sign say? It's so faint."

Mello followed her eyes to the faded piece of driftwood hanging above the double doors.

"Hotel Paraíso," he said with a grimace.

"Of course."

As they entered the grand foyer Mello felt a familiar eeriness envelope him. Even though Beacon had converted the stone building impeccably, he was never able to shake the knowledge that it had begun as a paramilitary fortress, not an opulent hotel. Its architectural beauty was ironic, almost sad. The arched ceiling drooped over them, tired and peeling. A single beam of light poured through the top of the dome creating a bright circle on the mosaic tile floor. He inhaled the glittery dust motes and looked around.

Today there was an unusual bustle of people inside bringing vibrancy to the space. Sirens hurried back and forth across the foyer, up and down the stairs carrying boxes, fresh linens. Someone placed a large bouquet of sandflowers and dried kelpweed below a nearby mirror. At first glance, it appeared like a regular hotel. But the air was charged with tension.

"Mello!" Cora rushed toward him. Her hair silvery hair, which normally fell in a smooth bob to her shoulders, fell haphazardly around her face. She combed her fingers through it and smoothed the folds of her wrapped tunic. "They're on their way here. We're preparing the rooms. God, I hope this is the right thing to do. Are you okay?"

"I'm fine, Mom. This is good. This is what we should be doing." He squeezed her shoulders. "Until we can see their cards and decide our next move."

"Come, I want to show you all something." Cora led them through the lobby to the backside of the hotel and onto another patio. Sam was already outside pacing.

The bright sun reflected on the white tiles, blinding Mello momentarily. He sidestepped into the shade of some tall date trees lining one edge. As his eyes adjusted, memories flooded back to him. The vast courtyard below had been such a treat to visit as a child. Before he heard the stories of how it was haunted by the ghosts of dead humans from Beacon and Portugal, he had found solace in the place. He remembered sitting in his mother's lap reading a book. *The Little Prince*. How it had made him yearn to explore the world. It seemed such an innocent reverie.

Now Mello looked out at the sprawling grounds and saw darkness in the unkempt spaces. The bamboo forest beyond the courtyard spread out endlessly in a dense tangle, thickening to a jungle at the foothills of the Vulcan. The gardens below him looked smaller, more confining. Lush tropical greenery, wild and tangled, dominated the stone courtyard. Precocious vines smothered concrete benches and crawled up crumbling dry fountains.

Several sirens milled around within the walled space. Some sat on benches, others paced the winding paths. Mello caught eyes with a man leaning against a tree trunk, his arms crossed and his foot tapping against the loose stones. They exchanged nods.

"There are more than I thought," Mello said, turning to his mother.

"What are they doing here?" asked Lorel.

"They are volunteers. At least twenty from each island have come." Cora gripped the rail and looked down at them. "This will show how cooperative we can be. But remember, all our islands are prepared and armed should things turn in the wrong direction."

"But what if . . ." Lorel's eyes grew wide.

"We will *not* allow any of these people to be harmed," Cora interrupted. "We're going to make it very clear to Galton that they can take blood samples, run observations, but under no circumstances can they do anything more invasive." She lowered her voice and looked at Mello. "Like what they did to you."

Mello put his arm around his mother, and she lifted her finger to run it along a scar on his forehead. Blood rushed to his face. "We won't let that happen."

Lorel tilted her head. "Sam, correct me if I'm wrong, but that should tide them over for a while at least. Usually with genetic engineering, the first round of testing just involves analysis of blood cells."

Sam shifted uncomfortably. "If we had more details, we'd know better. George has been trying to hack into DiviniGen's Mandate, which lists all of the plans, but it's been impossible for him to penetrate. He was able to hack into the lead geneticist's email account though, and we've pieced some things together. It appears the project will go in two major phases. First, they want to create a pill to give humans—"

"You mean *sell* to humans," Lorel said.

"Right. A pill that will modify the human genome so that essentially they are a hybrid, like Lorel."

"So they need siren genes to create the pill," said Cora.

"Yes," Sam continued, "they will, but the most valuable genomes they can get their hands on would be a hybrid's. That would give them a blueprint for the optimal molecular pattern. The formula, so to speak, for the perfect aquatic human. After all, they are in the business of mutating genes to create the best species. I like to think of it as unnatural selection."

Mello noticed a cloud of worry pass over Lorel's face. He thought of Isla's unborn child. At least they were here in Rodinia, under the protection of the sirens. Still, the danger was real.

"What's the second phase then?" Mello asked.

"Phase two," Sam continued, "is another pill that can be sold to these newly created hybrids so that when they mate, only the siren genes will be expressed, and they will be guaranteed a pure and selectively bred siren child."

Everyone was silent.

"They really want to create a new race," Cora said.

"But why can't they just assimilate sirens into human society and the process could happen naturally?" Lorel said. "It could be a beautiful thing."

"It would be," agreed Sam. "But think about it, there's no profit in it for DiviniGen that way. No pill to sell."

"And that's what it all stems back to," Mello quipped with a bitter tone.

"So the bottom line is, this will buy us time." Sam gestured to the sirens in the courtyard. "DiviniGen needs these sirens for now. But, they'll be after more soon."

"And if they want hybrid prototypes, won't they also need humans to experiment on?" Lorel asked with a raised brow.

"Yes," said Sam. "Essentially, they would need to infest the human germline, especially if they don't already have a hybrid blueprint."

"We're not all scientists here," said Mello. "Germline?"

"The germline is the set of cells that we pass along in reproduction," Lorel explained. "They are the cells that make us who we are. Human. Or . . ." she trailed off, blushing.

"It's more than just cells that make us who we are," Mello said softly. Her eyes flitted to his and lingered.

Sam thrust an index finger in the air. "But, the cells are susceptible to mutation or modification. If a germline is modified, then the new genes are passed to the next generation and so on. So infesting the germline is basically injecting foreign, in this case *siren*, genetic material into the human germline to create a new species."

"Lorel is right." Cora tilted her head. "They would need human subjects in addition to sirens. But surely they wouldn't bring their own kind here to experiment with."

"I once would have said the same thing," Mello said, crossing his arms.

"It would be tough to get away with in DC, or anywhere on the mainland. But what better place to do it than on a secret island?" Lorel bit her lip. "Sam, do you think they would?"

"We'll have to see how this all plays out," said Sam. "The details we have simply aren't enough. It's impossible to guess exactly how they plan to carry out this experimentation."

"But there is a Mandate, right? If we could somehow get our hands on it," Lorel said, her voice quickening, "we could figure it out."

"We will. Cameras are all over this place, and we're adding more." Cora nodded to a man in the corner affixing a tiny camera to the bark one of the palms. "Finding the Mandate will be a priority for the monitoring teams. Until then, we have to hope Sam and Lorel are right, that all they need is blood."

"If only blood were enough." Mello clenched his fists on the rail and looked down at the volunteers who had offered up their bodies for the sake of their people. He looked at his mother. "I should be down there. I owe it to them."

"No, Mello," said his mother, placing a hand on his forearm. "We need you. Here."

Mello glanced at Lorel. His eyes followed her long auburn hair down to her waist where a sheathed knife was fastened to the belt loop of her jeans. She knew being a hybrid made her a target. But she was tough, at least on the outside. Still, Mello wasn't going to let her out of his sight for a second.

With a sigh, he put an arm around his mother. "Come on, let's check out the operations inside."

Mello spent the next hour checking every guest room on all three floors, ensuring the sirens had hidden the cameras properly and that the building could be monitored from every angle possible. Then he headed out to the front veranda of the hotel where the others were surveying the beach.

Lorel leaned on the railing, staring out at the water. She greeted him with a sullen smile, then pointed.

"They've deployed their boats."

Mello swept the horizon with his eyes and detected a movement in the mangroves between Baltra and the neighboring island. His breath hitched. A loud and unnatural sound disrupted the calm. It vibrated across the water, sending his heart in a lurch.

From a narrow opening in the mangroves, motorized rafts zoomed out into the Eye, one after the other.

"Here we go," Mello muttered under his breath, trying to suppress the panicky feeling that racked his gut.

"It looks surreal, doesn't it?" Cora rushed to the edge of the veranda, leaning over the edge with them to watch the boats cut across the water leaving V-shaped wakes in their path.

"There must be dozens," whispered Sam, adjusting his darkening eyeband.

Mello squinted. Each boat appeared to be holding six to eight people. They approached Paraíso in frothy white trails and began sliding ashore with engines still rumbling. People spilled out onto the beach lugging bags and briefcases. Some heaved giant trunks. Mello noticed one marked "Microscopes—Fragile." Another read "Multi-species Stem Cells."

Two armed PanElites carried a long black box up the beach. He shivered at the label. "Nia." It sounded like the name of a person.

A shaky hand slid into his and he looked over at his mother. "This is going to work, Mom."

"Lalique seems to agree. I hope you're right this time," she said, her gaze still locked on beach below.

"I'm going inside to alert the setup crew that our guests have arrived."

Mello felt his heart pound at the sight of the strange people on his beach, his island. Humans. They looked out of place amid the serene tropical landscape. Their attire varied, reflecting the span of different professions that Galton had chosen to participate in the special operation. Everyone seemed busy, going about their tasks with intense focus sneaking only the briefest glances around to soak in the scenery. Mello couldn't help but marvel at the well-oiled machine Galton had created. Surely they were the cream of DiviniGen's crop.

Some wore business suits, some white lab coats, and others sported jeans and T-shirts. Mello couldn't decide who looked more foreboding, the PanElite men wearing black and gray camo from head to toe and draped with automatic las-guns, or the scientists. A flashback of Dr. Wong running her long pink nails down his arm sent a chill through him. Mello's muscles tightened just thinking about how he would be face to face with Galton soon. Would the spineless man even recognize him standing upright and not chained to a cot with stitches all over his body?

Below, the humans had begun making their way up the path toward the hotel. Mello knew Galton would not be among them. He would make his entrance with an entourage of guards, the same way he traveled on the mainland. The three-hundred-year-old hotel would not be the five-star accommodations he was used to.

But you'll be right where we want you, Mello thought

spreading his fingers wide on the railing until his webbing turned white. The sirens just had to remain in control, not miss a beat.

The consul of Paraíso had met with Madelyn and Lucas the previous night to discuss logistics and accommodations. DiviniGen's original plan had been to set up a few camps on the outer beaches and operate primarily from their ships, *not wanting to intrude*, as Madelyn had so politely explained. They had to have been surprised by the unexpected hospitality, though Madelyn was too smooth to appear ruffled. But no one could hide their surprise when Lalique announced there would be a morning feast to welcome the new guests.

Mello glanced behind him toward the eastern wing of the hotel where the aroma of seasoned fish and steaming breads wafted from the windows. His muscles tensed thinking of the long banquet table that would soon be filled with people so strange to one another. This was not how he had pictured coexistence.

The influx of thundering motorboats tapered off and the surface of the Eye smoothed out. Mello frowned as he noticed the sun glint on a large patch of swirling oil just off shore.

Then Galton's boat appeared, breaking the short stretch of quiet. It was the same motorized raft as the others since that was the only kind nimble enough to maneuver the outer rocks and penetrate the mangroves, but it was obvious from the armed PanElites that this was the VIP craft.

Lorel appeared next to Mello, brows knitted together.

"What if he recognizes me as the hybrid they were searching for in DC?"

A line creased his forehead at the idea. "You've never met him in person, right?"

She nodded. "Never."

"Then you shouldn't worry."

"I know, it's just that," her face scrunched up and she raked her fingers through her hair, "Galton never pursued me himself. He had people do it for him, of course. But he must have a file on me, pictures of me. Although, I used to change my appearance a lot. Stupid PAPs." She laughed. "Would you recognize me with a pink bob?"

Mello couldn't help but smile. "I would recognize you anywhere. But, Galton, he just sees through people."

Lorel sighed, fiddling with the silver coin that hung around her neck. "Right," she said, eyes cast to the white tile floor.

Mello squared himself to her and gripped her arms. Her skin felt soft and smooth over firm muscle causing his fingertips to tingle. "Hey," he said.

Her eyes flashed up to his and he saw hope. Their gaze locked, and Mello pulled her into a tight embrace.

"Don't worry. He won't be looking for you here anyway." He pressed his lips against her hair, smelling the sea, then pulled back to look at her. "Lorelei Phoenix is dead, remember?"

THIRTEEN
LOREL

September 26, 2098
Paraíso, Rodinia

A N UNAPPETIZING SCENT OF raw fish and seaweed filled the hotel's grand ballroom, but Lorel was beginning to appreciate the siren diet. Along one wall, adorned with panels of peeling muted floral wallpaper was a long buffet table lined with steaming solid gold platters. An elaborate display of exotic fish, colorful seaweed salads, raw oysters, conchs in pink shells, and jumbo lobsters awaited the brunch attendees. In the center was a gelatinous purple substance that could only be the superfood of Rodinia, the *porphuraphyceae*.

Lorel found it fitting to serve DiviniGen employees the algae. It was a reminder of the peaceful relationship the two species could have had. Not that it would have an effect on Galton. Lorel remembered how stoic he had appeared on the centennial video. A PanDivinity-bred

CEO. And now he had brought along his zombies to carry out the dirtiest work.

What would he say today? What story would he spin to make their visit sound noble? Whatever it was, Lalique was smart enough to see through it. Lorel had grown to admire the queen. She may not have had much human interaction, but her instincts were razor sharp. Still, the thought of her and Galton in the same room made Lorel uneasy.

The long banquet table in the center of the room was filling with people. Half were sirens—senior members of the Sieve Council, the consuls of all five islands, and a few others Lorel didn't recognize. The other half consisted of DiviniGen executives and scientists. Lorel watched the buffet platters puff plumes of steam, their gold tops teetering with soft clanks, and felt dizzy. Her arms were dry, almost chilly from the sea breeze that blew in from the open French windows, but slick sweat drenched her armpits the same way it did when she was on a bullet train. She shook her head, letting her long hair fall around her face.

The din of strained small talk was dimmed by a beautiful melody wafting from the far corner, where three sirens dressed in white played strange string instruments. Behind the musicians a wall of windows facing the Eye cast bright sunbeams that reached to the dining table. Crystal glasses, gold cutlery, and plates of smooth manganese gleamed in the light.

Lorel could not get over the ubiquitous presence of such precious metals in Rodinia. Even the chandelier above stretched elegantly over the table, its arms of diamond-encrusted gold held flickering candles that emanated a woody aroma. The hotel was certainly old and decrepit, but it exuded opulence. The Portuguese must have wasted no time in extracting the island's most dazzling resources for their fortress.

Lorel kept her head down as she ambled through the buffet line. It felt strange to be among humans now. With shaky hands, she filled her plate with a variety of saltwater cuisine then spotted an open seat between Mello and Sam. She headed to the table just as the double doors at the back of the room parted with a *swish*.

The music stopped, then resumed in a different key. Lalique entered with Siri and Assyria. The Triumvirate. The ladies at her side were just as lovely, and ethereal, as though the very air they breathed was of another realm.

Lalique's eyes met Lorel's from across the room, then flitted away to stare ahead. They seemed to focus on some faraway object no one else could see. As she walked her white gown trailed behind her. Her fiery red hair hung in soft curls, partly contained by thick braids that gathered at the crown of her skull. The crystal diamond on her forehead caught the sun as she walked toward the table shooting tiny rainbows around the room. But beneath the ornate beauty of her face was an imposing countenance.

Lorel's breath caught as she watched the queen slide into her chair at the head of the table. Siri and Assyria seemed to float into seats on either side of her like settling clouds.

"How are you doing?" Sam whispered to Lorel. They

had not had much chance to speak since he had revealed her true identity a few days ago.

"Hey, Sam." She took the linen napkin, folded like origami on her plate, and placed it in her lap. "I'm doing fine. Mello has been incredibly helpful. I just hope this goes well."

"Be careful and lay low," he said out of the corner of his mouth.

"I can take care of myself."

Sam glanced down at her thigh and smiled. "I see."

"I can't take Link everywhere." She grimaced, with a hand on her knife in its leather sheath.

"Lorel, these people are good at protecting. It's what they've done for centuries."

"Protecting themselves or others?"

"Point taken. But you are one of them. Don't be afraid to let them in."

"Of course," she said, biting into a bread knot drizzled in squid ink. Mello shifted in his seat on her other side, deep in conversation with another siren. His elbow bumped hers gently casting a ripple of pleasure through her midsection.

She had already let someone in. More than she wanted to admit.

"Lorel, there are people here that care greatly about you. I just . . . hope you know that."

"I do know that. Everyone here, every experience here up until right about now has been wonderful," she said, poking the algae with her gold fork and watching it jiggle, "but I don't belong here. You and I both know that. Once this is all done, I'm going home. To my father."

"I have no doubt," Sam said, glancing down as she met his eyes.

"With or without your help," she said, not caring how the words came out. Didn't he realize her father's life was at stake? *Days, a couple weeks at most,* the nurse had said.

"Lorel, I—"

"Never mind, Sam. You warned me fair and square. Let's just get through this morning," she said, exhaling through pursed lips.

At first glance around the table things looked normal, but close examination of any one face betrayed the gravity of the situation. Across from Lorel an attractive male siren with long braided hair and a brown tunic sat next to a human woman in a black business suit and pink lipstick. The anxiety was painfully obvious, but so was the intense desire to simply look at one another. Interact. In another world they could become friends, even lovers. But here they were strangers gathered only to discuss the boundaries meant to prevent a breakout of primitive violence.

Shouldn't we have progressed since the Neanderthals and early humans? she wondered. It seemed like the more similar the species, the more intolerant they were of each other.

Red las-gun flashes shattered her thoughts. She turned to see the double doors *swish* open again. Several PanElites marched in, all tall and muscular men with shaved heads. *Not unlike the tattooed man in black that had attacked her in DC,* she realized with a shiver. They propped their oversize weapons on their shoulders and lined up against the wall of the ballroom. The room fell silent. Lorel glanced at Lalique. Her face was still and unreadable, her chin held high as she watched the CEO enter.

He was tall, much taller than Lorel expected. His shock of white hair, interwoven with threads of gray, was impeccably formed in a marble wave. He strode in as though he was entering his boardroom. Lorel squinted at him. *Why did he look so familiar?* Seeing him in person jarred her. Resisting the urge to gape, she blinked rapidly and looked away.

Lalique set down her goblet and stood, smoothing the bodice of her white gown. "Mr. Galton, please take a seat." She gestured to the only open seat left at the opposite head of the table. As he sat, Lorel noticed a look of unease befall the faces, not of the sirens, but of his own people.

"Thank you." He nodded politely and gestured for the two PanElites still flanking him to recede.

Galton took several moments to situate himself in a methodical manner, unfolding his napkin and smoothing it across his lap, running a finger over one of the pieces of gold cutlery set before him, and finally steepling his hands beneath his chin to stare across at Lalique with cold blue eyes. Lorel studied his face from beneath her lashes as a siren approached to ladle some food onto his plate. She felt reluctant fascination with this man who was such a major leader back home. Not a good leader, but undeniably a powerful one.

PanDivinity was known for a lack of transparency when it came to its executives, or any employees for that matter. There were no faces or names to put to the people operating the most powerful organization—and in Lorel's mind the most evil—in the world. Its child companies, like DiviniGen, were not much better. There were names, but barely faces. CEOs and board members mostly lingered in the shadows of the public eye, letting the mammoth conglomeration with its talons so deeply embedded in the public's mind, operate on autopilot. The whole had become so much bigger than the parts, maybe the executives felt marginalized on some level.

Or maybe it was calculated, she thought. *Maybe they didn't want people to know them, recognize them. Maybe they were afraid people would see that beneath their polished masks of leadership they were just regular people pedaling a megacorporation's lies.*

Whatever the reasons, it remained that although Galton was CEO of the largest biogenetics company on the planet, he could walk through a crowd unrecognized. She remembered watching the holo at DiviniGen's Centennial. He had spoken about the Poseidon Prototype, how it was going to save the world. His face had been shadowed, a dark silhouette against the backdrop of the city outside his office window.

But now, as she stared at him under the grand chandelier, something sparked recognition. His gestures. The hard line of his jaw. The arch of his cottony white brows. Suddenly she sunk down low in her seat, then grabbed Mello's knee under the table.

"I *have* met him!" She hissed under her breath. "He was the man who threw me off the beach in New Charleston. Mello, he has to know where your daughter is. He was *there*."

A darkness flickered in Mello's eyes and Lorel could hear his breathing pick up, but he remained still.

"On behalf of the sirens here today, and all of Rodinia, we welcome you in peace," Lalique began, returning Galton's icy stare with her own.

Lorel's breath quickened and fresh layer of sweat broke out under her arms and the palms of her hands. She gripped the napkin in her lap. Everyone stared at the Queen with bated breath.

"You all have come on a long journey from the United States, and we welcome you to Rodinia. To Hotel Paraíso."

The humans around the table nodded with cautiously appreciative expressions.

Lalique continued, "But let us not pretend. You are here uninvited, and it is of our own free will that we have chosen to welcome you into our home. There was a time when your ships would not have made it within a mile of our outer shores. But we invite you in good faith that you will show us the same respect that we show you today. Should you abuse this privilege in any way and force our hand, you do so at your own risk."

Lorel liked the threat. Deep down maybe she wanted to see DiviniGen ensnare themselves in the sirens repressed talons. To see them fail. But then, in the end, no one would win.

Galton stood up, smiling to reveal perfect teeth as white as his hair, and offered a slight nod. "Queen Lalique, let me first say . . . thank you. To all of you." He spoke with a deference Lorel did not buy for a second. "And we appreciate your candor. It is good to know where we stand. Please know that we do not mistake your hospitality for ignorance. And while we certainly have all the means necessary to sustain ourselves aboard DiviniGen's fleet of ships and in the portable camps we've transported here, we gladly accept your invitation to stay in Hotel Paraíso." He gestured around the room. "And what a paradise you do have here. We look forward to touring the rest of the island."

Dozens of eyes darted from Galton to Lalique as they conversed across the long table. The music had softened to a gentle background of melodic vibrations. People lifted drinks silently to their lips and picked at the food on their plate.

"This is not a *tourist* destination, Mr. Galton. Nor will it ever be. Which brings me to our stipulations. Your entrance into Rodinia comes with restrictions."

"Of course, please, go on," he said with a nod.

"First, we know about your plans to create an *aquatic human*. We are flattered." She smiled. A few sirens around the table stifled grins. "But whatever scientific means you plan to use to create this . . . *Poseidon Prototype*, I believe you call it, they will not place our people in harm."

Galton stared at the queen in bemusement. For an instant Lorel saw lust in his eyes.

"Let me make one thing clear, to all of you," Galton said, gesturing with a thumb to underline his words. "Our aim at DiviniGen is to make this world a better place, to help people live better, healthier lives. With the oceans forcing our cities inland and resources becoming scarcer, the ocean is a place that offers hope for us. You, all of you here, are part of that hope. For that reason, we are grateful to you, we thank you. And we would never, ever, think of harming a rare and precious species such as yourselves. That is the last thing we want."

Lorel had to snatch her mind back from believing him. His words flowed out so smoothly, like fresh water. And therein lay so much of his power. As she glanced around, she found comfort in the fact that the sirens present did not appear convinced.

Jett, sitting a few seats down from Lorel, cleared his throat and stood. "Then what exactly do you want?"

"We only want to create a *seed*, if you will, for a new genetic formula that we can offer to the world. As soon as we get what we need, we will take leave of your lovely island."

"That brings me to my second stipulation," said Laliqe. "We require a guarantee that our home, and our existence, will not be revealed to a human soul. If you cannot convince me of this most critical —"

Galton interrupted her with a wave of his hand. "Let me alleviate you of this worry immediately. Our interests are already aligned. DiviniGen is a company that prides itself on having sole propriety over its product lines. We would never want to disclose our source for fear competitors may enter the game. In fact, in the interest of a long-term relationship, we are prepared to make a generous offer."

"You already squandered that relationship when you tortured one of our own. One who had put his trust in you." The queen looked at Mello, who stared at Galton with steely eyes. "That is not the kind of long-term relationship we are looking for, Mr. Galton. If only you had kept our original agreement. But you are only human."

"Human, yes, I admit that fault." A few people in white coats snickered. "But torturers we are not. We are professional scientists. Our goal is to discover. I would like to personally speak with Mr. Seaford during my visit, see what I can do to make it up to him. I apologize if my scientists may have treated him as less than . . ."

"Human?" Mello interjected with clenched jaw, dropping his fork loudly.

"I was going to say," his eyes shot daggers at Mello, "less than a *person*. A person deserving of the liberties bestowed upon us. You see, we are all the same."

Lorel heard Mello curse under his breath, but aloud he said, "We don't need to speak any further. But thanks for the offer to chat."

"And we will not be considering any more offers of the kind," added Lalique. "You are here on business. Do it promptly and respectfully, and then be gone."

Galton's pinkish face deepened to red. He looked down at his goblet and swished the wine around slowly before finally addressing Lalique with piercing eyes.

"Dear Queen, would you be interested in a private, undetectable air route with which to import any man-made goods directly to Rodinia? Your people could have unlimited access to anything they desired, no matter how big or small—clothing, jewelry, holograms and tablets, cars, building materials. You could start a small city here. Grow into a real country." His eyes sparkled with a contagious excitement. "And in return for DiviniGen's ongoing use of your island. We would have access to the algae, along with all other natural resources of the island, and the opportunity to observe—with the utmost respect—your people at any time. All for exploratory purposes, of course."

The table erupted in hushed murmurs of discussion. He was good at what he did, Lorel had to give the guy that. The faces of sirens around the table connected with quizzical glances, silently wondering what the others thought.

Lalique's lips curled into a half smile and her head tilted to the side. "Rodinia is not for sale." She lifted the goblet to her lips, maintaining eye contact with Galton. Sunlight caught on the bright ring of crystals that lined the edge of the glass.

The CEO's back straightened and he took a breath, preparing to speak. "Queen, perhaps we can continue this—"

"The only offer on the table is mine," she broke in. "Think about it. We will need some sort of guarantee. You are a businessman. I will leave it to you to draw one up that satisfies me and my counsel," she gestured to Siri and Assyria who stared at Galton with unflinching faces. "Otherwise, none of you will leave this island."

The entire table fell quiet. Lorel curled her toes in her sandals beneath the table. She couldn't help but feel the warning was directed at her as well. Sentenced in a paradise she would never be able to fully realize.

Lalique looked around with a disarming smile and lifted her arms winged with sheer fabrics. "Please, everyone, enjoy the food. It is Rodinia's finest."

The diners responded with a relieved clattering of glasses and utensils, and the casual, if not forced, chatter picked up to a normal volume again.

Across the table, at the far end next to Galton, Lorel noticed a man staring at her. She looked away. Not only was it critical she avoid Galton now, but all of the visitors. They may wonder why she looked different than the other sirens, why her eyes weren't quite as large, her fingers unwebbed. No one could be trusted. She sunk into her chair as she felt his eyes burning into her from down the table.

"What is it?" Mello whispered, leaning in, his breath tickling her ear.

"Is that guy still staring at me? The one with the slicked-back hair next to Galton."

Mello shifted his gaze down the table. "That's Lucas Keating. He was probably staring at me, remembering how he screwed me over."

"Lucas . . . Lucas. Oh my god." Lorel put her hand to her mouth. "I met him at the Centennial. I didn't recognize the name at first, but his face. That's him for sure. I think he must have recognized me."

She yanked a napkin up to her mouth as the man's gaze aimed again in her direction.

Sam turned from his other conversation, eyes wide. "Did you just say someone recognizes you?"

"We need to get her out of here." Mello looked pointedly at Sam. "All this mess started because of him. He turned me in like I was some washed up animal, knowing exactly what would happen. I should've known. Now I know better." He pressed a hand to her knee under the table. "I won't let him touch you."

Lorel thought back to the Centennial, her flee to the roof terrace to escape the madness inside. Lucas Keating had hit on her, in his sleek business suit and shiny cufflinks, then dismissed her when he had learned her position within the company was not high. He had given her a slimy feeling from the moment they met. Little had she known how slimy he was.

"You're right. She should go," Sam said.

Before Lorel could reply, think of a reason not to leave, Lucas Keating rose from his seat.

"You bastard," Mello muttered, his eyes burning into Keating as he circumnavigated the table.

"Play nice, Mello. We don't want to draw attention to this," Sam hissed.

Lorel dropped her head. *Dammit. Please say he's just going to the buffet,* she thought. But within seconds he was leaning over her and Mello. She could smell the same musky cologne he had worn on the roof.

Mello stood, stuck out his hand though his jaw

remained clenched. Lorel noticed as he towered above the businessman how different they looked from one another. Mello's long unkempt hair, his skin, tanned from a life beneath the sun, and sinewy muscles that twitched under a cream-colored tunic made from native fabrics. His hand firmly gripped Lucas's, whose wrist flashed with a holo watch and shiny cufflinks pinned to a starched white sleeve. "Keating," he said behind a locked jaw.

"Nice to see you again in the flesh, Seaford." His eyes darted away as though he couldn't look Mello in the face. His attention averted to Lorel.

"Hannah?"

Lorel craned her neck around to face him. "Hi. It's Lucas, right?"

"Yeah. I didn't know you were on this trip. It's level black." He looked pleasantly surprised.

"I'm just helping with some of the IT stuff." She crumpled and squeezed the cloth napkin in her perspiring hands.

"Ah, IT. Right. So, what do you think?" he whispered, placing his mouth near her ear, his breath hot on her cheeks. "This is some crazy shit, isn't it? These people, God Divine. They look so much like humans . . . yet *not*."

"Yeah, totally. So, maybe I'll see you around. I have to run to the ladies room."

"I look forward to it. What room are you in? Maybe we could meet on the veranda later for a drink."

"Haven't gotten my room number yet, but I'm sure I'll see you around."

"No doubt," he replied, patting her shoulder as he walked away. Lorel turned and sunk back into her chair relieved the exchange was over. She looked from Sam to Mello, who were both staring at her. "From now on, call me Hannah."

The two men glanced at each other. Mello's face had changed from seething to concerned.

"You are not to come back to Paraíso, *Hannah*. This island is too dangerous for you. If they find out who you really are . . ." Mello's voice faded.

"But if I'm Hannah, I'm not Lorel Phoenix. It's the perfect cover! And I really don't think Galton would remember my face." Lorel reasoned, not ready to be quarantined again.

"He's right, Lorel," Sam said. "I think the safest place for you is the bunker on Baltra."

She suddenly felt as though she'd been sentenced to prison. Just when things were escalating, she was relegated to the dungeon. But they were right. Paraíso was too risky now.

As the brunch wrapped up, Lalique stood again to say some closing words. "Mr. Galton, let me address the elephant in the room. As a show of good faith, you will find we've gathered a group of sirens who have volunteered to participate in your scientific exploration of our species' genetic potential. They offer their blood samples and the right to observe them, but no more. We ask in return that you share your findings. Do not cross the line."

Galton froze with his spoon of purple algae in midair.

A few gasps could be heard around the table from the scientists. "Your generosity is unprecedented. An unexpected offer to say the least. We are truly honored."

The DiviniGen scientists at the table beamed in agreement.

"That makes Stage One very easy for us all, does it not?" He addressed his employees with raised brows, then to Lalique, "And not to worry, for Stage Two we have brought our own volunteers. They're enjoying themselves in port aboard their own special vessel, the *Celebration*."

Lorel noticed a few scientists smiles fade at his mention of the volunteers. She felt her stomach drop. That could mean only one thing.

"Quick, go now!" Mello ordered as the brunch attendees poured out the front door of the hotel and onto the sunny veranda.

Lucas Keating halted just outside the door and put his hand up to shade his eyes. His head rotated like an eagle searching for prey. He was looking for her. Lorel could feel it. The attraction he felt for Hannah Ledger had been obvious the moment they met on the roof. She darted around the back of the hotel where the beach narrowed to a small rocky inlet nestled into an overgrowth of vegetation. Silas was already waiting for her in the canoe.

"Ready?" He began pushing off before she could pull both her feet inside.

"Yeah, go." She glanced back at the veranda full of people and breathed a sigh of relief. What had she been thinking, showing her face there? She should have known the danger. But it was too tempting. Galton was her enemy too, and had been longer than she realized. There was no way she would have missed his appearance in Rodinia. But what she wanted to do was spit in his face and tell him who she really was, that she had gotten away from him. Again.

Instead she was going into hiding. At least the bunker had the security monitors for viewing. She would not be completely cut off underground.

"So what was it like in there?" Silas asked shyly as he paddled across the Eye toward Baltra, hugging the perimeter of the mangroves to keep a low profile.

Lorel stared down through the clear water at the pebbles below. A school of yellow fish darted from the shadow of the boat like bats out of a cave. "Have you ever seen a human, Silas? I mean, besides Sam."

"Well, I've seen half of one." He smiled.

"Yeah, I guess I'm not exactly representative of the species." Lorel laughed. "The brunch went fine. Lalique laid down the law for them."

"Nice." Silas looked proud of his queen. "So they weren't forceful, with those PanElites and all? I guess I imagined them kinda trying to strong-arm sirens and stab needles into them or something."

"Silas, humans that work for these megacorporations are extremely educated, intelligent people. Their first play is always a sales game. They want the sirens to *want* them here, *trust* them so that they can get what they want with the least resistance. They're too calculated to come wielding swords, you know?"

Silas was young, still trying to understand the parallel universe that existed on the other side of his planet. One to which he was naïve but hopeful.

"Yeah, I get it."

Lorel could tell he didn't, at least not yet.

"But, Silas, Galton and his crew, they're not representative either. Humans are good people. Sometimes they become corrupted by these illusions the material world dangles in front of them. They forget what makes them human, what the ground feels like beneath their feet. But some people have the strength to resist the smoke and mirrors and stay grounded."

Silas stared back toward Paraíso. Lorel could make out the reflection of the hotel, even the volcano beyond it in his big round eyes.

"Like you," she went on, "like all of the sirens I've met. You have a special place here. I know you want to be a part of the human civilization, but there's no place as close to the earth as this."

"Yeah. It just makes me feel ignorant sometimes. I think that's what we all feel, the younger sirens at least."

"But you're not. Look, sirens think on a higher level than most humans I know. You educate yourselves so you can harness the land, own your environment without destroying it, live peacefully together without wars. Your trusted Council carefully chooses what material things enter your lives to keep yourselves from losing sight of who you are. You live in a world that is just as beautiful as the day it was created, while we are literally drowning in our own self-inflicted destruction. Not to mention, you even have a library of real books!"

He chuckled, raising a skeptical eyebrow. "We're not geniuses. Or saints, you know."

"I know." Lorel thought of the sunken ships outside the island ring, the Dark Submersion. "You're flawed just like we are. But at least you've found a way to suppress the dark side, right?" She looked up at him, smiling.

"Thanks, Lorel. I'm glad you came here." The canoe scraped ashore on Baltra, and he reached his hand down to help her out. She grabbed it.

"I'm glad I came too. But I better run." She jumped onto the hot white sand.

"Do you remember how to get to the bunker?"

"I think so."

"Just follow the trail to the Waterfall Tree and wrap around to the east," he said, pointing toward the forest.

"Thank you, Silas." Lorel kissed his cheek in a burst of gratitude. He reminded her of a young Jake, questioning life and existence rather than just accepting the norm.

He stood barefoot on the sand, blushing, as Lorel darted through the thick umbrella of sea grape trees and into the woods.

She felt a pressing urge to see what was going on inside Hotel Paraíso. They were probably setting up their lab equipment now, ushering in the siren volunteers, getting them settled into their experimentation rooms. And Galton had no clue the Council would be watching it all. *Would he even care?*

Back home DiviniGen had regulators breathing

down their necks, auditing their business operations, overseeing their research and development tactics. Even their fortress of underground labs was not impervious to the occasional bureaucratic inspector despite their deep governmental ties. But here it was free reign, no man's land. They could do anything they wanted, to humans or sirens. The thought sent a bolt of fresh energy through her.

Still jogging at a steady clip, her tunic now tattered and soiled by the branches along the path, she reached Mello's hut. She wound around the other side of the kapok tree then tore away the vines hiding the bunker doors. Quickly entering the numbers into the sundial lock, she released it and heaved open the iron door.

An ear shattering scream pierced through the hollow space. Lorel's heart stopped.

"Isla!" she yelled frantically, tearing into the main room.

The cavernous space was empty but for a few sirens who sat around the bank of monitors, staring at the security screens with headphones on.

The screaming grew louder, more hysterical. It was coming from one of the tunnels. Lorel ran toward the noise. The tunnel was dark, but she could see a dim light at the other end.

"Ahh!" She winced as someone, or something, rammed into her, slamming her body to the ground.

"Lorel?" said a small voice.

Someone scrambled to their feet in front of her, but she couldn't see anything.

"Who is that?" Lorel called into the blackness.

"It's Harper. Isla's sister," she spoke quickly. "She's in labor."

"Now? She isn't due for another week. Is everything okay?"

"She was fine until she started to push. The baby . . . it won't come. It's stuck. She needs to get to the water."

Lorel's stomach flipped. No doctors. No hospital. Only their bare hands to count on. And instinct. "Let's go."

"This way. In the kitchen." Harper turned and ran down one of the tunnels that branched off from the central room. Isla lay on her back in the middle of a lacquered concrete floor, legs spread, heaving and screaming in pain. Tears poured down her reddened face and sweat beaded on her forehead and upper lip. Sam would never forgive himself. He had been so hesitant to leave her for even a few hours this morning.

"Isla!" Lorel rushed to Isla's side, kneeling next to her. Isla grabbed her hand and squeezed so hard Lorel winced. "Hey. You're going to be fine. We're going to do this together, okay?"

"I think the cord is wrapped around its neck! It feels so still," she choked out in a whisper. "A siren always births in the water. I need water."

Lorel's heart raced, but she couldn't let Isla see her panic. The baby had to come out as soon as possible or it would suffocate. There was no time for transferring Isla to the beach, or even to the lagoon.

"Hey, don't worry. This baby is half human,

remember?" Lorel smiled assuredly. "He'll know what to do."

"He?" Isla raised her blonde brows.

Lorel shrugged. "I must have said that for a reason, right? Harper, grab her on the other side."

Harper and Lorel together gently lifted Isla up into sitting position.

"Isla, we need to get you in a more natural position for birth. Can you squat, like a frog? We'll support you."

Isla heaved herself into a squat, still squeezing Lorel's hand with all her might. Her blonde hair spilled down over her face and across her contracting belly.

"Now breathe . . . and push!" Lorel demanded.

Under Harper's and Lorel's support Isla squeezed her eyes shut and pushed. She pushed harder, crying out in pain, shaking until her face turned purple.

"My back. Oh god, my back is on fire. I need water, please just take me to water." Her eyes fluttered and she struggled to contain her breath.

"You can't give up now. You're so close, Isla. I promise. Here," Lorel pressed firmly against her lower back, then downward on her hips. "Does this help?"

"Yes. But here comes another one." Isla squeezed her eyes closed again and pushed until her face was the color of a beat. Lorel kept glancing down, but there was no sign yet of a head.

"You can do it, Isla!" Harper cheered, but her face was blanched white. "A few more pushes, I know it."

Several minutes passed, but they felt like hours. Lorel could not release a breath until she saw the baby's face, heard its first scream.

Suddenly the tip of a head appeared.

"Isla, it's crowning. You can do this. We need a really big push now, okay?" Lorel pulled her hand away from Isla's and repositioned herself. "Harper, hold your sister's hand. I'm going to catch the baby."

The baby slid out in silence and Lorel's blood ran cold. The umbilical cord was wrapped around its neck and its tiny face was blue.

"Give me some scissors!" Lorel yelled.

Harper rifled through a drawer and then handed her a pair of kitchen scissors. Lorel snipped the cord, disconnecting Isla from the baby, and began to carefully unwind it.

The baby erupted in a healthy, wailing scream. The capillaries in its face bloomed into a rosy red. Isla burst into tears of relief.

"It's a boy," Lorel announced, handing the baby to Isla who brought him gingerly to her face and smothered him in wet kisses. She put him to her breast and he began suckling, suddenly quiet.

Instincts, Lorel thought as a dam of relief broke in her chest. The lights in the room seemed to brighten, shining down on Isla and the baby. The air felt more breathable.

"My sweet Dylan." Isla caressed his tiny head as it bobbed eagerly at her breast.

Lorel held back tears. The situation could have gone so many other ways. Now all she could hope was that the baby stayed safe.

"Hello my little nephew," Harper murmured, putting

her face up to his. "You're beautiful. I think you're going to have your daddy's eyes. They're blue now, but they look so dark."

"Brown eyes," Isla smiled, "like someone else we know."

Lorel smiled. It was true. The baby was just like her, half in one world and half in another. What would his life be like? Where would he belong? Rodinia hung in the balance, everything seemed so uncertain. She reached out her arms. "May I?"

Isla handed her the tiny white bundle. Lorel's breath caught in her throat. Dylan gazed up at her with shining eyes and slowly puckered his pink lips. Her heart felt as though it would burst at the hope of this little child. He symbolized what could be . . . a union of human and siren. Suddenly she felt the weight of what Mello wanted for his people. It was the same thing she wanted for hers. She kissed Dylan on his fuzzy head.

"You are a miracle if I've ever seen one, sweet baby," she said, then added in a whisper, "and we are the start of a brand new race."

A full day had passed and Lorel was beginning to feel anxiety from being pent up inside the bunker. What was happening over on Paraíso? She had been incessantly wandering around the security monitors to see if anything was going on. So far, it seemed uneventful, but she was hoping for an update from Mello when she got him alone.

Lorel drummed her nails against the metal table of the bunker's kitchen. Sam, Mello, Harper, and Lorel all hovered around Isla in the kitchen admiring the baby. Harper had placed a tiny ring of blue flowers around his neck adding floral notes to the fresh scent of new life. A few of the sirens from the security post had wandered in as well. Coffee brewed on the stainless steel counter.

Lorel stood up. "I hate to leave the excitement, but I've got to go back to my hut and get Link."

"Wait, you can't go by yourself." Mello held up his hand in protest.

"But someone has to oversee the monitoring out there," Lorel pointed out.

The sirens in the room exchanged nods of agreement. Everyone in the Baltra bunker had come to rely on Mello for guidance and analysis of DiviniGen activity. No one wanted to miss a move the scientists made, but they did not want to jump to conclusions either, and much of it was new to them.

"Sam can help out. Harper can stay here with me and Dylan, keep us company," Isla said, looking at Sam. "It's okay, darling. I'll be fine."

Sam opened his mouth like he was about to disagree, but then stopped. "All right, just yell if you need me. I'll only be on the other end of the tunnel." He released her from his embrace and kissed her and Dylan on their heads. The other sirens followed him back to the main room.

"We'll be back in an hour," Mello said as he and Lorel left. "Need anything from up above?"

"We'll be fine," said Isla, barely looking up from the baby nuzzling against her chest.

They stepped out the iron door to a buzzing of insects. It was dusk and light fought to get through the canopy of leaves above.

"So you haven't seen anything out of line from them yet?" Lorel asked, whacking a branch away as they hiked swiftly along the path.

"Not yet. They've been taking blood samples from the volunteers as we expected. And there are a ton of white coats staring into microscopes and studying holos of DNA strands. But no attempts to get more invasive. Yet."

"So far so good," Lorel replied, short of breath. They had reached the steepest portion of the trail leading to the cliff huts.

When they reached the plateau, a starry sky blanketed the vast meadow that stretched out to the edge of the cliffs. They arrived at Lorel's hut, and she pushed open the door.

"Link?"

No sound or movement.

"Link!"

They began searching the area for him. Finally, Link pranced out of the woods dragging an oversized, half-dead rodent. He dropped it at Lorel's feet. She rubbed his head affectionately, but her face wrinkled in disgust.

"Thanks, buddy. Let's just leave this here for now."

Sensing Lorel's ungratefulness, the cat responded with a disappointed bow.

"It's getting dark, we should go," said Mello.

The moon, cloaked in a passing cloud, hung low over the ocean as the three retreated down the path headed back to the bunker. They treaded downward in silence surrounded by the hissing and buzzing of the woodland life. It was dark, but the forest at the base of the path had become so familiar to Lorel in the short time she had been in Rodinia. She inhaled the crisp smell of pines that interspersed with the saplings and hardwoods.

As the ground leveled out, Lorel paused. Where was the buzzing of insects, the chirrups of the birds and monkeys? It was quiet but for their own footsteps.

Mello moved fast, anxious to get back to the bunker and Link padded along at his heels. She sped up to keep pace. As the trees thinned out and sand replaced soft dirt and pine needles, Mello stopped abruptly in his tracks, throwing his arm back to keep Lorel from going any farther.

"Shh!" he hissed.

They could see the beach through the trees and the glassy water of the Eye beyond. Link crouched low on his hindquarters, growling.

"What is it?" Lorel didn't notice anything at first, but then she heard it. A group of people on the beach just on the other side of a grassy dune. "Link, be quiet!" she whispered, unraveling his leash from her arm.

He growled again, slightly louder.

"Get the leash on, now," Mello said, pulling a curved

knife from its sheathe on his hip.

As she knelt down to undo the latch and secure it to Link's collar, the people rounded the sand dune, coming into full view.

"I swear I thought I heard something over here," said a woman's voice. "Damn, this whole place freaks me out."

"Probably just an animal," responded a deep voice. Then the sound of guns chambering rounds.

"*Just* an animal?" It was the woman. "Who knows what kind of creatures are on this island. I mean, look at the freak-of-nature people that live here."

The sight of DiviniGen employees on Baltra caused Lorel blood to run cold. Lalique had laid out the boundaries very clearly at the brunch. Galton and his people were not to leave Paraíso. If they had broken this rule, what else had they done? What other boundaries had they crossed?

Lorel's hands began to shake as she watched the PanElites pace on the sand. Their silvery las-guns circled the air as though waiting for any moving object, hungry to release their load of bullets. There were three mercenaries. With them were a man and a woman dressed in business suits. She recognized the man as Lucas Keating and glanced at Mello. He put a finger slowly to his lips, eyes wide.

Clumsily Lorel clicked the leash around the metal clasp of Link's collar, but before she could grab the loop the cat bolted forward.

"Link, no!" Lorel cried, lunging toward her beloved

pet.

But arms of steel wrapped quickly around her and a warm hand covered her mouth. "Shhh! Lorel, you can't," Mello whispered roughly, his lips brushing against her ear.

She struggled to escape his grasp but the scene was already unfolding before her eyes. Link charged out of the palm trees and directly at one of the PanElites. Lorel watched in slow motion, her mind freeze framing the magnificent mane of fur silhouetted against the moonlight. For a moment it looked as though he would leap right over the people and into the Eye.

The shot rang through the atmosphere like the universe had just exploded, shattering every cell in Lorel's body. Red light flashed. Blood sprayed from the animal's majestic head, and he fell like a boulder to the sandy ground.

Lorel collapsed in Mello's embrace. His hands tightened around her mouth as she screamed in silent agony. Tears gushed from her eyes and she squeezed them shut, trying to block out the horror of what she had seen.

This wasn't happening. If she could go back in time, only a few seconds, she could grab the leash. She could stop it.

"It's going to be okay," Mello whispered, stroking her hair. He still gripped her so tightly she could barely move.

On the beach the group of people rushed over to Link's body, eager to examine what it was that had jumped out at them in the night.

"It's some sort of wild beast," said one of the PanElites, kicking the body over so Link's belly faced skyward. His head lolled loosely back on the bloodstained sand.

Lorel and Mello watched as Keating knelt down, pushing the PanElite out of his way. "Wait, this is one of our bio-products. Madelyn, come look."

The blonde woman in the business suit walked cautiously over and knelt down next to Keating.

"Oh." Her hand flew to her mouth in shock. "It's a DiviniGen mutant cat. How could it be possible?"

Keating shoved his hand under Link's limp torso and pulled out the pink leash. "And look at this. He's here with his owner."

They all began talking among themselves in a feverish cluster, casting suspicious glances into the woods, pointing in various directions. Their confusion was obvious, but it would be short lived if Lorel and Mello did not get back to the bunker in time.

"Let's search. Call for backup!" Keating demanded to the PanElites. Within seconds they were running toward the woods.

"Let's go!" Mello released Lorel.

Her legs felt like jelly, and she still couldn't take her eyes off Link, his body now lying alone on the beach.

"Lorel, you can do this." He gripped her shoulders gently. "Or I can carry you."

The offer snapped Lorel from her state of paralysis, and she grabbed his hand. "No. I'm okay."

Together they broke into a run, light-footed and swift,

winding through the woods until the voices behind them faded to crickets.

"Do you think they saw us?" Lorel asked as they slowed to a brisk walking pace.

"No. As long as we get inside the bunker we should be good. But we have to warn Lalique that DiviniGen is on Baltra now, if she has not already seen on the cameras."

Within minutes they had reached the bunker doors. Lorel gasped for breath as Mello fiddled to get them open. They climbed down the stairs. Inside it was eerily silent, only the soft hushing sound of static on the console screens could be heard. The sirens that had been monitoring the security cameras sat in their chairs around the bank of computers, headphones on. But their unusual stillness caused Lorel's stomach to drop.

"Mello, something is wrong." The air had a distinct chill in it from a draft that wasn't there before. Her hair stood on end.

Mello bolted to the siren sitting nearest to them and grabbed his shoulder, spinning the chair around. Lorel watched in horror as the person's head lolled forward, blood dripping from a las-gun hole in his at his temple.

"No," she whispered, shaking her head.

Mello didn't speak, just stood for a moment looking up at the ceiling dotted with lights. Lorel watched the blood boil behind his face and a vein on his forehead bulge. He dashed around the console, checking the other sirens. All dead. He began tapping the blackglass beneath a monitor.

"The security system has been deactivated." He

glanced at the tunnel leading to the kitchen. "Isla," he whispered, already halfway across the main room. Lorel followed, averting her eyes from the dead bodies as she rounded the console.

In the bunker kitchen Sam, Harper, and Isla sat back to back on chairs, their hands bound together and their mouths covered with tape. Lorel's relief that they were alive quickly vanished.

"Where is Dylan?"

Adrenaline surged through her as she stood frozen in the middle of the room. Link. The dead sirens. How could things have gone wrong so quickly?

Mello untied the all three of them, then ripped the tape from their mouths unleashing the hysteria.

"My baby!" Isla screamed, repeating it over and over. Harper and Sam tried consoling her, but she was in a frenzy.

Sam glanced at Mello, his eyes full of rage. "We have to do something. Now!"

Mello filled them in on the tragic scene beyond the tunnel, shoving his hands through his silvery hair. "How the hell did they get in? Did you hear anything?"

"They came through the main room first, must have expected resistance from the sirens out there. We heard the shots," Sam explained. "We're lucky to be alive, but . . ."

"Why do you think they left you alive?" Mello interrupted.

Sam shook his head. "They muttered something about being under orders, that since we're blood relations to the subject . . ."

"Dylan. The testing. They must have planned this from the beginning." Mello looked back and forth between Isla and Sam. "We will get him back."

"How could they have gotten in?" Lorel frowned, drawing Harper under her arm. "I thought this was fortified, hidden."

Isla spoke between sobs. "They came in so quietly, we didn't even see them. They had huge las-guns and were wearing black camouflage."

"And they all had shaved heads." Harper added. In her trembling hands she held the ring of blue flowers Dylan had been wearing.

"There must be a way in we don't know about. A passage inside one of the tunnels or something." Mello stopped his pacing, looked up at the ceiling. "But even if there is, how could they have known about it?"

"He was born only hours ago. And they knew. They've been watching us." Lorel's head spun.

"One step ahead. They always are." Sam said through a clenched jaw, drawing Isla closer and shoving his glasses up his nose. "I will get our baby back, my love."

Mello's lips pressed together in a slight grimace, and he blinked a few times before addressing the room. "We have no communication here now. We're on our own unless the Council saw this on camera, but there's a good chance they killed the cameras down here on their way in. What we must do now is get to Hotel Paraíso. That has to be where they've taken Dylan."

Everyone nodded in agreement.

"Harper, begin scoping out the bunker. Search every closet, every crevice in the walls. Find their way in, and we'll follow them back. Sam, I need your help out in the control room for just a few moments," Mello said lowering his eyes. "We must tend to our friends . . ."

His voice faded away in Lorel's mind as she realized what she must do. If they wanted a hybrid, they would get it. But it would not be an innocent child. Slowly she backed into the tunnel leading out to the main room then turned and ran. In the chaos, no one noticed.

The main room was empty and the bodies were gone, but she could hear Sam and Mello in another tunnel. Its label read "Incinerator/Janitorial." She assessed her surroundings. A flashlight hung from a latch next to the exit door, which was now sealed shut. She grabbed it then fingered the knife still hitched to her waist.

A dank draft chilled the air that before had been evenly circulating through the venting system. She licked her finger, holding it up to determine the direction of the airflow. It was from the one tunnel she had never been down. The overhead lighting strip flickered emitting only a faint glow. A metal plate above the door read "Commissary Facilities."

Lorel darted into the corridor. She did not have much time before they realized she was gone. And no one would have approved of her plan.

Her feet tingled in uncertainty as the dark tunnel sloped downward. She clicked on the flashlight and shined it around. Where did the passage end? Another gust of cold air raised goosebumps along her skin. A draft. That meant an opening.

She crept forward as quietly as possible in order to listen for any air movement. This area of the bunker seemed less modernized than the rest of the facility. The faint sound of water dripping echoed a few feet away. As she approached, the air gusted again causing a hollow groan. She kneeled down by the wall, scraping her knees on the rough surface.

Then she saw it. A round opening the size of a manhole was cut into the side of the wall. She ran her fingers along its perimeter.

"Ouch!" She brought her finger to her mouth and sucked the pinprick of blood.

Little pieces of metal curled toward her the way aluminum peeled from a can of food. It was obvious from the direction of the shards that someone had cut into the bunker from the outside. Another entryway. No wonder Mello and the sirens were not aware of it. Beacon must have constructed it with some purpose and never finished the connection. Or they were hiding something. It seemed there were things the secret organization had chosen to keep secret from the sirens.

Why? she wondered. But now was not the time to get pensive.

Lorel wiped the grime from her hands and leaned in, shining the flashlight through the makeshift hatch. It was another subterranean space that appeared to tunnel ahead like a passage. Just as Mello had guessed. This was where the PanElites entered. Lorel swallowed thinking of how exposed the sirens had been this whole time. It was as though Galton knew more about the land here than its native people did.

She crawled inside trying not to slice her back against the rough edge. At her feet she found a round metal disc that had been cut from the wall. She replaced it in the hole as well as she could, covering her tracks and blocking herself inside. The temperature was frigid and the hair on her skin prickled. She rubbed her bare arms, then took a deep breath of the dank air and proceeded forward.

The sides and ceiling were some sort of metal, probably steel, and a thrumming sound could be heard beyond them, steady like a beating heart.

Or like churning tide?

It was possible she had transitioned from subterranean to submarine. The ground was gritty with sand or dirt and her feet scraped, abrading the rough surface like sandpaper on brick. Water dripped at short intervals from above with unnerving echoes. She hoped the tunnel was safe. When did Mello say Beacon had built all these structures?

A few hundred years ago at least.

The tunnel declined steeply and she tripped, causing her heart to lurch as though she had stepped blindly off a curb. She regained balance, wondering if it would be better to just slide. But after a while the decline leveled off and the ceiling rose to a height where she could stand up and walk.

Where was this leading her? Another island? A bunker? She pictured the map of Rodinia. A gut instinct told her it was tunneling underneath the mangroves to one of Baltra's neighboring islands. Atolla perhaps.

Or Paraíso.

The drumming sound had grown to a crescendo and now the rushing sound of water was undeniable. This was a submarine tunnel. Her heart pounded as she warded off a feeling of claustrophobia.

Finally, the ground began inclining again, and Lorel climbed upward steadying herself with her hands at the steepest points. Her flashlight still shone brightly and she could see in the distance that she was nearing the end of the passage. She was no longer underwater at this point, which meant she had probably reached land. If the tunnel spit her out on Paraíso, she'd be able to find her way to the hotel. And to Galton.

She clicked the flashlight to the dimmest setting. This was going to be a surprise visit.

A clean circle of light came into focus ahead, leaking through the frame of another circular hatch. Lorel drew in a breath, stifling a cough as the damp air rushed her lungs. That had to be an indoor room, but based on the incline, it probably was not deep enough to be a bunker. So where was she? She palmed the surface as though her touch could provide the answer. It felt warm.

Aware that she could be entering a danger zone, she leaned down and pressed her ear to the metal surface. Silence. She pushed the hatch open and stepped through to find herself in a dark empty room. The damp smell and mustiness told her it was still subterranean. An old hand painted sign on one wall read:

AMMUNITION STORAGE & SALTPETRE

It *was* another bunker. Lorel pivoted to get a full view of the space and hoped she was alone. It was possible that all five islands were connected by these tunnels. DiviniGen people could be anywhere. Everywhere. As her eyes adjusted to the dim lighting, she noticed a pile of crates with labels in Portuguese. Footsteps sounded above.

Suddenly she realized where she was, and a knot twisted in her stomach. But this was good. Hotel Paraíso was exactly where she wanted to be.

The ceiling above had been retrofitted with a series of steel support beams. The Portuguese had hastily erected the building over the top of one of Beacon's old bunkers, which was now used as a basement.

On instinct Lorel headed toward some rickety stairs on the opposite side of the room. Light seeped in through a door at the top. Muffled voices sounded on the other side. As she approached, the faint sound of a baby's cry sent a chill through her. Dylan. With one hand on her knife and another on the cold knob, she froze.

"Dr. Wong, take it to the testing room immediately!" a deep, gruff voice commanded.

"Yes, sir," said a woman.

Lorel recognized the man's voice as clear as day. It was Galton. *Not only had she been led directly to the hotel, but she was right outside the lion's den.*

Feet clicked across the floor.

Lorel had to act before it was too late. She turned the knob slowly and pushed, but it was locked. Backing up on the landing of the steps, she brought her knee to her chest then released her leg in a powerful sidekick. The door swung open and light flooded in.

Without hesitation she stepped inside and found herself face to face with a woman in a lab coat. The woman looked Asian with jet black eyes, high cheekbones, and hair pulled into a tight ponytail that fell below her shoulders.

Lorel's gaze fell immediately to the baby in her arms. "Wait," she yelled breathlessly before she could even perceive the rest of her surroundings. "Please!"

"Who the hell are you?" The woman gripped the baby tighter, gaping at Lorel in shock, then called over her shoulder. "Mr. Galton!"

The dim room glowed with floor to ceiling holos of DNA helices that rotated in dizzying spirals. Projected against the back wall, beyond an ancient looking wooden desk, Lorel recognized a species genome map. Dots connected to dots like constellations in an endless universe of virtual genes. A title across the top of the map read "Siren Genome Project."

They had wasted no time.

Francis Galton stood from a chair in the corner of the room and smoothed his pants, then placed his tablet on the desk. Even at the late hour, he wore his business suit, black with a green and blue checkered tie. His marble white hair reflected the kaleidoscope of colors dancing around the room.

"And who, may I ask, are you, young lady?" He approached her in smooth strides, his head cocked to one side.

Lorel flashed back to the last time she had been face to face with him. The morning on the beach. He had worn an eyeband that day, but now he stood before her once again, looking her up and down just as he had a month ago, with piercing blue eyes.

"Do I not look familiar?" She straightened her back and returned his stare.

Galton pulled back slightly with a frown, struggling to place where he had seen her before. A flicker of recognition lit his face followed by confusion.

"Just picture me standing among a bunch of dead orcas. And a dead girl."

Before Galton could respond two men flanked her. She winced as one cocked his las-gun into her side. Thoughts began jumbling in her mind and she felt herself losing focus as fear kicked in.

Remember why you are here.

He watched her for a reaction but she gave him nothing more than an icy stare. His brows furrowed deeply and he edged closer, examining her as though she was an object behind glass. "I remember. You're the one who broke her statement and called the media. I had to put a whole team on that mess. You were a thorn in my side. A small one though. Why," he asked narrowing his eyes, "and, more importantly, *how* have you gotten yourself to this place?"

"Sir, she may have escaped from the *Celebration*," Dr. Wong said, freeing one hand from her grasp on Dylan to pull a tablet out of her pocket. "I'll call the captain."

He ignored her, too engrossed in staring at Lorel's

face, searching for answers as though she were a difficult math problem he was about to work out.

"Let me start with the *why*." Lorel dropped her neck in a deep bow so that her hair fell away exposing the blowhole, then looked up again. "To get the hell away from you."

The color drained from his face.

Dr. Wong gasped.

"Leave her," he commanded the PanElites. They returned their las-guns to their sides and stepped back into the shadows. Lorel let out a short breath of relief.

Galton approached her. "So you're the hybrid girl we have been looking for. But I thought you were—"

"Dead?" she finished for him. "Not exactly. We'll call it reborn."

He froze, mouth agape, and stood speechless. After staring at her for what felt like an eternity, he pressed a curled finger to his lips. "Well. How nice to meet you *again*, Ms. Phoenix. On this island, no less. Someone here must be on your side."

She crossed her arms, denying the hand he extended in front of her. "Do not touch me."

"Fair enough," he said, lowering his hand. His eyes dropped to her hip and a bemused look lit his face. "You won't be needing that knife. You know better than to think we are savages."

"Of course not. Savages wouldn't stoop so low." Lorel pulled the knife from its sheath and dropped it to the carpeted floor. She wondered if it had ever been in her to use it. "I know what you did to Mello, what you plan to do here with these sirens, this innocent baby. And with me." She clenched her fists. "You've been following me."

"Yes, Ms. Phoenix, you are correct. My people have been following you for some time. We would have pressed charges against your boyfriend for what he did to Chan, but things had to remain quiet of course. He got what he deserved, I am sorry to tell you."

A wave of dread passed through her. "What do you mean?"

"I mean that he was meddling. And this is a very important operation. He is dead. Well, if the PanElites did their job. But they always do."

Lorel's heart fell to her feet and she gripped her belly to stop the churning. She looked at the knife on the rug. Too far away. Her mind turned fuzzy with grief and suddenly the man before her began to bend and sway.

"I am sorry for your loss. I wish it had not had to happen. But you must understand. What we are doing is for the good of everyone. It would be wrong to let one person get in the way of that, you understand." He looked at her with softening eyes, then motioned Dr. Wong over. "Please get Ms. Phoenix some water."

Lorel straightened her back, speaking in a controlled tone. "Just give the baby back to his mother."

He shook his head. "If only I had gotten more involved myself, I would have known it was you on the beach, right there before me. Maybe we could have just worked out an agreement."

"Agreement to do what? Use me as a science

experiment?" She kicked the knife lying on the carpet and threw her hands in the air. "Well here I am. Unarmed, unprotected. On an island where the sky is the limit for you, right? No feds or municipals breathing down your neck. I'm all yours. You don't need the baby now."

His head jerked back in surprise, then he sighed heavily. "Ms. Phoenix, you seem to underestimate the importance of what we are trying to do. Do you understand the shape this world is in? Why it is imperative that we look to new frontiers for human settlement?"

"I understand what shape PanDivinity has put the world in. And I am not one of the people under its spell. I don't believe in any of your lies."

"Why are you standing here right now?"

"Because I want you to give this baby back to his mother."

"But why are you standing here, on this island at the end of the world? What do you hope to get out of it?"

Lorel opened her mouth, but her words caught in her throat. "It doesn't matter anymore. Now, return the baby and do what you wish with me."

"Sacrifice. An outdated virtue in this day and age. What went wrong in your life that you learned to be this way? It only leads to unhappiness."

Lorel grimaced. "And humans have a divine right to happiness. Whatever the cost, right?"

"Exactly."

"Like I said, I never bought into what PanDivinity was selling. And I'm sure I'm not the only one."

"Well, maybe you should start a revolt."

She responded with silence, her feet planted firmly apart.

He crossed his arms, staring at her with lips pressed thinly together. "As I thought. You are less useful than you think in this world, Ms. Phoenix. You better hope you never have to face a PanDivinity rep."

"They have no face. Neither do you," she spat.

A laugh erupted from high in his chest, but no smile accompanied it. He gestured for Dr. Wong to approach. "Transport this infant back through the tunnel. The PanElites will escort you."

"No," Lorel said, "it has to be a siren. The PanElites have done enough damage."

He frowned. "Quite demanding. Dr. Wong, retrieve one of the subjects from the experimental wing."

Dr. Wong handed Dylan to Lorel and turned with a flip of her black hair to leave. Her heels clicked loudly out in the lobby. Lorel stared down at the tiny face now sucking intently on a rubber pacifier and smiled. "Hey, little one," she whispered then kissed his soft apple cheek. His eyes grew wide in recognition.

"I hope that satisfies you, Ms. Phoenix." Galton folded his arms.

Lorel remained silent, rocking the bundle in her arms. She would not be satisfied until Dylan was safely in the arms of a siren on his way to Isla and Sam.

Dr. Wong returned with a woman in a blue hospital robe wearing padded slippers. She had long dark hair and deep green eyes cast downward. Something in her expression bothered Lorel. What had this woman been through in the past twenty-four hours?

Lorel approached the siren and placed a hand on her shoulders, cradling the baby on her other arm. "This is Dylan. He's not even a day old. What's your name?"

"Mira." Her large round eyes searched Lorel's face, unsure what to think of her.

"My name is Lorel. I'm from the mainland but I've come to Rodinia at the invitation of your queen." Lorel placed the bundle in Mira's arms. "I need you to return Dylan to his mother."

She pulled the flashlight from her back pocket and handed it to Mira. Galton and Dr. Wong had crossed over to the genome map on the far wall, already back to business, but the PanElites near the doorway watched with beady eyes.

"Over here," Lorel said gesturing to Mira. She opened the door, casting light on the stairs that led into the bunker. "Go down these stairs and cross to the far side of the room. You will find a small round hole cut out of the wall. Crawl through it and you will be in a tunnel. Follow it to the end. It's dark and slippery, so use the flashlight. It will take you all the way to an underground bunker in Baltra. There you will find Mello Seaford as well as Isla and Sam Bishop, Dylan's parents."

Mira, who had already used the blanket to wrap Dylan in a pouch against her chest, nodded. Her eyes widened and Lorel could see so many questions in them. And fear.

"Thank you, Mira. Thank you." Lorel tried smiling to reassure her, but she knew her own eyes revealed the same fear.

Mira placed her hand on the knob. Out of the corner of her mouth, she whispered, "You cannot stay here. They will harm you."

Chilled air gusted from the bunker.

"Mira, listen to me," Lorel whispered.

"Let's not take all day," called Galton, then returned attention to Dr. Wong who was nodding and tapping furiously into her tablet.

"I have to stay here," Lorel continued, breathlessly, "There is no time to explain why. But they cannot come back for me. Tell them that if they do . . ." her eyes glanced up to the ceiling, "then Galton will take the baby for good."

"But, Dr. Wong said they don't—"

Lorel shook her head. "Just do it. And tell them—tell Mello—I'll be all right, I can take care of myself. Please."

Mira tilted her head and stared at Lorel, then nodded. "I will."

"Thank you," Lorel sighed, standing back to clear the way for Mira. "Now go quickly. And be careful."

With a quick smile, Mira started down the stairs with Dylan quiet on her chest. The dark space illuminated with the glow of the flashlight.

"And, Mira?" Lorel's voice echoed into the dark space.

"Yes?"

"Tell Mello thank you. For it all."

"Of course," she replied.

Lorel felt a lump rise in her throat as she watched

Mira disappear into the blackness. She swallowed hard then turned to Galton.

"What now?"

"Let's get to know each other." He smiled and walked over to his desk as though she was there to interview for a position.

Dr. Wong slinked out of the room with her head still buried in her glowing tablet. Lorel followed Galton to his desk. He seemed very settled in, and she had to blink to remind herself she was in Hotel Paraíso and not an executive office. The room, still aglow with scientific hologram images, was adorned with a couple of Louis XV style lounge chairs and an elegant coffee table. The Portuguese must have intended it as a cozy lounge off the main lobby.

"Please, take a seat." He sat in the upholstered chair and crossed his legs. Next to him was a mirrored side table with a decanter of amber liquor and a couple of crystal tumblers. He poured two glasses and handed her one.

Lorel lowered herself into a similar chair across from him and leaned back. The knife she had dropped now lay on his desk, a reminder that she had relinquished the last possible hope of defending herself from what was to come. Not that it mattered with PanElites everywhere. A calm resignation replaced the frantic rush of nerves that had been flooding her system for the past half hour.

"How did you know about me, before I knew myself?" As much as she hated to enter into a civil conversation with him, it was possible he had some answers.

"Well, Ms. Phoenix—" he began, uncrossing his legs and leaning forward.

"Why don't you cut the whole polite CEO act? I know who you are. I know you've killed people—Jake, the sirens in the bunker. And sirens *are* people, by the way. So just cut the goddamn act."

His brows darted upward, then fell, casting his face into a softer form that made Lorel's skin crawl. "I suppose it is nice to be myself," he said with a half smile.

"So. My question."

"I learned of you from the man who was supposed to protect you from . . . well, people like me." Galton chuckled, bemused. "He wasn't as good at protecting your secret as he thought. Poor Ben, always caught in the crossfire. If only he knew you were alive. And here, of all places."

The hair on Lorel's neck prickled and adrenaline coursed through her veins. "Ben?"

"You can't blame him. He did try."

"Blame who? Who is Ben?"

"My old associate. Ben Reshing."

"Reshing?" Lorel felt short of breath and abruptly took a gulp from her glass. It stung all the way down.

"Of course, you couldn't have known," He said, a sympathetic smile sweeping his face. "But Ben Reshing was your guardian."

FOURTEEN

JAKE

September 25, 2098
A day earlier
Atlantic Ocean

THE SAILBOAT TOSSED ABOUT like a toy boat in the South
Atlantic as Jake sat at the bolted in table below deck.
His beer sloshed within its can threatening to spill.
He chugged the remainder, then crushed the can in his
fist and tossed it into the trash bin across the room.

A loud rumbling shook the boat accompanied by a
flash of blue light. The thunderheads had shown their
purple faces as the sun descended, and Jake was hoping
for mercy in what looked to be a strong gale. The waves
were choppy, and he had been forced to cut the engine
well below maximum speed. Earlier that afternoon the
boat had passed the remaining landmass of Trinidad,
blasting over the water on hydrofoils in the fair weather.
It was now veering south by southeast in order to

241

circumvent the tip of South Africa and continue due east toward the coordinates of the island.

Their swift progress was due to the hydrofoils, solar panels and hi-tech diesel engines on the catamaran. His SEAL friend, who had loaned him the state-of-the-art vessel, had not exaggerated in saying the boat's speed was unmatched in its class. Jake, who prided himself on the mastering the art of sailing, felt like he was cheating. But this was not a cruise. It was a rescue mission. He ran exasperated fingers through his salty, windblown hair.

Had he been too hasty in dismissing Reshing last night? The man was a snake, but still, Jake could have gleaned more intel from him. Like a timeline. When exactly would DiviniGen arrive on this island? It would be crucial to get to Lorel before they did. He had a nagging feeling that he had not thought things through properly.

Jake rubbed his eyes wearily and slid his finger along the table to retrieve the holomap of his programmed route. The virtual seas quivered and a red dot flashed representing his location, far from any inhabitable land. Despite the high speed, he was still days away. And worse, something in the back of his mind kept torturing him. The thought that maybe Lorel did not want to be found. Reshing had mentioned she had a connection to this place, and Jake had already begun to feel resentment toward the invisible string that tied her there.

A violent cough came from the tiny bedroom beneath the stern followed by a loud thud. Jake glanced at his watch. Three in the morning.

"Henry? Are you okay?" He strained to hear over the

pelting rain and thunder.

Lorel's father emerged from the small door with a blanket around his shoulders and a germ mask stretched across his mouth and nose. His face still looked gaunt, almost gray, and his frame looked too fragile for the violently rocking boat. Jake had been shocked when he stepped out of a cab in his hospital gown at the marina. But at that point he could not turn the man away. Henry had sensed some sort of urgency in Jake at the hospital that had prompted him to follow.

"Just got tossed off the bed." He chuckled, wobbling on his bare feet as the boat dipped. "Still rather be here than in that stuffy hospital room."

"Beer?" Jake asked. He grabbed a cold can from the mini fridge.

"Ah, now that's something the nurses never offered." He cracked open the beer and slid into the booth opposite Jake. "So how far are we?" His face alit as he stared down at the holo.

"A few days away. We're here right now." Jake swiped a little puddle of beer distorting the tiny red holo dot. Henry tapped it and the coordinates 8.276, -43.138 flashed in red then faded.

"Back in my day it would have taken us a month just to get here. Amazing what they can do with these engines now." Henry shook his head at the rapidly increasing numbers on the odometer.

"Supplemented with solar power too, so we never run out of juice," Jake said.

They stared in silence for a few moments as the boat

sloshed back and forth.

"Henry, are you sure you have no idea why Lorel may have come to this island? I mean, if this turns out to be true," he added, being careful not to get Henry's hopes up. "Her boss seemed to think it was her decision."

A cloud darker than the afternoon's thunderhead passed over Henry's face, and he looked down.

"Henry, you're hiding something," Jake pried. He was trying to be gentle, but this was no time to hold back information.

Henry's eyes darted up again. "So are you." He frowned. "You know more than you're telling. You know if she's alive, she's in danger. So do I. We've just arrived at the information differently. I didn't realize until you said she had gone to an island to . . ." His voice trailed off and he began muttering something to himself.

"How do you know she's in danger? What do you know, Henry?" Jake clenched his fist in his lap, trying to refrain from banging it on the table.

Henry let out a long, muffled sigh through his germ mask. It was cut short by a brutal cough. Jake shoved on his own mask that hung around his neck and waited patiently for the coughing to subside.

After a long swig of beer, Henry recovered. He looked Jake with widening eyes, pulling a hand through his beard. "I planned to tell Lorel before I died. I suppose I've cut it close, but I have wanted to tell her for so long. So long, son."

Jake leaned forward with a galloping heart. "Tell her what, Henry?"

"The story of her other side. Her mother. What little I know, at least." He looked up at the ceiling and shook his head. "Her mother did not abandon us. Something much darker happened. See, her mother was not normal, not completely human."

Jake's breath caught in his chest. Not human. Was this one of the missing puzzle pieces? He nodded at Henry.

"I met her when I was stationed on a dig in the United Kingdom, around the time that the sea was lapping up the last of the old beach towns. The cliffside ones were safe, but we were working at an exposed beach called Brighton. About an hour outside London." Henry's eyes glazed in memory.

"She was the most beautiful woman I had ever seen, an ethereal creature. She was walking down the beach in a bathing suit with a sheer white tunic, just gazing out at the sunset. I was on the beach, sitting on a towel examining an artifact I had found in the excavation earlier that day. A shipwreck coin. It had a tiny figure of Neptune riding a dolphin on it. Probably from a few hundred years AD. I had seen a lot of shipwreck coins— they were usually turned into necklaces and sold for thousands—but never one so old, so precious.

"When she walked closer I was startled by her eyes. They were larger than any I had ever seen, and a blue deeper than the ocean. There were other things, her skin, her height . . . I remember feeling almost under a trance as she approached. Her hair was the color of the sunset, long and wild in the wind. As soon as I saw her, I knew I had to give her the coin."

Henry stopped, lost in another world.

"Go on," Jake said, touching the man's trembling hand.

"Sorry." Henry shook himself from the daze and lifted his mask to sip his beer. "I somehow mustered the courage to speak to her. The next evening she was wearing the coin on a gold chain and sitting across from me at a seaside restaurant, laughing. I still remember her laughter. It was like the sound of bells in heaven. This woman, this beautiful woman, became my wife only a few months later. She was desperate to leave the United Kingdom. She said it was too dangerous for her, but she would never tell me why. I still remember her so adamantly insisting. She said 'If you want to be with me, you must accept me with questions unanswered.' And how I wanted to be with her.

"She told me she had run away from home. When I asked her where home was, all she would tell me was that it was a 'secret island.' Then she would smile, distract me with her eyes, kiss me. She always made light of it, but I knew she was different. I knew she was from a world different than my own.

"Back in the states she was happy but always on guard. When she got pregnant, the fear compounded to the point of paranoia. She said people were following her. I never knew if it was true or if she had a vivid imagination. But I feared for her. And I began to fear for our unborn child as she grew more uneasy, and unstable. The birth was long, difficult. It didn't come natural for her. We almost lost her. Between the screams of labor, she would mutter that they were at the window watching. That they were coming. I thought it was just feverish talk, from the stress, you know?

"And then Lorel was born. Auburn hair. Eyes large and lovely like her mother's, but dark like mine. As soon as she was born, her mother burst into tears and held her for hours, staring at her, singing to her in a voice I can still hear today. But she looked at me that night with a heavy heart and said, 'If anything happens, don't ever tell her about me or her life will be in danger, Henry.' I never fully understood why."

Jake swallowed hard. The information was still gelling in his mind, but he was starting to realize Lorel's connection to this place. And to its people.

Henry's forehead glistened with sweat and Jake worried he would faint before finishing, but he continued. "The next morning she was gone. Just vanished from the hospital room without a trace. I held Lorel in my arms, gave her a bottle, a million kisses, but nothing really soothed her. The loss of her mother affected her deeply. She understood, even at a day old. And we never saw her mother again. I looked, for years. When Lorel was about ten, a man came to me, threatened me, told me I didn't know what I was dealing with. He said I should stop looking for her, that she was dead. And then he handed me the necklace with the coin, so I knew. He was telling the truth."

A tear rolled down Henry's face, pooling at the lip

of the germ mask. "I have been lying to my daughter. The doctors told her she has this disease, this mosaicism. I've always known my baby wasn't defective. She was just her mother's daughter. Different. But I did know that with the essence of her mother came an undefined danger. My lack of understanding, and the sudden loss of her mother, made me fear it even more. And so I let Lorel believe that she had this disease. Even worse, I let her believe that her own mother abandoned her. She grew up hating her."

Henry dropped his head in his hands, elbows propped on the table. "I wanted to, *meant to*, tell her the truth one day. But I had to protect her. Now I fear she has found out on her own." He looked up at Jake, eyes glistening and cheeks slick with tears. "I fear she's found her mother's homeland."

Jake scooted nearer to the sick man who looked as though he would choke on his grief. The sobs turned to coughing again. They were sinister coughs that came from deep within, escaping from his soul like demons. Henry was the kindest man Jake had ever met. It was heart wrenching to see him suffer in what were likely his last days. He put his arm around Henry's shoulder.

"You'll see her again. I know it. And then you can tell her everything."

The storm had calmed and Jake crossed to the navigation board to rev the engine to its maximum speed again. Every second counted.

The sun had not yet risen when Jake heard it. A deep sonorous horn sounded in the distance like a dying whale. He scrambled from his bunk and ran to the upper deck. A large ship was approaching the catamaran at a menacing pace, its bright lights slicing through the dark dawn. Jake's breath caught in his throat.

Pirates?

He was prepared with plenty of ammunition and arms, courtesy of his SEAL friend who had loaned him the boat, but the approaching ship was sizable. He and Henry were floating shark bait.

"Shit!" Jake paced the deck, which was still slick from the night's storm.

A cold breeze blew from the northwest, chilling him to the bone. *Maybe it was just a freighter gone off course. Maybe not.* He had to protect Henry, had to get to Lorel. His mind raced. He couldn't call the navy because he had basically gone AWOL.

The ship neared at a fast clip, looming on the horizon. The sun peaked above the water in a sliver of brightness. Jake squinted at the vessel. It appeared to be a navy warship or some official type of boat. That did not seem like pirates.

Jake grabbed his binoculars. The boat was now close enough that he could read the letters on the bow. *The Nautilus.*

It seemed like an official ship. And it was clearly heading directly for the catamaran. Jake dashed to the stern where the window hatch allowed a view down into Henry's bedroom. He banged on it.

"Henry! There's another boat approaching us. Stay down there and do not come up until I give you the word it's safe, okay?"

Henry looked up at Jake through the hatch bewildered but nodded in agreement.

Jake ran down below deck again, grabbed a semiautomatic las-gun from his stash, and slung it over his shoulder. Then he returned above and stood with his feet planted on the starboard. He was ready. He stared into the horizon as the enormous ship barreled forward like a steamroller. With a gasp, Jake realized the vessel was a C22Galleon, a twenty-second-century modern galleon.

He snatched his binoculars again and pressed them to his eyes. He had only heard about the C22s but didn't realize they actually existed yet in sailing condition. She was the ship of the next century, still a couple years away. A ship for all purposes under the sun, equipped with every capability the modern world offered. They called her a hero-ship for her superior ability as well as her look. Her body was sleek and black, made of a special alloy of steel and platinum. Her masts waved in a holo-active material of shimmering metallic evoking the image of a sixteenth century galleon. She was majestic.

Armed men stood guard around the perimeter decks. Jake could see their modernized las-weapons erected, the sharp harpoon metals glinting in the rapidly rising sun.

"Jake Ryder." A voice boomed over the water from an unseen sound source.

Jake dropped the binoculars and his hands clutched the chest strap of his gun with white knuckles. He watched in fascination as his face appeared on the holographic fabric of the rippling masts. His SEAL headshot.

In awe, Jake slowly raised his right hand, then pulled the gun from his body and lowered it slowly to the deck. This was no pirate ship. Whatever it was, he and Henry were at its mercy.

The magnificent vessel, now so close Jake felt dizzy, slowed to a stop and drifted toward the catamaran like an iceberg. Two armed men lowered automated anchors with steel hooks that looked like giant claws. The hooks gripped the railing of Jake's boat, binding him to the *Nautilus*. He gazed up at the men who towered at least twenty-five feet above him from their midlevel deck. Before he could make out their faces, they receded and another man's face appeared.

"Hello, Mr. Ryder."

Jake froze. Adrenaline surged through his veins. He felt like a fly trapped in a spider's web. Benjamin Reshing stared down at him unsmiling.

"Gone AWOL, have you? Don't worry, I cleared your status with the navy for the next several months." He awaited a reply but got none. "Care to join us? We'll be arriving in Rodinia by midnight tonight."

"Why are you doing this?" Jake yelled up to him, anger welling in his stomach.

"I tried to tell you why, but you wouldn't listen. This is bigger than you and Ms. Phoenix. A lot hangs in the balance. And I've had to call in Beacon, not something I wanted to do. But as you can see, they have the best resources in the world." He spread his arms wide in display of the grand vessel on which he stood. "Come with us, Mr. Ryder. We need you."

"Why? I assume you know the coordinates now. What do you need from me?"

"Because you love her. You will risk your life for her."

Jake looked down. Of course he would, but that was irrelevant. He still did not trust the man.

"And," Reshing paused, "now that Beacon is aware you know about Rodinia, they cannot let you return home. Nothing personal, they're just enforcing island policy."

"That's ridiculous. I will come and go as I please." Jake glanced down at the shiny anchors that hooked around his boat like an eagle gripping its prey.

"Well, why don't you tell that to Mr. Harnott yourself?"

"Who?" Jake asked.

"Richard Harnott, Guardian of Rodinia."

An hour later Jake stood outside on the windy deck in front of his cabin. His room was a tiny cubic box hemmed within the central portion of the ship. Large enough to fit no more than a bunk and a washbasin, its platinum walls were plated with blackglass and the doors slid open by voice command.

Henry was already sleeping in the cabin next door. A red holo scrolled across its door that read "Infected — Quarantine." The excitement had greatly weakened him, and Jake was worried about the speed of his deterioration. A nurse from the ship had visited him a few times already.

Jake gripped the slick chrome rail and looked down. The water was so far below he could not get a feel for its conditions. At the hull of the mammoth vessel, Jake glimpsed the side of his catamaran as it was tugged along behind. It looked like a tiny ragdoll next to the *Nautilus*.

Jake was still in awe of the ship. It belonged to the elusive subsidiary that Jake, privy to most secret organizations and rogue under societies around the world, had never heard a whisper of in his life.

Beacon, Jake mouthed the name under his breath with a frown and then shook his head. Remembering what Reshing had said about how they originally spawned from the East India Company, it made sense they owned such a ship. They were obviously powerful, but who were they really? How had they stayed under the radar all this time? And how far did their span of power reach?

Suddenly Jake felt nauseated.

The massive ship skimmed across the water at a dizzying speed. They would be there within hours and Jake's anxiety was mounting. He dropped to the floor and began his push-ups, a healthy distraction from the foreboding unknown.

"All settled in?"

Reshing sauntered down the breezeway and stopped in front of Jake squinting down at him. His skin was pallid under the midday sun as though being exposed to natural light was a rarity. "I want to share some things with you."

Jake looked at Reshing suspiciously but detected no deception in his tone. He hopped up from his plank position.

"Overdue. But go ahead." Jake used his T-shirt to wipe a layer of sweat from his forehead then slung it over his shoulder. Reshing clasped his hands behind his back and began walking toward the main deck. Jake fell in step next to him.

"I didn't want to involve Harnott because I didn't want to have to tell him that the pact has been broken. See, the people of Rodinia made a deal with DiviniGen, which is what ignited this unfortunate relationship with the megacorporation in the first place. But, the Beacon-Rodinian pact clearly states that the sirens are not to reveal themselves to the human world without express permission from Beacon.

"But didn't you say that's what they want anyway, to stay hidden from humans?" Jake glanced over his shoulder as they reached the end of the sleeping cabins and passed by a smooth blackglass wall. It displayed various maps and live feeds of strange rooms and tropical landscapes.

"Historically, yes. But people change. Once Beacon

became involved and began using Rodinia as their secret paramilitary base, they also became vested in keeping Rodinia a secret."

Jake nodded. "I see, so the pact has lasted so long because it has always been mutually beneficial."

"Any good pact is. Also, Beacon's roots are corporate so naturally profit is part of its motivation. The pact also says that the sirens may not share their indigenous resources with any other country or entity before Beacon. They have first right of refusal, if you will, to every grain of sand or nugget of gold on the island."

"And the sirens have not honored this?"

"No. They have been sharing one of their most precious resources."

"With who, DiviniGen?"

"And with us. The United States. At least we are supposed to be the recipients. However, you and I and Henry Phoenix will never see it. DiviniGen has been hoarding the resource to control the market."

"What is it?"

Reshing paused next to a cylindrical glass room labeled "Global Nautical Hub." Several people stood facing a bank of virtual screens, too engaged in operation to notice the two men peering inside.

"Erbium's active ingredient."

Jake pulled back in surprise and his eyes widened as a puzzle piece slid into place. This was why Lorel had gone to Rodinia. He thought of her obsession with concocting Erbium, her desperate and unyielding search for any amount of the miracle drug. She planned to save her father. "Erbium has disappeared from pharmacy shelves everywhere, out of stock in the entire US. Even the richest of the rich can't get it."

"Things went terribly wrong," said Reshing, resuming his stroll down the deck.

Jake stared down at the water churning below them in dark sapphires as they passed. "The pictures you showed me, of the people in Leo's factory. Those were the sirens."

"Yes. Galton began to set his sights on more than the island's resources. On the people themselves."

"The *Poseidon Project*. A new achievement. That's the lifeblood of all PanDivinity's children. Growth. New business opportunities grow the family."

"And increase their power," Reshing added. "See, my goal ever since I learned this was to find a way to make Erbium available to the entire world, not just the privileged few. I was secretly using my position within the Department to identify the enigma behind the purple algae's growth and discover if it flourished anywhere else in the sea besides Rodinia. If I could find another source, we wouldn't have to rely on the sirens for it and thus could use it freely without putting them at risk."

"Did you say *purple algae*?" Jake's skin tingled. "So that's what Lorel was helping you with, her top-secret assignment?"

"Analysis of the *porphuraphyceae*, yes. I was forbidden from divulging any details to her, of course. But I have been racing the clock with Galton. And when my private eye learned that he had discovered the existence of the sirens, and then activity at the factory started, I knew something had to be done."

"Leo." Heat rushed to Jake's cheeks. "Galton just disposed of him like he was nothing."

"He had a bullseye on your forehead too, you know. You can thank me later for diverting that one."

Jake stared at him, his face blanched. *He'd had his eye on the wrong enemy this whole time.*

"Galton will not let anyone get in the way of his grand plans," Reshing shook his head, a look of sympathy in his eye. "Don't worry, the search has ended. I was able to solicit a John Doe in your same dimensions from the morgue—both Ryder twins dead. Galton's PanElites will be none the wiser."

"What did I ever do to that man?" Jake banged the chrome rail with his fist.

"You killed his best henchman. Chan Sang Wu."

"The man at Lorel's apartment."

Reshing nodded. "He was PanElite. Undercover."

"She had indicated he was some random attacker, but I knew it had to be more. She has been in danger for longer than I realized. I should have—"

Galton put a hand up. "Do not blame yourself, Mr. Ryder. These are powerful people. Once you know the game they play, you have to find a way to beat them at it. Or you will lose. We have all been in danger."

"So why couldn't you get Beacon to help earlier?" Jake asked. "Aren't they protecting these people?"

Reshing's face flushed red in a rare moment of vulnerability.

"Years ago, Beacon dismissed me just before I was set to become Guardian."

Jake cocked his head in surprise. "You were going to be Guardian? In charge of protecting the sirens? And you ended up not even knowing how to get to Rodinia. Why?"

"I helped someone against the rules of the pact. It was someone very important in Rodinia. Someone very special." He glanced out at the ocean with a distant stare. "I bowed out gracefully, signing a contract to never disclose anything I had learned, relinquishing any access to information about Rodinia. Most regretfully, its location. That is when I threw myself into my research and focused on ocean conservation. I knew what was out there."

Jake felt touched by the tenderness in Reshing's voice, the sincerity.

"When I learned that the sirens had broken the pact by making contact with humans, through a PanDivinity company no less, I feared for them. I know what Beacon is capable of, if betrayed. I knew how angry Harnott would be. He feels exposing the sirens to the human world is a threat to both species."

"A threat how?" Jake asked. There was more to this story.

"In ways I cannot get into," he said with a frown. "Anyway, I did not want to tell them what the sirens had done. But I had to. That was the only way to get the island's coordinates, which have been kept under lock and key."

"I see." Jake bit his lip. "I'm sorry. I should have given you the coordinates, I should have listened."

Reshing waved a hand in the air. "What's done is done. The sirens will have help now."

Something about the expression on Reshing's face caused Jake's stomach to dip. At what cost would that help come?

"So if Beacon doesn't succeed in ending Galton's game," Jake said, "DiviniGen will have a monopoly on the algae *and* on its people. And Erbium's prize ingredient may be exploited to extinction."

"Yes," said Reshing, "a fate the same as the rest of the world's resources."

Jake glanced back at the cabin area of the ship where Henry lay dying. This rescue mission was about more than Lorel. More than Henry. It was about everyone. "What are we going to do?" he asked.

"Come with me. There's someone I want to introduce you to." Reshing turned down a breezeway leading toward the center of the ship. A silvery mast nearby flapped loudly above him as he mounted an inner stairway, gesturing for Jake to follow.

The images on Jake's puzzle had begun to form a fuller picture with an evolving narrative. A PanDivinity logo of the Gemini twins hovered in his mind, floating in a pool of blood. A hooded man who once appeared sinister and dark now stepped into a beam of light, illuminating the ugliness around him. Ben Reshing was not the man Jake thought he was. He pulled his T-shirt back on and followed him up the stairs.

"Jake Ryder, meet Master Richard Harnott," Reshing said as they entered the sleek stateroom at the zenith of the *Nautilus*.

Cool air washed over him as Jake entered the strange room. It looked like a mix of a spaceship control center and a corner executive office with a view of the vast sea beyond. The floors and all four walls were platinum, shiny and sleek. A stern-faced man with midnight-blue hair and dark eyes sat behind a platinum desk.

"Welcome to the *Nautilus*. On board here, you can just call me Captain Harnott." He winked, and a chill passed over Jake's skin. "Take a seat."

"Thank you." Jake and Reshing both sat down in the translucent bucket seats across from Harnott.

"So Reshing tells me you're a SEAL?" He raised his brows to sharp points.

"Yes, sir." The Naval Officer in Jake came out as he felt an automatic deference to the man before him.

"What ranking?"

"Lieutenant Commander. I lead a team assigned to combat pirate activity on a global level."

"Yes, yes, I know all about that." He clasped his hands neatly over a pile of holosheets on his desk. Jake noticed a glass paperweight on them just like the one he had seen in Reshing's penthouse.

"Ben informs me that you were on your way to this island already. That there is someone there you care for?"

"Yes, sir."

"Good. We don't know how things are going to play out on this operation, but we will need your help. The situation is disheartening. Deeply disappointing to be frank. I don't know what will come of the pact now, but that is a discussion for later. Now, we must focus on getting to the island."

"I will help however I can. That's what I was on my way to do anyway," Jake stated, straightening his back.

"Start by familiarizing yourself with the information on here." Harnott handed him a microchip. "Dock this into the wall of your room. It contains the map of Rodinia. It also has Galton's *Mandate List*, something best read in private. The details are . . . disturbing to say the least."

Jake took the microchip and shoved it into his pocket. "Thank you, sir."

"You are under our command now, Lieutenant Ryder." Harnott leaned back in his chair, with his hand on the paperweight. "Understand, you cannot leave this ship, or the island, until you have our permission. And Lalique's, of course. It is in the bylaws, and the bylaws must be strictly adhered to. That is how we've made the pact work for so many centuries, you see."

"Who is Lalique?" Jake asked, skirting the first part of Harnott's statement. This man may think he was in control of Jake's freedom, but he was mistaken. Jake had no commanding officer on this mission.

"She's the queen of Rodinia," Reshing clarified.

"*Queen?* So they have a whole governing structure?" Jake asked, scooting his chair closer.

"They are highly sophisticated, Mr. Ryder," said Harnott. "We are not arriving on an island of tribal primates, or the lost society of surviving Neanderthals.

This subspecies of human, I would go so far as to say, are *higher level*," he whispered the last words as though ashamed to admit the inferiority of their own species.

Could that be the threat Reshing had alluded to earlier?

Jake glanced past Harnott, his eyes ensnared in the vast expanse of sea ahead of them. *Who were these people?*

Back in his cabin Jake slid the microchip into a small docking port on the wall, then stood back as the hologram materialized. The *Mandate List* emerged on the blackglass first. As Jake skimmed the document his stomach churned.

.

CLASSIFIED
Property of DiviniGen Inc.
Mandate List for Transgenetic Experimentation on Live Subjects*

Round 1
-Collection of Siren Blood Samples
-Live Organ Biopsies and Gene Collection
-Examination and Analysis of Genotype
-Testing of Species Capabilities

Round 2
*-Intake of Human Volunteers***

-Infestation of Germline
-DNA Injection Tests (Bioluminescence, cold blood, etc.)
-Leg Fusion Experimentation
-Gill Implantation
-Poseidon Prototype Implementation

*Need Live Hybrid Species
**Confined on *Celebration*

With mouth agape Jake scrolled through the pages of the document. It only got worse. The company had grand plans, grander than Jake could ever have imagined. Details of the plans were highly classified with explicit instruction from Galton that no one at PanDivinity, their own parent company, could know. They had several iterations of "product" to roll out with the first "output" to hit the market in 2100.

First it would be a GAP, a Gene Altering Pill. Similar to a PAP, which temporarily altered a person's genetic phenotype, the GAP would cause the permanent mutation of their mitochondrial DNA. In a period of six months, a human could develop aquatic survival capabilities similar to the siren species. With these adaptations, they could begin to repossess some of the coastal cities that were submerged but they would still be limited in breathable time underwater to three hours.

Still not their perfect prototype for underwater living, Jake thought.

He scanned the development section. It appeared

that live human subjects were needed to infest the human germline, essentially mutating their genes. *How could they possibly do this to people without harming them?* Jake swiped back to the asterisks on the first page.

*Intake of Human Volunteers** led to:

**Confined on the* Celebration

His mouth went dry. They had their human subjects. And Jake would bet his life they were not voluntary. Galton was far more sinister than he could have imagined. He planned to use this island to get away with torture in the name of scientific research.

Jake scrolled his fingers down the blackglass, scanning the document, and shook his head in disbelief.

The next iteration would be the germline transfection, a process in which genes would be transferred from one cell to another. Siren to human. During this process DiviniGen would choose the most desirable of the siren genes to transfer, creating a new species superior to both human and siren. Parents could birth a super aquatic human through in vitro fertilization, with the purchase of the patented seeds. This offspring would have aquatic capabilities exceeding the offspring of two GAP mutated individuals, breathing underwater for up to twelve hours.

And finally their grand finale product — the Poseidon Prototype. This completed prototype would serve as the model for what all humans could then achieve, upon purchase and consumption. The new and improved aquatic version of themselves that could live in the underwater city of the future. That was the grand vision.

Restore the drowned cities, colonize the sea floor. Create an empire.

Jake flashed back to his conversation with Leo on the back porch of their old house. They had discussed undersea colonization, an idea abuzz in the news among radical politicians and companies. How far away and unbelievable it seemed back then. If they had only known how much those fantastical plans would change their destiny. Grief constricted his throat and he swallowed hard, then swiped to the next page.

The Poseidon Prototype "deliverable" was due to hit the market by 2102. Even as a biologist himself, Jake had a hard time comprehending how this creature was to come to fruition. It appeared the plan was for this humanoid to exist as a superior being to the siren-derived aquatic human. It would have retractable gills, scales that appeared in water, an eternal tolerance for oceanic depths and lengths of time underwater. It would be the "human of the future," the pioneer settler of the undersea cities.

Galton's vision seemed to be that humans over time would literally morph as a race into this species. A race adapted for survival in a damaged world. But this was no natural selection.

Jake clenched his jaw, swiping to the last section, *Marketing & Investor Relations Strategy*. The first and "most critical" step to garner investor support was to acquire a hybrid species. The hybrid was to be taken on a private roadshow to prove to potential investors that this was a credible venture worth pouring billions into.

It would be essential for commercial success. His eyes skimmed to the last line in red font.

"Hybrid Candidate: Lorelei Phoenix, Age 25, Washington, DC." Then a comment next to it: "Operation Cancelled — Deceased."

Jake shivered and a horrid realization flashed into his mind. These bastards were targeting Lorel.

FIFTEEN
LOREL

September 27, 2098
Paraíso, Rodinia

L OREL STARED AT GALTON in awe. All this time Reshing had been watching over her? It couldn't be true. It made no sense. How could she trust what this man was telling her anyway? Galton was a master of lies and manipulation. Selfish and greedy. And so was Reshing.

Wasn't he?

She set her jaw and thought of her father. *Focus on what matters now.* She didn't have time to dwell on the past. Still, a prick of guilt stung her and she realized she would never see him again and could never reconcile — if Galton spoke the truth.

Galton glanced down at his watch, gold with flashy zircon crystals around the face. "It's getting late and we have a big day tomorrow here in paradise. Let's show Ms. Phoenix to her room."

He stood up, gesturing to the PanElites.

"How convenient that you already have a room for me," she quipped as the two muscular men rushed to her side.

"This room has been waiting to be filled by someone like you for a very long time," he said as he walked out the door.

Following at Galton's heels the PanElites escorted her out into the hotel lobby and down a carpeted hallway that branched off toward the east wing. Gold paint peeled from the humidity-exposed plaster walls and a musky scent mixed with the salty indoor air. All the guestroom doors were closed, but she could hear faint moans and see slivers of strange light coming from some of them.

"So I saw you have quite an expansive genome map already. Do you plan to make one for hybrids too?" she asked, mentally preparing for whatever lay ahead.

Galton slowed his pace to walk next to her.

"Oh, you misunderstand. It is not your genes that we need now. We have already found plenty of desirable phenotypes and obtained a blood sample from the infant. Your value lies simply in your presence. We need you for something much more important. For now I hope you'll be comfortable as we do a bit of stress testing. Nothing to be scared of. And please, take care of yourself. Your physical appearance will be critical once we are on the road."

Lorel stared at him, but his face gave away no answers. This was a curveball. Her hair prickled and she halted in place, but one of the PanElites jabbed her back with his gun.

"Move," he barked.

They came to an elevator bank and stepped into an open cab then descended to the bowels of the old hotel.

Galton looked at her. "I can't tell you how happy I am that you showed up here, Ms. Phoenix." He smiled and his eyes rolled over her like molasses.

"Where are you taking me?" she asked as the PanElite squeezed his fingers into her shoulder and pushed her forward. Galton stood unfazed as the elevator doors parted. The need to run was hard to resist, but this was her choice.

"I want to show you one thing before we take you to your room. So that you understand." Galton said as he switched on the overhead lights of a long concrete hallway. The air smelled dank and Lorel sucked in air through her nose as the PanElite clutched her shoulder again.

"Can you tell this brute to get his hands off of me, please? I already agreed to come. You don't need to treat me like a prisoner," she said, casting a searing glance at the bald man.

The PanElite grimaced. Galton nodded and he released his hold on her with a grunt.

They reached a set of double doors that Galton swung open to reveal a dimly lit room with concrete floors. They were back in the underground bunker, which had been repurposed in this area as the hotel kitchen. The smell of rusted metal mixed with mildew. The air was chilly and Lorel hugged herself tightly as a shiver passed over her.

The heels of Galton's shiny leather shoes clicked on the floor as he led them into the recesses of the kitchen. They passed at least three antiquated ovens, shelves filled with copper pots and pans, a giant porcelain sink. At the end of the last room a stainless steel door with a long latch shone metallic in the light. The freezer.

Galton paused in front of it. He straightened his back, ran a hand down the front of his suit as though preparing to step into an important meeting. "Come," he beckoned to her.

Lorel stood unmoving. One of the PanElites shoved her toward Galton and she stumbled, bumping the freezer door. He snickered. "Don't worry, Ms. Phoenix. This is not your room. It is already occupied."

"I'm not worried. I have no doubt your accommodations will be great," she replied with an icy stare. Something told her she did not want to see what was inside the freezer.

Galton's eyes scanned the length of her legs, her stomach, her breasts as they heaved up and down over the butterflies winging through her chest.

"You are quite attractive. I had no idea. But after seeing these people it makes sense. There is something otherworldly about their beauty. Of course, you possess only half." He laughed. "And not nearly that of the queen. What a woman. She is PanDivinity material."

Lorel saw a dark flicker of lust in his eyes. "I doubt that."

"Anyhow, your looks will be helpful for the roadshow. We want to dazzle and delight the investors."

"What do you mean *roadshow*?" Lorel narrowed her eyes.

"Patience, Ms. Phoenix." He returned his attention back to the freezer and began unfastening the door. "You know, when I found her I thought she was the only one who existed, at least within our reach. But then I learned of you and my search began. When I thought you'd drowned, I feared it would never work. But then we found Mello, and our way to the island," he lowered his voice to a whisper, "and here you are."

He let the chain of the freezer door drop with a clang and the door parted a few inches letting out wisps of chilly air. Galton reached his hand out and caressed her face, her cheeks. His fingers felt rough and cold.

"Your skin is oddly smooth, like theirs. Hairless and thick. Your eyes, so large. It's a beautiful gene blend, is it not, Christopher? I'm ashamed we didn't engineer it ourselves. Even just a PAP for the stunning eyes."

"It would have sold like wildfire, sir," said the PanElite then grunted in salacious agreement, running his tongue lewdly along his upper lip. Lorel flinched.

Galton swung the freezer fully open with a chilly gust and walked inside, then turned to her. "Well? Won't you come in and meet her?"

Lorel stepped inside. Cold air washed over her body. She let out a breath that immediately condensed in a thick cloud of vapor. The spacious freezer was a temporary morgue. Displayed on a table was a body sliced cleanly into several sections. Thin sheets of glass divided each one enabling a cross-sectional view of the internal organs. The girl's head was intact and well preserved. Silvery blonde hair, neatly groomed, shimmered in the cold fluorescent light. A thick black lock twined through the hair on one side, framing her face.

Lorel's head jerked back. *It was her.* She prayed silently that Mello would never see this. Her stomach roiled, and she felt like throwing up though it had been hours since she had eaten anything.

"This is Nia. Isn't she lovely?" Galton mused, circling the young girl's body and peering inside her upper torso with fascination. "The billion-dollar discovery just washed ashore right at my feet."

Lorel backed away from him in disgust, her hands finding a frosty wall. The CEO had reached a new level of ruthlessness. The door was closed and escape was not an option with the PanElites outside.

"Oh don't worry, you won't end up like her. Sadly, she was already dead in the orca's belly when I found her. Remember?" His eyes glittered. "But she was a rare find, a diamond in the rough. Until we found you."

"Please . . ." Lorel wanted him to stop. She needed to get out of the freezer, away from this poor girl's butchered body.

"It has been a long day, hasn't it?" He straightened up and pushed open the door open.

Lorel stumbled out, gasping to inhale the fresher air. Before stepping out, he whispered something inaudible to the severed corpse, then turned to the PanElites.

"Christopher, please show Ms. Phoenix to her new room now." He smiled at Lorel, his teeth glowing as white as his hair under the lights. "Sleep tight, my dear. Pray your friends are satisfied with the return of their infant and do not come looking for you. We begin Stage Two tomorrow and cannot afford to be disturbed."

With that he turned and walked away, his heels echoing down the lacquered concrete to the elevator bank. One PanElite followed him leaving Lorel alone with Christopher who was digging into the pocket at his massive thigh. Lorel watched in alarm as he pulled out handcuffs. Before she could blink he had jerked her hands behind her back. Cold metal cut into her wrists as he clasped them, and she winced.

"Shut up," he snarled.

He grabbed her shoulder, nearly pulling it out of socket, and dragged her out of the kitchen. They took the elevator up to the lobby level. It was dark outside, but through the windows Lorel noticed the perimeter of the building and the beach were filled with PanElites standing guard. DiviniGen had turned Hotel Paraíso back into a fortress.

Lorel thought of the sirens. *Had they transitioned to Plan B?*

DiviniGen had already relinquished their right to a peaceful visit. Lorel wondered how much had been seen through the hidden security cameras. If Baltra's bunker had been compromised, perhaps others had as well. Likely there was no trace of her whereabouts. And Mello had probably already received Mira's warning not to come after her.

It was what she had wanted, insisted on. But at the

273

thought Lorel suddenly felt weak. Why was she here now? It *had* been an act of sacrifice, a way to give herself in exchange for Dylan. To save him. Now it seemed Galton didn't even need her. Not for the reasons she had thought. Dylan was returned home, Galton had his hybrid blood sample, and she was being dragged to god-knows-where by a henchman.

First chance she had, she would escape.

Christopher loosened his grip as they passed through the empty lobby. She glanced over her shoulder at the hotel entrance.

"Don't even think about it," he said tightening his grip.

She cursed under her breath then picked up the pace so he wasn't dragging her. Shadows loomed from corners, and the damask wallpaper seemed to have eyes embedded in the ornate pattern. They rounded a corner, exited through a side door and descended a curving limestone stairway into the empty courtyard. Only yesterday morning Lorel had stared down at the siren volunteers there.

Moonlight cast a bluish hue across the crumbly stone paths and empty fountains. The sweet smell of jasmine permeated the hot air giving Lorel a fleeting sense of comfort. White orchids glowed like tiny ghosts in the night, peeking out from tree branches and vined walls of shrubbery.

"This way." Christopher had loosened his grip on her and was now leading them down a narrow footpath that cut through a thick forest of bamboo.

After a few minutes the shoots became too dense to traverse the path. The ringed poles bent so low that they crisscrossed at eye level, creating a leafy barrier. With a groan of frustration, Christopher pulled a hand machete from his belt full of weapons and began slashing. Lorel could hear animals screeching and scattering in the surrounding forest.

"Where does this go?" she asked, afraid to hear the answer. The hotel was now several yards behind them.

"A tourist attraction," he said curtly.

"How do you all know the layout of this place so well? You've been here for what, barely three days?"

"A PanElite recon team with DiviniGen resources, lady," He scoffed. Then, unable to resist the opportunity to gloat, he continued, "We have holo scanners that can spit out a 3-D map of this entire freak of an island, from sea level to the top of that damn volcano within seconds."

"Oh." She gulped. His gloating had worked. Reconnaissance technology was beyond her comprehension. And unfortunately for the sirens, beyond theirs too. No wonder DiviniGen had gained the upper hand so swiftly. It was impossible to hide.

Christopher continued slicing away at the bamboo in a figure eight motion. Lorel cringed every time the blade passed within inches of her head in his backswing. He seemed to enjoy it more than necessary. Finally, the path ended at a set of French doors. He shoved the machete back in his belt and kicked one of them open with ease.

She looked up. It seemed like a building made entirely of glass, like a giant greenhouse. It was tucked deep in the woods on the farthest perimeter of the hotel grounds. She would not be surprised if they were connected underground somehow. Even the stucco trim and certain architectural features were the same as the hotel. The Portuguese must have built it to be some sort of appendage to the original building.

They entered the greenhouse to a small foyer. An old wooden sign read "Bem-vindo ao Arboretum" in faded letters. Off to one side she could see trees and flowering vines, an indoor botanical garden area that had grown wild, long neglected. Branching off the foyer on the other side was a narrow hallway. Another sign said "Aquário" with an arrow.

With a jerk, Christopher shoved her toward the hallway. One side of it was a glass wall facing outside to the thicket of bamboo. A polished wooden bench ran along it. The other side was also a wall of glass, from floor to ceiling, but its interior was dark. Christopher flipped a light on and Lorel saw her reflection in the glass. She looked so small next to the colossal mercenary. Her eyes slowly adjusted to the space beyond.

The room was large and empty. Its dirty concrete floor sloped down to a circular drain in the center. On the back wall, which was painted a pale aqua, a cluster of rubber hoses dangled from a ledge toward the ceiling. Suddenly Lorel realized what she was staring at. Christopher was not totally wrong. This had been meant at one time to be a tourist attraction. The room in front of her was an enormous tank. If filled, it would be large enough to hold a school of dolphins, maybe even a whale.

Before she could comment on her observation, Christopher was unlocking her cuffs. He yanked open a small side door leading to the empty aquarium.

"Get in," he demanded.

She stood frozen, shaking her head in defiance. "No."

"Get in there, bitch, now!"

He shoved her inside the tank, and she stumbled on the sloped floor.

"You'll get breakfast brought out in the morning. If you're lucky." His voice bounced off the bare walls. Then he slammed the door with a bang and cut the lights. Lorel watched him saunter down the hall and disappear into the path of bamboo.

Fighting back tears, she sunk to the floor and pulled her knees to her chest. She had been abandoned in some sort of giant fish tank in the middle of the night and not one siren knew where she was because she had been so foolish. Imagining Dylan in Isla's arms was her only consolation.

She thought of Jake and a fresh wave of grief washed over her. Had Galton really had him killed? Nothing the man said could be trusted, yet she would not put it past him.

"Jake." A heaviness crushed her heart as she whispered his name aloud. *What did you do to get yourself involved in this?*

Now she would never get the chance to feel his embrace again, to tell him all that had changed about her. To tell him who she really was.

And how was she going to get back to her father

now? She had thought that Galton would be done with her once he had extracted her hybrid genes. But he had other plans in store for her, plans seeded well before she came to the island. Helplessness engulfed her like a cold blanket. She had made a terrible mistake and now there was no turning back.

Too tired to resist any longer, she let the tears fall. Images of her father lying alone in his hospital bed tortured her. Had he lost his daughter as well as his wife? So many secrets he had kept from her all this time. Lorel knew it was to protect her and because of that she could forgive him, but it was harder to shake the lifelong resentment she had built up toward her mother.

A monkey crept up to the window outside with a tiny baby clinging to its back. It looked in the window, and upon seeing its own reflection, screeched and scampered back into the woods. Lorel sniffled. Something about this place, this journey, had opened up old wounds. Now knives twisted inside them with excruciating bursts of emotion.

Lorel took a deep breath, trying to calm herself. In her nose and out her mouth, slowly. *Slowly.* Her long breaths echoed in the darkness and her mind mercifully went blank. With each exhale the tiny embers of resentment that had been smoldering inside her for so long escaped until finally she was left with a bittersweet yearning for a mother she did not remember.

A siren. A woman. A mother who had not abandoned her after all. Hours passed until finally she laid her head peacefully against the hard floor and fell into a restless sleep.

"To what do I owe the honor?"

A man's voice awoke Lorel with a start. It sounded far away. Bright morning sunbeams sliced through the bamboo forest beyond the aquarium casting shards of light against the aqua floor and back wall of the tank. Lorel felt groggy and her body ached from lying on the concrete. She glanced around, her nerves shooting to a heightened sense of awareness. There was no one in sight.

Was she hearing things?

But there it was again. And this time a woman's voice too. She looked up. The sounds were coming from a vent in the ceiling. The air duct system must be connected with the hotel.

"Release her," the woman spoke with authority.

Lorel heard what sounded like a door closing. Then the man let out a sigh.

"Our aim has been to satisfy. I thought you had come here to say thank you."

Sarcasm dripped from his every word. The man was Galton, Lorel was certain.

He continued, "We have almost completed Stage One, quite successfully I'm pleased to say, with your people unharmed —"

"Unharmed? There were five people dead in our bunker on Baltra. Blood has been shed. We have been watching your every move. So thank you for your *humane* treatment of our volunteers, but the damage has been done. You will sorely regret what you have unleashed."

"I am truly sorry about your people in the bunker, but had they been more cooperative it would not have come to that. We never intended to harm the infant, of course."

"The baby is back with his mother now. But you have stolen a very special guest of ours."

"All of the siren volunteers will be released from Hotel Paraíso tomorrow. Then we admit our human subjects and the real work begins. Surely you have no concerns about how we perform research upon *them*."

Lorel's heart lurched at the implication.

"And which category have you put her in?" the woman asked.

"Ah, good question. Ms. Phoenix will return with us to the United States. She will be part of our . . . marketing effort."

Lorel swallowed as she remembered his plan for her. The roadshow. As desperately as she wanted to get home, it was not going to be with Francis Galton, as his secret marketing slave.

"She belongs here. Release her."

"Unfortunately there is nothing you can do about that."

"We have been nothing but cooperative, but it has been by choice, not by force. You have no idea what we are capable of. What this island can do to you."

"The island?" He scoffed. "Let me lay it out for you

in business terms. My team is well equipped and well resourced. We want no harm to come to any of you. We only want what we came for. Do not resist, and no more blood will be shed. We are business folks, not savages."

"We are all savages inside. We just have the decency to suppress those instincts. Unless it is warranted."

"You are a wise woman."

"Return Lorelei Phoenix to us." The woman lowered her voice.

"Why is this girl so important to you? You all have no need for a hybrid. In fact, from my research I thought it was rather unaccepted in your culture to . . . dilute your precious genes," Galton said. "You must hate her. Do you want to do away with her, is that it?"

"On the contrary, I love her. She is my daughter."

At first the words entered Lorel's ears uncharted. Then an explosion of joy shattered through her body and tears welled in her eyes. She stood up with a rush of euphoria.

Her mother. Her mother was alive. Her mother was here *. . . for* her.

"Lorelei Phoenix, your daughter?" said Galton with amusement, then added in a pensive voice, "So you were Reshing's downfall. It all makes sense now."

What did he mean by that? How could there possibly be a connection between Reshing and this siren?

Suddenly Lorel's senses kicked into overdrive. She paced back and forth inside the tank straining to hear the conversation. Who was this woman? Her voice had sounded familiar but Lorel couldn't place it.

S I R E N S

The conversation resumed from the ceiling vent and she froze, feet planted askance over the drain. Her reflection in the glass stared back at her like a statue.

"Leave Benjamin out of this. That is in the past," the woman said.

Galton stopped laughing. "Now I see why you've come alone. This is your little secret, one you have been hiding from your own people. You have broken the golden rule," he condescended as though reproaching an employee from behind his desk.

The woman responded with controlled rage. "Release her or I will unleash this island against you and your people."

"I'm sorry, but I cannot do that."

If he was threatened by her, it did not come through in his voice.

"What do you want?"

"Oh it is not about what *I* want. It is about DiviniGen Incorporated. What does our *global customer* want?" he said with the rhetoric of a corporate speech. "A good CEO is always looking out for the next big product. Do you think you can provide that? Does this *island of plenty* have more for DiviniGen?"

Lorel could see him steepling his fingers, raising one bushy white brow.

"We can continue to supply the algae. Anonymously, of course," she bargained. "And we can teach you how to farm it. Only a siren can harvest it, you could never extract it on your own. But we could help."

"Tempting, but no. The truth is that Erbium is on the

282

backburner as we have something much more lucrative in the pipeline now."

"But with Erbium, you would have the entire human world as your loyal customer. Aren't those the kind of global profits you are looking for?"

"I like your thinking. Too bad you aren't working for me. You may be surprised to hear, though, that it is more than profits we are after. We want to change the world. Don't you see? Humans will soon begin populating the floors of the ocean. Forget building cities on the moon!" His voice began to take on a manic quality. "It will negate the need for Erbium, considering the siren species' superior immune system and life span. In essence we are effectively *upgrading* the human race. And between you and I, the human population has gotten out of control. What are we now . . . thirteen billion? A little pruning is necessary, don't you think?"

"What then? There must be something you want. Not for your company but for *you*." She was digging for a hook, trying to appeal to any human desire Galton may have.

There was a sound of heavy breathing. He responded gruffly, his voice lowered. "I'll tell you what *I* want."

There was a pause, then a shuffling of feet as he continued, "How lucky I am you came here alone."

Suddenly there was the sound of a struggle. Furniture turning over and then muffled screams.

Was he hurting her?

"Get off me!" the woman yelled in a muffled cry. The scuffle continued. Cloth ripping. Grunting.

Lorel's blood began to boil, imagining the worst. She ran to the glass wall and began banging, screaming. But it was useless. She dropped to the floor of the aquarium and pulled her knees to her chest.

Then another cry came. It was from him.

"Go ahead," said the woman in a cold voice. "Call in your mercenaries."

"I . . . I had no idea of your strength. Your skill," he spoke between moans. "It is not often that someone surprises me."

"Sirens learn to defend themselves at a young age. It is the call of nature."

"Your kick certainly has a bite." He let out another pained sigh.

"You are nothing but a weak old man with the illusion of power. If you think you can have me you are mistaken," said the woman.

"How old are you?" he sneered.

"Decades beyond you."

"Yet look at you. Your hair, your skin . . . this face."

"Step back."

"Forgive me. You're just so beautiful. By the way, where does *this* come from?"

Lorel strained to picture them in her mind. What was he referring to?

"From a place you will never go."

"Is it the same place the gold comes from?" he pressed. "Because ever since we arrived here, I have had my people scanning the surface maps, x-ray maps. Nothing. No mines. No buried treasure troves. Can you dispel this mystery for me?"

With a jolt, Lorel remembered her conversation with Mello. *DiviniGen will never find out about the mines, much less penetrate them . . .*

"I can, but I will not," the woman returned. "You and your people will never understand this island. It demands respect if it is to reveal its mysteries to people."

"Quite all right. I have a knack for unraveling mysteries," he said.

"Misunderstanding can come at a high cost. I warn you."

"Understand this. If wiping you and your people from this forsaken place is what we must do, then we will. And I would be only too happy to start with your daughter. She is not so rare as I once thought."

A loud clap echoed in the room. Lorel bit down on her lip so hard she drew blood.

"How dare you?" he bellowed. "The first time was amusing, but this I find no humor in." After a pause, he called, "Enter!"

Lorel could hear the sound of a door opening, then boots shuffling across the floor.

"No please . . . let go of me."

"Your power here means nothing to us, understand? You are the one who has underestimated. We will take what we need from this island with or without your help. You want to see your daughter? Let's go."

Lorel's limbs began to shake and a mix of excitement and terror pulsed through her veins. *They were coming.*

The woman winced. Then a door slammed. Then

silence.

She froze but her body buzzed with adrenaline. Instincts told her to run but there was nowhere to go. After a few minutes the door to the hallway opened. Galton stormed in ahead of two PanElites who dragged a woman behind them.

At first Lorel could only make out the ruffling of pale green fabrics that trailed along behind her and a streak of red hair. Then the door to the tank swung open and the PanElites shoved her inside. She stumbled forward toward the drain just as Lorel had the day before. The door slammed shut with a dampened echo.

"Here!" Lorel reached out a hand and the woman quickly steadied herself with it, then lifted her head.

For an instant Lorel was blinded by a flash of light. A crystal. Then a face, a beautiful face. The eyes staring back at her, deep blue and flickering with anger, were the eyes of the siren queen.

Before Lorel could react, Lalique flung her arms around her and squeezed. "You're okay, thank god you're okay," she said.

Suddenly Lorel's world disappeared. The glass walls melted away and she was standing under the warm sun. She felt enveloped by a love she had never consciously felt before. Maternal love.

"Is it true?" she said, pulling away. "Are you my mother?"

Lalique met Lorel's eyes. "It's true."

A part of Lorel wanted to fall into the arms of this

strange woman before her, but something stopped her. The anger she had been holding onto for so long would not depart so easily. She backed away from Lalique, shaking her head. "You're alive."

"Lorel, I have so much to—"

Lorel put her hand up, her expression hardening. "I thought you were dead. My father thinks you *are* dead. But you're alive, on this island, this paradise," Lorel said, not caring how disgust filled her voice.

"I couldn't come for you, it was impossible. You have to understand."

"Understand? You abandoned me. Us. I grew up without a mother. And my father, he was in love with you." She narrowed her eyes, stepping closer to Lalique. "Now I see why I'm really here. I'm of no help to the sirens. You brought me to this island on the other side of the world because I'm your daughter."

Lorel meant it as an accusation, but she felt a conflicting sense of gratitude. Her mother *had* brought her back. She had never stopped loving her, Lorel knew it. She could see it written all over Lalique's face and feel it in her presence.

"I will explain everything one day, I promise," said Lalique.

Lorel sighed, stubbornly unwilling, or unable, to let go. She said nothing in response, only turned her back, looking out the aquarium glass to the bamboo with crossed arms. Seconds passed, or maybe minutes. Lorel couldn't tell, her heart was beating so fast. Lalique approach her from behind, then gently place a hand on her shoulder. Lorel turned back around to face her.

"Lorel, I have been terrified of this day. The moment I kissed your forehead in the hospital and said goodbye, I knew you may never forgive me. That you may grow up hating me. But I have dreamt of your sweet face every night since, and kept you in my heart every waking moment. You are my daughter, and I never wanted to leave you, you have to believe that." Lalique's lips quivered and she blinked several times trying to hold back tears. One spilled over despite her efforts to prevent it.

The sight was too much for Lorel to bear. Lalique, the queen who had always remained poised, stoic, even cold, was now filled with emotion. Love. Before Lorel understood what was happening inside her, forgiveness rushed in, engulfing her whole being.

"Lalique, I—" The lump in her throat had grown so much that words ceased to be possible.

"You don't have to say anything," Lalique said, holding out her arms.

Lorel succumbed, allowing her body to fall into an embrace that she never wanted to end. Soft sleeves of light green silk entwined with dirty muslin, and wet cheeks pressed tenderly together.

A deafening noise interrupted the moment.

Still holding each other, the women spun their heads around to see where it had originated. A gurgling sound exploded above and they looked at the ceiling. The rubber hoses began to wiggle and lurch as though coming alive.

Then water gushed from them with the force of a fire hydrant.

Someone was filling up the fish tank.

SIXTEEN

JAKE

September 27, 2098
Indian Ocean

T HE *NAUTILUS* SLICED THROUGH the darkness like a ghost
ship. A thick layer of softly glowing clouds cloaked
the moon. Jake leaned against the deck rail letting
the tropical night winds wash over his skin and ripple
his clothing. He squinted.

It was difficult to discern whether the orb of blackness
in the distance was land or just a dark mirage holding
false hope of Lorel's presence. He glanced at his navy
watch. The compass needle pointed northwest and the
coordinates revealed that the *Nautilus* would fulfill its
promise, arriving right on time. Ten minutes to midnight.
He marveled once again at the efficiency of Beacon's
ultramodern galleon.

It was late and the rest of the ship was quiet. At
dinner earlier in the evening, Jake had been frustrated

to hear that Beacon planned to pass the night outside the perimeter of Rodinia and assess the conditions of entry at dawn. Dawn. *Why had they bothered rushing here?*

Maybe Jake was being hasty, but he wanted his boots on the ground as soon as possible. Which was why his heart thumped violently against his chest in anticipation.

He had his own plan.

With a surge of anxiety he adjusted the gun holstered to his belt. It was fully loaded. He had considered wearing a wetsuit but had settled on clothes, jeans and a black cotton tee. The water would be warm, and although he was unfamiliar with the dress of the island inhabitants, he would surely be more conspicuous in diving gear. Not to mention it would be tough to conceal his gun in a skintight outfit.

The *Nautilus* had now slowed to a drift and the clouds above had passed allowing moonbeams to penetrate through. They seemed to spotlight the land ahead as though beckoning him there.

Jake drew in a breath as Rodinia emerged from the darkness, silvery in the moonlight. *Was he dreaming?* The sight before him was majestic.

High spires of mountains reached ominously for the sky. Below, miniature rocky versions pierced through the surface surrounding the shore. The eddying water around them looked rough. No wonder the sirens were so protected from the outside world. No captain in his right mind would risk navigating his ship in such hostile waters for a seemingly meaningless, uninhabited island.

The *Nautilus* began changing course, curving to the

west rather than directly toward the dangerous rocks. Jake breathed a sigh of relief. As it circumvented the island from a healthy distance another piece of land came into sight. It was a tiny islet, no more than a mile wide, with a smooth sandy shore. He frowned. It appeared as though it was being used as a port. Several massive ships clustered in anchor a few yards from the islet.

"DiviniGen," Jake whispered as his heart dipped.

They had already arrived. How long ago?

Jake punched his palm with an angry fist and emitted a slew of curse words, then glanced around. Henry was inside his room sleeping along with most of the ship's occupants.

With the agility of a sports car, the *Nautilus* came to a sudden halt causing Jake to nearly fall over. He grabbed the rail. A large wake swelled and crested below. Beacon planned to pass the night here. Between the hostile shores of Rodinia and an islet full of corporate zombies.

A strong wind gusted, lifting Jake's hair. He stared wide-eyed through the darkness at the scene in the near distance.

One boat in particular seemed to be alive with activity, and a festive blue and green flag waved from the top. DiviniGen's signature colors. But it did not look official like the others in the fleet. Jake strained his eyes, searching for a clue to the boat's identity. Faint sounds of voices carried across the water. Laughter and music. It seemed odd, out of place. He was ready to do some reconnaissance. If this was DiviniGen's fleet, it was possible Lorel could be in their possession on one of these ships.

Jake kicked off his sneakers, tied the strings together and secured them to his belt. He pulled on the flippers and climbed over the railing. With his flippers dangling off the edge, he looked down. He stood at least forty feet above the water, but he had done higher. With a deep breath he squeezed his arms tightly to his side and jumped feet first.

His body slid into the water like a bullet. It was warmer than he had expected. But clear. He did not think about the predatory sea-life that likely cased Rodinian waters. He let himself plunge downward until the momentum waned. Then he clicked on his watch light, oriented himself to the direction of the surface, and shot forward with all his strength toward the islet.

The swim was only about half a mile, but Jake had to surface several times for air. Noises from the ship carried in a loud ruckus across the water. Joyful yelps, singing like drunken sailors, and the sound of steel drums cut abrasively through the otherwise quiet night.

Finally he reached the boat, panting heavily. He swam around looking for the repair ladder and upon finding it on the starboard, began to climb. Halfway up he hung onto a rung with one hand and switched his shoes back on, swinging the flippers around his neck. Something told him he did not need to worry about being spotted. These people were having too much fun to notice a guy in wet clothes climbing aboard in the shadowy corner of the stern. With a silent grunt, Jake heaved himself onto the deck.

The wind had picked up, but he smelled the unmistakable aroma of greasy food and booze. He hung back for a few minutes to squeeze the water from his clothes then sauntered casually toward the crowd. Just as the sounds had depicted, people were singing, dancing, slushing colorful tropical drinks around. Most were half clothed or in bathing suits. Beyond a doubt they were humans, in all of their glory.

Jake realized he had been hoping to discover sirens aboard. The species was still so unreal in his mind that he was anxious to see one in the flesh. *In a way he already had,* he realized with a chill.

This strange seafaring journey had brought him closer to Lorel, within an arm's reach. It was a dream come true given that only a few days ago he thought he might never see her again. But the closer he got to finding her, the further away he felt.

Who was this girl he had come for?

The Lorel of their New Charleston days seemed an ephemeral image in his mind, someone who no longer existed. He felt a flutter of desperation at the thought, an urgency to get her back and soak up every morsel of her being like he had always wanted but never had the courage to do. Looking into her eyes, he had always felt vulnerable. Weak. The byproduct was often resentment and then stoicism. But when he found her, he planned to look all the way into her soul. And show her his.

A woman with bare breasts walked by him and pinched his buttocks.

"Hey, darlin'! Looks like you just went for a dip." She

smiled, twirling a strand of cotton candy pink hair in her index finger. "Want me to help ya outta those?"

"No," Jake answered curtly.

"Suit yourself." She flipped her hair in his face, then turned and joined the dance mob, her hips swaying slightly off beat from the music.

He stared at her curiously. Her accent sounded like someone from the Skirts. People there were poor and uneducated and often had their own dialect of broken English. Shaking his head in bewilderment, Jake headed into the promenade area where most people were clustered.

A large swimming pool surrounded by plastic lounge chairs lit up the center of the activity deck. A couple to Jake's right writhed on a chair, grunting and breathing heavily. Naked people swarmed the pool. Some dove sloppily in or dipped their toes while sipping drinks. Others splashed around in the water like fish in a barrel. Jake stared in wonder.

Why would there be a cruise ship anchored outside the most secretive island in the world?

A scantily clad waitress shoved an icy drink in his hand that glowed with liquid luminescence. "Drink up! You look way too sober, young man." She winked at him.

He took a hesitant sip of the strange alcoholic substance inside. It was sweet and tasted of pineapple and rum. *When in Rome,* Jake thought. If he was going to blend in, this was a good way to start.

He spent the next few hours scouring the guest cabins of the ship. Most were unlocked, and many were empty, but there was no way he could search them all. The elevator buttons revealed that the vessel had twelve floors. After searching the first five, Jake felt exhausted. His gut told him Lorel was not on this ship anyway. It did not make sense. And its presence still perplexed him.

How and why was this booze cruise here? The people seemed clueless to the fact that this place was anything more than a random tropical island. They were definitely not corporate zombies. They were party zombies with tunnel vision of endless libation and debauchery.

Did Beacon know about this?

As the thoughts rushed through Jake's mind they became blurred together. A dizziness overcame him and the dimly lit hall began to undulate. The alcohol had gone to his head and physical exhaustion was doing him in. He peeked into the nearest cabin to find it empty and collapsed in the tidily made bed.

Jake awoke to a blaring intercom announcement. "Occupants of Floor Number Five, you have been selected."

Floor five. Wasn't that his? Selected for what?

Spotting the empty glass he had been drinking from the night before on the side table, he bolted up in bed. There was something engraved on it that he had not noticed last night—*The Celebration*.

He thought of the Mandate List. *Stage Two: intake*

of volunteers . . . from Celebration. It was the name of the ship. He remembered the list of experiments DiviniGen planned to conduct on the humans. Leg fusion and fin implantation were two that came to mind. His stomach rolled.

The jaunty female voice over the intercom continued.

"You are the lucky ones chosen to embark on that beautiful tropical island that you see in the distance and partake in the world's most powerful drug, Erbium. Please listen carefully for instructions. Our stewards will be collecting you from your rooms in twenty minutes. Begin preparing. You may carry one small bag onto the island. And don't forget your bathing suits!"

Out in the hall he could hear yips of joy and a commotion of doors opening.

His heart skipped a beat. Wasting no time, he bolted from the room and headed down the hall toward the nearest elevator bank. Two armed men wearing black camouflage were guarding the entrance. He was trapped.

"Sir, please form a line here. The stewards will arrive shortly to lead folks to the water taxi," said the burlier one, straining to sound friendly.

On impulse Jake reached for the gun hidden beneath his tee shirt, but a higher instinct stopped him. *Play along and you'll get a ride straight to ground zero.*

He shoved his hands in his pockets and looked at the men with an innocent grin. "A free ticket to paradise and a sip from the fountain of youth? Man, I sure am lucky."

Within minutes Jake was bustling along in a line of people dressed for a trip to the beach. They whispered and buzzed in a fervor of excitement. Two women behind him were discussing whether or not nude beaches existed on the island and if so, would they have enough SPF for their bare bottoms.

"What's the name of this dang island anyway?" one said between smacks of gum.

"It don't even matter. They're all the same. Sunshine and white sand and hot men. Hey, how does my ass look in this thong?" She flashed her sundress up and they collapsed in a fit of cackling laughter.

"Hun, that extra baggage will be gone in a jiffy after that pill they're givin' us," her friend replied.

The corralled group of occupants, consisting of at least a hundred people, were led like a gaggle of geese up the elevators and across the promenade deck toward a fleet of water taxis. The taxis had been lowered from the neighboring ship, which loomed menacingly over the *Celebration*, casting it in shadow.

As Jake patiently waited for a woman ahead of him to lower herself down the ladder, he heard a man's voice call after her.

"Have fun, babes! Don't get a sunburn." The man stood off to the side, a sunburst morning drink in hand.

"Bye, hun! Maybe you'll get called next." She blew him a kiss and disappeared below the deck.

Jake followed her down into the waiting taxi. His chest felt tight. These poor people had no idea they had won a lottery ticket to hell, not paradise. He hoped the *Nautilus* was making arrangements to infiltrate the island soon. The clock was ticking.

SEVENTEEN
LOREL

September 28, 2098
Paraíso, Rodinia

"WE'LL HAVE THREE HOURS underwater before our oxygen runs out," Lalique said. The words stung Lorel, but her mother's eyes revealed a tender sympathy. "Maybe a little less for you."

Lorel nodded in understanding and looked up at the ceiling. Its peeling aqua paint was now inches from her face. The drain, now several feet below, regurgitated spouts of dark cloudy water, spewing chunks of debris from the ancient pipes. Water continued gushing loudly from the rubber hose. A chilly sputter of it splashed her face.

"Just talk to me. Tell me anything." Lorel licked her lips tasting strong chlorine. Her heart fluttered.

She needed a distraction from the rising water. Even if these were her last true breaths of air, she found solace in the fact that they were being spent with her mother. But her heart broke knowing it wasn't enough to cover a lifetime of questions, to get to know each other. Within minutes they would be submerged, and Lorel's lack of ability to use her biosonar would prevent them from anything but rudimentary gesturing for communication. "I want to know you."

Lalique drew in a deep breath. "If there's time, I'll tell you everything."

Lorel could tell it was not often that this woman exposed her soul. It was one that had been long guarded for self-preservation. An old soul, but bruised. Lorel was still in awe to see the face of the queen so soft, so suddenly familiar. She could see her own reflection, head bobbing, in Lalique's troubled sapphire eyes. They had grief behind them. Regret. Lorel's heart twisted in longing to understand this woman that was her mother.

"It was my journey to Elizabeth," Lalique began in a voice soft and unguarded, "so I was very young when I met your father. We both were. But we were in love. And he accepted me blindly. He knew I was not normal, he *had* to know, but he let me be who I was. It was that deep intuition he had that warned him not to pry or ask questions about my background. I loved him for that. But I was naive to think I would be able to stay in the human world. After all, my father was the head of the High Council, the siren king. And I was his only child.

"When I found out I was pregnant with you, I prayed every day that a miracle would happen, that they would not find me." She smiled. "And for a while they didn't.

A man, a very kind man, took mercy on me. He was next in line to be Master Guardian for Beacon, and against all rules of the pact, he helped me stay hidden. He would meet me in secret, let me know how much Beacon and the sirens knew. He risked everything in his own life to help me."

"But . . ." Lorel said, knowing how it ended.

"But Beacon found out what he was doing, and then found me. They told my father, and it was all over." She stopped and drew in a long breath. "That was the hardest thing I ever did, leave you. Not that I was given a choice. Two members of Beacon had been assigned to follow me, waiting for me to give birth so that they would not bring a forbidden hybrid into Rodinia. The very night I had you they whisked me from the hospital in a whirlwind. They took me kicking and screaming all the way to my furious father's arms. He never forgave me."

Lorel stared at her mother, shaking her head in disbelief. Water gushed in her open mouth and she spit it out. "How horrible . . . couldn't the man have warned you?"

This was so different than how she had imagined her mother. A selfish, unfeeling woman who had purposefully left her because she was too young to deal with the inconveniences of a baby. Lorel always had the guilty feeling that she had stolen her mother's youth. That hateful person never existed, only a young woman in love hoping to remain in a world that she knew could never be hers.

Lalique continued, now lost in another time. "They

found out he was helping me. And he lost everything he had worked so hard for. They kicked him out of Beacon, ripping away all his privileges and connections with Rodinia. He had angered my father and the Master Guardian to the point of rage. But he had been so kind to me, had made it possible for you to be born in safety. And he gave me the time I had with you and your father. Still it was not enough. It could never have been enough." She shook her head.

"The night before I was taken, he came to me. He promised me that he would look after you. It was the only thing I have held onto all this time. I knew you had a secret guardian who could protect you from those who may discover your identity, try to exploit you. It's dangerous to be a siren among humans. That is why I never told your father everything. The less both of you knew about Rodinia, the safer I knew you would be. That's why . . . why you've never really known who you are." Her voice broke. "I am so sorry for that."

"This man was Benjamin Reshing, wasn't he?"

"Ben. Yes."

Galton had been telling her the truth. "All this time I thought he had cruel intentions, that he was just another Galton. I wish I had known. I wish he would have *told me*!" Lorel frowned.

"He couldn't tell you. He could only do his best to keep you safe." She ran her finger along Lorel's wet cheek. "And he did. Here you are."

Lorel closed her eyes and lowered her chin. "Here I am."

"But Lorel, you must forgive him. He put himself at risk doing me a favor. He lost his chance to be Master Guardian, a role he had been seeking his whole life. He did it all for me, for us, and never told a soul. The few that knew about the whole debacle in Beacon kept it secret."

"But why did Reshing never reconnect us? Or somehow put us in touch, tell me about the island . . . something!" Lorel felt her anger at Reshing resurface despite the new information.

"He couldn't. He never knew where Rodinia was. I had no way of telling him." She shook her head. "The only thing I could think to tell him was that we were the one place in the world where the purple algae grew. If he could find the source of the algae, he could find me again."

"It all makes sense, why he recruited me, assigned me to the purple algae. Maybe he was the one who granted me the scholarship to the marine sciences program at the university."

The scope of Reshing's influence on her life hit Lorel like a pile of stones. She shook her head.

Lalique continued, "I always latched onto the hope that maybe he would find me, so that I could find you. I was never able to keep track of you after I left, but I knew that any hybrid on mainland—because surely there were others like me that had not been caught—had to be protected, because they could be you."

"But how did Sam know?"

"He was hacking into hospital records, searching for any unique congenital diseases documented in patients."

"My mosaicism," Lorel whispered.

Kaleidoscope shards of her life seemed to spin and rejoin in new shapes before her. It was dizzying.

Lalique had given her a secret guardian. He had known her mother and seemed to have developed a lifelong obsession with finding her again, and uniting Lorel with her. Maybe it was some crazed love for an otherworldly beauty he had met so long ago. Or maybe it was his dedication to a simple promise to do the compassionate thing for a grieving mother.

Whatever his reasons, Lorel felt an overwhelming sense of gratitude. And forgiveness. Reshing was a stoic man, appearing cold and nefarious on the surface. But there was a kind soul beneath. And though he had had no choice but to keep Lorel at a distance, she regretted that she had so deeply misjudged him.

"So none of the sirens ever knew about me besides your father?" Lorel asked.

"Never. It would be a confession of one of the greatest sins, mating with a human and *tainting* the purity of our species." She grimaced. "Not to mention I was inheriting the throne. My father protected my reputation by keeping the entire escapade a secret, but he made me promise that when I took the throne I would banish the Choice forever. I think he knew that it would always serve as a temptation for me, a dangerous *in* to the forbidden human world. He knew my daughter existed in that world, and a man I had fallen in love with."

"You mean you banished the Choice because of your past?"

"I never wanted to, I was forced to."

Lorel cast her eyes downward. *Mello*. How hard he had been on himself, blaming his own mistakes for the loss of one of the sirens' most precious privileges. Hopefully she would have a chance to tell him. He had borne the burden for so long, for nothing.

"Lalique, I am so grateful, despite what's happening right now, that you helped me get here. But you should know something. I came because I wanted to help the sirens, but the ultimate reason was because my father is dying."

"Henry," Lalique murmured. Tears welled in her eyes. "How is he? I promise we will get him all the algae he needs to heal if . . . do you think there will be time?"

The question cut so deeply that all Lorel could do was laugh bitterly in response. "If miracles happen in Rodinia, then yes."

The water now lapped at their chins and tiny debris floated around them. She began shaking, and Lalique grabbed her hands. "Please forgive me," she whispered.

"I forgive you. Of course I forgive you," Lorel whispered back.

Her last words were silenced.

Lorel now stared at her mother through the dirty tank water, her heart pounding in her chest. She had not even taken one last deep breath. With an uncontrollable shudder, she succumbed to her siren instincts. Her lungs expanded. Every vessel in her body distended like a swelling river as they flooded with oxygenated blood.

Lalique began swimming languidly around the

aquarium, the greens of her dress swirling around her like a living watercolor. Despite the hopelessness of the situation, a peaceful calm enveloped Lorel. They still had three hours. Anything could happen.

EIGHTEEN
MELLO

September 27, 2098
Twelve hours earlier
Baltra, Rodinia

L OREL. WHERE THE HELL *are you?*

Mello was furious with himself. A few hours had passed since they had last seen her. In all the chaos of Dylan's kidnapping, no one had noticed her slip away. But he should have. It was his job to keep Lorel safe. Had Galton's men come for her too without him noticing?

Self-loathing welled in his gut as he thought of his incompetence. People were looking up to him and he was letting them down. Again.

To make matters worse, he and Sam had discovered that the doors to the outside of the bunker were barred shut. Someone had locked them inside and they were now hostages in their own safe-house. The security cameras were destroyed and the bodies of the dead sirens lay near the door awaiting proper burial.

DiviniGen had gained the advantage on the sirens' home turf, or at least on this particular battleground. Mello felt blindsided. *How had they known about the bunker?*

"Ahh!" He bellowed loudly in frustration, his voice echoing inside the dark tunnel that led from the bunker's main room toward some storage spaces. He leaned his forehead against the wall and took a deep breath. The metal felt cool against his skin.

An unexpected sound perked his ears. *Was it a voice?* He knocked on the wall and an echo reverberated on the other side, then a clatter. This was supposed to be an underground tunnel surrounded by dirt, but there was hollow space on the other side. So there *was* a hidden passageway. But who was in there?

Suddenly he heard a shrill cry, then a woman's faint voice. "Hello? Please help!"

That cry had to be Dylan's. It was Dylan and Lorel. She had gone to rescue him! Mello felt a rush of relief and admiration.

"Lorel, stay there. I'm coming to get you!" he yelled through the wall. "I just need to find a way in."

Frantically, he ran his hands along the cold concave surface. The sheets of metal that formed the tunnel were filled with grommets, screws, and rough joints where the panels were welded together. But there had to be a way through. His fingers brushed across a different protrusion, and he began to trace its circular shape.

"Ouch!" he cried.

He yanked his finger back to see blood oozing from a thin slice in his skin. Sucking his finger to slow the bleeding, he looked closer. Metal shards jutted from the wall as though the circle had been cut roughly with a blunt object.

He pushed against the smooth center, and to his surprise the sheet fell out like dough from a cookie cutter. It clanked on the ground on the other side making a loud echo in the dark space.

"Hello?" He poked his head through but could barely see a thing.

"I'm here," a meek voice replied. Then he heard footsteps approach from the recesses.

Dim light from the bunker tunnel illuminated the figure of a woman holding a baby. Mello's heart jumped with joy. Lorel and Dylan were back.

As she crawled through the hatch and stood upright in front of him, his stomach dropped. A confluence of relief and disappointment flooded his chest. Before him was baby Dylan, safe and sound. But he was in the arms of a woman Mello had never seen.

"Okay, Mira, tell me one more time, are you *sure* it was Lorel and Galton that you spoke with? And she was there, with him?" Mello's brows furrowed in a struggle to understand.

Mello, Harper, and Mira sat around the kitchen table

trying fretfully to piece together the events of the past few hours. Sam and Isla were across the room snuggled up with Dylan in a blissful family reunion.

"Yes. And she said to tell you *not* to come for her. She said . . . they'd come back for Dylan if you do."

"Eat up. Please, you need it," said Isla, nudging the dish of algae closer to her. Mira took a bite but her fingers still shook.

"She offered herself in Dylan's place. Dammit, Lorel!" Mello slammed his fist on the table and the girls jumped. "Sorry," he muttered in apology, but his mind was racing.

So Lorel did not want anyone coming after her. Why? He wanted to respect her wishes, but what did she think she was going to do? Galton's intentions with her could be nothing but sinister. He had been searching for her for so long, and she somehow evaded him on the mainland only to walk directly into his arms in Rodinia.

Where they were supposed to keep her safe. Mello felt sick thinking of what Galton could be doing to her at this very moment.

He had to get to Paraíso. They may be locked in the bunker from outside, but now he knew the secret passageway. And according to Mira it led right into the basement of Hotel Paraíso.

Mello stood, glancing around the table at what should have been a nice moment. A new baby. His best friend. Tea steaming on the counter next to a big bowl of algae. But in the back of his mind he saw the dead sirens. Could still smell death on his hands. He grabbed his knife from the side table and shoved it in his sheath. "I'll be back. Someone close the hatch behind me."

Isla jumped up. "Mello, you can't go after her. It's too dangerous!"

"She's right," said Sam shaking his head. "Let's discuss this. We can make a plan."

"There is no time for planning." Mello turned and walked out. He could feel their eyes burning into his back as he left, but he had to do this. He crossed through the central control room, now eerily quiet, and entered the tunnel containing the hatch.

Without warning the ground beneath him rumbled ever so slightly, and he heard a distant gurgling sound.

Could it be the Vulcan?

A quick glance around revealed nothing unusual. He shook his head at the thought. Impossible. An eruption would shake this island chain like dice in the hands of a giant. *It must be the piping,* he thought with a grimace.

Halfway through the tunnel, he found the hatch again still secured firmly in place. He and Sam had created a makeshift lock for it with some wire and a crowbar in case anyone from DiviniGen attempted another visit. He knelt down and quickly unfastened it, tossing the crowbar aside with a loud clang.

The low gurgling sounded again, closer this time. Mello put his palm to the center of the hatch, ready to push it through.

Before he could act, it blew open with such a force Mello hardly knew what hit him. A torrent of water gushed into the tunnel, knocking him to the ground. As

311

he frantically struggled to get back on his feet, he heard footfalls.

"What's going on down here?" Sam dashed to Mello and pulled him to his feet. There was no need for a response. The scene rendered them both speechless.

Water gushed through the hatch and into the tunnel at an alarming rate. The sound was deafening. Mello looked down in horror to realize their ankles were already covered in water. His heart sunk as he looked at Sam.

"Sam, we've got to get you out of here. Now." He raised his voice over the violent cascade. "See if you can close the hatch. I'll go get everyone. At this rate, we'll be underwater within the hour."

Sam nodded, but his face had gone pale. "All right."

Mello flew down the hall toward the control room leaving Sam pressed up against the hatch. The water pressure had been substantial. He knew Sam would not be able to hold it for long.

Someone had purposely flooded that passageway, and Mello was pretty sure he knew who it was.

The three girls were already in the main room clustered next to the table of blank security monitors in a flurry of nervous chatter and fitful hand gestures.

Isla had wrapped Dylan tightly to her chest with a muslin sheet. "Mello, what's going on? We heard all these weird noises!" she cried, her eyes lavender saucers.

"Follow me. All of you," he demanded, then swiveled toward the tunnel just as a shallow river of water poured into the room.

Harper gasped. "Where is that coming from?"

Isla's jaw dropped and her hand flew to her mouth. "Sam!" She pressed Dylan's cheek against her chest and ran into the tunnel, splashing after Mello. Mira and Harper followed at her heels.

As Mello expected, Sam had been unable to keep the hatch shut. Water gushed through the opening. He stood wiping his glasses on his shirt while water pooled around his shins.

"Sam, are you okay?" Isla ran up to him and threw her free arm around his shoulder.

"I . . . I tried to hold it back. I'm sorry."

"We're not underwater yet," said Mira, placing a hand on Sam's shoulder.

"Let's get out of here and swim through it," Isla said, bouncing Dylan on her hip to keep his whimpers from becoming cries.

All eyes turned to the hole in the wall gushing gallons of water by the second.

"No," Mello said, lifting up one leg to yank his boot off. "We can't. Not yet. It has to rise above the hatch before we can swim through."

After twenty long minutes the water swirled well above their waists, churning and frothy. The hatch was well submerged.

"All right, the incoming current should be weaker now. We have to go under and swim through. It's going to take all your strength, but you can do it," he assured everyone.

Wet, worried faces stared back at him.

"What happens when we get through?" Sam shouted. "Isn't it just another tunnel?"

"We'll find the source of the leak and exit through it. This is seawater, probably from the Eye. It can't be too deep here. Sam, you'll make it out of here." He looked at Isla who was desperately trying to calm the screaming infant. "And so will Dylan."

Isla wrapped her arms tightly around Dylan, her voice quivery. "Mello, I don't know how he will react in the water."

"I do. He'll use his submarine breathing by instinct. Just like a siren would. He will know, Isla. Trust me."

She nodded and her face relaxed. Dylan began suckling on her pinky finger. Sam looked at Mello gratefully and for a fleeting moment Mello felt a burst of pride. But he humbled himself quickly.

Focus. Or fail.

The water now reached chest level, swirling in a violent eddy around them.

"All right, on the count of three," Mello yelled. "One, two, three!"

Isla and Dylan submerged first, then Harper and Mira, and finally Mello who held Sam firmly by the wrist. Swimming through the hatch felt like going head first into a riptide, but it only lasted a few seconds and the pressure lessened on the other side. The water was pitch black, but Mello knew the sirens could easily adjust. His own eyes widened and the dim surroundings took shape.

The passageway was narrow and sloped downward,

augmenting the intense feeling of claustrophobia. He swam to the front of the group and gestured for them to follow. Sam was kicking in smooth strokes with his legs while Harper and Mira pulled him along by the arms at a swift pace.

Feeling for the currents, Mello located the source of the leak, which was a gaping rip in the ceiling of the tunnel. That would be the way out. He led everyone toward it. Luckily, the opening was large enough for them to fit through, and soon they had exited the tunnel and were swimming in open water toward the surface.

The fact that Mello could see the moon, its light distorted by the water, meant they were in the shallows. He emitted a puff of bubbles through his nose in relief. Sam would be okay.

Within seconds their heads were bobbing in the moonlight. The sirens released sprays of water through their blowholes and it came raining down in a cool shower. Mello looked around to orient himself. They were in the Eye, in a cove between the mangroves and the western beach of Baltra.

"Everyone all right?" he called in a rasp whisper, unsure who lurked onshore in the darkness.

The sirens all confirmed with breathy nods, water glistening on their relieved faces. Only Sam looked as though his struggle was not over. He gasped and coughed but managed a "thank you" between sputtering breaths. Mira and Harper gripped his shoulders keeping him afloat.

Dylan began to whimper. Isla nuzzled him, laughing

softly. "You did it. You are amazing, my little love. And so is your daddy," she said, smiling at Sam through teary eyes.

Silently the group swam to shore. One by one they collapsed on the beach, exhausted from the traumatic exit. Microscopic organisms glowed in the sand, making it glimmer as though reflecting the stars above.

"Well, that was an unexpected way to escape the bunker. All is well that ends well, I suppose." Isla sat cross-legged on the sand with Dylan cradled in her arms. His tiny head bobbed against her chest, feeding peacefully.

Mello knelt down next to her, smoothing his hand over Dylan's head, and cast Isla a warm smile. "All *will* end well."

She returned his smile, but he noticed her lips quiver. He stood up, shoving his wet sleeves up his arms. "We've been cut off from communication with the Council and the other islands for hours now. Hopefully their security control centers are still operating, but we don't know. You all have to go to Lalique's cavern. Tell her about Dylan, and that Lorel is still in danger. Tell her to send help to Paraíso immediately. It's time for Plan B."

"Past time," Sam mumbled, squeezing out his wet shirt on the sand.

"What about you?" Isla looked at him with concern. Her eyes were pools of black, still fully dilated from the swim. "Aren't you coming?"

He gazed across the Eye at Paraíso. The peak of the Vulcan was engulfed in a passing cloud, and a dark silhouette of mountainous spires dwarfed the hotel at its base. He could see DiviniGen employees still at work inside the building. Its windows glowed dimly through the distance daring him to approach. The shore itself appeared dark and still, but the place had to be surrounded by PanElites.

"No." He clenched his fists. "I'm going to find Lorel."

His friends disappeared down the beach leaving Mello to his own journey. He felt good knowing they would be safe with Lalique. Once she and the Council found out the extent of what DiviniGen had done, things were going to heat up. It would mean war. Mello suddenly felt more isolated than ever.

Had it really come to this?

He kicked a nearby conch shell, sending a spray of green luminescent sand up from the beach. DiviniGen Incorporated had been nothing but a curse on Rodinia. Their people did not reflect any of the humans he had met, had none of the beauty of the human cultures he had experienced. Theirs was a culture of greed and callousness. What a shame the sirens could not have connected to a more peaceful part of humanity.

Now humans would be feared and hated more than ever. Sirens had progressed so much since the Dark Submersion. They were ripe for a kinship with their fellow species. But this whole experience was hurtling them headfirst into the past – a darker, more lonely place. Mello's dream of peaceful coexistence would never be realized.

An unusually cool night breeze fluttered against his wet clothes sending a chill down his spine. He could feel a repellent presence in the air affirming the reality that Rodinia, for the first time ever, had allowed the enemy within.

His mind raced to devise a plan of action. First, find Lorel. Then find Galton and see what the hell he had done with his daughter. A fresh surge of anger bubbled up again, but he needed to focus. He knew the hotel like the back of his hand, having spent his childhood playing in the wild gardens, roaming the ancient library, and visiting the herbalist or doctor on rare occasion. There were enough nooks and crannies that he felt confident he could enter unseen by the PanElites.

Mello walked into the water, staring ahead at the hotel in the distance until his chin, his nose, his eyes became fully submerged. Then, propelled by raw determination, he swam toward the shore of Paraíso.

He covered the mile distance in minutes and, as stealthily as possible, crawled through the shallows to shore. The rocky enclave near the mangroves where he had sent Lorel to join Silas was the perfect entry point. It formed a concealed inlet and was located inconspicuously near the backside of the hotel. To Mello's relief there were no guards between him and the subterranean door he planned to enter.

He scurried over the dunes and across an expanse of

unkempt lawn toward the hotel. As expected, the door was unlocked. He slid inside in silence. The basement was pitch black, but turning on lights would be foolish. Going on memory, he headed toward the elevator bank. Galton's headquarters was on the ground level, and that was where Mira had last seen Lorel.

As he crept down the hall, Mello noticed the kitchen light was on. For no apparent reason, a chill shot through his body as he passed. His hair prickled. Something made him want to look inside, see what was there, but he had to remain focused on finding Lorel.

Father.

Mello stopped cold. It was a voice in his head, he knew. He had heard it before in his dreams. But now a feeling of someone's presence overwhelmed him. *Her* presence.

Spinning on his heels, he headed back toward the kitchen. The room was chilly and the faint scent of lemon cleaning solution masked the mustiness. Stainless steel surfaces of shelving and countertops gleamed in a soft light seeping from the far wall. He crossed the room to arrive at the door of the walk-in freezer, and placed his fingers on the cold metal knob. His hand shook in hesitation.

He pulled the door open to a burst of frigid air and the smell of formaldehyde and stepped inside. The sight of the girl lying on the table brought him to his knees. A pain unlike any he had felt before gnawed at his gut and weakened his limbs. Lifting his head, he found himself face to face with his daughter. Her eyes were closed in half-moons of fringed lashes, and her skin was unnaturally pale, but her heart shaped lips turned up ever so slightly as though she was smiling at him.

"What were you doing out there?" he whispered to her. "I would have crossed a million oceans to find you. I *should* have, not you." His voice broke. "Not you."

A shiny black lock of hair framing one side of her face caught his eye. Just like his. The rest of her hair glowed silvery under the dim light. She had Lea's nose, and his chin. But her face shone with a beauty that surpassed them both. Looking at her, he felt pride well in his heart followed by an unbearable heaviness.

She deserves a proper burial, he thought. If he could take her now, dress her and . . .

Mello stopped himself. A lump filled his throat with the realization that this was where his moment ended. This was all he and his daughter would have together. There were people that needed him, people alive and in danger. With trembling lips he kissed her forehead.

"Goodbye my love. I am sorry, so sorry."

Goodbye.

Letting the freezer door slam behind him, he darted out of the kitchen and headed back toward the elevator. He stepped inside, mashed the L button, and held his breath as it ascended to the lobby, hoping no one would be there when it opened. The pain of leaving his daughter threatened to weaken him to the point of uselessness, but he had to go on.

The doors parted to a deserted lobby, and he took a deep breath. Ready. A strange smell, like medical equipment and burned flesh, had replaced the nostalgic scent of salt and musty air. Mello entered, swiveling his neck around like a falcon. The grand columns cast long shadows everywhere and bluish light streamed through the windows creating a glowing patchwork on the marble floor. A cacophony of strange and disturbing sounds drifted into the airy space. It seemed to be coming from the hallways that branched off from the lobby. The guest rooms.

As the sounds became clearer Mello realized they were cries, wails, coughs, and whimpers. People in distress. He shuddered.

What were they doing to the sirens?

As he wandered down the nearest wing of rooms, the cries grew louder. Mello clenched his jaw as scenes from the basement of DiviniGen's headquarters flashed through his mind. His own hellish violation. Masked doctors holding live organs. The fear, the pain, the blood.

Here it could even be worse. On mainland the scientists were kept somewhat in check, the chance of a surprise visit by the feds always a lingering possibility. These sirens, the ones that had so bravely volunteered, sounded like they were in pain. What few moral restraints DiviniGen had had disappeared like a puff of smoke once they entered the unparalleled privacy of Rodinia.

Mello stopped at the first guestroom door then swallowed hard, preparing himself for what he may see. Inside the dark room a man lay on a hotel bed moaning. His eyes were closed and he seemed to be in a trance. Mello balked at the sight of his body. The man's legs were crudely stitched together, the skin pulled taut and fused with cauterization. The room smelled of burned flesh. He pulled the door shut behind him before the man noticed his presence.

As he walked away, Mello realized something with a shock. That man was not a siren. *He was a human. But why . . . how?*

In a state of bewilderment, Mello moved to the next door and opened it. Inside was another surreal scene. An oversized human woman lay on the bed in a skimpy bikini, either passed out or heavily medicated. Her skin was glowing in a hot pink luminescence that reminded him of the deep-sea lanternfish. But on her it was unnatural, grotesque. She had multiple bandages scattered across her abdomen with blood seeping through. It looked like ink in the black light.

Mello noticed a sign on her nightstand that read: "Dermal Luminescence Gene Injection. Experiment in Progress."

He backed out of the room, again unnoticed. As soon as he found Lorel, he needed to get back to Lalique's cavern, make sure the others knew what was going on. This torture had to be stopped. *How could humans treat their own kind like that?*

A voice interrupted Mello's thoughts. It was faint, wafting across the airy lobby and down the hall to his ears, but Mello could sense a frenzied excitement in it compelling him to investigate. He scurried back across the lobby then paused and flattened his back against the wall. His heart pounded. Next to him were the double doors of Hotel Paraíso's grand library.

Who was inside?

One door was ajar. A sliver of light spilled through the doorway. Had DiviniGen set up a lab in there? The labyrinth-like space did not seem suitable for that. Mello exhaled slowly, perking his ears to listen.

The library was the only room in the building regularly visited by sirens. Within its vast mahogany aisles of floor-to-ceiling shelves were books. To sirens, they were windows into the soul of human civilization — the ever evolving cultures, histories of wars, the rise and fall of empires around the world and throughout time. Languages. Religions.

No book was too ancient or too modern, from classic literature to scientific texts and periodicals. Even popular culture novels and hologram comics were a part of the canon. Once books had gone out of print, the library adapted to the new technology to ensure the flow of knowledge into Rodinia never stopped.

Mello's favorite part had always been the Nook, a hidden library within the main library. Its contents solely regarded the history of the siren species, the geological past of the Rodinian landmass, and important historical records from art and culture to scientific and mathematical advances unique to Rodinia. Access was highly restricted.

Mello's mother used to take him in there on special occasions and show him the beautiful original texts and maps tucked inside. Musty and covered in cobwebs, the space had to be manually lit with hanging lanterns fastened to the kapok-wood ceiling. But the treasures within it were marvelous. The very first map of Rodinia. Letters of correspondence between the first human to step foot on Rodinian soil in the sixteenth century, Sir William James. And the most ancient piece of parchment, never to be replicated for the sake of its preservation and protected by a thin sheath of glass, was the map of the Abyssal Plane. It was adhered to the far wall of the Nook under a sheet of glass.

Mello still remembered his mother taking him through it in a hushed voice, sliding her index finger along the intricately scribed topography. It was then, the night before his first deep dive to the Abyss as a young child, that she told him the story of the undersea land at the base of their microcontinent, of its precious treasures and abundance of life-giving resources that the rest of the world could only dream of. The map was detailed, labeling every undersea mountain range, unique topographic features, the lava streams and falls.

Like many children, Mello had been most intrigued by the Vulcan Traps, the geologically formed steps that ascended to the seafloor base of the Vulcan Volcano. The map had been constructed hundreds of years ago when the shaft of the volcano was accessible to the sirens for mining purposes. But Rodinia was situated on a hotspot. Since then their island had shifted on its conveying tectonic plates, and the shaft was no longer safely accessible. The entrance to them became locked forever.

Today, among the young sirens, it loomed a mystery. Some hardly believed the volcano had ever been open to enter, but the proof was there in the precious metals ubiquitous on the island in all forms. The Vulcan Traps were permanently blocked off now, and the enormous Golden Doors at the top of the Traps remained locked with arms of steel and barricaded by a fence of chains. It looked like a mirage in the distance, wavering and distorted by the intense heat of the water in its proximity. As tempting as it was to swim beyond the forbidden borders and climb the steep steps up to the Golden Doors, every siren knew the danger. Those doors could never be opened again.

Mello inched closer to the polished wooden door of the library and pushed it farther open. The familiar smell of dusty books and old mahogany mixed with the scent of human inside. He peeked in just as the man released a bellow of laughter.

"It's just so ironic!"

Mello's ears perked up. It was Galton. And he was talking to a woman, her voice giddy with excitement in contrast to his chilled tone. "I can't believe it was her. I was sure it was some idiot who had somehow escaped the *Celebration*."

The sound was muffled by several rows of bookshelves. Mello began creeping in their direction, the voices becoming clearer.

"I had just received a call from Lucas Keating," Galton continued, "warning me a human girl was on the island, claiming to have come with us. And then I pieced it together. Lorelei Phoenix was in Rodinia. I'd almost given up on her, had Madelyn revise the marketing strategy already, but suddenly there she was standing before us."

"So where is she now?" The woman's voice sounded familiar.

Mello tiptoed down one of the dark aisles toward the back area where they were talking. Slowly, he pulled a book off the shelf at eye level to get a view. Peering through the narrow slit, he could see the CEO, his gray suit as sleek as though he was standing before his board, and the familiar Dr. Wong in her white lab coat.

Galton chuckled. "The girl is quite a handful. In fact, it got me thinking . . . how much do we really need her at this point? She would be a valuable marketing tool. A siren-human hybrid of exceptional beauty displayed next to our Nia would be quite a compelling story for the investors." He clicked his tongue. "I suppose I should decide soon. She and the queen are floating around in the aquarium as we speak."

The woman was silent. Her face seemed to turn pale. "They can't stay underwater forever though, sir. The species has a limit."

"And soon we will know that limit."

"How long have they been in there?" she asked in a hesitant voice.

Mello gulped. *Lorel and Lalique were in the old aquarium!* It could not have been three hours yet, but he needed to get to them out. Before it was too late. As he turned to go, something stopped him.

"Enough questions, doctor. You take care of the science experiments and leave the business operations to me."

"Yes, of course, Mr. Galton," replied Dr. Wong.

"Now, the update?"

"Yes, sir. The research team is breeding the siren genes with the humans' as we speak. The Poseidon Prototype will be ready to launch very soon."

"Well done, doctor. The Poseidon Project should hit its target roll out date without a snag." His voice lowered to a confidential tone. "And now that it's well underway, we need to start thinking about the next venture for DiviniGen. Implementation is nearly upon us. Once we begin colonization, we will need the algae farms started. And slaves to harvest. What's the status on the Subservience GAP?"

Mello's eyes narrowed. *What else did they have up their sleeve?*

"It is nearly complete, Mr. Galton. Mr. Seaford's frontal lobe tissue samples have been quite cooperative and the Subservience GAP has proved to be effective in the testing."

"The pill," she continued, "will turn the most stubborn siren into an obedient farmer within two to three days. It is record mutation time in terms of brain tissue and behavior modification."

"Good, good. I want to start tonight. All siren volunteers are cordoned in the basement now ready for testing. The sooner the better. Let's take a look at the map, shall we?"

Mello's blood pressure spiked. Something had to be done.

With a snapping motion Galton unfurled a large piece of parchment paper, and Dr. Wong huddled close. Their backs were to him so Mello could not tell what it was, but he shuffled back a step as he realized where they were standing. A faint feeling washed over him.

Just beyond them was the secret door to the Nook, and it appeared to be slightly open. For a second he could not believe his eyes. It was impossible. How could they have known about the hidden library, much less gotten into it?

The entry was disguised as a wall of books, blending in with the rest of the library. Mello and those with access knew to look for the Charles Dickens book, *A Tale of Two Cities*. Behind it was the pad requiring a keycode that changed after every entry. Only Lalique knew the code.

Would she have had reason to give it to him? Or did he somehow force it from her?

Galton scanned the paper in front of him again, then tapped it.

"So here it is."

Dr. Wong released a long breath. "Wow. It's like an entire underwater landscape!"

"Yes, and a very fertile landscape. Can't you imagine humans inhabiting it one day?" Galton traced his finger around the paper.

"Poseidons everywhere, hmm," she purred in lurid enthusiasm.

"And here's the spot, at the top of these things that look like steps."

"'The Golden Doors,'" she read aloud.

Mello gasped. They were holding the undersea map of the Abyssal Plane. Galton was talking about accessing the old mines inside the Vulcan shaft.

Mello shook his head, stupefied. Dread overtook him. This could be disastrous.

Galton held the map up higher, giving Mello a full view. "Once we get down to those doors, the possibilities will be endless. All the gold, manganese, diamonds, and whatever the hell else they have down there, will be property of DiviniGen. And with an island full of obedient sirens, we will have our entire labor supply for mining, farming, whatever we need."

"I'm sure DiviniGen will pay competitive wages. Right, Mr. Galton?" She laughed, but Galton stared intently at the map unsmiling.

"Pen please," he demanded.

Dr. Wong reached into her breast pocket and pulled out a pen. Galton took it and, pressing the map up against the wall, marked an 'X' on the parchment. Mello stared at the ink, a sacrilege over the rendition of the Golden Doors.

"Well, you should be getting ready, Mr. Galton," Dr. Wong said. "The aquatic PanElites are setting up the fleet of deep-sea submersibles as we speak. You submerge at daybreak."

"And the crew count?"

"Twelve PanElites will be escorting you. Not that we expect any interference down under," she spoke confidently.

"What about the ballistic?"

"The missile will be fastened to yours. So you can do the honors. I wish I could be there for the grand opening," she gushed.

"I better suit up." With a twitch of his lips, he rolled up the map and tucked it under his arm.

Dr. Wong slid closer to him, her eyes hooded.

"This could be dangerous. Are you sure you want to do this yourself? The team is well equipped to—"

"I want to be there, see it with my own eyes."

Mello realized how much Galton himself wanted to be in the skin of his own product. It was more of a personal obsession than he had imagined.

"But thank you for your concern, doctor."

"You have always been hands-on. How about a little treat before you go?" Dr. Wong dropped her white lab coat to the floor and began unbuttoning her blouse. Within seconds she was standing before Galton, naked. On impulse Mello became entranced by the sight of the bare human woman before him. She looked strange and exotic, and in spite of her despicable character, beautiful.

The sound of Galton's zipper ripped abrasively through the hallowed space. As Dr. Wong knelt to the ground before him, Mello disentangled himself from the scene. Turning in disgust, he darted silently back down the aisle and out of the library.

Out in the hall he paused. It was clear what Galton intended to do. What he did not realize was that he would never get far enough. His journey would end at those doors. Everyone's would.

Mello leaned over and grabbed his belly, trying to

stave off the riptide of nausea that clenched his gut. It seemed like a bad dream. More was at stake than Lorel, than finding the body of his daughter. The life of every siren in Rodinia—in the world—hung in the balance. Galton had to be stopped. And Mello had to be there to stop him. DiviniGen's submersion team would be on the beach by sunrise.

He sunk into the shadows as Galton and Dr. Wong walked past him out of the library.

"You will need a good breakfast, sir. It's waiting for you in the ballroom. And the submersibles tech would like to go over a few things with you and the team."

"I need to freshen up first. Inform them I will be joining in fifteen minutes," he said, smoothing his suit and heading toward the eastern wing of guest rooms.

"Yes, sir," she nodded as they parted ways. "See you shortly."

Lorel. He may have enough time. With one hand on his holster, Mello bolted out the back door of the hotel. As silent as a ghost in the night, he flew down the winding stairway and across the courtyard toward the annex.

NINETEEN
LOREL

September 28, 2098
Paraíso, Rodinia

S HE LOOKED OUT OVER *a green meadow of tall grass that rippled in the wind like calm waves. The sparkling sea lay just beyond in the distance. A cool breeze brushed across her skin, gently warning that the dark puffy clouds in the distance were on their way. She did not care that a storm was coming. She had shelter.*

She lifted an icy glass to her lips and cold, sweet liquid swirled around her tongue, lemony and tart. Cubes tinkled like chimes as she set it back down. A rhythmic creaking lulled her mind and a pleasant dizziness penetrated her tired body. Her left hand rested on the smooth wooden handle of a rocking chair. Back and forth, back and forth. The breeze bristled her arm hair and a giggle escaped her lips.

A hand reached across to her, knitting its rough fingers through hers. She looked down to see wrinkled hands entwined, both speckled with age like the delicate shell of a bird egg. Her fingers squeezed back, trembling gently, and a feeling of euphoria rushed through her at the happiness she felt. A bolt of lightning flashed on the horizon in the darkening afternoon sky, and large raindrops began to plop down on the velvety green grass below.

"I love you," said the man holding her hand.

The rocking chairs creaked in sync with each other and she felt a smile slide slowly across her face.

She turned her head to face him. "Is this a dream?"

The man laughed softly, caressing her hand. "The best I've ever had."

She laughed back. "I love you too."

Bliss. Peace.

He stared ahead at the storm rolling in, the features of his face a blur. His hair was the color of snow. She leaned closer, her own hair tumbling over her shoulders, wiry and gray. A warmth emanated from his body as she neared his cheek and he turned to face her.

Lorel's eyes flew open and her entire body flinched, sending a ripple of vibration through the surrounding water. It felt hot.

Had someone turned up the temperature?

She had been somewhere else for the past few minutes, maybe longer. The dream was such a pleasant escape from reality, but as ephemeral as any reverie, it faded before she could remember the details.

Lalique swam up to her with a knitted brow and questioning eyes. Lorel nodded in assurance. Her chest felt heavy, compressed, but her body had enough oxygen. Evolutionary wonders were keeping her alive, for now. The siren genes, selected generation after generation as the early humans hunted deeper into the sea, had made their way all the way to her body, in the year 2098.

Time could create anything given enough of it. But to the individual it was only a droplet in a vast and endless sea, its full scope beyond comprehension. *Deep time.* And right now, it was not on her side.

She began swimming in circles around the tank to feel her blood flow, reminding herself she was alive. It still seemed like a miracle that she could exist this long in water. That her skin had not turned to prunes and her lungs to water balloons. How long had they been under now? It seemed like no more than an hour, but her perception could be distorted.

Suddenly a movement beyond the glass caught her eye. The figure of a man appeared in the hallway and a dim light flickered on. Lorel froze, gripped with fear. But as he came into focus, she felt a burst of joy.

Mello.

He ran to the glass and peered inside, his webbed palms pressed firmly against the tank. Their eyes locked immediately, brown eyes lost in azure. They stared at each other unblinking. A lump rose in her throat, of immense relief. And profound longing.

She wanted desperately to talk to him. There was so much she needed to tell him. That he had never failed the sirens. That he was one of the most admirable people she had ever met. That he *did* have the virtue and the power

334

to lead his people out of isolation and into a harmonious relationship with the human world. That it would all work out, somehow.

As he looked into her eyes, she could see that despite everything, Mello still believed in the beauty of human beings. And Lorel believed in him.

Lalique swam over in a flurry of green to greet Mello and began making frantic but purposeful gestures. Even stuck in a tank, she still maintained an air of majestic authority.

Lorel blinked, unlocking their gaze. Although she did not have the ability to communicate with Mello, Lalique did. The queen began clicking and nodding her head. Mello responded with similar motions, pressing his forehead against the glass so that his biosonar waves penetrated the water.

What were they saying? Was he going to get them out of here?

Lorel watched Lalique's face for clues. The queen's brows drew to a sharp point, a worried expression clouding her face. She was learning news from Mello. And it did not seem good. He nodded vigorously, lines of concern creasing his forehead. Could it get any worse, Lorel wondered? She tapped Lalique's shoulder, eyebrows raised in question.

Lalique shook her head, a glimmer of fear in her eyes. Seeing the siren queen with such a look of dread sent a fresh wave of panic through Lorel. They still had a couple of hours before depleting their oxygen, but something was happening beyond their watery prison that was bigger, more dire.

What?

Mello began pounding on the glass, kicking it with all his might. He ran to the small door and did the same but to no avail. Dropping to his knees, he scanned the floor as though looking for a clue, any way in. His hand rested on some sort of hidden panel in the baseboard. Lorel's heart jumped with hope.

But then, something caught Mello's attention outside. Lorel watched as he ran to the opposite wall of glass to look out. It was still dark outside but she could make out a blurry streak of men rushing through the bamboo. PanElites.

Mello's face looked suddenly tormented. He glanced outside, then at Lorel and Lalique. Lorel's stomach sunk. She did not know why, but she knew he had to go. Whatever was going on, he needed to stop it. Lalique nodded her head at him in solemn command. But he stood frozen in place, staring at Lorel. She realized he was waiting for her blessing.

With a heavy heart she nodded. *Just come back. Please come back soon.*

The sincerity in his eyes assured her that he would. *I will not leave you,* she could hear him whispering in her mind. Lorel fought back tears, swallowing hard as he bolted out the door and leaped into the bamboo forest like an animal in chase.

It was all out of her control now, she thought with a sense of surrender. The fight in her was weakened, battered down by the loss and trauma she had already experienced on the island in such a short time. An image of Link entered her mind, the shape of his majestic body leaping toward the DiviniGen people on the beach, then the stillness of it lying on the sand. Jake's image lurked even darker beneath, his reality, his existence so uncertain in her mind. Her heart ached. It seemed there was only so much more she could take. But then she thought about how much she still had to lose.

TWENTY

JAKE

September 28, 2098
Paraíso, Rodinia

JAKE EYED THE DOORKNOB of the hotel room he had been thrown into earlier, his mind fighting to keep focus. The wails and screams outside had finally died down after the initial shock of their reality set in for the "lucky" *Celebration* tourists. They had been introduced to their tropical excursion with the jab of a needle and handcuffs binding them to their beds. But the tranquilizing medicine was setting in, sedating everyone into complacency.

Jake resisted the peaceful calm that emanated through his blood instructing him to give in and rest his head against the soft hotel pillow. Both of his arms were cuffed to the bedposts behind him, and he knew it was only a matter of time before the dark-haired man in the white lab coat returned.

On the table next to his bed was a holosign that read

"Scale Implantation Experiment." Next to it were several stainless steel tools laid out on a square sheet of cotton. A plastic container labeled "Placoid Scale Sample" was full of hazy liquid with tiny shimmery discs suspended inside it.

Leaning forward with a strain that threatened to pull his shoulders out of joint, he reached his navy watch with his mouth and pulled out the cuff needle. He had been trained for moments like these. Holding the needle steady in his teeth, he inserted it into the cuff's lock and jiggled until it unlatched. Within seconds both arms were free.

Jake jumped up, feeling a queasiness wash over him. The medication was powerful, but he could not submit to it. With lead feet he shuffled toward the door just as footsteps approached down the hall.

There were two people. They stopped outside the door finishing up a conversation. Jake slid against the wall on the hinged side of the door breathing as quietly as possible.

"This one is a young male. We will be implanting dermal denticles into his posterior distal leg. Followed by a submersion endurance test."

"Fascinating. Good luck and carry on. Any resistance, do not hesitate to inject the serum."

"Yes, sir."

Jake's heart slowed and his mind went blank as the door opened. "Mister. . . ." A man squinted down at a clipboard, then cleared his throat. "What's your name? We don't seem to have record of . . ." The scientist stopped in his tracks as he stared at Jake's empty bed.

Jake slowly pushed the door closed and the man turned to face him in awe. As the man reached into the deep pocket of his white coat, Jake lurched forward and slammed him down on the bed. He covered his mouth and pulled out the gun, shoving it into the temple of the man's shaking head.

"Please," the man whispered, his eyes bulging from his reddening face.

"Shut up," Jake growled, cocking the gun. "Don't make me use this."

Holding the man down with his knee and pressing one hand over his mouth, Jake cuffed him to the bed in the same position he had been in only moments before. Then he tied a pillowcase around his mouth as a gag. Part of him knew he could kill the man now. It would not be the first time he had killed another person, but something stopped him.

He did not *need* to. He was not like them.

The scientist continued flailing and kicking like a donkey, bouncing frantically on the bed. Jake grabbed the other pillowcase and tied his legs together.

"How's that for leg fusion?" he snarled as he took the white coat and slung it on himself. It was a perfect fit.

"I'll need these too." Jake snatched the glasses off the scientist's face and shoved them on. The intense magnification induced a sudden dizziness and he slid them down the bridge of his nose a little.

The man just stared at him with wide eyes. Jake flipped the light switch off.

"Sweet dreams, doc," he said, pulling the door shut quietly.

He shoved his hands in the pocket of his crisp new uniform, which smelled of formaldehyde and alcohol, and slipped out into the dark hallway. His fingers grasped something in the pocket and he pulled it out. A syringe with fluid inside and a needle still encased in its plastic sheathing. He shoved it back in, just in case.

To Jake's relief the hallway was empty. But he could hear faint moans and the whir of medical machines and delicate clinking of stainless steel instruments. Scientists were at work despite the late hour. The air smelled pungent, a mix of stringent chemicals and human flesh.

Now he was free. What next? He glanced down the hallway toward what appeared to be a lobby. First he needed to get his bearings, reconnoiter the interior of this strange new land. He headed down the hall across the lobby and pulled open a heavy front door. A veranda of smooth white limestone gleamed in the moonlight, but before Jake could soak in the view beyond, a voice came from beside him.

"Good evening, sir."

Jake turned to face a man in the same black uniform he had seen on the escorts from the *Celebration*. A large las-gun hung around his shoulders, its red lights blinking to signal readiness. But the weapon looked small against the man's bulging chest. Jake had seen enough of these men to know he was a PanElite. Hiring a private army of mercenaries indicated one thing: no one was going to interfere with their operation.

341

Jake's heart raced, hoping he would not be recognized as an imposter. "Evening," he murmured with a simple nod then continued across the porch. He slid the glasses up his face staring straight ahead as he passed a few others. DiviniGen had this place on lockdown. And not a siren in sight.

Weren't these people guarding their island? Jake wondered what they were like. Hostile? Naïve? Peaceful to a fault?

He paused at the top of the stairs. The view caused his breath to hitch. Under the moonlight a vast panorama of shimmering water spread out before him. It was enclosed by a landscape of rugged land. The spiring mountains he had seen from the outside created a calm and protected haven within.

Jake scanned the dark horizon, tracing the shadowy profile of the island against the starry sky. The surrounding land seemed to be broken up by some sort of forested areas making it impossible to see out to the open ocean. It was an archipelago of distinct islands chained together in a perfect ring. An otherworldly energy seemed to emanate within the basin. It felt like a separate universe. With a shiver he realized the marine desert in front of him was the surface of a rare blue hole, the deepest in the world according to Reshing.

He clambered down the winding stairs of the veranda and traversed the path down to the beach. Dunes towered on either side of him like sandy walls. The still air smelled salty and mixed with the fragrance of exotic flowers that peppered the high shrubbery bordering the path. Jake stumbled onto the sand and leaned against a nearby palm, still feeling dizzy from the medication. And the sky did not help. The stars above were so numerous and layered that the sphere above him seemed to undulate in several dimensions.

The island closest to the one on which he stood looked to be at least a mile away. It bore sheer cliffs that jutted out over the water, and a thick line of trees hovered at the edge of the cliff like a hanging forest. On the western side a massive waterfall cascaded down the rocky cliffs, dividing into three silver threads, then merging, then dividing again to create a thrashing tidal pool below.

Rodinia was breathtaking. Jake could only imagine the marine wonders that existed below, all kinds of fish and aquatic life that had ceased to roam most waters on earth. This water was isolated, a safe shelter from all the smothering green algae and dangerously warming currents. And the lush tropical land above completed the paradise. If only he were here for other reasons. He could live out his days in this place with Lorel and be content to never leave.

He thought of Henry. How he would love to see his wife's—and his daughter's—homeland. *If all went well . . .* but Jake stopped himself from entertaining the thought. Nothing was going well yet.

Jake tore his gaze from the mesmerizing view. He turned back to face the hotel and frowned up at the sky. Framed in the distance, a giant mountain with a flat top loomed high above the building. It was hard to tell in the darkness, but it looked like swirls of smoke rising from the top. Suddenly his senses deciphered something in the air. The faint smell of sulfur.

That was no mountain before him. Rodinia was a volcanic island. It had probably not erupted in ages or the island would have been tracked and flagged by the navy, Jake reasoned with comfort. Still, there was something unsettling about standing at the bottom of an exhaling volcano.

Jake looked around the beach he stood on. It extended into darkness on both sides. He headed westward down the beach toward the backside of the hotel, determined to search every square inch inside and out until he found Lorel.

A high concrete wall surrounded the back of the hotel. It looked like a good place to start. A few guards milled around it, but Jake was skilled in scaling walls. Plus, he knew they were likely at the end of their night shift and exhausted. It was only a couple hours before dawn.

As soon as the opportunity presented itself, Jake bolted across the lawn and scrambled up the wall. Pausing for a moment, he looked behind him at the beach. The *Nautilus* seemed so far away, beyond the mountainous island walls of Rodinia. What were Reshing and Harnott doing right now? Had they infiltrated the island yet or were they reconnoitering from afar? They would surely be here soon if not already. The feeling that any moment Jake could be caught and taken back into the custody of DiviniGen made him anxious for backup.

With a quick assessment of the ground below, he

jumped, landing with a thud on a gravelly path. He swiveled to take in his new surroundings. It was a vast courtyard with stone paths twisting around mature gardens overgrown with tangles of weeds and wild shrubs. Something about it reminded him of a graveyard.

To Jake's relief, it appeared empty in the moonlight, though he could not discount the shadows. The place was eerily quiet, but beautiful in a wild abandoned sort of way. The flagstone path was worn and weed tufts poked through at intervals. Loose white stones rustled loudly under his feet as he made way toward a dry crumbling fountain.

The garden had lots of nooks and crannies that he would need to explore. A few yards down the path beneath a sandbox tree was a shed. In the distance, on the far side of the courtyard, was a building of glass with a steepled roof reaching just above the surface of the trees. Jake tried to make out more details, but most of the building was engulfed in a thick forest of bamboo.

Lorel could be hidden anywhere out here. He would start with the shed.

A drape of sweet-smelling creeper vines covered the old wooden door. Jake took a deep breath and pulled them aside. It opened with a creak. The room was no more than what it appeared to be from the outside. Storage for shovels and gardening tools. A loamy stench of rotten wood and old soil hung in the air and Jake swatted at a bug that crawled across his face. Gossamer from a spider's web clung to his forehead as he backed out of the shed.

One more place to check out before he went back inside the hotel. He gazed across the courtyard at the peaked roof, its glass panes reflecting the moon above. It seemed like a huge greenhouse built within the courtyard walls. A soft glow of light emanated from the left side of the roof.

Someone was inside.

Jake darted down the path leading into the bamboo forest and entered to blackness. The bamboo was so overgrown it was difficult to maneuver, and his feet shuffled against loose branches strewn along the ground. The faint woody scent told Jake they were not cut very long ago. Someone had recently hacked them off to make the path passable. Leafy shoots swished against each other as he pushed them aside.

Feeling safely out of the enemy's sight, he clicked on his watch light and shined the small LED beam around. Tiny eyes of lizards, ground birds, monkeys, and other tropical critters glared out of the darkness. Jake had not noticed the jungle sounds before, but now shrieks, hollers, and strange clicks surrounded him in an unsettling chorus. Above, the bamboo rose into the dense branches of banyans and brazil nut trees. Jake was sure he saw a coiled lime-green body dangling from a branch, its beady eyes glaring down at him. The hair along his arms prickled.

Several feet ahead on the path was a set of ornate glass doors — the entrance. He switched off his watch light and dashed toward them.

A loud rustling sounded along the path behind him,

and then light footfalls. They stopped abruptly. Jake could feel the presence of someone standing in front of him. He froze in the blackness. Every hair on his body stood on end. Barely breathing, he reached for his gun, but someone beat him to it. The singing *whoosh* of a knife being yanked from its sheath echoed through the forest, silencing the cacophony of critters.

Suddenly Jake felt a blow to his chest, like the punch of a fist. Whoever was there could see him, but Jake still felt blinded by the night. He fell to the ground, the wind knocked out of him.

Jake squinted up in the direction of his assailant, struggling to see, to steady himself and fight back. The man holding the knife slowly came into focus. He was tall and of large breadth. His disturbingly large eyes almost glowed in the dark, and his hair was long and strangely light colored. A dark streak shocked through it. His steely expression was indecipherable but caused Jake to shudder. There was no doubt that the man before him was a siren.

"Wait!" Jake cried.

The siren loomed over him, pointing the large knife directly at his chest. "Who are you?" he demanded in a gruff whisper.

"My name is Jake Ryder." Jake held his hand up to shield his face. "I — I've come for someone."

It seemed absurd, telling a strange man in a strange land his proper name like it could somehow matter.

"Jake . . ." The siren muttered the name as though waiting for recognition, but his knife stayed pointed at his chest.

"Please, I've come to help. I know what's going on, what DiviniGen is doing."

"So you're saying you're not with them?" He eyed Jake's white lab coat suspiciously.

"No. I'm here to find a girl. Her name is Lorel Phoenix."

The man froze. Slowly, he lowered the knife to his side.

"You're here for Lorel?"

"Yes. She's my girlfriend," Jake replied.

The siren was silent for a moment. Jake thought he detected a look of anguish or sadness in his eyes, but it was fleeting. They stared at each other and the silence thickened. He shoved the knife back in its sheath, then extended a hand to help Jake up.

"I'm Mello Seaford. I know Lorel."

"You know her?" Jake's heart skipped. "Please, can you tell me where to find her?"

Mello breathed heavily. "I was just on my way back from the beach, returning to her. I should still be back there, but I had to come help. I hope it's not too late. They don't have much time left."

"Much *time* left?" Jake asked, confused.

"She's been submerged in a room full of water with the siren queen. Galton has locked them inside."

"Shit." Jake's stomach dipped like a roller coaster.

"I think I know how to get them out, but it's tricky."

"You said you shouldn't have left the beach. You have something else you need to do. Let me help." Jake needed to free her himself, feel her alive and safe in his own arms. "Just tell me how to do it."

Mello was silent, hesitating as though unsure whether to trust Jake. He glanced down the bamboo pathway, a torn expression on his face, and then sighed.

"There's a hatch in the floor that leads to a crawl space which I believe contains the pump. The space runs underneath the aquarium floor. Somewhere inside on the ceiling you should be able to find the base of the drain. But as soon as you release it, water will rush in. You'll have to get up through the drain against that current. And then you'll have to wait for the aquarium to drain. Can you manage this?"

"I'm no siren, but I have a little experience underwater. I can do it."

Mello nodded. "Okay then."

Even in the dark, Jake could see sadness flash across Mello's face again briefly. An icy determination replaced it as he stared back down the path. His eyes were large saucers of ebony in full dilation. Flames flickered in their dark centers.

"Thank you," Jake whispered, feeling an overwhelming gratitude for this mystical stranger.

Mello pointed to the double glass doors. "You'll find them in there, in the room marked 'Aquário.' Go!"

Before Jake could respond, Mello dashed down the path toward the beach.

"Wait, where will we find you?" Jake called, but he was gone.

SIRENS

Jake entered the glass doors of the greenhouse structure to find himself inside a foyer of polished brick. To his left was a sign marked "Aquário." A hallway stretched out before him flanked by glass walls. A wooden bench ran along the outer side facing the bamboo forest. The inner side was a giant wall of water enclosed in glass. The aquarium. The rhythmic whirring sound of a pump bellowed in his ears. Jake felt as though he was underwater already, or dreaming.

At first glance the murky tank appeared to be empty. He paced the length of the glass scanning its shadowy depths. The sun was not yet up, but the blackness of night had receded to gray providing some light. He pressed his face against the glass to get a better look inside.

The image appeared slowly like an apparition materializing before his eyes. As it came into focus, Jake choked on his next breath. Two people huddled in the far corner of the tank. Their bodies were still. The only movement he could detect was long locks of hair swirling among tentacles of green fabric.

He banged on the glass with his fists. "Lorel!" he cried. "Lorel, it's me!"

The glass was thick and double paned, but from the blurry motion inside the tank he could tell they had heard.

A woman swam across the tank like a bolt of green lightning and at first Jake thought his eyes were playing tricks on him; he was face to face with her. Her enormous eyes begged him for help, crimson hair swirling around a pretty pale face. One large crystal glistened on her

350

forehead.

The siren queen, Jake realized. In her arms she held Lorel.

Jake's knees turned to jelly as he looked at her, his own queen, and his face contorted in horror. Lorel's body was limp. It was in the same damsel-in-distress pose he had held her in only weeks ago, just after they made love in her apartment. But this was no joke.

Her head hung back and her eyes were shut. Her mouth fell slightly open but, alarmingly, emitted no air bubbles. A bluish hue flushed her face. Her lips were even darker. Now he understood what Mello meant about time running out.

Snapping back to reality, Jake remembered what he needed to do. Hopefully it was not too late.

TWENTY-ONE
MELLO

A S MELLO FLEW THROUGH the forest, his heart became progressively heavier until it felt like lead slowing him down. An image flashed through his mind of Lorel watching through the glass, waiting for him to return. Maybe she had already begun to doubt him.

He could not think about that now. All that mattered was that she ended up safe. The man had come a long way to find her, and as much as Mello did not want to let go, he could see it in the human's eyes. He would save them. And he had showed up just in time.

Mello anticipated the moments ahead and fear mixed with his festering anger. The bamboo had given way to sparsely scattered trees toward the backside of Paraíso. Streams of gray light penetrated the thinning canopy to reveal the dawn. He burst through the forest and out onto the beach just as the sun peaked above the horizon, splashing an array of oranges and reds over the Eye.

Before anyone noticed him he halted, planting his bare feet into the sand. They were preparing to enter the water, just as he suspected. When Mello spotted Galton earlier, he and the small group of PanElites were suiting up for their descent into the blue hole. Crouched behind a small dune, Mello had stared in awe at the strange machinery.

The "submersibles," as Dr. Wong had called them, were underwater rockets sized compactly for single occupants, shaped for speed. The vehicles looked like a fleet of mechanical sharks. Their shiny medal rudders now glinted in the rising sun.

Mello's heart raced as he watched the men begin to ease the sleek black capsules into the water. Galton lingered behind near an outcropping of rocks. He was speaking with a small man in a lab coat on the beach. The man held a tablet, which he tapped between vigorous nods to the CEO. Mello could hear a muttering of *sirs*.

Galton stood barefoot in his sleek black wetsuit holding flippers in one hand and gesturing authoritatively with the other. DiviniGen's logo was emblazoned on his back in green and blue outline. The symbol had come to stand for so much ugliness it made Mello's blood boil just looking at it.

As discreetly as possible, Mello darted across the beach and hid behind the other side of the rock jetty. He watched as the aquatic PanElites passed through the clear shallows and into the sapphire water with their submersibles. With a shrill whistle, Galton held up a hand commanding them to wait. Obediently the men floated in place just off the cuff of the Eye Atoll.

"All right, sir. Submarine communication is activated. My team and I will be standing by in case you need anything," said the man with the tablet. He shuffled back up the beach leaving Galton on the shore alone. With a quick glance around, Galton shoved his watercraft into the shallows and waded in.

Mello scampered up the jetty and looked down on Galton from his perch above the water. "What the hell do you think you're doing?"

Galton's head spun around. His eyes widened in shock, then recognition.

As their eyes met, Mello's mind flashed back to the moment Galton had introduced himself. How his smile had at first given him such relief, then terror as he realized the man was not an ally but an adversary. It all seemed so long ago. And here they were again. But this time Mello was not chained to a hospital bed.

"This is not of your concern, Mr. Seaford." His silver brows dipped into a deep frown. "If you'll excuse me, we have business to attend to." He pulled a mask over his face and turned toward the men awaiting him in the distance.

"Wait!" Mello shouted. "You're about to do some damage you will not walk away from."

Galton paused as though pondering whether he should engage or ignore him. Slowly, he turned and waded back toward the jetty with one hand steadying the submersible by his side. He pulled off his mask and squinted up at Mello.

"You don't own these waters any more than we do."

"We may not own it, but we understand it. We respect it." Mello glared down at him with gritted teeth.

"Well, pardon me if I seem disrespectful, but I think this land can afford to spare some of its resources. There are people in this world in need, something you all may not understand here in this tropical bubble. So, please, spare me the dramatics."

"People will die," said Mello.

"Die?" The CEO's brows wrinkled in distaste. "And how is that exactly?"

The sarcasm in his voice was disconcerting. *He didn't believe him . . . or didn't care.*

"The mines are compromised. If you open those doors, it could destroy the whole island."

"Really? I notice your people have had no hesitation in using them." A bushy white brow rose to a sharp point.

"We stopped mining centuries ago. The island . . . it moves. We're on a hotspot. Please, you can't open those doors."

"Of course you would say that. And believe me, I understand your motives, Mr. Seaford. But the gold, the algae . . . it belongs to us as much as you. You people want to hoard everything, even your way of life and your adaptations. DiviniGen wants to bring it to the world." Galton's voice carried across the water as naturally as it would through a corporate auditorium.

"Right, the way you brought them our algae? We

protect. You hoard." Mello clenched his muscles to prevent them from shaking with anger. "DiviniGen doesn't give a crap about helping the world, you want to run it. You purport to have this divine providence, but really you just want to take every remaining resource hostage to exploit."

"Mr. Seaford, you obviously do not know how this world works. You're naive. But understandably, that is just a byproduct of isolation. People are scared in this world. They look to PanDivinity's children, like DiviniGen, to take care of them, help them survive."

"You're the one who is naive if you've convinced yourself of that. PanDivinity's megacorps are no better than tyrants. You've taken over on a global scale rendering governments useless and pushing this beneficent façade. But it's bullshit. People are not fooled. They're just oppressed. Their choices have been taken from them, and self-serving philosophies have been shoved down their throats, telling them how to live, promising them they were created as superior to other species. PanDivinity has created quite the story."

Galton's eyes narrowed in anger. "What we do is enable human beings to evolve. And at a rate nature could never accomplish. You think there is any such thing as natural selection? You want to know the dirty little secret about evolution in the twenty-first century? There is nothing natural about it. *We* select who survives in this world."

Mello kneeled down to move closer to the CEO. "I think you'll find you're wrong. There is a process taking place. You're just too blind to see it."

Galton turned away, the water swirling around his waist. "Good day, Mr. Seaford."

Mello ran his finger along the knife in his pocket, then called out, "What would the world think if they knew sirens existed?"

Galton's head swiveled back faster than Mello could blink. "The world will *never* know your existence."

Then it occurred to Mello why. It was so clear . . . the existence of the sirens would shatter the entire PanDivinity belief system. It would yank the carpet of power from beneath them in a split second.

"One day humans will discover the truth about our existence. And theirs. That there is common descent. That we're all the same."

"Again, so naive. People believe because they *want* to believe. Common descent, evolving from apes, it's all so . . . pedestrian."

"People will learn. They're not stupid." Mello said between clenched teeth. "No one needs PanDivinity rationing their food, their medicine, their genes. They need the truth. They *want* the truth. I know, because I've met humans. Good people. That's what the world mostly consists of. But somehow, on your path to what you call civilization, the good ones let power slip into the hands of the corrupted few. You call yourself human, but you delude yourself. You have no idea what humanity is. You're just a cog in the machine."

Galton's lips pressed into a thin to a line. For a moment Mello saw a flicker of some buried emotion in his eyes. He clutched the floating submersible as a gentle wave caused it to swell, and looked behind him at his men. "Go home, Mr. Seaford. Call it a day."

Mello's heart lurched as he watched the man wade into the deep. There was only one thing left to do now. But something stopped him from jumping in. His bare feet dug into the rough rock as waves lapped below.

"Just tell me one thing. What did you really see when you found my daughter on the mainland beach? Did you see a person or just dollar signs?"

Galton turned slowly back around to face Mello. His head tilted to the side with a half smile. "Nia?"

Although it was a mystery to him, deep down Mello needed to see compassion in Galton, just a shred of humanity. Something told him if it was there, it was tied to his daughter. *Nia*, Galton had named her.

"The answer to your question is easy. Nia is worth the price of saving the world. She is our seed. A seed that will grow lots and lots of money. And I suppose you are the very one who planted it," said Galton.

Not a shred, Mello thought.

Mello tore his eyes from Galton and looked back toward the hotel. Something twisted in his gut. *His daughter lay just beyond the dunes. Cold and alone.*

He looked to the east, the Isle of Sleep. In the distance he could see the glistening of the siren cemetery, a vast expanse of golden pillars clustered along the mountainous peaks. They overlooked the open sea where sirens were sent off into their eternal slumber. *She deserved a pillar there.*

"I am sorry, Mr. Seaford. It's a shame the sacrifices that have to be made in this life." Galton pulled his mask back on and began paddling through the gentle breakers to join the others. Together they continued out past the atoll and into the deep.

Mello watched motionless from the rocks. All he could hear was the beating of his heart and the loud silence of fury in his mind.

In a flurry of splashes and bangs the men sealed themselves inside their submersibles. A burst of noise cut abrasively through the air as the engines ignited, polluting the morning calm. Within seconds the surface erupted in a torrent of bubbles as the aqua rockets launched toward the sea floor.

Mello felt paralyzed, entranced by the presence of his daughter and the desire to go to her, see her face one more time. It was a cosmic pull, like the tide toward the moon.

But no. This time he was not going to jeopardize his people. He would not let the sirens down. He had to move forward, toward the enemy and away from everything, everyone he loved.

His heart felt the weight of the sea. He had hoped it would not lead to this. With one pained look behind him, he soaked in Paraíso, the hotel, the Vulcan looming high above in the distance, and then dove in.

Don't look back.

Cool molecules of water rushed over his body sending prickles of energy through his muscles. His scales erected along his wet skin in microscopic flashes of reflecting light. Spreading his digits wide to maximize the webbing, his arms flew to his side and he cut through the water like the manmade missiles he planned to follow. *You get one shot at this,* he thought. Deeper than his undaunted determination to save the island was something darker and more self-serving — a chance at redemption.

He reached the atoll abruptly, weaving in and out of netlike fan corals and fingerling sea plumes, slithering between the branches and blades of hard spiny coral colonies. Schools of awakening fish scattered like leaves in a strong gust of wind as he passed. As the water darkened and the sandy floor began to slope toward the drop off, he halted.

With a swift flip he turned upright, creating a swirl of current, and planted his feet into the sand with curling toes. His hair floated in silver streamers, reaching toward the surface now several feet above. He clenched his jaw and lowered his chin to his chest then stared ahead in stillness.

With full concentration he built up a series of aerated clicks in his nasal cavity until it felt as though his head would explode from the pressure. He flung a blast of sonar from his frontal lobe, swiveling his forehead to encompass the full circumference of the Eye. The high-frequency sound waves sliced through the water like a million tiny knives.

Mello squeezed his eyes shut and covered his ears as his broadcast reached the corals and nearby grottoes, bouncing and reflecting in all directions in ear-piercing pings. The underwater scream prolonged itself in a reverberant summoning. Spooked fish dispersed in all directions, hiding in shells and burrowing beneath the sand or coral. As the echoing pings subsided Mello looked around at his deserted surroundings. Bright morning sunbeams streamed through the softly rippling surface. His chest heaved up and down from the effort, and his heart pounded wildly beneath it.

Would they come?

The water was calm, too calm. And there would be no sirens to hear his call. They had all taken to the Land Realm in a position of defense. Little did they know that they had miscalculated the breadth of the battleground.

Weren't humans the bipedals of land? And sirens masters of the sea? Things were falling out of balance.

He thought of the ship graveyard that surrounded Rodinia. They had always been untouchable from the sea, but DiviniGen was a new kind of beast that knew no boundaries, could penetrate the core of the earth if they wanted to. And now they were heading directly for the heart of Rodinia, a needle plunging into the pupil of its eye.

Mello glanced ahead to the precipice of the continental shelf's gaping hole. Not a trace of bubbles remained in the path of the submersibles. From the time-lapsed return of sound waves he pinned their location to a hundred feet down. There was not much time with the rate they were moving and the current was on their side.

Mello held his breath and waited. Suddenly he heard it, a clattering of sonar and clicks. *Here we come.*

And then he saw them. At first only a few peeked

their heads above the edge of the cliff, smiling faces and beady black eyes filled with loyal determination. But more continued to rise from the depths. Dolphin after dolphin until there were hundreds. They hovered in excited swarms above the abyss, faithfully awaiting Mello's command.

He exhaled a flurry of bubbles through his blowhole in a burst of relief and propelled himself into the mass of allegiant creatures.

Thank you, he clicked in reply.

With a vigorous flip of his feet, Mello glided down into the blue hole in a corkscrew motion leaving a trail of guiding currents. He looked back up through the foamy bubbles unfurling in his wake. Slowly the chaotic mass of dolphins morphed into a churning circle, their dark shapes silhouetted against the sunlight high above. They swam faster and faster in a delirium of flickering light. Then in impeccable syncopation the circle stretched into an elongating spiral.

His heart jumped with promise. They were following his lead.

Soon there were dolphins at his heels. The diameter of space between the limestone walls had narrowed to a vertical cave, augmenting the aural constellation of clicks and sonar pings. Below he had closed the distance enough to see specks of light. The submersibles still barreled toward the bottom with the currents ushering them along.

But the cyclone of dolphins at Mello's ankles had begun to turn the tide. At the counterclockwise swirl of his hand the dolphins increased momentum, spinning the currents into a reverse whirlpool.

He waited to feel the pull. First the current neutralized and Mello felt himself stalling. Then it came. The vortex had created an updraft. Downstream had become upstream as though some planetary force were siphoning the blue hole toward the sky itself. *Galton's fleet would be powerless once it reached them.*

Inches ahead of the funneling siphon, Mello swam downward in a pulsing stroke. Dim lights from the Abyssal Plane began to illuminate the water and the shaft widened, weakening the upward pull. *Would it work in time?*

After a few minutes Mello felt a change in the water pressure. They were close to the Event Horizon. He released a stream of bubbles through his nostrils in frustration. The whirlpool would be nulled there.

The siphon had to reach the fleet. Now.

The distance was closing in on them, but not fast enough. Perhaps he had miscalculated something. Their engines were perhaps stronger than he thought. All he could do was keep going. He pumped harder, then assumed a streamline position riding his momentum downward like an eagle toward its prey.

But too soon he arrived at the Event Horizon. The shaft's walls disappeared altogether and the current dissipated to neutral. Mello and the dolphins were suddenly dwarfed in vast expanse of water that spread out before them. The dolphins struggled to keep the whirlpool spinning, but Mello could see it slow. The heaviness of failure began weighing on him, and he relaxed his muscles in surrender, allowing himself to float.

The dolphins continued circling above. Mello closed his eyes. But then it started to happen. His eyes shot open. The lights of the submersibles seemed to grow larger. *Yes. The current was enough. The siphon was working.*

Within a few moments they had risen to Mello's level. But instead of being pulled up through the vortex as he had hoped, they slowed to a stop. Plumes of bubbles surrounded them as the men revved their engines, trying to resist the suction but only maintaining equilibrium.

Mello looked down toward the Abyssal Plane. They were all suspended a few hundred yards above the mesa. He flashed back to a recent memory of taking Lorel's hand and diving off the edge. He had felt her euphoria. How long ago that seemed.

Now he found himself face to face with wicked men encased in strange capsules. The humans stared at him, then up at the swirling mass of dolphins with bulging eyes. The fear he saw in their faces fueled him with a jolt of courage and an animalistic instinct surged through his veins.

Welcome to my territory.

He looked from one horrified face to the next until finally he landed on Galton's. It was red with rage. White hair glowed inside the tiny cavity. The two men locked eyes through the glass shield. Mello swam up to Galton and pounded his fists against the glass.

Embracing his rage, Mello felt no inhibition. They had forced his position. He gritted his teeth and emitted a blast of high frequency sonar. To his surprise the glass withstood the blow, but the sound waves had penetrated. Galton cringed in pain and trickles of blood began dripping from his ears. His face shook in anger as the rivulets ran down his neck.

Mello looked at the other men, all gripping their ears in pain. *You're done down here.* He turned back to Galton who ensnared him in a piercing glare. Something in the man's pale eyes sent a wave of dread through Mello's core. In a flash the tides began to turn again, this time in the wrong direction.

A strange cone shaped device rose up from Galton's submersible and began blinking red. Mello watched in horror as plastic casings on every vehicle opened like eggs to reveal naked missiles. This was not supposed to happen. His sonar should have crippled them by now. They should be hurling up through the whirlpool, powerless to stop themselves. Catastrophe averted.

Slowly Mello lifted his hands up. His hair swirled around in the stillness of the water and he closed his eyes.

Sunlight. Lea—a flash of his past. A gust of salty air. Cool sand beneath his feet. Lorel—a dream of his future.

He opened them to see the missiles cocked upward on thin metal arms, ready to fire. His heart sank. Even enclosed in a capsule miles under the sea, Galton exerted his unbending authority. He was acquiring Rodinia for PanDivinity's empire. He would not concede.

But Mello was not ready to give up. Seething, he blasted another wave of sonar, swirling in circles to ensure the piercing sound waves reached every capsule. The humans winced and writhed in pain behind their glass shields.

Blood trickled from Galton's eyes. But he was still alive, the glass intact. Above, the dolphins continued swimming in circles. Mello watched helpless as the missiles' red lights began blinking at a rapid rate. In a deafening explosion they released shooting upward and then detonating in an array of sparking fireballs.

Mello screamed in a burst of sonar. A warning. But it was useless.

Clouds of blood exploded and the body parts of dolphins began to rain around him. A bloody fin banged into his left cheek and a torso spun past him.

Then he saw a head.

A smile.

No, no, no.

The upward current weakened to nothing, releasing its hold on the submersibles. Mello watched in horror as they shot down to the mesa and then soared into the Abyssal Plane heading straight for the Golden Doors.

Game over.

There was only one thing left to do now. Maimed dolphins swarmed in a confused frenzy around him, the water thickening with their blood. *I am sorry.* With a heavy nod, he clenched his fists and shot toward the surface.

Mello broke through the surface of the Eye cresting like a whale. A forceful fountain of water gushed through his spout. He had ascended the blue hole in record time and every muscle in his body screamed out. His legs felt like flames, twitching and stinging from the overextension. But there was no time to rest. And the remainder of his journey was uphill.

As his pupils constricted to tiny dots in the bright sun, Mello swiveled his head, soaking in the beauty of the surrounding island chain.

His home. His country. His world.

He looked up at the Vulcan towering high above the hotel, the zenith of Paraíso's mountainous backdrop. The volcano was such a part of Rodinian landscape that often he forgot it was there. The sleeping giant. Its tiny spews of lava, so subtle they could hardly be seen during the day, had always reminded him of shooting stars, a stream of never ending wishes that turned to ash and floated away with the clouds.

Now they looked ominous, fiery omens portending their source deep inside the volcano's throat . . . all the way down to the Golden Doors. Mello saw a sea of lava in its bowels, bubbling and churning in his mind.

Shoving his hands through his slicked hair he swallowed hard between panting breaths. He did not want to think about what was happening below. It was now out of his control. It always was. Galton would blow open the Golden Doors, disturbing the delicate balance, and Mother Nature would take her course.

Man's interference, he thought with a surge of anger. *No, Galton's interference.*

He scanned the Vulcan's profile trying to spot his destination, and his breath hitched as he caught sight of it. Among the trees that tapered off toward the mouth of the crater was the old stone lighthouse. Only a tiny dot near the top of the volcano, barely visible. No one had set foot inside the old tower in decades, maybe more. Beacon had built it just before the Dark Submersion. It had one purpose and one purpose only.

Mello never in a million years thought he would have cause to go there, but there was no time to mourn the reason. He tore his eyes from the lighthouse down to the hotel far below it. Squinting, he noticed people on the terrace and scattered along the beach in some sort of commotion.

Had the sirens taken to fight?

Whatever was going on inside Hotel Paraíso did not matter anymore. If the sirens had started to fight back, they might as well lay down their weapons.

The body of his daughter lying cold and lifeless on a slab of frosty metal flashed through his mind again. It also did not matter. She was gone. It was only her body. *Still, it was his own flesh and blood.* The temptation called to him even stronger than before, but again he resisted.

There would not be time.

In a fluid porpoise stroke Mello swam, emitting a

series of violent spouts between long subsurface glides. The water swelled above him. He headed for the far side of Paraíso, the western end where the beach narrowed into a lush tangle of mangroves. It was where the path started. Mello could only hope he would recognize it, that it had not been swallowed by creeping vegetation over the years. Even so, he would find a way up to the lighthouse. Nothing mattered anymore but getting there.

Nothing.

As soon as the water became shallow and his feet could touch the ground, he bolted, toes digging into sand and water spraying from his body in tiny beads. He reached the narrow shaded beach and leaned over to catch his breath, but nothing could stop his heart from pounding, and a lurching feeling racked his stomach.

You can do this.

A strong wind had picked up, which was unusual inside the mountainous walls of Rodinia, and despite the beating sun Mello could feel cool shards of rain pelt against his skin. Flurries of dark purple leaves, rich with algae from their sea suckling roots, swirled at the sandy fringes of the mangrove trees. His skin began to tingle in some sort of premonitory warning.

Had Galton opened the doors?

No. He would know that moment beyond doubt.

On instinct he glanced behind him once more before disappearing into the dark shade of the mangroves. An enormous rainbow soared over the expanse of the Eye, from the northernmost island peak to the southernmost. Its arc enclosed Rodinia in a sphere of beautiful light.

Beyond the glorious half orb of colors, purple clouds were accumulating, pulling a blanket of darkness across the sky as though tucking in the island. The gusty wind whispered faint lullabies, licking the water of the Eye in a sheet of ripples.

The weather was often a reflection of the undersea, or even deeper—whatever churned far beneath the earth's crust. Mello shuddered thinking of the storm that brewed below. The soles of his feet burned at the thought. Spotting the path with a rush of relief, he bolted toward it.

It was slow going at first, and his feet slipped and slid on the swampy surface as he grasped for vines and low branches to balance. A tree root came out of nowhere, tripping him. He flew to the ground. The taste of salty mud filled his mouth and he spat, his face an inch from the muck. His legs catapulted his body forward and he ran, covered in mud.

Finally the path began to wind farther inland, transitioning from the swampy edge of the mangroves to a sturdy floor of deciduous trees. Mello picked up more speed on the firm ground. Soon the elevation kicked in, and he was winding his way up the Vulcan in a series of switchbacks and jackknives.

Patches of sky began to show through as the trees thinned, and Mello knew he was close to the summit. The lips of the crater loomed above him, startlingly large up close. The air smelled pungent with sulfur, and Mello could hear the loud hissing of the fissures inside the crater. He frowned noticing that the billows of white looked more opaque than usual.

As the path ended, Mello found himself standing before the majestic lighthouse. Its gray stone matched the sky now, which had turned menacingly dark. The single iron door was ajar.

Without wasting a moment he ran inside. As he hurdled the cast iron steps of the spiraling stairway, he felt something. A tremor. It was small, but there was no doubt. The Doors had been opened. Mello swallowed back the metallic taste of fear.

There was little time now. With a fresh burst of adrenaline he dashed all the way up to the catwalk. A mighty gust of wind greeted him outside, a challenge to turn around. But Mello knew he had reached the point of no return. He felt another tremor followed by a sinking feeling of doom in his stomach.

A wave of emotions threatened to seize his faculties, but he fought it. He had to persist, had to do this. None of his other failures mattered if he could get this right.

Through unshed tears he looked at his surroundings. He was close to the highest point in Rodinia and the gaping crater exhaled only a few yards above him. The air was hotter than fire, and beads of sweat covered his body, dripping from his brows and into his eyes. On the western side the open sea spread to infinity. Even from his pinnacle, he could see the ocean was rough, angry. On its surface strange formations danced around like tiny funnels of water.

Waterspouts!

They seemed to be growing in size and strength and

the low thunderheads dipped down in scattered funnels to meet them, marrying sea and sky.

Another tremor shook the lighthouse. It was much stronger this time. He could feel the stone structure shift and loud rattling sounds came from inside. Mello grabbed onto the guardrail to stay balanced and looked down to the east. Rodinia spread out before him. From here the water looked truly like an eye, staring back at him blue and unblinking. Its calm dark center foretold nothing of what was happening beneath, but dark clouds were rolling in from the ocean. The rainbow still cut through the strange light creating a halo around his beloved land. He had to smile at the irony of it, the sheer beauty.

With an aching heart, he turned toward the center of the lighthouse. The gong emerged from the shadows before him. It was suspended from the lantern room by thick ropes and hung above the forty-foot shaft of the spiral stairs.

How long had it been there, untouched, just waiting to be struck and fulfill its only purpose?

A giant mallet hung next to the seven-ton bronze disc. Mello reached out for it, hands trembling. The instrument was heavy, and it took all his strength just to lift it into position. Once there he paused for a moment, gripping the mallet with his arms cocked back, ready to strike. He took a long slow breath and held it. The sounds of the forest, the animals, the hissing of volcanic fumes usurped his senses and a welcome blankness flooded his mind.

Release.

His arms swung full force, and the mallet hit the center of the gong. He stumbled backward, catching himself on the railing of the catwalk. The sound of the gong penetrated the atmosphere, quieting everything in its path like an invisible tsunami.

He ran back out to the balcony to watch. At first the Rodinian landscape was still, as though frozen in time and space. Mello held his breath in anticipation. Then finally, far below, the beaches began to fill with sirens. From every crevice of rock, every green blanket of forest, they poured. And then slowly, in gradual crescendo, Mello began to hear music mix with the resonating gong, distant voices floating like sea foam on the wind.

TWENTY-TWO
LOREL

September 28, 2098
Paraíso, Rodinia

A MYSTERIOUS FORCE SHOOK LOREL violently, yanking her from a deep subconscious state. Strange vibrations emanated through the water. Her lungs screamed out for oxygen.

Was she imagining things?

There were no visual clues to reveal the source of the shaking. She was not in her right mind. Despite the oxygen deprivation, she had not lost consciousness, but she was delusional. A moment ago she saw a school of bright fish swim by, their brilliant scales flashing in reds and oranges of a sunrise. But the tank was as lifeless and empty as it ever was, aside from her and Lalique.

Her mother still held her tightly under the water. Her fingernails now dug into Lorel's arm. Something more powerful had awoken her, paralyzing them both with

374

fear. *Was that the earth trembling?*

She turned her head to see the glass wall of the aquarium crack. Tiny jagged lines spread gradually across it until the entire surface looked like a slab of shattered ice. The wall was still holding, but for how long?

Precious air awaited them on the other side, but Lorel was not sure they could withstand the torrent of broken glass that would surround the violent release of water. Suddenly it felt like the only question left was how?

How was she going to die?

Drowning? Laceration? At the hands of a PanElite? How had it come to this? A deep sadness suppressed the instinctual panic. In panic there was at least hope, a fight. Lorel did not think she had any fight left in her. It was easier to let go.

Lalique tugged on her arm, pointing down at the drain. Lorel looked below then retracted herself upward with a jolt, the panic returning. She stared in horror. Fingers from beneath the floor curled up around the iron drain cover, then shoved it aside. Giant bubbles floated ominously upward accompanied by a deep gurgling sound.

Someone had come for them.

The shadowy figure of a man crawled up through the open drain, slowly and with effort. Through the cloudy water she could see he was dark haired, clothed, and from the way he moved . . . human.

Not a siren. Not Mello.

Her toes curled in horror and she back paddled as

close to the top of the tank as she could to keep distance. Was it Galton himself, or had he sent a PanElite to come to finish them off?

The tank gurgled again and a swift suction threatened to slurp them down through the gaping hole. Lorel struggled to hold onto Lalique as pangs of terror riddled her body. She felt like shark bait, squirming like a worm on a hook. Visibility in the murky tank disappeared entirely as the turbulent water swirled and fizzed around her.

Suddenly another tremor reverberated through her bones, the source somewhere beyond the aquarium, somewhere more cosmic. It felt like the very ground below them was shaking and shifting, trying to shove them off.

Then, through the chaos Lorel heard the strident sound of glass shattering. The aquarium wall had given way. Her stomach churned as she watched her small universe collapse in slow motion.

This was it.

Water gushed from the tank like a dam, and Lorel was hurled downward as helpless as a ragdoll. The fall seemed never-ending. Until her body slammed against concrete. Shards of glass pierced through her arm then her thigh. She clutched both wounds screaming from the sharp pain. All she could feel beyond the pain was concrete, glass, and . . . air.

Hands, a man's large rough hands, grabbed her, pulled her close. Her mind ordered her body to kick, scream, resist, but there was no energy left to power her muscles.

Defeated, she stared at his face struggling to focus on her enemy. Through a fuzzy haze, it materialized. Black hair, chiseled cheekbones flanking a strong roman nose. Dark blue eyes, bloodshot and full of emotion.

Jake. Her lips moved but no sound came out. *She must be dreaming. Or dead.*

"Lorel!"

She blinked slowly as he pressed his lips to hers and vigorously exhaled. Her chest heaved like a balloon and suddenly she felt alive. Blood rushed to her head returning her to full awareness.

"Jake . . . you're here!" She flung her arms around him, smothering his wet cheeks with kisses. The pain in her arm and thigh vanished. "I can't believe you're here. You're alive. Galton told me—"

"Not me. Leo. I couldn't let them take you too."

"Oh no. Jake, I'm so sorry."

He pulled her close. "Me too."

Then tears came, a burst more powerful than the dam that had just freed them, and she sobbed into his shoulder. For the love she had always kept so bottled up, the future she had always been scared to hope for. For the unveiled truth of his dedication.

He had come for her.

Too fast Jake pulled away, gripping her shoulders tightly. He looked her in the eyes with startling intensity, a fear she had never seen in him before. The ground shook again and the whole building rattled. Jake looked up at the ceiling of glass panes. The morning sky was darkening at a disturbing pace.

"Lo, listen to me. We have to get out of here. I don't know what's going down on this island, but it's something big."

"Yes. Something very big." Lalique walked over to them, unscathed from the violent exit of the aquarium but for a few scrapes on her arms. Her dark red hair was plastered to her pale skin and thick rivulets of water streamed down her chest and dripped from her dress. The crystal on her forehead flashed a ray of light into Jake's eyes alighting the deep blue of his iris.

"Jake." Lorel weakly squeezed his hand and looked up at Lalique. "Meet my mother."

He looked up at the queen with his mouth agape.

"Hello, Jake." Lalique kneeled down next to Lorel and looked at them both with wide eyes. "We need to get out to the beach. Now." She glanced at Lorel's wounds, and drew in a sharp breath. "Oh."

"It's not as bad as it looks." Lorel glanced down the length of her body and felt faint. "My leg just hurts a little."

Together Jake and Lalique worked swiftly to extract the shards of glass that had lodged inside Lorel's muscle tissue. The pain was excruciating, but the adrenaline pumping through her arteries took over in numbing relief. Lalique ripped some fabric from her dress and tied it around Lorel's arm and upper leg to stop the bleeding.

"Ready?"

Lorel nodded, and within seconds Jake had scooped her into his arms.

"Follow me," called Lalique, already halfway down

the hall. "We'll go the back way through the woods."

Together they ran out of the greenhouse and into the bamboo forest headed toward the beach. The air was hot and still, a pungent odor mixed with the sweet woody scent of flowering vines and bamboo.

"What's that smell?" Lorel asked, wrinkling her nose. "It's nauseating." She gripped Jake's neck bouncing along in his gallop, and nuzzled her face into his hair. His scent was comforting.

"Sulfur," Lalique called from ahead.

Lorel and Jake exchanged confused glances.

Suddenly a booming instrumental sound reverberated through the air. Lorel could feel the vibrations emanate through her body and her hands went instinctively to her ears. But it was all encompassing, impossible to avoid. There was a beauty to the low sonorous din but a foreboding sense of doom belied it.

"What is that?" Lorel cried over the incessant resonance.

"It's the gong. We must hurry. We're almost to the beach." Lalique had picked up her pace significantly. Jake ran in full stride with Lorel in his arms but was falling behind.

"Jake, let me down. I can run." She was holding them back like a dead weight.

"No way." He picked up speed, gripping her even tighter, and she felt a flurry of relief.

Soon they were surrounded by tall grassy dunes that occluded the view of the beach beyond. Lalique was a streak of green ahead, winding in and out of the giant sand hills. Finally they reached the beach, and Lorel jumped down from Jake's arms, determined to push through the pain.

"Here, just hold onto my shoulder." Jake extended his arm for support and they hobbled forward together.

The gong's baritone ring still persisted, drowning out most other noise, but another sound was emerging. Lorel's ears perked.

Beyond the crickets chirping in the dune grass, melodic voices floated on the breeze, swirling in gusts around them like a ghostly serenade. They wove in and out of the monotone gong as though harmonizing with it. She was reminded of the celebration on Baltra's beach, the throng of singing sirens. It had sounded like a melodic thunderstorm, like a product of Mother Nature herself.

"Do you hear . . .?" Before Jake could finish he stumbled into the back of Lalique almost knocking her over. She stood like a statue at the opening of the dunes. Beyond her was the glittering expanse of Rodinia.

"Whoa! Look at that," Jake whispered to Lorel.

Her eyes immediately drifted skyward landing on the most vivid rainbow she had ever seen.

"It's beautiful." She suddenly wanted to cry. The rainbow glowed, illuminating the water with its colors. But the sky was a deep gray and funnels dipped down from the low-lying thunderheads in the distant sea beyond. "Jake, look. Over there."

"Water spouts." Jake frowned, worry lines creasing his forehead.

A gasp came from Lalique and her hand flew to her mouth. A few yards away two bodies lay on the beach, blood seeping from unseen places into the sand. One wore black camo, the other was in plain clothes. Several yards down it appeared there were more.

Lorel balked. She could not bring herself to look closer, to discover which were sirens, which were human. Did it even matter? A battle had begun.

And something stopped it.

The beach was lifeless but for the distant shouts and gunfire sounding from the hotel. It was several yards down the beach, but Lorel could see PanElites running frantically back and forth among scientists in lab coats. Black and white blurring to gray. Lights inside the hotel flickered on and off and shadows of people could be seen inside.

Where were all the sirens?

As though she had asked the question aloud, Lalique pointed out at the water. "There," she whispered.

Lorel tore her eyes from the hotel. Not far from their feet, angry waves lapped and frothed against the shore. They were unusually large for the inner beach, but the view of the Eye itself was what captured her breath. "Look at them all!" She gasped. "What are they doing?"

The water was filled with sirens as far as she could see. On the farthest islands she could see them marching like ants into the water. They streamed from the beaches, the cliffs, the mangroves. Those closest to Paraíso were swimming fast, diving and spouting like schools of dolphins as they headed toward the deeper water. All the while, they sang. There were so many that the water was hardly visible among the frolicking bodies.

Lorel, Lalique, and Jake watched in silence.

"They're fleeing land as though the jungles are on fire!" Lorel cried.

"And singing. The sound is beautiful," Jake murmured, staring ahead.

Lorel ran to Lalique who spread a calm arm out like a wing.

"Come." The queen drew her in then placed a hand on Jake's shoulder.

Silky green and aquamarine fabric, now dry and light as a feather, rippled from her gown. Lorel felt as though her mother was a part of the sea itself. *But why was her demeanor so tranquil? Why did her neck crane to look fixedly inland?*

Lorel examined Lalique's ethereal face. Tears welled in her sapphire eyes and one fell, streaming down her cheek.

"Lalique?"

"This is the energy of our terrain," the queen murmured to no one. "The battle may seem hopeless, in disarray, but there is order in the chaos. There is purpose." She touched the diamond on her forehead.

Lorel recognized the phrase from a book she had read long ago, a leather-bound edition of the *Art of War*. "He or she proffers the bait and the enemy is sure to take it." She stared at her mother in awe. Lalique knew this was going to happen, whatever exactly it was.

"They will be brought down by their own greed,"

Lalique murmured. "We all will."

Lorel followed her mother's gaze to the top of Paraíso. She stiffened as her own eyes landed on the point of focus. The large volcano that towered above the island was spewing large chunks of lava. The Vulcan. A black cloud of smoke swirled from its mouth, slowly engulfing the western end of the rainbow. The source of the rumbling.

Lalique nodded, her face somber. Jake squeezed Lorel's hand hard as they stood together in silence. An unrelenting wind gusted as though trying to push them to the ground.

"Lorel!" called a man's voice above the echoes of the gong and the wind. "Lalique!"

Lorel's heart jumped to see Sam running wildly toward them from the direction of the hotel. Isla followed close behind with Dylan wrapped tightly to her body. They stumbled up breathlessly on the sand.

"You guys are here! I was so worried. Are you okay?" Isla cried.

"We're okay. For now." Lorel managed a meek smile, gripping her bloody shoulder.

Noticing the perplexed expressions on Sam and Isla, Lorel introduced Jake, but there was no time for explanation.

Isla frantically tugged at her sling to tighten it after her run down the beach. She looked at Lorel and Lalique with pursed lips and lifted her palms in the air. "Suddenly you were both just gone! We were afraid something terrible had happened. We just came from the hotel. It's chaos inside."

"It looks like chaos out here too." Sam stared wide-eyed at the water full of sirens, then over to the bodies near the dunes. "We were lucky to get out alive."

"You should not still be here." Lalique stared at the little family, shaking her head, then pulled Isla aside.

They began whispering in hushed but frantic tones. Lorel noticed Lalique lean down to kiss Dylan's forehead. A streak of joy fleeted across Isla's clouded face and the two sirens embraced.

Sam stood next to Lorel, staring up at the volcano with the veneration and awe of a scientist.

"Sam, I thought you said this was inactive!" Lorel hissed under her breath. "Why is this happening?"

He turned and looked her in the eye. "Lorel, this is a consequence of tampering. *Human tampering* with the island, not any sort of natural geo-reaction."

"What do you mean? DiviniGen has done this?"

He nodded. "The sirens used to access their subterranean mines through doors at the undersea base of the volcano, but a few centuries ago the tectonic plates shifted. One swallowed the edge of another effectively shifting the floor's topography and the island's location. The mines were swallowed into the earth's core and now all that remains is a vacuous space of pent up gases. They've been building up ever since." He drew in a sharp breath. "The sirens closed and locked the doors to the mines long ago."

"And these doors are at sea-floor level?"

"Yes, the submarine base of the volcano is at the

Abyssal Plane. A set of natural stairs leads up to them."

"The Vulcan Traps," Lorel whispered, remembering the surreal step formations she had seen on her dive.

"If those doors are ever opened, a terrible chain reaction would occur."

"So the volcano would erupt." Lorel took a deep breath to quell the fear bubbling in her chest. Sulfuric fumes permeated the air.

"Yes, but not just any eruption." Sam looked up at the sky, closed his eyes for a long second. "It would be a super eruption. There is a thin membrane of lithospheric crust separating the chamber of gasses from the inner volcano."

"The Core Mantle Boundary," Lorel said with a nod.

"Yes, and if seawater is introduced to the pressurized environment, the water molecules would break down releasing hydrogen atoms. Then the gasses would ignite creating a molten mantle plume. This plume would eventually punch a hole in the sea bed and shoot through the shaft of the volcano until it hit oxygenated air, at which point it would become an explosion of massive scale."

"And how long is *eventually*?" Lorel arched an eyebrow, exchanging a worried glance with Jake.

Sam raked his fingers through his hair and looked over at Isla and Dylan. "God, my family," he whispered. "How will I keep them safe? I'm out of my element."

Lorel shook her head feeling her blood pressure rise. "We all are. How long *do we have*, Sam?"

He sighed. "It should take about twenty or thirty

minutes for the gases to build up, and then . . . boom."

Boom. The word rang in Lorel's ears.

Lalique walked up to them. "We need to move quickly. There is still a chance."

"What do we do?" Lorel's voice shook. She was almost afraid to hear the answer. With a slippery palm she squeezed Jake's hand. He squeezed back.

"The only safe place to be when the Vulcan explodes is under water," Lalique replied.

No one could ignore the elephant in the room anymore and all eyes looked somberly at Jake and Sam.

Lalique looked at Sam. "You may not survive this. We must be submerged because the gases will smother all oxygen in the air . . . and there is no telling when resurfacing would be viable again." Her eyes searched the beach as though a solution were somewhere to be found.

"I know," Sam groaned, kicking the sand. "Isla had a boat ready for us. But we couldn't leave without finding you two."

"A few humans took the boat," said Isla. "I don't know where they were going, but they just paddled out to sea."

"Lalique, is there some other way for Sam? Anything?" Lorel said, noticing Isla's chin tremble.

Lalique looked out at the water. "Soon, land will no longer be an option." She shook her head with a sigh. "Even if you made it to outer beach, without a boat, there is no escape route for a human."

"Wait!" Jake held his hand up. "On my way here I

noticed there were a couple DiviniGen's motor rafts on shore. If you could get to one, then you could get to the *Nautilus* and take harbor there."

"The *Nautilus*?" Sam asked.

They all stared at Jake with questioning eyes.

"It's a futuristic galleon ship. And it's out there," he said pointing finger in the direction of the sea.

Lorel looked at him. "Is that how you got here?"

He nodded. "I have so much to tell you."

"Do you mean to say they are here?" Lalique's face turned ashen.

"Yes, Beacon. They're stealthing about a mile off shore." Jake looked at Isla and Sam. "If you can get there, they'll take you in, and you can warn them too. Tell them to get as far from here as they can, immediately."

"They already know. They always know," Lalique said pressing her lips into a thin line.

The queen's face was a constant puzzle to Lorel but she thought she saw hopeful expectancy. It gave Lorel a glimpse of hope. Her trust in Lalique was consummate, but something bothered her about what Jake had said.

"Hold on. Jake, you have to go with them."

He set his jaw. "I will not leave you again."

"But Jake, this is beyond your abilities. Humans can't—"

"Lo. I'm staying."

Lorel shook her head at him, tears brimming in her eyes. *Why was he always so stubborn?*

"Sam, let's go! This is our chance." Isla's lavender eyes brightened.

"No." Sam frowned, and her face fell. "You and Dylan would be safer to submerge in the Eye. You two must stay. I'll make it to the *Nautilus*." He clasped his hands around Isla's shoulders. "And after all this, I will find you."

"We can't separate. We *all* go to the boat, as a family," she said, feet planted in the wet sand. "Please."

Sam let out a long sigh of defeat.

"Thank you!" Isla hugged him fiercely, squeezing Dylan between their chests.

"Just remember, the DiviniGen ships are in port on the nearby islet. Steer clear of them," Jake warned. "You'll find the *Nautilus* about a half mile to the northeast of there."

"Thank you, Jake," Sam said, placing a hand on his shoulder.

"Go now!" Lalique said without tearing her eyes from the volcano. "Every second will count."

Isla swiveled around. "Wait. Where is Mello?"

The question hung in the air like a dark premonition they had all been avoiding. Something had kept Lorel from asking it herself, as though the answer would change everything.

A huge gust of wind swept across the beach spraying water against them. Silence. Lorel's heart beat in slow motion, echoing in her ears.

Did anyone know?

"Mello has chosen higher ground." Lalique pointed a long slender finger up to the volcano. "There."

Lorel squinted upward scanning the balding portion

of the Vulcan's zenith until she saw it. A lighthouse. The towering stone structure rose above the tree line just below the mouth of the crater. A tiny lantern room at the top caught her eye, its metal roof reflecting a stray sunbeam that penetrated the dark clouds. Sulfuric white smoke swirled around it.

He was up there? Now? It was far. Too far. The way down, which appeared treacherous with jackknifing cliff trails, would take far longer than a half hour. Lorel felt a ball of wax form in her throat. She closed her eyes and could see him looking down on them, hair rising on the heated wind, coalescing with the white tendrils of smoke.

Mello.

"He rang the gong," Isla whispered, looking at Lalique. Her face contorted. "But that means . . ."

"Yes." Lalique shook her head, her eyes forlorn.

"He knew. He knew he would never make it back down to the water in time." Isla covered her face with her hands and Sam pulled her close, his face pale.

"But he gave *us* time. We must use it wisely." As Lalique spoke the ground beneath their feet shook violently.

"Look, over there!" Jake pointed at the islands in the distance.

Large rocks started falling from the cliff sides, boulders tumbled from mountaintops. Landslides cascaded down from the highest elevations, swallowing silver waterfalls in brown avalanches of mud. The islands were trying to disencumber themselves from the very crust they were wrapped in like a dog shaking mud off his back.

"Run!" Lalique shouted to Sam and Isla.

The family took off up the beach and into the woods. Lorel squeezed her eyes shut, praying they would reach the open sea.

Alone together on the beach again, Lorel, Lalique, and Jake stared up at the Vulcan. Instinctively they backed toward the water and away from the angry volcano. Large chunks of lava spewed from it with loud booms. A few glowing streams of liquid fire spilled from its mouth like drool.

This was still just the lead up, Lorel thought with dread. *The main event was yet to come.*

Muffled screams drifted from the hotel and she could see people running from the building. There was nowhere for them to go. She looked away.

"Listen, they're still singing," Jake said, nodding out toward the water.

"Yes," Lorel murmured, barely able to talk.

More spouts had formed above the Eye, spinning around each other like a ballet. They seemed to sync with the reverberating aural symphony that filled the air. The water's surface was still rough from the splashing sea of sirens, and rain had begun pelting down from the sky.

Lorel glanced around the tropical panorama from one atmospheric threat to another. She could only make out remnants of the rainbow, ultraviolet and infrared fighting to exist in the impending grayness.

"We need to join them," Lalique whispered to Lorel then walked into the shallow water toward the sirens.

Lorel and Jake followed, kicking off their shoes and

stepping into the cool froth. She glanced at his face, wondering if he had felt the same jolt of electricity she had. The water seemed alive today. Jake took the waves in wide strides. His face was set and his eyes remained fixed ahead, but Lorel saw worry in his tightening jaw. Soon waves crashed against their knees.

The earth rumbled again.

Lalique turned to Jake. "You still have time to reconsider. Resurfacing will not be an option after . . ."

His eyes sparked. "I told Lorel, I'm not leaving." He looked at her. "I won't let you out of my sight again. The risk is mine to take."

Lalique nodded and Lorel noticed admiration flicker in her eyes.

"I hate you for this," she said biting her lower lip.

"I know," he replied. "But you'll forgive me."

Water lapped at their thighs, and as they waded deeper, Lorel began to feel sick. What was his record time underwater, ten, maybe twelve minutes? If anything happened to him she would never forgive herself. Her mind raced, fighting to think clearly, come up with a solution. There had to be a way.

"I am going to get you through this."

"I'm ready, Lo. I got this far, didn't I?" He smiled but his eyes faltered.

"You did. But I'll get you the rest. And then you will owe me a serious back rub."

"Deal."

They had reached chest level. Water sprayed their faces and the wind pelted shards of rain against their skin. Out in the center of the Eye the waterspouts grew, rising from clusters of sirens as though they had spouted the cyclones themselves.

Lalique swam a few feet ahead, almost at the atoll. She looked back every few moments to check on them. Lorel stopped, drawing in a quivery breath. It would be time to submerge soon. But they had to wait until the last second. For Jake.

His arms encircled her and squeezed so tightly she could hardly breathe. The gong had softened and Mello's warning slowly faded away. Now only the song of the sirens filled the atmosphere, a sonorous backdrop to the horrific scene unfolding before their eyes. Its notes were building, coalescing into a victorious anthemic sound. The intensity was almost too much to bear. Her heart pounded with the rhythm.

Then all at once, like some subterranean force had sucked them under the water, the sirens were gone. An eerie silence fell upon the entire land.

Tha-thump, tha-thump, tha-thump.

Lorel's stomach dropped like an anchor. Something electric in the atmosphere prickled every hair on her body. Jet black smoke began shooting from the mouth of the Vulcan. The gentle streams of lava started to gush. And then the flashes of light began.

TWENTY-THREE
MELLO

September 28, 2098
Paraíso, Rodinia

THE GONG HAD DIED to a quivering muted vibration. Mello stared in anguished reverence at the display before him. Black smoke poured gracefully from the Vulcan's crater. It tumbled in slow motion toward the lighthouse like a gaseous avalanche. An inhumane heat enveloped his body in a cocoon of sweltering sulfuric air, mercifully bestowing him with a peaceful numbness.

The oxygen in the atmosphere's chemical composition was swiftly dwindling, atoms being swallowed greedily by the carbon monoxide filled sulfur clouds. Methane and carbon monoxide now leaked out of the Vulcan like demons. Rodinia itself was metamorphosing.

It won't be long now. He sucked in a toxic breath and closed his eyes.

The flashes were so bright they penetrated his lids

in a blinding radiation of light. When he dared open his eyes, his stomach roiled at the apocalyptic sight before him.

A shuddering rumble sounded as boulders began tumbling down the mountain. Mello's hands shook on the rails and he felt the vibrations penetrate his bones. It was more powerful than he imagined. And this was only the beginning. In the distance he could see it happening on all the islands. Small rocks and boulders pelted into the water, hurrying along in landslides or hurling from cliff tops.

This was it. The sky was falling.

Slowly Mello felt himself leave his body, defying the laws of nature. He floated like a feather above himself, undulating with the resonance. Tiny musical vibrations shook his vision and everything looked like a dream world. Colors more vivid. Space and time affixed to different dimensions.

In the Eye far below him, the sirens submerged all at once like the grand finale of a magic act.

They were under. They would make it.

An agonizing love reverberated in Mello's heart and relief flooded his body. All was wrong and all was right with the world. The sirens would survive. Individuals would be lost to the circle of life, but that was the way things were supposed to be. The species would go on, strong, able, and ready to adapt to whatever new earthly environment faced them.

Another tremor shook his body so hard the ground beneath his feet disappeared. Black smoke and fire wiped out all sight. Suddenly he felt himself falling backward, into the shaft of the lighthouse. A voice called to him in his mind.

Father.

He closed his eyes and saw a face sweeter than life itself. A face so similar to his, so familiar. She beckoned him downward, toward the blinding light, and he was in freefall. A glorious wave of elation washed over him as he smiled.

TWENTY-FOUR
LOREL

September 28, 2098
The Eye of Rodinia

BOOM.

The explosion was a fiery plume that surged from the Vulcan like a blooming mushroom. Its black cap spread a blanket of ebony over Rodinia, emitting a magnificent display of light and heat. And then the sky was on fire, flames licking at cheeky black clouds. It looked like another universe glittering with bright orange stars. But the stars began to fall like rain.

Lorel stared in awe at the cataclysmic sight above her, lingering for a moment on the spot where the old stone lighthouse was. Now only liquid magma could be seen cascading over the mountainside, smothering the trees and everything else in its path. Swallowing hard, she suppressed the sharp stab of heartbreak. Nothing could be done to change things now. Survival was all that mattered.

Adrenaline whooshed through her veins preparing her for the swim of her life. She stared wide-eyed into a face clenched tight to hide the fear.

"You can do this, Jake!" she yelled above the deafening roar of the volcano.

Coconut-size fireballs pelted the dark water where they treaded in the pupil of the Eye. Lalique had taken off toward the seafloor to join the rest of the sirens. Despite her offer to wait with them, Lorel had insisted that she go. The Abyssal Plane would be the safest place.

Jake raised his brows at her as another rumble shook them.

"Not yet," she said, shaking her head. Every second would count for him. The air was gauzy and already beginning to feel sparse with oxygen. A few more minutes passed as they both struggled to keep their heads above water. They were wasting energy.

Lorel had to make the call. "Ready?"

"On the count of three!" Jake cried back, his hair plastered against his wet face.

"One, two . . ." they chanted in sync.

Jake's eyes flickered with reds and oranges, reflecting the chaos. Lorel looked into them. No words were necessary. *I love you,* she thought with a pounding heart.

She gave him a gentle nod and their stare lingered a second longer.

"Three!" Lorel shouted.

Jake sucked in an enormous breath, then sunk below the choppy surface.

Lorel followed, taking only a second to glance up at the volcano through dripping lashes once more. *You will be remembered . . . you will be revered.*

Goodbye, Mello.

Goodbye, Rodinia.

Cool water swirled around her head silencing the fiery maelstrom above. From below Jake's hands slid along the side of her belly indicating his location. *He was a blind man from here,* she thought as her eyes slowly adjusted.

The dark abyss stretched out below them. Flipping her body head down, she grabbed Jake's hand tightly and they paddled into shaft of the blue hole. On his wrist she felt his navy watch and clicked the light on.

Two minutes.

Lorel's pupils dilated to saucers and she looked at his face. His brows pinched, eyes squinted and cheeks puffed out. But she saw courage, and determination. This was the moment he had been training for. *Come on FTX.*

She looked at the watch again, pumping hard with her legs.

Three minutes.

Water rushed them downward, faster. Colder.

Four minutes.

She squeezed his hand, and he returned it weakly. He was losing steam. He clicked a button on his watch and it displayed their depth: 327 feet. Lorel looked around.

Where were the grottoes?

The walls of the shaft shifted by them in shadow.

The water was so much darker than the last time she had made the descent, which had been a day with sun — not a day when the sky was turning black and falling.

Seven minutes.

Jake's fingers went limp in hers.

No. She yanked his arm in an effort to stimulate his blood flow then pulled them both into an upright position. The current still pushed them gently downward. She twisted her body, squinting to see the details of the limestone walls that surrounded them. The façade of toothy stalactites and stalagmites emerged in her sight. Large gaps and crevices seemed to stretch out in blackness behind them.

The grottoes!

Lorel sighed, emitting a plume of bubbles, and pulled Jake over to the nearest cave. The stone structure was jagged and close-knit, and it felt like they were slithering through a submarine labyrinth. Jake's eyes were open but his face looked confused as if he had left reality. She grabbed him from behind, linking her arm beneath his, and gripped the bulge of his pectoral in her left palm. Her nails dug in as she tugged and pulled with her free hand.

Thump . . . thump . . . thump . . . His heartbeat beat in slow motion. She pumped her legs, dragging him with all her might. Suddenly he would not budge. His body felt like stone. Lorel glanced down. His foot was caught between two stalactites.

She let go of his chest and slithered over to wrench

it out. A quick glance at his face and darkening lips told her he had only seconds left.

You said you wouldn't leave me. I'm holding you to that.

The cave crevice was narrowing and had turned pitch black. Even with her adaptation, she could not see a thing. After struggling inward a few more feet she noticed a green glow. *The bioluminescence of an air pocket!*

She hugged Jake around the middle and shoved his body upward, then swam up herself. Splashes sounded as their heads popped above the surface and into the small oxygenated cave.

Jake's head hung limp.

Don't leave me.

She grabbed his hair, lifting his chin out of the water, and looked into his face. It was still and glowed a pale greenish white in the dimness of the illuminating organisms. She slapped him hard on one cheek, yelling his name.

Nothing. She grasped his jaw in her hand, steadying his head and breathed out, exhaling into his mouth.

Suddenly he kicked, his arms flailing around. Then he began gasping for breath. Coughing. The sounds of life echoed in the small air bubble.

"Jake," she cried, choking back tears.

He looked at her, stunned, his breath still unsteady. Then a smile slid across his face and he pulled her close to him, cupping her cheeks in his big hands.

"Lorelei Phoenix, whoever the hell you are, will you marry me?"

At least an hour had passed and the air in the small grotto felt heavy. And thin. Lorel shivered and Jake pulled her closer. They had hoisted themselves out of the water onto a shallow bank of smooth rock.

Lorel kicked at a pebble and it splashed, echoing through the space. "How am I supposed to plan a wedding stuck beneath an island of fire and brimstone?" She tried to laugh, but her heart was too heavy.

"You mean they don't have Internet down here?" He rubbed her shoulder.

She sighed. "I don't know what to do next, Jake. I'm sorry."

"I can breathe. I think this was a good first step."

"And maybe a good second step would be that backrub," she said, nudging him.

"Come here," he said pulling her close.

She relaxed into him, letting her legs stretch out and her toes swirl in the water as he began kneading her shoulders.

"I say we wait a few hours, then try to swim out again." Jake said, sliding his knuckles along her spine.

"No way, the air could be toxic. One breath up there could be our last, Jake."

"It has to dissipate eventually. I'll wait here until the oxygen runs out, and then I can go back up. And you can swim to the Abyssal Plain and join the sirens."

She stared at him. "No. I'm not leaving you either. Plus, I worry for the sirens too. They can't live down there forever."

"Stubborn as always," he said, brushing a strand of wet hair behind her ear.

"Funny, I was just thinking the same about you." She said, then took a deep breath. It felt labored.

"I guess we'll just have to make the best of this little love nest then," he said, raking his fingers down her thigh.

She laughed, for real this time, surrendered to the feeling of helplessness. As she shifted position on the rock bed to scoot in closer to Jake her hand landed on something cold and hard. She picked up the object and stared. Big round eyes filled with worry stared back at her.

"It's a mirror!" She gasped with surprise, clutching the small treasure in her hand.

The oval looking glass had a handle and frame of tarnished gold. Encased in the curves of the metal were tiny pearls and gems that glistened in the greenish light. Somehow Lorel felt as though she were holding the most precious thing on earth. Goosebumps prickled along her arms.

"But how?" Jake stared at the object in her hands.

"There is so much I could tell you about these people. The sirens live down here. Well, many live above land now, at least the younger ones do, but this cave system has been their home for centuries. It's filled with little suites. Maybe we're near one."

A burst of excitement swelled in her. "Hey, what if there are sirens around here?"

"Wouldn't they all go down to the Abyssal Plane to get as far from the explosion as possible?"

"I'm sure most of them did. But it is possible. We're pretty far below land. If we could find someone, maybe they would know of an escape route, some sort of tunnel that would lead out to the open sea."

"Then we could get to the *Nautilus*." Jake's eyes glimmered with hope.

"And we could get home, to my father," Lorel whispered, casting her eyes down.

Jake opened his mouth as though he were about to speak.

"What?" she asked. "He was still okay when you left him, right?"

Jake's gaze lingered a moment longer before he said, "He's still hanging on."

"Thank you, Jake. For taking care of him," she said, feeling defeated. The idea of saving him seemed so far away. Lost.

Jake had stood, his head inches from the ceiling of rock, and was feeling along the cave's surface. His hands rubbed off the glowing organisms leaving messy trails until the wall looked like a child's finger painting.

"Lo, come here," he said into the wall, squatting. "I can see into another room. It's too dark to tell what's in there though."

Lorel scampered over to where he was peering through a large gap in the rock. He moved aside to let her look. Her eyes felt like the lens of a camera straining to focus. Finally, some familiar items took shape.

"It looks like a bedroom." The shape of a bed and dresser materialized in front of her. But it was empty, no trace of being lived in for a long time. She shook her head. "Never mind. It's one of the abandoned ones."

"I don't know how we could get in there anyway." Jake sat back down against the wall and took a loud breath. It sounded wheezy and strained.

"Jake," She looked at him and he averted his eyes. His lips were turning blue again.

"I'm okay."

She breathed deeply to the same effect. Every breath she took triggered the desire to gasp for more. A small bud of panic bloomed in her chest. "Let's find a way in there. It's a bigger space, there will be more oxygen."

"How would a siren enter?"

She chewed on her lip. "Through the water. I see a little pool in there, but where does it connect? This place had a one-way tunnel in." She slid to her knees against the cool stone staring at the water.

Jake caressed her head. "We're going to find a way out of this."

"Of course," she said.

In the silence that followed, all that could be heard was the wheezing of their breath.

Lorel put her head in her hands, unable to look into his eyes. The life they could have had loomed in front of her like a mirage, shimmering then vanishing. They were almost going to be married. Almost going to grow old together and sit on a porch and watch a storm roll in. Everything she wanted in life was almost within her reach. Almost.

Wanting makes you weak. She swallowed hard. *Think about now.*

"Jake, I'm going down into the tunnel. I'll find a way in and then I'll come back and get you—"

"No, it's too dangerous. You could get stuck."

"But what choice do we have?" She threw her hands in the air. "We have to do something!"

"Lo—" he started but his eyes lost focus as though he forgot what he was saying. He shook his head then drew in a weak breath.

"I have to, Jake. I'll be back."

He looked at her, nodding slowly, but said nothing.

She sat at the edge of the water and began sliding her body in. It felt colder than before. She took a deep labored breath and hoped it would be enough oxygen. Just as her chin lowered beneath the water a low wailing sound reverberated inside the cave.

"What was that?" Jake glanced around with a jolt of awareness.

Their limited sight revealed nothing of the source. Lorel's body tensed as she paddled in place in the frigid water. "Could it be another eruption? An earthquake?"

It came again, louder this time and accompanied by beeps. The water rippled with the vibrations.

"No. It's manmade." Jake raised his brows at Lorel. "A submarine?"

"Maybe." She bolted upright. "We have to go. Both

of us. Can you swim again?"

He nodded with heavy lids, but his body said otherwise. She kneeled over him. "I know it's hard, and I know you're depleted—we both are—but you have to take as deep a breath as you possibly can."

Still slightly bewildered, he walked to the water and took a long slow breath, then lowered himself in.

"I'll lead you," she said, grabbing his hand. Without waiting for an answer she pulled him down with her. As they slithered downward through the narrow tunnel she felt something cold in her hand. The mirror. She clutched it tighter, unsure why.

The tunnel ended and toothy stalactites and stalagmites spread out before them, the last divide before reaching the shaft. Using the thin ends of the coned rocks to grab onto, Lorel pulled them toward the open water until they were free. The current immediately pushed them downward. They held tightly to each other's hands letting it take them.

But where was the source of the sound?

Suddenly it erupted again like a whale's bellow, low and sonorant. A few feet below Lorel could make out something white, and disturbingly large. Its surrounding light glowed like a halo in the dark water. As they came closer her heart began beating wildly.

Jake was right!

It was larger than a whale and floated upward toward them in a controlled motion like a spaceship. Lorel turned to Jake and they exchanged looks of relief. Within seconds the behemoth machine was before them.

On its underbelly a large bubble of glass protruded. It opened up like a mechanical jaw, air bubbles spewing out. A green light blinked, beckoning them inside.

They swam toward it. The glass jaw closed slowly until they were encased within the bubble. Soon the water began to drain until it was empty and they found themselves standing in cool air.

Lorel sucked it in with loud gasps, water dripping from her hair and clothes. She looked over at Jake who was steadying himself on the mobile surface. His face was white with undertones of blue. "Are you okay?"

He gulped the air in a series of fast breaths, gripping his neck, then coughed. "Yeah. You?"

"Yes." She straightened up, trying to maintain balance as the vehicle moved. "It's them, isn't it?"

"Beacon," Jake confirmed between gasps. A rosy bloom of color was returning to his cheeks.

"How could they have gotten in? The blue hole is sealed off from the ocean, top to bottom."

"This must have come from the *Nautilus*. This was their entry plan the whole time," Jake murmured, his now pink lips parted.

The vehicle began beeping and their eyes shot upward toward the sound. A set of white stairs descended smoothly from the underbelly of the submarine. Bright halogen light poured through the opening, inundating Lorel's exposed pupils. She winced, squeezing her eyes shut for a moment, then slowly walked up the stairs with Jake following behind. Her hands shook as she gripped the cold metal handrail to steady herself.

Once they reached the top, the steps rose up sealing them inside a bright space. It was like no submarine Lorel had ever seen, or even imagined. But what caused her heart to lurch was the familiar man standing before her.

"Welcome to the *Sub-Nautilus*." His voice was diminished by the whirring sound of the engine.

Sleek white walls sheathed in a thin layer of smart glass curved inward like the contour of a whale. They seemed to breathe in and out. Lorel felt dizzy and instinctively reached backward fingering the wall of steps.

Every surface shimmered with nautical hologram maps, radar and satellite detectors, and statistical charts. People milled about, busily sliding fingers along the glassy surfaces. Oblong windows displayed a view of the dark water outside. Curtains of white foamy bubbles filled each window and lit up in varying colors. Even the floor itself was glass. Lorel stared down at the swirling water beneath her feet.

When she looked up, the man still stood there, hands folded neatly in front of his waist.

"Ben?" She blinked several times to make sure it was real.

"Lorel." The unfamiliar tone of sympathy in his voice jarred her. "Forgive me. I always wanted to tell you . . ."

"I know." She shook her head, her face flushed as she stared at her boss. Her guardian. "Lalique told me everything. I owe you an apology . . . and my gratitude."

"Don't think of it. I would have done anything for your mother."

A heaviness tugged at Lorel's chest and she glanced out the window. Where was Lalique now? Had Lorel found her escape only to lose her mother once again?

"Ben, we need to find her."

He smiled wistfully and his expression betrayed a hint of longing. "We already have."

"She's here?" Lorel's head spun around. "Where?"

On the other side of the marble floor a blackglass door slid open and the queen entered the room. Her green dress had dried and floated behind her as she approached.

"Lorel!" Her eyes glittered with excitement and she grabbed Lorel's hand, squeezing tightly.

"I thought I lost you again," she said, hugging her around the neck. The smell of the ocean, the sea breeze and distant notes of something musky and warm filled her senses. The familiarity of a primal yearning. Her mother's scent. She had smelled it before, locked it into her memory twenty-five years ago. Tears filled her eyes.

Lalique pulled away. "Here," she said as she took Lorel's hand and placed something cold and slimy into her palm. "I was just about to use this on a patient. But now you are here, you should give it to him."

Lorel looked down at a gelatinous substance quivering under the halogen lights in a deep violet hue. *A patient . . .*

She looked back at Jake. A shiver of elation shot through her. "He's here?"

A smile swept Jake's face. "I brought him along for the ride."

"But you must hurry," Lalique said. "He's not doing well. He keeps slipping into unconsciousness, and we can't get him to open his eyes. He's in there." She pointed to the door across the room she had come through.

Lorel ran, nearly slipping on the smooth marble with her wet feet, to the door. It slid open upon her approach. She stepped inside a small, dimly lit room. The door slid closed. Her father lay on a bed of white sheets before her. A germ mask covered his lower face. His eyes were closed, but his chest moved slowly up and down.

Lorel rushed to his side. "Dad!"

He was still but his lids fluttered, struggling to open. She put her ear to his chest. The thump of his heart was faint, and an ominous rasping sound dominated his chest cavity. Her blood ran cold. He was close to death. She hugged him tightly around his neck but drew back quickly. There was no time to waste.

She grabbed a germ mask for herself from his bedside then pulled his off. With a gentle lift of his neck, his jaw dropped allowing his lips to part. She placed the algae in his mouth and closed it.

"Just swallow," she whispered in his ear then rubbed her forehead against his and waited.

Suddenly a horrible thought occurred to her. What if it didn't work? What if all this time, she had been mistaken to think that she could interfere in the circle of life. That she could play God.

Raspy breaths filled the room and she could smell the ashy scent of death. She clasped his hand and brought it to her heart, then began telling him everything that had taken place. The truth.

"And that is why you are not going to die, Dad. I promised you, didn't I? That morning on the beach," she said, remembering.

The morning that started everything. And brought us to this moment.

She brushed his hair back. His breathing slowed and agonizing seconds passed between raspy inhales. She swallowed hard and gripped his hand tighter.

Please, Dad, I love you.

Slowly his breathing began to clear. His cheeks flushed with pink as though every capillary was welcoming a burst of cleansed blood. She leaned over him, placed a hand on his chest. His heartbeat strengthened beneath her palm.

Her father was going to live.

A dam of relief flooded her body, and she began to sob against his chest. He stirred beneath her weight, and she sat up to witness his eyes open, clear and calm. With a vibrant look of shock, then joy, he pulled her into a tight hug.

"Oh, honey, I thought you were . . ."

"I know, Dad. I'm so sorry I put you through that. I had to come here."

"I know. I'm just sorry I never told you who you really are." His eyes begged forgiveness.

"I understand, Dad," she whispered. "I understand it all now."

He exhaled a long silent breath then hugged her tighter. "Thank you. Forgiveness means everything to an old man."

She laughed through her tears. "How many times do I have to tell you, you are not an old man!"

He smiled, a smile that reached all the way to his sparkling brown eyes.

She stood, clasping her hands together. "Dad, there's someone here I want you to see." She glanced behind her to see Lalique's figure lingering behind the blackglass.

"Come on in," Lorel called softly.

Lalique entered, pausing a few steps into the room. Lorel noticed her hands shake as she smoothed the green silks of her dress, but when her eyes landed on Henry they lit up like fire.

Her father bolted upright in bed like he had seen a ghost. "Lallie?" His voice sounded quiet and brittle as though she would disappear if he spoke too loud.

"Henry!" Lalique cried softly, approaching the bed.

Lorel retreated as her mother and father embraced each other. Shoulders heaved with sighs, and sniffles sounded intermittently between fierce whispers. She watched as her father's hand stroked Lalique's red hair, just as he had done with her so often. The spinning kaleidoscope of her life suddenly slowed and melted together into a single color—yellow. It was blinding sunshine and penetrating warmth. It was a new day. Joy emanated through her body as she joined them in the tender embrace.

This was her family.

A hand squeezed her shoulder and she turned to see Jake, his eyes filled with tender adoration.

This was her future.

The *Sub-Nautilus* descended swiftly toward the Abyssal Plane then shifted into forward motion along an expansive stretch of sea grass. Steadying herself against the nausea, Lorel stared out the floor-to-ceiling window. Sirens filled the underwater landscape. Some walked along the ground in fields and along pulsing lava streams. Others swam in large groups like schools of fish. Cutting languidly through the water, they looked like strange mythical creatures, as ephemeral as the stars. It still did not seem real. These were her relatives.

Our relatives, she thought. *Would the rest of the world ever know their kin under the sea?*

In the distance, ascending into the acclivity of some low seamounts, her eyes followed the Vulcan Traps all the way up to the Golden Doors. They stood wide open, their edges jagged and charred. An orange glow emanated from within, but it was just calm embers. The volcano's rage had been spewed upon the land leaving the Abyssal Plane intact. Rodinia's most precious gems still remained. The magical underwater world. And the sirens themselves.

Lorel jerked her head from the window as a large gray body occluded the view. It turned to face her, and she stifled a scream as the jaws snapped open, then closed. She squeezed her eyes shut but the image of razor sharp teeth stayed seared in her mind.

Lorel grabbed Lalique's arm next to her. "I thought there weren't any sharks in the blue hole."

"There weren't," Lalique said, pursing her lips.

They both stared in silence as the prehistoric predator swiveled from the window with a flick of its tail.

Lorel pressed closer to the glass. "Look, it's after something."

A figure floated a few yards away. Lifeless. Dark inky blood flowed from the head clouding the face. *A siren.* Lorel prepared to squeeze her eyes shut as the shark closed in on its easy prey, but something caught her attention. Marbled white hair flashed in a swirl of movement. A wetsuit.

Galton.

Lorel's hand went to her mouth. Lalique pulled her close and they stared out the window. Part of her wanted to turn away, but she needed to see it. This was the circle of life. This was natural selection.

The sympathy she felt as the shark devoured the body of the CEO who had once been on top of the world was no different than that she would feel watching a cat eat a mouse. One was no better than the other. It was too bad he had never understood that. She sighed, placing her fingertips to the glass as the shark followed a trail of blood to another floating body in a wetsuit.

She sighed aloud. *It didn't have to be this way, Galton.* Blood had been shed needlessly. No one had won. But he chose his path, and his faithful employees had followed in his wake.

"Lalique," Lorel said, breaking the somber silence. "What will happen to the sirens? Sharks or no sharks, they can't survive down here forever, even with the air pockets, right?"

"Right. But look . . ." Lalique pointed to where the *Sub-Nautilus* was headed. They were now level with the sea grass, which thrashed in the vehicle's wake. Ahead was a gaping hole in in a rocky wall.

Lorel squinted. "Is that a tunnel?"

"Yes." Lalique's voice quivered with what Lorel thought was excitement. "We've connected."

"So it leads out to the ocean?" Lorel watched the gaping black hole draw closer.

"Where Beacon's ship is waiting."

"So that's how the sub got inside." Lorel said. "It must have tunneled through the seabed from the other side."

"And that's how *they* will get out." Lalique raised her hands to the glass, fingers splayed to reveal the full span of her webbing, and stared out at the sirens.

"To the open sea." Lorel said. She listened to her mother drawing unsteady breaths.

"The Realm once forbidden." Lalique turned to Lorel with widening eyes. "I can't leave my people. I have to get out of here."

"Lalique, it's too dangerous, you —"

Before Lorel could finish Lalique cried, "Richard!"

A deep, calm voice came over the intercom. "Lalique, what is it?"

"Richard, I can't do this. I need to leave. I have to be

with my people right now."

"I'm afraid that's not possible, we've sealed in and pressurized for ascent. We can't change course now."

Lalique stared at the speaker on the shiny white ceiling. "Richard, they need me. I am their leader, their queen. I can't leave them like this. What if they don't make it out? Or beyond the Open Sea Realm?"

"Even if we could, it's too dangerous for you. Look out there," Richard said over the speaker.

Lorel, unsure what to do, glanced out the window. Three large sharks circled in the distance. Lalique paced back and forth, shaking her head in distress. *What must she feel like*, Lorel wondered with a pang of sympathy. A queen, once so dominant yet loved. A ruler whose land had been ripped from under her, whose people were right before her eyes, but so far out of her reach.

Before Lorel could find the words to comfort her, Richard's voice came over the intercom again. "Remember who your people are, Lalique," he said. "All that you've taught them as their leader. Strength and wisdom. Survival. Every siren is a leader inside. And remember what we discussed. I'll make sure you're reunited with them. You know I stand behind my word."

Lorel watched in awe as her mother's breathing slowed, calmed by this man. Who was he exactly? Lalique's eyes lowered from the ceiling to the window again. "I know," she said softly.

A few sirens swam up to the submarine, attempting to peer in the windows, but it was obvious they could not see inside. One banged on the glass with his fist before darting away with the rest toward a crowd in the distance. Lalique turned away.

Lorel placed a hand on her shoulder. "There are other people that need you, Lalique. I need you . . . and my father needs you. I know it's hard to sit back and watch, but maybe Richard is right. Maybe you should have faith in your people. You've been a great leader to them. Trust that they will save themselves, and that they will find you again," Lorel said, hopeful. "Come with us and finish the life you started long ago."

"I know, he's right. They'll leave the Realms of Rodinia. They'll ride the tides, and they'll find a place."

"Do you have an idea of where they will go? Are there other islands the sirens know of nearby?"

Lorel worried there was no place in this world for the sirens. Not yet. Their one attempt to integrate with humans had been met only with hostility and greed.

"No. They will go wherever the currents take them. Some distant shore, perhaps."

"What will they do then?"

"What all living things do. They will adapt. They will survive. And I will reunite with them, if it's the last thing I do," she said, her jaws tightening.

Lorel breathed a sigh of relief. At least she wasn't losing her mother again so soon. They would just have to hope the sirens made it.

Silently, they stared out the window as the submarine slowed in preparation for entering the tunnel.

"I have something for you. Come." Lalique took her hand and led her to a white console table. On it was a large clamshell, closed and still soaked from seawater. It smelled of fish.

"Open it." Lalique placed the shell in Lorel's hand.

The mossy green algae on its surface felt slippery and cool. She pried her nails into the clamped shell and pulled it open. Inside was a cluster of dark purple stems.

"What is it?"

"A gift. One you've been waiting for," Lalique said, her eyes bright.

Lorel shivered with a thrill of euphoria as she realized what she was holding in her hands. *The magic.* She fingered the algal stems.

Her mother leaned close and whispered. Lorel's ears tickled with her words. "This is how you will germinate it. This is how *you,* Lorelei Phoenix, will bring it to the world . . ." she began.

Jake and Lorel entered the control room of the *Sub-Nautilus* to a *whoosh* of cool air. The ship's control panel flickered with an array of red lights. Halogen bulbs above cast a soft glow against the white walls. Lorel shifted awkwardly behind the man at the helm as he swiveled in his high-backed leather chair to face them. He leaned back, crossing his legs, and glanced from one to the other.

"Welcome aboard," he said after a moment.

Although the man smiled, Lorel felt a wave of unease pass through her.

He stood up, ducking his head to avoid hitting the ceiling, and nodded to Jake. "Nice to see you again, Mr. Ryder."

"Likewise, sir," Jake replied. "This is Lorel."

The man reached out a hand to her. "Richard Harnott."

"Lorelei Phoenix," she said, returning the shake.

"Mr. Harnott, we want to thank you for saving us," Jake said, his tone formal. "And for taking us home."

The man nodded.

"Yes. Thank you for everything," Lorel added. "When can we expect to arrive in the States?"

Harnott tilted his head, a gleam in his dark eyes. "First, I have a proposal for the two of you. The answer to your question depends on whether or not you are . . . interested."

Lorel stole a sideways glance at Jake. *What could the leader of Beacon possibly want from them?*

"My organization has a need for people like you, people with your skill set. Undercover roles with very important missions. I can't go into detail here, but you would be very well compensated."

"What type of missions?" asked Jake with narrowing eyes.

"Let's just say we have a strong interest in helping the sirens in their quest to remain hidden from the human world," he replied.

"The sirens just lost their home," Lorel said, pursing her lips. "Their priorities may be changing."

"You are correct. Though, I think we both know,"

he grimaced, "they were changing well before the tragic destruction we all witnessed today. Nevertheless, Beacon's priorities remain the same. The sirens must stay hidden."

Lorel jerked her head back, staring at Harnott. "Oh really?"

"People knowing that we have a sister species so similar to ourselves would, hmm, how should I say this . . . weaken our story."

"What do you mean, 'your story'?" Jake asked.

"The story of human origin," he said matter-of-factly.

Lorel felt her face redden. "Are you referring to the story or the truth?"

"I know you are scientists. As am I. But why crush others' beliefs?"

"You mean illusions," Jake said, an edge creeping into his voice. "Whatever this mission is, we're not interested."

Harnott tapped his fingers on the chair, looking between the two of them. "Let me spell this out for you more clearly. Discovering the existence of the sirens would disappoint quite a lot of people, turn their whole world upside down. There would be pandemonium. Our story holds the world together. It gives people hope where there is none."

"*Your* story? Let's give credit where credit is due," Lorel said in a sharp tone. "Beacon may be powerful, but PanDivinity is the one pulling the strings, controlling this world full of puppets with their lies and —"

A smile crept slowly across Harnott's face.

Lorel's voice trailed off and a bitter taste formed on her tongue. She swallowed hard as the man's eyes locked with hers.

"Exactly, Ms. Phoenix. And I am the puppeteer." He extended his hand again. "I believe a more thorough introduction is due. Richard Harnott, Master Guardian of Beacon, and Chairman of the Board of PanDivinity."

EPILOGUE

THE SATELLITE CAMERA ZOOMED in on its target location, coordinates -6.111, 72.085. An island appeared from a distance as a dark hazy smudge on the glassy surface of the Indian Ocean. The operator shoved his glasses up his nose, straining to see the image magnify and resolve in the virtual approach. Down through the black smoke he zoomed like a plane descending through storm clouds. Finally the view materialized, drawing a gasp from the man.

A thick layer of pyroclastic ash and pumice covered the island ring. It looked like an old black-and-white photograph. All color had been wiped out. No green to the trees, no yellow sand, or blue water. Only a spectrum of grays. The water appeared swampy and black, lifeless. The camera panned across the surrounding land. All was still as though frozen in time. An object caught his eye and he zoomed in. A building. Figures of people strewn across the beach, the dunes, along the verandas and in the grassy perimeter of the building.

He located one particular figure on the shore and magnified her image. It was a woman, or more a statue of what once had been a woman. She had been flash frozen in gray ash, preserving the shape of her body in desperate attempt to reach the water.

Scanning the beach, similar images appeared. Human or siren, it was hard to decipher. People in the midst of running, holding arms over faces, splayed out on the ground. Some even peeking out windows or standing in doorways of the building. Two people held hands looking up to the sky. The operator shivered at the expressions of horror plastered on their stony faces. He aborted and zoomed out, leaving the island of ash behind. What was there once was no longer.

Across the ocean, on some distant shore overcrowded with people, a boy looked up from his sandcastle. He shaded his eyes from the bright sun and stared out at the water. At first the figures were difficult to decipher as they emerged from beneath the waves. Their heads were slick and shone in the sun and their skin glistened like crushed diamonds. There were so many that he could not begin to count, and they kept coming, rising from the water. The tumbling breakers did not cause them to falter as they approached shore.

One of them, a child like the boy himself, walked directly toward him. Her eyes were large round seashells and her hair was wet silk. She reached out her hand to him, and he noticed a delicate webbing of skin stretched between her tiny fingers.

"Hello," she said.

The small plastic shovel dropped from his hands.

AUTHOR'S NOTE

Thanks so much for reading *Sirens: Lost World*! Reviews are extremely important to the success of a novel. I would be grateful if you would go on Amazon. com and review my book. And if you do, please email me your address and I'll mail you a *Sirens* bookmark as a way to say thank you!

Also, feel free to drop by my website and say hello at www.tlzalecki.com.

Best,

T.L. Zalecki

ACKNOWLEDGEMENTS

I could never have undertaken this book without the initial support of Catherine Wittmack. Her publication of *Eliza's Shadow* in 2012 was an inspiration. Catie, thank you for helping me launch "The Manphibian Project" and for bringing it home at the end. Thank you to Trey Harris for his epic brainstorming session. To Charlie Bray at the Indie Tribe for his early feedback on my partial first draft. To Andrew Bouve for a killer cover.

I can't express how helpful my beta readers were in developing this story. Thank you to my early ones: Leah Cooney, Annie Miller, Mike Zalecki (AKA Dad), Catherine Wittmack, Tyler Sandberg, Susannah Shive, and Emily Wilson. To Quoc Nguyen and Jim Jones on book two. Extra appreciation to the ones who read the story thus far (Books 1 and 2) from beginning to end: Andrew Bouvé, Heather Shive Hunt, Amanda Botha, Kim Harris, Cathy Fisher, Missy Metzl Sandberg, and John Aranguren.

My mother, Michelle Zalecki, stands in a category of her own having read the story three times. She also provided key ideas for the story ("message in a shell" and the "three phone calls" prologue) as well as recommendations for celebrities that should star in the movie. John, my husband, also deserves special thanks for putting up with a messy house and the emotional turmoil that comes along with being a writer. John, you supported me the whole way through—thank you. And thanks for being my "secret" editor.

Thank you to my trusted critics in the *Adams Morgan Writing Club*—you guys came into my life at the perfect time and helped me fall in love with the craft of writing. To Maxann Dobson, my first editor, who touched my story with a magic wand. The quality of editing, insight, and critique she provided was superb. Max, I could not have brought this to a place I was proud of without you and the folks at the Polished Pen.

Thank you to the folks at Kindle Press, especially my editor, Stephen, whose thoughtful insights and critiques pushed me to improve both *Rising Tide* and *Lost World* when I thought I had done all that could be possibly done. My journey through Kindle Scout and my experience with Kindle Press has been nothing short of wonderful.

Finally, to Will and Ava, for napping when Mommy needed it most.

ABOUT THE AUTHOR

T.L. Zalecki spent several years in the corporate world working with global "megacorps" before moving on to her most important job, raising her two children. During naptime, she created a world to escape to in *Sirens*. She enjoys using science to create fantastical fiction, packing sophisticated and sometimes controversial themes into stories of adventure, and twisting ordinary legends. She lives with her family and some tropical fish in Washington, DC.

52252565R20261

Made in the USA
Charleston, SC
23 February 2016